CW00524545

The Child of Good Fortune

TOM DE HAAN

The Child
of
Good Fortune

JONATHAN CAPE
THIRTY-TWO BEDFORD SQUARE
LONDON

First published 1989
Copyright © 1989 by Tom de Haan
Jonathan Cape Ltd, 32 Bedford Square, London WC1B 3SG

A CIP catalogue record for this book
is available from the British Library

ISBN 0 224 02586 4

Phototypeset by Falcon Graphic Art Ltd
Wallington, Surrey
Printed in Great Britain by Mackays of Chatham PLC

*TO KEN AND BILLIE ADLAM
WITH LOVE AND THANKS*

Contents

Prologue

One summer evening, in the thirty-fourth year of his reign, Michael Andaranah Tsyraec, King of Brychmachrye, was stabbed in the chest by one of his guards as he sat down to dinner in the Palace of Tsvingtori. The sharpened blade cut through skin, fat and muscle, carving back a triple layer of pink on white on red to lay bare the heart pumping within its birdcage of bone. Skidding on a rib, the knife failed to penetrate its original target, and instead punctured the left lung before slicing cleanly through the pulmonary artery. The others present – Councillors, noblemen, Guards, ladies, servants – were immobilised, some by complicity, others by amazement. None of them had seen a living human heart before. The King's heart, exposed to their gaze, was a purple lump of raw meat, tough and glossy, sprouting tubules. It thumped energetically as the King slouched forward.

And my heart, is mine like that? each onlooker marvelled. *A creature of independent movement?*

Dark blood frothed from the wound. The lungs, drowning in blood, coughed scarlet streams through the mouth and nose. The King was turning blue. Blood gushed into his soup-plate, overflowed, pooled in his lap, washed over his knees and soaked into the carpet. His heart emptied, and stopped beating. The King fell out of his chair. All this took perhaps twenty seconds, by which time Basal Rorhah, nineteen years old, elder son of the Fahlraec Hans of Rorhah, Guardsman, murderer, and claimant to the throne, had thrown away his knife, run outside to where his closest friend Edvard filcLaurentin was waiting with two saddled horses, and set off for the east at a gallop, where his army was assembling under the lieutenantship of Gilles Mehah.

The two years of civil war that followed proved that young Basal Rorhah was without doubt the greatest military genius and most gifted politician of his generation. While the Andaranah opposition was riven with factions and jealousies, Basal Rorhah's charismatic leadership swept the rebel armies through victory after victory, until at last the only parts of the country not under his control were the north-west provinces of Peat and Mindarah, parts of Floriah, and small pockets in the central mountains. The Andaranah dynasty, directly descended from Michah the Conquerer and rulers of Brychmachrye since the Conquest, had been almost eliminated: of King Michael's eight children only the three youngest, the Princes Henry and Asah and the Princess Ursula, remained alive.

Lord Thomas Floriah, a handsome and spirited man who by deaths and default of competition had become Commander-in-Chief of what remained of the Andaranah armies, realised that the loyalists' only hope was to smuggle the royal children out of the Kingdom. Tom Floriah had no illusions about the immediate future. The war was as good as lost. Basal Rorhah was riding on a wave of popularity and was, for the moment, invincible. As long as the Andaranah Princes lived, however, he would never sit easy on his stolen throne. To this end Tom Floriah had dispatched envoys to foreign powers to beg for aid in the form of a ship which could carry the children to safety; but Tom had no way of knowing whether these envoys had succeeded in leaving the country. Weeks passed as he waited for a reply, shifting his headquarters from stronghold to stronghold.

Without Tom Floriah the disparate elements making up the Andaranah resistance would have cut their losses and made their separate peaces with the new power in the land. Tom alone held them together, urging them on with his passionate refusal to accept defeat that was as compelling, in its way, as Basal Rorhah's invincibility. Tom Floriah took the war personally. He was thirteen years Basal's elder, and had been the young man's Captain in the Palace Guards. He had noticed and admired Basal's ability, befriended him, brought him to the attention of the King, recommended him for promotion. He had nurtured a traitor in the bosom of his affections. So much goodwill abused, talent squandered, potential dishonoured – it had destroyed Tom's faith in his own judgment. And so he fought on with his back to the wall, unable to forgive or surrender.

The Rorhah ran him to earth in Mindared. Mindared of the famous walls, never scaled, never fallen, against whom even Michah the Conquerer had had to admit defeat, was from Tom Floriah's point of view no bad place to weather a siege. It stood less than a mile from the western coast, and the ocean was clearly visible from the top of the castle keep: if a ship did come, it would not be impossible for them to fight their way through to it.

10

Meanwhile, Basal Rorhah made camp. Several days later his friend Edvard filcLaurentin arrived at the head of reinforcements, who were at once set to work digging entrenchments and building ramparts. Inside the walls the Andaranah kept their heads down, scanned the western horizon, and took no action.

In the second week of the siege a boy of about ten years was seen leaping to his death from the battlements. His red hair stood out boldly against the sky as he fell: Basal Rorhah guessed who he was and sent some men up to retrieve the body.

'It's Henry Andaranah,' said Edvard, looking at the dead boy lying in Basal's tent. Edvard's nausea was partly relief: he had not liked to think about how the Princes would be disposed of.

In Prince Henry's pocket they found a letter written in the Princess Ursula's hand. It was headed 'Amanah-in-Peat', and contained all sorts of false clues, such as how she hoped he and Prince Asah wouldn't be too lonely without her, and how the Rorhah would abandon the siege when they realised she had left Mindared, and how pretty the northern moors looked at this time of year.

'Do you think Tom knew?' asked Edvard.

'What do you think?' laughed Basal, tearing the children's trick up.

'Poor Tom,' said Edvard.

At the beginning of the sixth week the Rorhah camp was stricken by an outbreak of siege fever. Hugo Floriah, one of Tom Floriah's elder brothers, was among the first to die. His and other corpses were taken upstream and placed in the river which ran, through a subterranean tunnel, into Mindared to supply it with drinking water (Mindared well-water was notoriously brackish). Basal sent a herald to the foot of the walls to announce, 'Tell Ursula Andaranah not to drink the water.'

'Thirsting them out is quicker than starving them out,' Basal remarked to Edvard. The two friends strolled at a leisurely pace with their arms round one another's shoulders, observing the alarm that had been stirred up on the town walls.

One night in the middle of the eighth week three strangers appeared in the camp. They were soaking wet, although it had not rained for weeks. 'We want to see the King,' they said.

Basal stroked the black stubble of his first beard. 'How are things in there?' he asked them.

'Dreadful, Sir. They're dying of the fever.'

11

'How did you get out?'

'Through the water-tunnel, Sir.'

'Could we get in that way?'

'Impossible, Sir, it's too narrow. Your Grace couldn't get more than one man through at once.'

Basal smiled. His broken nose edged sideways on his face. 'I take it you have a better idea?'

'We will open up the gates to your army, Sir.'

'How much do you want?'

They named a sum, the ransom of a city.

A date, three days hence, and a time were agreed. Difficulties were anticipated, discussed, disposed of. Then Basal called for extra guards to be mounted around the entrance to the water-tunnel, and these soldiers escorted the three men back the way they had come. The traitors took with them a favourable impression of two able, serious-minded young men: a King who knew how to take advice and a friend who knew how to give it.

Alone together, Basal and Edvard let rip, throwing punches at each other, stomping and hooting for joy, while the guards on duty outside Basal's tent grinned knowingly at each other and the rumour spread through the camp that the end was in sight. Without warning Basal jumped on to Edvard's shoulders; Edvard's knees buckled and he sprawled across the floor with Basal on top of him, the two friends laughing and wrestling until they had exhausted the first frenzy of their delight. As a child Basal had been prone to uncontrollable fits of high spirits in which, often, things got broken and people were hurt, but latterly he was able to confine such displays to moments, like this, when he was alone with Edvard (and to his solitude? wondered Edvard jealously). Breathless and sweating, they lay side by side on the trampled grass and dry dirt that formed the floor of Basal's tent.

A suspicion occurred to Edvard. He was reluctant to spoil the moment, but it had to be said. 'Are you sure we can trust them?'

'Of course we can't. It doesn't matter as long as we know that. If there is an ambush we'll be prepared. All I want is a chance to get inside. I have three times as many men as Tom has, and mine are healthier.'

'And suppose they do turn out to be trustworthy?'

'When they come back for their money, they'll be killed.

12

And don't argue with me, Ned. One way or another they're traitors. You save your tender heart for people who deserve it.'

'Yes, Sir.'

Basal laughed, and dug Edvard in the ribs.

Awake in the night, Edvard reflected on this and thought, Tom was right, we didn't really know what we were doing. How much longer will I be able to rough about and laugh with Basal, as if he were not a King? Will the day come when I call him Sir and he doesn't smile? Will our children feel about him the way we once felt about King Michael, when we were young and new at Court, trembling in awe of him, most at our ease when we were prostrate in front of him? But Basal was always a King, more of a King than any man I ever knew. If he were not, none of this would have happened.

Next morning Basal rode out on a tour of inspection. During the course of his circuit around the walls one of the Andaranah archers succeeded in planting an arrow between his shoulder-blades. He pitched forward on to his horse's neck, but immediately recovered, and after Edvard had broken off the shaft he insisted on finishing his rounds.

The arrow had hit high. No vital organs were threatened, and when the fear that it might have been poisoned proved groundless Basal refused to have it taken out, saying that such an operation would impede his shield arm more than the present wound. Forty-eight hours later Edvard could see that it was giving him trouble, and demanded to have a look. The flesh had puffed up and smelt bad, so he called in the camp doctor who was hovering outside the tent. The Learned One sniffed Basal's wound and said cheerfully, 'Doing the Andaranah's work for them now, are you, Sir? You'll be buried lucky if you haven't poisoned yourself. I did tell you, Sir, you should have let me take it out while the blood was fresh. It'll have to come out now, and this bad pus won't make it any easier –'

'Go away,' said Basal.

'Stay,' said Edvard, grabbing hold of the doctor's arm. To Basal he said, 'You must let him take it out.'

'You want me to loll in my bed while you and Gilles take Mindared?'

'As if we could. There's no one else the men will follow. What would happen if you became really ill, if . . . Why do I have to say this to you? You know it has to come out.'

'It's not bothering me.'

13

'It bothers me.'

The operation was brief but painful. Basal lay on his stomach and did not utter one sound. The arrowhead was levered out, the wound cauterised, stitched up, washed with wine and bound in a linen strip that passed around Basal's neck, over his left shoulder and under his arm. Later Basal sat up and drank some beer. Flexing his arm he said to Edvard, 'I'll have to go without my shield.'

'You really think you're indestructible, don't you?'

'The important thing is that my men believe I am, don't you think?'

Edvard fought down the impulse to throw himself at Basal's feet and beg him to keep well away from any danger. Self-restraint was second nature to Edvard now: he had such impulses all the time and was practised at concealing them. He merely said, 'You've already lost half your hand, and you were lucky it was only your nose that was broken and not your neck. You really ought to take more care of yourself.'

'After tonight I will. Everything will be different.'

These were words for Edvard to brood on. More and more as the end of the war drew closer he suffered from bouts of despondency, aware that he had never really looked beyond winning the war, never fully appreciated how much he might lose thereby. He sought out Gilles Mehah, but found him crowing over their forthcoming annihilation of the Andaranah, and totally uninterested in what the more distant future might bring. Gilles had always been like that, forgetting yesterday, ignoring tomorrow.

Night fell. The attack began. Gilles Mehah sent diversionary assaults up the unfinished ramparts, while the main body of Basal's troops waited in the shadow of the woods for the signal to storm the gates. Basal's horse, an old campaigner, was sleeping on its feet. To Edvard and the other officers Basal said, 'If you run into Tom Floriah, try to stop him throwing his life away.'

The traitors were as good as their word: there was no ambush. At first Basal's soldiers found themselves up against townsfolk armed with picks and spades and kitchen knives, but gradually the castle guards were drawn into the streets by the fighting, and battle was joined in earnest. Dawn broke on the Rorhah standard of blue and gold fluttering above the castle keep.

They found the Princess Ursula in her bedroom. She was a

plump, pretty girl of thirteen, red-haired, with a scattering of freckles across her nose. Her dress was caked with dry blood. In her lap lay an eight-year-old boy. His throat had been cut. It was her brother, Prince Asah.

'If I hadn't done it,' she said, 'You would have.'

'You remember Edvard filcLaurentin, don't you?' said Basal gently.

'Oh yes, very well.'

'Let him take the Prince.'

She passed her brother over into Edvard's arms.

'You can come with us now,' said Basal, holding out his right hand to help her up.

> 'When the war is o-ver
> Our Rorhah will be King!
> He'll show those Andara-nah
> How to be a King!
>> He'll take Michael's daugh-ter,
>> He'll take her on the floor.
>> He'll break her in and screw her so-o-o
>> HARD she'll scream for more!
> So HARD she'll cry out RorHAH! RorHAH!
> Sir! Oh just once more . . .'

his soldiers sang in the streets below.

I

The Boxer

1

Summer again, the season for haymaking, pilgrimages, lovers. The sun is sloping westwards from afternoon to evening when three wagons roll on to a village green. Hungry farmers rise up from their half-eaten suppers; wives drop their washing; children abandon their noisy games; the whole village stands and stares. The red canvas hoods of the wagons are spangled with tin stars and crescent moons that catch the sunlight and are alchemised, like an actor, into something they are not, a fool's gold that will glitter only until night pulls down the curtain. As the wagons draw to a halt the butterfly fuzziness of their wheels resolves into spokes painted azure, purple, scarlet, saffron yellow. Down the left side of each wagon large white letters spell IDRIS OWENSON THEATRE COMPANY, and down the right side THE MOON AND THE STARS; but the villagers do not need to read to know that these are players' wagons. The strong smell of greasepaint, artifice and confabulation taint the air around them.

Ignoring the gawpers assembled on the edge of the green, the players climb over the tailboards and head for the inn, grumbling loudly. An hour ago they were turned back from the gates of a small market town up the road. The watchmen had said that, due to the recent death of the Lord of the Fahl, all public entertainments are cancelled – and those wagons, they added, are a parade in themselves. *Oh shit*, thought Brennain Swithsunson, as ten expectant faces looked to him, their leader, to sort this one out. Hadn't he been coaxing their goodwill for days with promises of the cold beer, hot bath-houses and deep feather beds awaiting them behind those locked gates? Bren shook his head helplessly. He has been a player all his life: he has bluffed his way through most of the scenes this world has to offer, and he knows, from many past and painful performances, what the upshot of trying to bargain with officialdom will be – once again uppity scum of the earth gets arse kicked by respectable citizenry. Amid howls of protest Bren turned his mules around, and tonight the Company will have to sleep rough under the wagons.

The players squat together at a distance, muttering and sending him dark looks. Bren sits alone in the driving box, mulling over his wrongs. What are they, donkeys, that they have to have a carrot forever dangled in front of them? No one forced them into this life. If they don't like it, let them leave. Let them learn how it feels to earn bread by the sweat of their brow. Let them be like this chicken-headed gaggle of peasants boggling as if their bleary eyes are about to pop from their heads. Then they'd see whether they had anything to complain about.

Or if they have to blame someone, why don't they blame their master? Idris is the one with the obsession for touring. Of course it's no skin off the old boy's nose to insist on this homage to the bad old days – he's laughing, wrapped up all cosy with his memories at home in Tsvingtori.

Glenda's voice rouses Bren from his bout of self-pity. 'Cheer up,' she says, handing him a mug of beer and a bowl heaped with food. 'It won't kill them to sleep on the grass tonight. Anyway they can't quit. They've got nowhere to go. By the time we get home they'll have forgotten it.'

'We have to get through this summer first.' Bren drinks deeply, and wipes the foam from his stubbled lip. 'I comfort myself with the knowledge of having been proved right. I told you I had a bad feeling about this summer, in my water, right from the start. At this rate we're not even going to cover our expenses.'

Glenda vaults neatly into the driving box with an agility belying her age, and bunches up beside him. She and Bren are the oldest members of the Company, relics from its heyday before the war. He is a big, beer-swollen man, intelligent grey eyes pouched in the folds of an ugly red face. Glenda has taken better care of herself. In her youth, when she was beautiful, she was a dancer and a King's mistress, and Bren's lover too, on and off. Now she takes the matron roles. Off-stage she plays mother hen to the rest of the Company, Asdura opposite Bren's beleagured Adonac.

'Everything's changed since the war,' says Bren. Glenda nods absently. This is ground they have covered many times. 'I don't just mean losing the Palace theatre,' Bren goes on, 'not having that any more, that prestige. But it's like everybody expects more all the time, bigger and better and newer. Everybody's so restless, like they're itching to run round the corner to see if there's something more exciting. We never used to have this trouble holding our audiences. Or maybe it's us. Us and our plays, both getting antiquated. We need some new blood, eh, Glenda? Glenda?'

'Shut up,' Glenda whispers. 'Look.' Covertly she points, a little way away, to where a beautiful child has just sat down under an elm tree.

At first glance Bren sees nothing unusual about the boy, aside from his remarkable prettiness. His hair is ash-blond, thick and straight, hacked off at different lengths all round his head. His smooth face and bare arms are golden-brown from the sun. In his lap he cradles a bloated burlap bag. Close to him a half-grown bitch puppy rolls yawning in the grass.

A quick movement may catch the eye, but absolute stillness arrests it. The boy has not moved or blinked. He hardly seems to be breathing. Bren and Glenda continue to stare at him, fascinated. He gives the impression of sleeping with his eyes open: they are dark blue, very bright, very vacant.

'Is he blind?' Glenda wonders. 'I think he is, I think he's blind. Oh, it's not fair.'

We'll see about that, thinks Bren. He shouts, 'Oi!' and flaps a hand across the boy's field of vision. The blue eyes blink twice. An intelligence appears in them, recognises itself as an object of attention. Immediately a pink blush fills the boy's cheeks. Glenda cannot help laughing aloud: the child is sheer delight to look at. The boy scowls at them both and stands up, teeth gritted, one hand braced on the tree trunk. He wants to turn his back on their laughter and walk away, but his feet – they have guessed it – are a mass of blisters.

This one's not used to walking, thinks Bren.

The boy's shoes, though well-made, are splitting at the seams. His clothes were good once, before they were rained on and slept in and rained on again. He's too well-dressed and has too much poise for a poor boy, and yet he's too foot-sore and travel-stained to be a rich man's son. He has the fair colouring and sturdy build of a native, coupled with the prickly pride of a young gentleman. All things and no one thing, thinks Bren, thoroughly intrigued.

At that moment the boy's stomach rumbles so loudly no one can pretend they did not hear it. His blush deepens to crimson, his eyes blaze, and that extraordinary burlap bag is pressed hard against an empty stomach.

Can't have eaten properly for days, thinks Bren. And that dog – if that's not a hunting dog, a gentleman's hound, worth as much as one of Idris' players can earn in a year, well, then Bren hasn't got eyes in his head, that's all.

21

He says, 'Come over here.'

The boy hesitates. Not so his dog, who smells food and has no shame. Tail wagging ingratiatingly, she trots up to the wagon and paws Bren's knee. After a second or two the boy follows, limping. Bren holds out his bowl of food. 'I can't eat this,' he says in the country native of his childhood. 'Eyes bigger than my stomach. Can't bear seeing good food go to waste – you wouldn't finish it up for me, would you?'

Expressionless eyes search Bren's face. Poor lad, thinks Glenda, maybe he's dumb. There is *something* wrong with him, something strange.

The boy says, 'Thank you, you're very kind,' and takes the bowl. His voice is pleasant, distinctive, slightly hoarse, and in it Bren detects the hint of an accent, the rounded vowels and slurred consonants of those raised in a more privileged language.

Two and a half centuries have passed since the Conquest. Brychmachrye's invaders have come to feel as much at home here now as the natives they rule. Andariah, where they came from, a corrupted version of whose language they still speak, is a foreign land to them. They are Brychmachrese; their language is Brychmachrese; and it is perhaps for this reason that the persistence of the old native tongue seems, to them, more absurd with each generation. They have banned the native from schools, law-courts, and Temple services, though not as yet, for what it's worth, from playhouses. It is useful to them only as an administrative tool with which to govern peasants too ignorant to acquire a less barbaric mode of speech.

This ragged boy speaks the native with the tongue of a nobleman. Bren glances at Glenda to see if she has noticed the accent. She nods, and in silence they watch as their suppositious young Lord picks all the chunks of meat from the pastry crust and feeds them to his dog.

Glenda's curiosity finally gets the better of her. 'Are you one of Isen Mathred's initiates?' she asks. It's a fair question: vegetarianism is a common eccentricity among that sect. The boy smiles. Apparently the idea amuses him. 'No,' he says, 'I just don't like meat.'

'What's your dog called?' asks Bren.

The boy says, 'Fern', which is an Andarian word. An Andarian name.

Among themselves the Company usually converse in

Tsvingtori street-patois, a bastard of a language that they call native, though most country folk would have trouble understanding it. Nevertheless they can all speak Andarian – court-speech – well enough to act in it. Most of their quality plays, as opposed to the mummery and farce they keep in repertory for tours like this, are written in the language of the Court. They have to give the City audiences what they are willing to pay for, those Guildsmen, merchants, clerks, temple priests and University Learneds eager to shake off their hick antecedents. Cunningly Bren phrases his next question in court-speech, '*Are you from around here?*'

The boy cocks an eyebrow the shape and colour of an ear of wheat. 'No,' he says, sticking stubbornly to the native.

'Where are you from, then?'

A full mouth prevents the boy from answering.

'Those shoes have seen a lot of road. Where're you heading?'

The boy shrugs, and keeps chewing.

'He's run away from home, haven't you, love?' says Glenda. She longs to reach out and stroke the boy's soft brown cheek, but doesn't dare. She wouldn't be surprised if he bit her. 'I bet your mam's worried sick about you.'

This, if true, does not seem to bother the boy.

Bren tries again. 'You're going to Tsvingtori, aren't you?'

Now he's on the right track. The boy's eyes twitch, and he swallows a mouthful. 'Bugger me,' Bren laughs, 'you think you're the first blue-eyed kid ever had that bright idea? How old are you? Fourteen? Fifteen?'

And, all unwittingly, Bren's hit on the one jibe the boy cannot ignore. 'I'm nineteen,' he glowers, 'nearly.' Clearly he has had enough of being cross-examined, for he now asks a question of his own, 'Are you Idris Owenson?'

So, thinks Bren, he can read. That's not so surprising, given the background his clothes and manner and accent suggest. Perhaps he is a merchant's son, with a mother from the petty nobility and a family that prides itself on the cultivation of court-speech and gentrified manners. There is nothing to be gained from teasing such a serious youth, so Bren gives him a straight answer. 'No. Idris is getting too old for this lark. He sends us out to sing for our supper and we bring him back the pudding.'

'What's "The Moon and the Stars"?'

Bren needs a moment to answer this. He looks closely at

the boy, wondering if his leg is being pulled. But no – there's no mischief in that perfectly-proportioned face, no gleam of humour in those self-possessed blue eyes. Bren hates being made to feel uneasy, so he tries to laugh it off and says, 'My, we are green, aren't we? You mean you've never heard of The Moon and the Stars?'

'Should I have?'

'What godforsaken backwater do you come from? You've really *never* heard of it?'

'Bren,' says Glenda calmly, 'he's never heard of it.'

'Good grief! What's this country coming to? I ask you. Never heard of The Moon and the Stars. And what about "Brennain Bellthroat"? You want to tell me you've never heard of him either?'

The boy shifts uncomfortably from foot to foot, and finally shakes his head. 'Hah!' cries Glenda, delighted. 'That's shown you, big-head. "Brennain Bellthroat" is him himself, love, as if you couldn't have guessed. Look at him, all puffed up like a great toad. Now don't you blush – he's a vain old bear and it doesn't hurt him to hear a few home truths. Bren's trouble is, he used to sing for a King, and he'll never let us forget it.'

Bren covers his face with his sleeve, playing at shame to hide his real discomfort. Maybe it is nothing but foolish pride – but, bury it, in Tsvingtori he *is* still well-known, and this boy's failure to recognise his once-famous name comes as more of a shock to him than he cares to let Glenda see. He is not, on the whole, a reflective man: he has never stopped to consider, as the years have gone past, that his life and the events he has lived through could be seen as history by someone else, someone young. He cracks jokes about being antiquated, expecting nobody to take him seriously. And now suddenly old age has popped up, close and real as never before, to stare him in the face through the nameless eyes of a beautiful child. 'Good grief,' he growls, 'I'll be buried,' and other nonsense, until he feels more like himself again. Then he drops his arm and gives the boy a direct look. 'So, what do they call you, blue-eyes?'

'Caryllac.'

'We've got a Caryllac, only we call him Carrots on account of his red hair. What do people call you? Cal? Cary? Caro?'

'Caro.'

'Well,' Bren twinkles, 'I bet you know this, Caro –

Caro, Caro, you sweet child of sorrow,
Sleep well in the moonlight, the world ends tomorrow.
Lie on the waters to carry you there,
With stars in your eyes and flames in your hair . . .'

Although past its prime Bren's voice is deep and powerful,
as lovely to hear as Caro is to look at. Bren ends the verse with
a triumphant flourish, an air of having thoroughly vindicated
himself, and is rewarded by a look of dawning respect from
Caro and fond indulgence from Glenda.

'Sure you know it,' Bren laughs. 'Everybody does. Now
I'll tell you something, Caro. That song was written before
you were born. Written for me. Peter the Black wrote it. Those
were the days when poets weren't too high and mighty to write
plays. They all wrote plays for me – Peter the Black, Conor
Aneurinson, Felix filcThomas . . .

> *Caro, Caro, you sweet child of sorrow,*
> *Age tires of dreaming, washed up the shallows.*
> *So many ships sail west on the sea,*
> *But none return east to bring Caro to me – '*

'What did I tell you?' Glenda sighs. 'Loves the sound of
his own voice.'

'*First Solstice*,' says Bren dreamily. 'That's one they haven't
got tired of yet. We still put it on, every winter, just for the
festival. So anyway, Caryllac what?'

'I'm sorry?' says Caro.

'Caryllac whose son? Come on, what's your father's name?
What's your village? What's your Quarter?'

'I have no father.'

The way Caro says this sends a little shiver through Bren.

Or is it the way the boy is looking at him, as if through
glass or water, or from a great distance, from the far side of an
uncrossable abyss? The cold self-confidence in his young face
defies Bren to feel sorry for him.

Or has it been dawning on Bren all this while, hand in
hand with the slow realisation that Caro's beauty is in fact
without flaw?

Such loveliness, the kind that can sap men's will and blind
their judgment, ought properly to be the portion of women,
who have no other weapon. For a moment Bren can almost

believe that the child is telling the truth: that he is, must be, something more significant than the chance result of the coupling of flesh and blood. One slip on the creator's part, a slightly larger nose or a different set to the chin, could have ruined this masterpiece; but the hand that made the boy never faltered. Caro's precarious perfection, like a stroke of good luck or a bizarre coincidence, cannot be dismissed as chance.

Certainly the little shiver in, as Bren would say, his water, is unmistakable. He has experienced it perhaps a dozen times in his life – when he met the woman who was to be his great love, and a man who became a friend he would have died for; and when, aged fourteen, Idris Owenson picked him out of the gutter. It feels like the finger of the Gods running up his spine: the abrupt premonition of another human being's importance.

Whoever this boy is, wherever he comes from, whatever he's running from, their paths did not cross by accident. Bren is sure of it. His' water is never wrong. It obliges him to take some action. Look at the boy. Dead on his feet and sick with hunger. Even without that premonitory shiver Bren couldn't just turn away and leave him here. The boy needs help to get where he's going. And so Bren says:

'You'll never get to Tsvingtori like that, Caro Caryllac. Your shoes are going to drop off and your feet are going to follow them. Bet you've got no money either, right? Bugger me, nothing changes. *I* was thirteen when I ran away to Tsvingtori. I'll tell you what, Caro Caryllac. You and your dog can hitch a ride with us, at least as far as Laurinyed – '

'Bren!' Glenda exclaims, laying a hand on his arm. She slips into their street-patois and says hurriedly, *'What do you think you're doing?'*

'We can't just leave him here.'

'You're pushing your luck already. The others won't stand for it.'

This was the wrong thing to say. Bren's eyes narrow and his lips purse. 'Who's in charge here, them or me? Yes, I am. Thank you. And I say that if Caro wants to come with us, he can. There's plenty of room.'

Glenda sighs. Quite what Bren wants with the boy she cannot imagine, but once he takes a notion in his pig-head there's no gainsaying him. She folds her arms and surrenders the argument.

'Fine,' Bren nods. 'Well, Caro Caryllac, what do you think?'

Whatever it is he may think, this boy born and bred to be

a hero from the golden hair of his head to the flapping soles of his shoes, it is nobody's business but his own. He merely smiles, and says, 'Thank you.'

2

A month passes. The Summer Solstice has come and gone; the days grow imperceptibly shorter; the brick-red city of Laurinyed, with its geranium window-boxes and war-scarred walls, is left far behind as the wagons head south, through flat fields of wheat and flax, into the parched downlands of Terenzah; and Caro and his dog are still with them.

At first the Company wasn't sure how to treat him. Glenda's warning proved to be founded on common sense, for with eleven people already crowded into three small wagons, they didn't welcome the addition of a boy and his dog, however winsome. He seemed unapproachable. His quiet aloofness was an insult to their robust camaraderie. His beauty made them feel ugly and awkward. His helpful obedience in completing any task they set him didn't make up for his secretiveness. He gave nothing away. He didn't try to fit in. He didn't belong with them. On the whole, they saw Bren's introduction of this stranger in their midst as yet another cause for complaint and, had they had their way, Caro would have been unceremoniously dumped out of the wagons.

Then, in Laurinyed, everything changed. The weather improved and the audiences were generous, and superstitiously the Company has given all the credit for this turnaround in their fortunes to Caro and his dog. Their original misgivings are forgotten. They rough and tumble all over him, and laugh at his gravity. They speculate about him to his face in the Tsvingtori street-native they believe he doesn't understand. They call him 'Little Lord Caro', and 'Our Lucky Charm', and tease him unmercifully about his good looks. They pester him for a peep inside his mysterious burlap bag. The girls are forever flirting with him. Squint Winnie won't let him alone. 'Give me a kiss,' she pouts, 'you're so pretty I can't stand it. Oh, you're breaking my heart, Caro, you love that dog more than you love me.'

He comes in useful in all sorts of ways. His deft fingers can bind a looseleaf script or mend a torn costume with equal ease. He copies out flysheets and lost pages in a quick, neat –

27

to Bren's eye, trained – hand. He carries out all his jobs quickly and thoroughly, with a discipline rarely seen in young men of his age. He knows how to mix paints. Sometimes, without reason or warning, he withdraws into the same state of rapt blue emptiness in which Bren and Glenda first found him, but he never loses his temper, and his patience makes him the ideal prompter and hearer of lines.

Above all, he is consummately skilled in the art of evading questions.

Bren asks him, 'You're a clerk, aren't you, Caro?'

'I've picked some things up.'

'Come on, I know training when I see it. They've made a good job of you. Where'd you work before?'

'Here and there.'

Glenda is dying to know, 'What *have* you got in that bag, Caro?'

'My personal belongings.'

The craft of acting, however, is a closed book to him. His one appearance on the stage, occasioned by the sudden illness of the other Caryllac, was an ordeal for cast and audience alike. All the same, his hopelessly wooden performance has done more than anything else to endear him to the Company. They are delighted to find something that Caro is not good at.

They have all forgotten that the original intention was to leave him, and his dog, and his great fat bag, in Laurinyed.

When he's in the mood, Bren fills Caro in bit by bit on the history of The Moon and the Stars.

The oldest and – for the Company will brook no contradiction on this point – by far and away the most famous of the three playhouses which survive in Tsvingtori as going concerns, The Moon and the Stars was first conceived by Idris Owenson more than seventy years ago. As a young boy he travelled to Pravarre with his father's theatre company, and there saw, for the first time, purpose-built open-air play pits. Every one of his actresses, actors, dancers and musicians knows this story by heart, for Idris never tires of telling it, and a lifetime twice as long as most men's has failed to dim his memory of the moment of inspiration.

IDRIS [*to father*]. We should have one of those pits in Tsvingtori.

28

FATHER. What have you got between your ears, thick- ^
head, wood? We wouldn't use it more than a quarter of the
year if we was lucky, weather we get at home. Be a waste
of bloody money.
IDRIS. We could build it inside a house, then.

Father walks away from his idiot son, laughing in a superior
manner. Idris is left alone to contemplate the new world his
vision could open up:

No more trudging cap in hand from town to town, shoulders
braced to the yoke because the mules have been sold, or eaten;
no more being rained on, snowed on, spat on, their feet covered in callouses, raw chilblains oozing on their fingers, their
clothes full of holes, freezing in the winter, roasting in the
summer, starving nearly always, giving birth in stables and
dying in ditches. His father always said that acting was a
disease: only madmen, lepers and players wander about the
country in all weathers, hoping for charity, and the first two
have no choice. His father always hated the fate that had
made him the son and heir of a player. His father had no
guts, no imagination, no passion, unlike Idris. Idris was going
to take that same fate by the horns and ride it up into eternal
glory.

Oh, the infinite scope of the productions he could mount,
if only he had a home for them. Once he was no longer
restricted to the few simple props that could be packed up
and carried, there would be no limit to the fabulous effects
that would be his to command. Oh, the scenery, the rolling
castles, moving boats, ocean waves and thunderstorms, hoists
and pulleys and flying machines, hidden rooms, rotating stages
– all the instruments of fantasy that Idris yearned to bring to life.
All he needed was a house.

For thirty years every investor the visionary approached
with his dreams laughed him out of sight. When Owen died
Idris inherited the Company, perpetuating the wandering way
of life while his heart was given over to perfecting ever more
grandiose plans for the world's first playhouse. He was forty-
two when he met Michael Andaranah.

It was the year of Michael's coming-of-age. Recently released
from the guardianship of a parsimonious uncle, and very much
in love with the arts, young King Michael was eager to make
his mark as a patron on the royal scale. When the excellent

reputation of the Idris Owenson Company reached his ears, he immediately summoned them to Court – according to Idris, so moving did the beardless King find their rendition of Conor Aneurinson's *The Death of Prince Foxfoot* that he afterwards sent for the Company's manager and in private audience offered to grant him whatever his heart desired. Recognising the chance of a lifetime, Idris did not wait to be asked twice. He would like his listeners to believe that he added, 'But I'm afraid I'm asking for the moon, Sir,' and that to this King Michael replied:

'Am I not King? What you ask for I can easily give; for the pleasure I have had from you this day I would gladly give you the stars as well.'

Thus was Idris Owenson's playhouse named before the first foundation stone was laid.

Over the years the friendship between the aging impresario and the young King flourished. Michael was fond of saying that when future generations considered his reign they would look upon The Moon and the Stars, and the other playhouses springing up in imitation of it, as his greatest achievement. (It was statements like this, made in all earnestness, which started begging the question in certain persons' minds of whether Michael was fit to be a King at all.) Michael's passion for the theatre – indeed for anything dramatically exotic or expensive – was such that, not content with having given his favourite a playhouse, he set about constructing a theatre at Court, with extensive workshops at the back where Idris could further his research into ever more elaborate pieces of stage machinery. Towards the end of Michael's reign Idris was living entirely at Court. This was the time when Bren and Glenda formed part of the 'Royal Court Company'.

Michael's subjects, however, were not prepared to go on indefinitely disgorging limitless sums in support of his patronage of the arts. After Michael's murder Idris, now in his seventies, fled abroad, and did not dare return for five years. When he came home, it was to find The Moon and the Stars occupied by a family of butchers. His legal struggle to prove rightful ownership of the property, though ultimately successful, used up what was left of the fortune a King had once squandered on him. Now he lives in semi-retirement, blaming his theatre's slump in popularity on the unwillingness of the general public to forgive *him* for Michael's generosity, and convinced that a renaissance in his personal and professional fortunes is due any day now.

'Which is why', Bren concludes, 'he's revived the summer tours. But his real problem is he hasn't got the plays any more. No good ones, I mean. It's the same with all the playhouses. Since the war playwriting's lost all the prestige it had in the days when Peter the Black and Conor Aneurinson were still alive. These days no poet with a half-way decent patron would touch playwriting with a bargepole. Vulgar, don't you know. So we rely more and more on the sort of crap we're doing at the moment, a few songs and dances strung along some pitiful excuse for a plot that even the huskheads can follow. And the more we rely on that, the lower our reputation sinks. We've tried reviving the old stuff, the good pre-war plays, but no one's interested. They think it's old-fashioned. They want novelty, and if we don't give the educated audience, the real audience, the real money, something to get their teeth into, they'll look for it elsewhere. They already are,' he finishes gloomily.

A little later he adds, 'Now listen, I'm not saying anything against our King Basal, he's a great King and he's putting this country to rights again – but old Michael, I guess he made some mistakes and all, but he was good to us. He would never have let an artist starve.'

Glenda and Bren are riding together in the driving box. As happens more often than not these days, they are discussing Caro.

'He slept with Winnie last night, you know,' says Glenda.

'About time too, poor girl. She was getting pretty desperate. Mind you,' Bren squeezes Glenda's knee, 'I wouldn't climb over you to get to her.'

'Chance would be a fine thing. According to Winnie, she's found something else that Caro's incredibly good at.'

Bren roars with laughter. Glenda is not amused. 'You never could resist a pretty face,' she frowns. 'If I didn't know you so well I'd wonder about you and him.'

'Oh come on, he's turned out all right. The Company love him.'

'They treat him like a toy, that's all. They don't really know him. None of us knows him. He's been with us for, what? Nearly two months, and we don't know any more about him than the day we picked him up. We don't know where he comes from or who he is, and the Gods know I've given up trying to get

31

answers out of him. We don't know how his mind works or what he wants from us. We don't even know if Caryllac is his real name. He could be someone's runaway servant or a thief – for all we know that bag of his could be full of stolen property.'

'Not the way he slings it around. It's not heavy, I can tell that much from looking at it.'

'Well, it doesn't have clothes in it. He didn't have anything to wear but what was on his back.'

'Now hold on, Glenda. I know he likes to keep himself to himself, but we've got no reason to think he's dishonest.'

'He's hiding something. Oh, I don't know, Bren. I know he's sweet and pretty, it's hard not to like him. I just worry about you. I don't want you to get too attached to him. I don't think people mean much to him, that's all. Sufficient unto himself is our Caro. He was a stranger when we met him, he's still a stranger, and he always will be. You mark my words.'

3

Caro sprawls across the tailgate, drowsy in the sunshine, watching the dusty road unroll westwards off the wagon wheels. Fern's muzzle presses a hot weight of love against his stomach. Bren, following on foot, with Glenda's words fresh in his mind, wishes the boy would trust him enough to confide in him. Caro's head is pillowed on that bag full of secrets. It's like an extra limb: Caro never lets it out of his sight. His brows are knotting fiercely and he chews his lips. What profound thoughts, what secret ambitions can be passing through his mind? Bren would dearly love to know. He can only guess, and in guessing, go wildly astray.

Bren has fallen so much into the habit of expecting the extraordinary from Caro, that he has forgotten he too was once eighteen. He has forgotten that the odds are against a young man's thoughts running, on this sweltering August afternoon, to anything more unusual than that universal preoccupation, sex.

Or love. Sex and love, poetry and deception.

Winnie keeps her neck and shoulders bare to display the contract, signed and sealed, of his love-bites. The other girls wonder if Caro does love her. He must do – for Winnie is certainly not the prettiest girl in the Company, and Caro could have had anyone. But he never made a move. They'd assumed he was an innocent. Now they have to take Winnie's word for it that they were very, very mistaken, and they're dying to know whether half of what she boasts about is true.

It would be easy enough for them to find out. All they would need to do is present themselves as Winnie did, with their bodices open and their skirts up, and Caro would oblige them with as much willingness and as little pleasure. But they don't know this. They think he must be fond of her. For the sake of peace in the wagons they respect Winnie's claim, and it's never been worth Caro's while to run after any woman.

When he was younger, fourteen or fifteen, and all he knew about love and sex was what he read in poems, Caro visualised it as a room or a house – a tavern with a great fire blazing in the grate, bright and warm with candles and happiness. To step over the threshold of this tavern, delicate hands helping you inside, was to step into adulthood and become a man. The sort of pleasure on offer in this tavern was not to be imagined, could not be adequately described. They had a wine there that put hair on your chest. You became drunk with a passion that sharpened all your nerves instead of blunting them. The deep sweet draught of ecstasy, no less, the poets called it. Until you've tasted that, you haven't lived. Everybody wanted to be inside that tavern. Sometimes Caro felt he was the only person on the outside. He pressed his nose against the window, but it was all steamed up and he couldn't see clearly.

He was sixteen before a girl offered to relieve him of his virginity. She was a few years his elder and knew what she was about, and her heartfelt praise of his performance was therefore not to be scorned, although it did slightly perplex him: he could not express an equal delight in the exercise. Nevertheless his disappointment didn't worry him unduly. He had always known that poetry requires dedication and practice, and he confidently expected to make it flesh soon with some other girl. It was only after he had slept with half a dozen girls, and all of them had congratulated him on not being like other men, that he began to suspect there was more truth in the statement than they could possibly guess.

He can do everything that other men do, and he can do it, so they tell him, better than most. Presumably he can even father a child, although no one's laid that particular disaster at his door yet. What he cannot do is feel, for himself, inside himself, any

33

part of the enjoyment he can see on the faces of his partners.

For other men, it seems, sex is about the only thing in life that never disappoints. For them, lovemaking is the closest they will ever get to poetry. It is the highest point they can reach on their endless, doomed climb towards immortality. In making love, their thoughts, their ambitions, their worries, their hopes, and even their consciousness of the passage of time are swept away on a transcendental surge of physical sensation, their minds are submerged in their bodies, and flesh and intellect, like man and woman, become one in an embrace so powerful nothing can prevent them from crying out. And when it's finished, and the two separate to tug them, as before, in different directions, they grieve because they feel only half-alive, half-dead. Or at least that's the impression Caro gets.

He has never found escape in the arms of a woman, and he has given up hoping it will happen. He never feels more detached than when he is making love. Only his loins are involved. His thoughts remain clear, and often wander away down the most tangential avenues. His self-control is untroubled by the least inkling of rapture. He becomes more of an observer than ever: and his observation is that sex doesn't feel like anything, much. He doesn't like it or dislike it. There is a certain mental pleasure, part amusement, part gratified pride, to be gained from watching his partner writhe and shriek. The thing he hates most about it is that it makes him feel so utterly alone with himself. Probably it's just as well that he has a gift for it. His girls are too busy having fun to notice that he is having very little fun. He could not endure it if they realised there was something wrong about him.

'What was it like?' he asks them.

'Oh you men, you're all the same. Couldn't you tell? Didn't you feel it?'

He used to mind. He used to feel cheated and angry, the way he did when he was a child and his father came home for one of those visits which were always unannounced and never lasted long. On these occasions his mother would say, 'Go outside and play, Caro.' The moment he stepped out the door she dropped the latch and refused to let him back in. They ignored his howls, and for his part Caro soon learned not to be so gullible. When he heard the words 'Run outside and play', he grabbed hold of the nearest fixed object and refused to budge. Later still, after he had started school, he understood why he was in the way and would slope off of his own accord to climb a tree. He had resigned himself to putting up with it. He knew it was only for as long as his father wanted to do *that* with his mother that they could count on him returning to them.

Caro has never told anybody about his failure to enjoy sex. He has never had anyone to tell; and in any case he now sees that it was always inevitable, as inevitable as Bren turning up on the very same village green in the middle of nowhere when Caro, sore of foot and heart and wondering which step his fate would take next, should happen to sit down on it. That Caro should be so good at something which does him no good is no more surprising than fate arriving in the shape of a fat, vain actor and three gaudy wagons. Caro takes these things for granted. They are of a piece with his beauty, and the knack he has of always finding a friend in time of need. Fate has kitted him out with everything he needs to smooth his path through life, bring him to his destiny, and achieve his immortality. Caro knows why he is alive, and it is not for the sake of enjoying himself. He accepts this, but he sees no reason to talk about it, any more than he should reveal to those around him the Caro inside his prettiness, the Caro who is ugly, and unlovable, and not like other people.

4

On the morning of the following day, as if to remind Caro that his life is a serious business – made, and preserved, with one object in mind – fate has so arranged it that Bren's itinerary brings the Company to the town of Farzaned, where the week of the harvest festival coincides with the celebrations for the marriage between Lord Farzanah's daughter and the nephew of the Fahlraec of Olivah. The town's holiday mood has been doubled by its excitement over a prodigy witnessed two days ago:

On that afternoon the groom and his uncle arrived to spend the festival week with the bride's family. They came in state across the countryside, banners high and trumpets blaring, and were welcomed at the gates of the town with presents and garlands and speeches by all the leading Guildsmen. Suddenly everyone was amazed to see a wild fox come running in from the fields, darting fearlessly between the legs of men and horses as if a pack of ghost hounds were on its tail. It was foaming at the mouth. People scattered before it, except for the man whose turn it was to speak next. Despite the confusion around him, this man stepped up to begin his speech. He had come to within less than an arm's-breadth away from Lord Olivah's horse. Apparently he never realised the danger he was in, until the fox ran right up to him and bit him, on the leg, so savagely that he cried out in pain and fear and threw up his arms, dislodging the sword he had hidden in his coat. All this took place in broad daylight.

No one tried to capture the fox, and it ran away. Mad foxes are sacred: they have the spirit of Prince Foxfoot in them. The failed assassin confessed everything. It transpired he was the cousin of one of the men condemned in the recent treason trials in Tsvingtori, and he had planned to exact revenge on the person of Lord Olivah – which is to say, on a limb of the King. Many people were of the opinion that he should be left to suffer the slow death the Gods had already punished him with, but Lord Olivah and Lord Farzanah promised him mercy in return for his confession, and this very afternoon he is to be buried alive.

You're in luck, a high-spirited townsman tells the Company. If you'd come tomorrow you would have missed it. Acknowledging that they are bound to lose out in the competition for audiences, Bren lets the Company have the afternoon off.

But where's Caro? They can't go without Caro. He wouldn't want to miss this. At last they find him curled up with Fern in the back of one of the wagons. Aren't you coming, Caro? Don't you feel well? Squint Winnie offers to stay with him; but when she touches him, he cringes. There's no talking to Caro when he's in a mood, so they leave him in peace and hurry off to make sure of a good view.

Caro's teeth are chattering. He wraps his arms around Fern's warmth and hugs her tight. He feels as cold and oppressed as if *he* were buried in earth. As indeed he will be one day, in all probability. It is not luck that has brought him to Farzaned on this particular day. His fate is always testing him.

Imagine it, Caro. The damp earth, the worms and centipedes, your bound limbs struggling fruitlessly, the pebbles rattling on your skull. Are you afraid of it? But you must embrace it. An assassin is keeping the earth warm against your turn.

Fate dangles terrors and temptations in front of Caro, as though to say, you need not accept the destiny for which your life was preserved. You could choose instead, as so many others have, an aimless, selfish life. Fate wants to make sure of his commitment. Fate shows him his life being woven on the loom of circumstances, none fortuitous, and forces his memory to look at the beginning of the pattern: another dog, equally faithful, dead from the stroke of a sword, and a fat man clutching a bitten arm while blood seeped between his fingers. *See, Caro, how it repeats itself?* I know, Caro answers. That is the way of swords. That is why I refused to have one.

Caro feels that basically the Company are decent people, if frivolous and unthinking. What then compels them, and the men and women of this town, and all his fellow countrymen, to make a public spectacle out of a murder, and to see death as a cause for celebration? Caro can't blame them. They know no better. They are as much victims as the man whose death they have gone to watch, buried alive while he still breathes, breathing until the weight of stones and mud crushes the air from his lungs. He is dying because he knew no better. He acted in accordance with what he was taught to believe; and he is being punished as a criminal when in other times and places similar deeds have been rewarded as acts of heroism. How many drops of blood is it going to take, spilled from generations of lives, to wash away the mistake on which the world is founded? I *was* right, Caro tells himself. Teeth and swords are not the answer. There has to be a better way.

He didn't try to argue the Company out of going to the execution, because he knew that they would laugh at him. Who is going to take it seriously when a charity child, their pretty foundling boy, tells them they are making a mistake? For now he must hold his tongue. One day they will listen to him. Fate has kept him alive for no other purpose, and fate will so arrange things that one day the whole country will sit up and take notice of Caro.

The others return from the execution in a properly sober and spiritual frame of mind, to find Caro perched cross-legged in the driving-box, polishing up one of the tin crowns from the props basket and whistling tunelessly.

Leaving Farzaned, the players turn their wagons homeward. Caro's birthday falls when they are still three days from Tsving-tori: they pile into a village tavern to drink and sing the night away, culminating in four consecutive performances of 'Caro,

37

oh Caro', roared in chorus by the entire Company. Later Winnie drags Caro outside, cheered on by guffawed applause, to give him his present. Making the most of him while she can, thinks Bren. She'll never hold on to him in Tsvingtori.

Next morning the Company set off on foot to walk off their hangovers, and Bren is left sitting alone with Caro in the back of a wagon. Caro is asleep on a heap of sweat-stained velvet costumes, breathing softly with his mouth open. The tan is peeling from his nose, leaving a fawn's dappling of pink patches and freckles. He looks like something ripening in the sun. Long golden lashes flutter on his cheeks. Fern dozes happily against his chest. Together they are the very picture of a clear conscience.

Bren, however, is wide-awake – more than wide-awake, in fact, as one who in the sudden presence of great joy or great danger is utterly alive, utterly concentrated in a moment frozen out of time. Headache forgotten, queasiness completely vanished, conscience thrown to the winds, curiosity astounded and dazzled with excitement, he has Caro's burlap bag, stolen from under Caro's sleeping grasp, open on his knees, and his hands are full of Caro's secret.

Poems.

The bag is stuffed with poems. Bren can hardly take it in. Poems covering both sides of a sheet of parchment, poems running round the margins, poems squeezed between the lines of other poems – an overwhelming clamour of poems calling out to poems as yet unwritten, dreams of poems jostling inside Caro's slumbering head. It's impossible for Bren to reconcile the Caro he thought he knew, pretty little biddable Caro, Caro who never uses two words when none will do, with this profusion of talent, this wild forest, this spring storm of poetry. Epigrams, sonnets, scraps of epics, dialogues and even hymns – hymns from the pen of a boy who has never displayed the merest rudiments of faith. And they are good poems too, works of a conscious artistry acquired by hard work and trial and error, infused with the youthful promise of greatness in maturity. Poems written in two languages, native and court-speech, each as fluent as the other – no, *three* languages, for here's a little one written in their street-patois! And Caro never gave a hint, not by the flickering of an eyelid, that he understood it! The sly bastard.

Caro – their Caro – a great poet? Bren's head is throbbing

38

with the effort of coming to terms with it. To look at him you'd never guess . . . Bren wouldn't have believed it if you'd sworn it on the King's oath. He still can't believe it. Just look at the boy snoozing there, all rosy and golden and innocent of guile. Hardly the picture of a tormented genius.

Of course there are strong traces in these poems of the masters who came before, from whom Caro has learned his craft. Again and again Conor Aneurinson's turns of phrase emerge, re-twisted and given fresh life; Felix filcThomas's original model reveals unexpected possibilities through being harnessed to a new line of argument, a new way of seeing. Peter the Black, obviously Caro's favourite, has been translated over and over again into the native.

Bren knew these men. He knows their poetry. The thought that he will now have to class Caro in their company is more than a human brain can hope to cope with in one morning.

Good grief, thinks Bren, he's bamboozled us all. We've patted him on the head and patronised him, laughed at his eccentricities, laboured the joke of his acting – and all the time he had this up his sleeve. Why didn't he tell us? Why did he hide them? He must think we're right idiots.

As the first shock of the discovery subsides, Bren's heart begins to swell with righteous indignation. The Company has offered Caro nothing but kindness and companionship, and this is how they are repaid: by lying and dissembling. He shoves his hand to the bottom of the bag and gropes around, wondering whether the boy thought it worth bringing anything aside from his poems when he decided to run away and seek his fortune in Tsvingtori. Ah – a book. Bren pulls it out and flicks through it, carefully, for the pages are crumbling and spotted with mould. It must be several hundred years old, written in the classical Andarian that bears about as much relation to court-speech as Tsvingtori street-native does. Who these days, aside from University Learneds, can read such stuff? Bren certainly can't. Mightily irritated, he slaps the book shut, and as he does so it disintegrates in a cloud of dust and dry glue, the pages scatter across the floor of the wagon, and Bren is left with only the empty bindings open in his hands to reveal, inside the front and back covers, the poem Caro has written about the prodigy of Farzaned.

Though less polished than the other poems, this one is so passionate and sincere it makes the rest sound like schoolroom exercises. The others were gem-stones, worked over and refined. This one has blood and breath and feeling. It addresses the people who seek to find the magic of a King in the madness of a fox. You must listen to me, it insists. There is no magic in a King, or anywhere on earth. The madness is nothing more than your own credulity, your thoughtless acceptance of everything your masters tell you to believe. Can't you see that the King and the assassin are one and the same, blood-brothers? Can't you understand that the error will continue to repeat itself, feeding on its own blood, until you find the courage and the will to change it? In a world where bloodshed is the only solution, there will always be Kings and there will always be assassins. Your devotion to this madness will bleed us all to death, unless we find a better way.

By the time Bren reaches the end of this wild howl of unabashed treason, he is sweating.

Men have died for less. Men have died for the mere suspicion of thinking along these lines. Stupid boy. Stupid idiot. No wonder he hid this. No wonder he cowered in the back of the wagon. He should never have written it. He shouldn't even think it. If anyone sees this poem, they'll bury him.

Bren's whole body is shaking with fear – fear for Caro, fear of that poem and the destructiveness it could unleash on its own author – and anger at whatever guardians allowed him to grow up so misguided. At one blow his new-found pride in his friend, the great poet, applauded and rich, is knocked aside by the vision of a beautiful child condemned, vilified, being rolled into the pit before he has even begun to live or understand what he has done. It's a cancer of a poem, a parasite taking advantage of its host's naïvety. Bren's one thought is to destroy it. Already his fingers are tearing at the bindings, ripping the thin board into chunks and the chunks into splinters, spitting on it to smear the ink. He works away busily for a minute or so, before realising that Caro is watching him. Impossible to know how long those blue eyes have been open. Caro has woken silently, without moving a muscle.

'What are you doing?'

'Finding out why you never let go of this bag. Caro, I –'

'Nobody said you could read them.'

'Yes, well – Gods! Caro, don't you know that this – this –'

No words can express it; at least, no words that Bren knows. He is forced to pause, and reflect. It is more than likely that

40

the boy really does not realise the sheer stupid dangerousness of what he has written. Bren knows that tact is not his strong point. This moment, when he's caught at a disadvantage, would be the worst moment to try talking some sense into Caro. Much better to hold back for now, think all the arguments through carefully, and then explain it to Caro, man to man. Our sins always rebound on us – Bren shouldn't have pried into Caro's secrets, and by doing so he has brought this awful punishment, the responsibility for saving Caro's life, upon himself. For Caro's sake he can't afford to put his foot in it. All right, thinks Bren, I'll humour him for now, and raise the subject when he's in a sweeter mood.

So Bren pushes the scraps of binding into his pocket, gives Caro a broad smile, and summons up enough false cheerfulness to quip, 'You are a little shit. Why did you hide them? They're too buried good to keep in a bag.'

Caro leaps into a sitting position – from the speed of his movement and the blaze in his eyes, Bren fears the poet is about to go for his throat.

'Do you really think so?' asks Caro shyly. He keeps forgetting that he respects no man's opinion.

Bren barely utters a word for the rest of the day. Hard thinking doesn't come easy to him at the best of times, and the morning's revelations have almost overpowered his reason. He needs to concentrate, and walks on his own at some distance behind the wagons. By nightfall he believes he's cracked it. He's come up with a plan. He can save Caro from the consequences of his folly, while incidentally doing Idris, and his own career, a good turn.

That evening the Company makes camp in a ploughed-over hayfield. After supper – baked hare for Fern and the players, bread and beans for Caro – Bren stands up and asks Caro to come for a walk with him. They stroll in silence along a hedgerow until they are out of the sight of the wagons, when Bren opens the conversation with:

'Given any thought to what you'll do when we get home, old man?'

Caro says nothing. Whether this is because he has no plans, or because he doesn't intend to confide them, Bren cannot tell, so he continues with, 'If you were counting on going on working for us like you have been, you can forget it. Idris won't

41

stand for it. If it were up to me I'd find something for you, but let's face it, you're pretty useless. Your acting is crap. You sing like a crow. You can't dance. In fact all you can do is write.'

'So?'

'So why don't you write plays? For us.'

'I'm a poet. I don't write plays.'

'Oho, what was good enough for Peter the Black isn't good enough for Little Lord Caro.'

'Don't call me that.'

'Don't talk bollocks then. Some of those poems are as good as plays, if you took out the bits between the dialogue. I'm not offering to do you a favour, Caro, Gods forbid. I wouldn't suggest it if I didn't think Idris would take you on, and he won't take you on unless he's as sure as I am that you can deliver the goods. You could write a good play, I know you could. A play I'd be proud to be in. Look, I think you owe it to me to at least try. Tit for tat – I introduce you to Idris and you revive my flagging career. How about it?'

'I've never written a play in my life. I've never wanted to write plays.'

'How else do you think you're going to earn a living? Not off your poems, that's for sure. Of course you'll have no trouble getting them accepted, but don't you know that the Official Publishers don't pay their authors anything? There's only two ways a poet can make a living – you can find a rich patron, easier said than done, and you'd have to write to his tune anyway; or you can take a retainer with a theatre company and write plays. That's how Peter the Black got started. Please, just think about it. You could walk a lot further before you got a better offer.'

A bat darts past their heads and they look up, following its flight across the moon until it vanishes against the dusk. The stars arrange themselves into constellations, as if they subscribe to a sort of order, have affinities, offer meanings.

Caro says, 'You tore up my poem.'

'And you know why. Who put those ideas into your head?'

'Nobody. I write what I see. I'm old enough to know my own mind.'

'Caro, I know I shouldn't have read them, but really it's a good thing I did. I don't think you realise how dangerous that one poem was. You could be killed for it if anyone had seen it.'

'Everybody has to die sometime. I'd rather die for the truth than die for nothing.'

'It's easy to say that now. Everybody thinks they're immortal when they're your age. Anyway,' Bren chuckles, 'dying for the truth isn't as straightforward as you think. I came pretty close to it – I mean, that's what I thought I was doing at the time. I fought in the war, you know. For the Andaranah. I thought they had the Gods on their side. I was in that battle where Prince Maxim got killed, Beacon Hill. We were acquainted in a manner of speaking, what with me being at Court and all. And we were the same age. After he died I lost the heart for it. I realised that it didn't really make much difference which side won. We're still natives and they're still Andarians. We're still their servants and they're still our masters, and the war was never going to change that.'

'Someone said the same thing to me once,' says Caro. 'He said it wasn't our war.'

'And he was right.'

'No, I don't think so. I knew many people, natives, who fought in the war and died. They thought they were doing the right thing. That made it their war. What I don't understand is, if Basal Rorhah was meant to be a King, why did thousands of men have to die to make him a King? Why was it necessary? And why should I believe in Gods who choose war as the means of achieving their ends? I don't want to believe in Gods like that.'

'Whoa, a philosopher!'

'Don't laugh at me.'

'Well, you should hear yourself. You're not the only person who's ever asked himself these things. Why are we born, why do we die, what's the meaning of life . . . You could waste your whole life wondering and never really live. There's no answer. You have to live with what you can't change. Life's to be lived, that's my philosophy, to have a good time and make the best of yourself. Now take you, for instance. I still can't get over your poems. They're so damned good. You've got every gift the Gods can give, and you don't know how lucky you are. You could really make something of yourself. You've got so much talent. I'm not just saying that to flatter you. Quite frankly you're too good to waste. And that poem was treason, that's the long and the short of it. You should get rid of all the ones like it. And don't try to kid me it's the only one. If you don't get rid of them you'll be found out, sooner or later, and all your talent will go

43

for that,' Bren blows a raspberry. 'They won't care that you're only young. Look, I don't expect you to change your mind about this immediately. You know what your life is worth to you. But I like you, Caro. I think of you as a friend. And as a friend I had to say this to you. All I ask is that you think about, just think about, the possibility that you could be wrong. That's all. Enough said. Now, about Idris. I think what we should do is let me pick out a dozen or so of your poems for him to read –'

'You do what you like,' Caro interrupts. 'Whatever you think is best. If you want a play you can have one. I suppose I do owe you that much. Can we go back now, please?'

Caro lies awake, curled in his blanket close to the smoking embers of the campfire. From time to time a charred log crumbles, and a whirl of orange sparks leaps upwards. Caro is thinking about what Bren said, and about death.

Not for the restless ghosts of traitors the soft berth in a rocking ship, the comfort of a bright fire, the salty waves purifying all wounds, both those given and those received, the journey swift as the wind and light as ashes to the eternal home. Traitors' graves are at once a punishment and a deterrent – depriving them of this life and of the life to come; that is, if you believe that what they are stripping you of is something that exists to be taken, and if your fear of death, of ghosthood, is so great that your skin seems worth preserving even at the cost of the truth. Hanged criminals are permitted a funeral. Only traitors are demolished as if they had never been.

Bren's concern distresses Caro more than he had expected. He should never have allowed himself to grow attached to Bren. Affection for other people, like any indulgence, can only make his task harder. Poor Bren, who could be kinder? He only wants what's best for Caro. He doesn't understand. Regrets are vain, but Caro can't help wishing Bren had got the better of his curiosity and left that bag alone. He knew it was too soon. He knew that Bren would laugh at him, and talk down to him, and fail to listen.

Caro presses his face into the grass, the smell of tiny flowers and crushed seeds tickling his nose delightfully. I must teach myself to welcome it, he thinks. Digging his fingers into the earth, he tells himself, a grave is better. If I had the choice, I would choose to be buried. I would choose to stay. These little periwinkles will grow where my eyes were, and the roots of these grasses will tangle round my finger-bones. The summer rain will water me. I will be a father to a little patch of Brychmachrye, flesh of her flesh, earth of her earth. I love this country. I will truly be a part of her. They will think it is my punishment, when it is my reward. They will be dust one day, every trace of them blown clean off these shores. And I will still be here, where I belong. I will be refreshed in the clear water of her rivers, ripen in the corn of her fields, taste sweet in the fruit of her orchards. I will still be here when thousands upon thousands of years have erased all memory of them. What more can I ask? Kings rise and fall, generations pass away and new generations take their place to be supplanted in their turn, but Brychmachrye will always turn to spring again. And I will still be here.

5

Everyone who does not live there knows two things about Tsvingtori: it is built on a cliff, and it is in consequence a wonder of the world.

Caro is forced to abandon the first of these misconceptions the moment he sets eyes on the City. Tsvingtori is not built on a cliff, although part of it is built under one. The oldest quarters stand on ancient terraces of earth thrown up against the cliff face. North of the waterfall that once formed the boundary of the City, the cliff slopes down to an alluvial plain carved by the Wastryl before it changed its course, and on this flat land the new city, airy and prosperous, is expanding in a curve around the bay.

The second misconception is lost somewhere among the alleys and terraces of the Old City. Bren and Caro head up from the docks, climbing streets that are no more than twisting flights of stone steps. Filth-encrusted pigs and mangy geese forage in the choked gutters. Black clouds of flies hover above butchers' stalls. The houses, built mostly of timber and plaster, are jumbled so close together on the slopes that in many places the red tiles of their roofs touch, casting the streets below into damp shadow. Caro hurries to keep up with Bren, elbowing through the crush of people, stopping now and then to shake a piece of rotten vegetable or excrement from his shoe, and whistling for Fern, who persists

45

in darting off to pursue the sources of all these noxious smells.

Tsvingtori is no different, no more wonderful, than any other city Caro has seen – it's only more overcrowded, and dirty, and noisy, and ramshackle, and seedy and cramped and starved of sunlight, and so big he doesn't think he'll ever find his way out again.

His spirits already depressed, Caro's first sight of The Moon and the Stars, decked out in the tawdry remnants of her better days, fills him with an inexpressible sadness. The brass-bound doors are worm-eaten and badly in need of paint. Silver leaf is peeling, like dead skin, from the plaster moons on the cornice, and all the stars have chipped their points. Two have fallen off completely, leaving a gap where a family of pigeons has made its nest, dropping messes on to the steps. On either side of the entrance cracked slates are fixed to the wall, chalked up with details of tomorrow's performance. Beneath one a passing critic has scratched the terse comment SHIT.

The entrance is locked. Bren leads Caro around the back. They stumble down a gloom-struck alley until they come to a blanket tacked across an open doorway. Bren lifts the blanket aside, takes Caro's arm, and pushes him through.

Inside the room is full of smoke, very dark, and smells of unwashed feet. The shutters are closed. A little light comes from a small fire spitting in the hearth. Somebody is asleep in an enormous four-poster bed pushed against the far wall. Along another wall is a bench. Bren motions Caro to sit down. The floor is strewn with hay, pieces of parchment, clothes, and books bound with string. In an armchair beside the fire sits a man with the head of a tortoise. Caro can't stop staring at him, bedazzled by the man's extreme antiquity. His scalp has exactly the same pink-and-liver spotted complexion as that bare bit of Fern's tummy behind her hind legs, and his nose is like a mountain. He is facing them, but he is reading, and seems not to have noticed their entrance.

After a moment he coughs, hawks a chunk of phlegm into the hay, screws up the page he is reading and feeds it into the fire. When three pages have been consumed in this way, Bren says, 'Idris, we're back.'

The sleeping person sits up and reveals herself as a naked red-haired woman. 'Bren!' she squeals, 'Bren, Bren!' making no move to get out of bed.

'Who's the kid?' says Idris.

'Isn't he cute?' she cries. 'Come over here, cutie, so I can see you better.'

'This is Caryllac, he's a friend of mine. Caro, at last you meet the famous Idris Owenson.'

'How do you do?' says Caro politely.

'Humph,' snorts Idris. 'I can see he didn't learn his manners from you, Swine's Son. What did you do, kidnap him?'

'My name's Morwenna,' says the red-head.

Suddenly Idris groans, 'What's THAT? A DOG? Get it out of here. I can't abide animals.'

Caro has some difficulty persuading Fern to stay outside. He returns to find that Bren has handed over the tour's profits to Idris, who stands weighing a bag speculatively in each hand as he says, 'You know I'm not interested in taking anyone on unless they can do something spectacular. Is he a contortionist? Can he eat fire? Fly?'

'If you don't want him,' says Morwenna, 'I'll have him.'

'You're wasting your time, darling, that kid doesn't look like his balls have dropped.'

Bren quickly lays a restraining hand on Caro's arm. 'Don't mind him. He likes you really. Idris, you'll want him when you hear what he can do. Caro's going to save our bacon. He's a poet.'

'And I'm the King of Andariah.'

'It won't cost you anything to listen, will it? You'll be sorry you missed this chance when one of the other theatres snaps him up. Look, read these – ' Bren takes the bundle of twelve carefully selected poems from his shirt and hands them to Idris, 'and then you tell me whether you don't think Caro could be worth anything to us.'

He pulls Caro on to the bench, and they wait.

Twenty minutes later Idris has read each poem twice.

He finishes the last, puts it on top of the pile in his lap, licks his lips, folds his hands, looks from Bren to Caro and says, 'Well, well,' and suddenly beams with the smile that once charmed a King, though there are only three teeth left in it. He puts four silver coins on the table. 'Get dressed, Mo. I want you to go to the vintners' in Sheep Square and get us a bottle of their best Cadini white – two bottles.'

'I think we've done it,' Bren whispers to Caro. 'The last time the old shit bought me a drink was before the war, and

47

even then he borrowed the money off me.'

Much later, when Bren and Caro are leaving, drunk and happy, Idris takes another handful of silver from his pocket, presses it on Caro, and tells the boy he has two weeks to make the outlay worth his while.

6

Caro's first attempt at a play is not a success.

He hasn't seen much of the City over the last two weeks, working all the hours the Gods send and, when he can't keep awake any longer, grabbing a few hours' sleep on Bren's floor. The ink has barely dried on the last page before he sets off, red-eyed with exhaustion but flushed with impatience and pride, to show it to Idris. Several hours later he returns. His face is white, his look murderous. Without a word he shuts himself into Bren's bedroom. Bren knocks once, twice. No response. Alarmed, Bren runs down to the Conqueror tavern and corners Idris. 'What happened?'

'Touchy little bastard, isn't he? I burnt his play.'

'You didn't! How could you? He worked his guts out for that!'

'Did you read it?'

'He wouldn't show it to me.'

'Gods preserve me from poets. They're always their own worst enemies. Sit down, Bren. Before we go any further I think you'd better tell me everything you know about this boy of yours.'

Bren's tale is soon done.

'Hmm,' says Idris. 'So he could be anybody.'

'He's going to be a great poet.'

'If he lives so long. And you knew what he was like, didn't you? You knew and you brought him to my theatre. If I wasn't such a sentimental old fool I'd give you the sack, Bren. You ought to know better after all we've been through together. Shall I tell you what his play was about, or can you guess? The war. The war, for fuck's sake! He can't even remember the war. I told him those of us who can don't want to be reminded. How did he think we'd get away with putting on a play about the war? The censors would have us all underground five minutes after we opened. When I said so he started to puff smoke out of his ears, and I told him he had to decide whether he wanted to be

48

dead or a poet. I have to watch my own step – and you're not entirely above suspicion either, you know. The last thing we need is some seditious lunatic trying to put one over on us.'

'He'll grow out of it.'

'I should hope so. Anyway I couldn't have put his play on even if it was Prince bloody Foxfoot. Strangest play I've ever read, if you can call it a play. Good writing, mind you, you were right there, and I may add it's the only reason we're still speaking. But no songs, no laughs, and all the acts were different lengths. Who's going to sit through that? Didn't that kid learn anything this summer, swanning round the countryside at my expense? I almost wish I hadn't burnt it, it's such a joke. Right at the end, the climax, the hero Lord Thomas gets cornered in some cottage where he's holed up, and this Commander character, his enemy, is threatening to chop his head off. Great opportunity for some really stirring speeches – the whole play's been leading up to it – and your boy just throws it away. The Commander says, "What's it to be?" and the hero says, "I'd rather die," and then the Commander says, "All right, get down," and the hero says, "I'm not going to kneel in front of you." I nearly split my sides, Bren, I'm telling you. And your Caro said, but that's how people talk. So big deal, I said, who's going to pay for that? They can hear how people talk in the streets, for free. I don't know whether your kid is a tragedy or a comedy, but he's certainly bizarre. If I had any sense I'd wash my hands of him.'

'You wouldn't – you won't turn him in?'

'Oh, you know me, I'm a soft touch. There's no love lost between me and the Rorhah, and anyway your little genius is too good to lose. But don't you dare tell him I said that. I don't think he'll try to pull any more stunts, now that he sees it's got him nowhere. I'm giving him another chance. I told him to take that poem about Vuna's Fan – you know the one, lust versus love, where she throws her Fan down to earth and every girl who picks it up is suddenly irresistible to men. Good stuff. Lots of potential. I think he wrote the beginnings of a play there without knowing it. I'll make a playwright of him yet, you watch me. Oh, by the way, I also gave him a copy of Peter the Black's last play.'

'*Brennain Bryach and Swanwhite*?'

'Yes, I told him he could learn something.'

'And what did Caro say?'

'What do you think? That if it was like the plays he saw this summer, Peter must have died of shame. Can you beat that? I told him that until he could equal his betters he had no right to badmouth them. That kid is either going to ruin us or make our fortune. I'm willing to take the gamble because if I don't I'll be ruined anyway, but I'm not going to be the only one at risk. If your boy cocks up again your job is on the line. Your round, Bren, I think.'

Early morning, and a mist hangs over the bay of Tsvingtori. Frost rimes the roof-tiles and the empty storks' nests. Out in the streets shopkeepers are throwing wide their shutters. Pulleys squeal and wooden pails clatter as housewives draw water from courtyard wells. Clogs on hurrying feet strike sparks from the cobbles. A pig screams in the butcher's. Across the Clerkden busy officials shout 'good morning' to one another, and down along the docks teams of donkeys, loaded with wool and ginger and cheese, shuffle their hooves and bray.

The Moon and the Stars sleeps on, its silence undisturbed save for the twitching of a rat's curious whiskers, and the flutter of a sparrow that has strayed through the open skylight, and the scratching of a dog at her fleas, and the soft breathing of a boy. Caro sits on one of the benches in the gallery, his feet scuffing among the discarded apple-cores, nutshells and withered herb posies left behind by last night's audience. From this height he can look down across the straw-carpeted pit, where standing-room costs the same as a loaf of bread, to the three-cornered stage guarded on either side by towers made of planks and painted canvas, and above it the great swathe of curtains concealing the oiled machinery in the rafters. Peter the Black's last play, thrice-read and learnt by heart, lies open on Caro's lap. He has been here for more than an hour, considering the theatre and pondering his fate.

He will make playwriting an art again.

The summer has taught him an invaluable lesson: people will laugh at anything. They are simply dying to laugh. The feeblest hint of smut, the crudest absurdities set them kicking their heels with glee. They can laugh around a pit in which a man is being murdered.

The plays Caro saw this summer offered the audience impossible situations and unbelievable characters to laugh at. 'She's in the trunk, she's in the trunk,' they would shout at the hump-backed cuckold, when even the worst idiot, if he was a real idiot, would know that the trunk was the only place to look – and would not have left his toothsome young wife alone with the handsome shepherd in the first place. Funny perhaps, but because it was ridiculous. Caro can do better than that.

The audience is safe in laughing at these characters, because that is all they are, characters, not your neighbour or your master or, possibly, yourself. They laugh as they might at a dog that chases its tail. No one says to them: look at your absurd selves.

Idris knows his business. People want to laugh. They can laugh at their neighbour if someone shows them how. And when the follies of their neighbour begin to pall, and every other object of amusement has been exhausted, perhaps, in their craving for laughter, they will look in the mirror and see what fools they have been made of. Caro can lead them on by subtle stages until they are laughing not down, but up, at officials, Learneds, priests, lords, the powers that be, Gods and Kings. Nothing is ordained: all things are possible, even laughing at a King. Nothing is too sacred for a laugh. And once they have learned to laugh at it, maybe they will start to think about it.

It will take time, of course, more time than Caro expected to have. Clearly this is going to be his life's work.

One week later Idris is presented with the finished manuscript of *The Marvellous Adventures of Vuna's Aphrodisiac Fan*.

'Well?' says Caro.

Idris is too much of an old stager to betray his satisfaction. The play isn't perfect, but it's getting there. It conforms to all the rules Caro's first play broke: there are three songs in every scene and a chorus to end each act, and the obligatory buffoons have been included, clowning around in the wake of the hero and dangling hopelessly after every girl who flutters the Fan. And there's more – there's an art to it, rough but vibrant, capable of breathing life into a tradition that had lost almost all its elasticity. Idris is intrigued by the device whereby the hero who lusts after the first girl should be the same character who marries the last one. He visibly grows up as the play progresses. The Fan does nothing but alert him to the girls' true qualities, and while the first girl is a rampant seductress who needs nobody's help to drive men wild with desire – mentally Idris has already cast Morwenna in the part – the modest maiden virtues of the heroine, who has been in love with the hero from

51

the play's beginning, pass unappreciated until she picks up the Fan. Very clever. Just so long as the audience don't realise they're being preached at . . . Still, all ends happily with the inevitable wedding, and that's what they'll remember.

'Well,' says Idris, 'I think we can do something with this. All right, Caryllac, you tell that crafty Swine's Son he's got his rooms to himself from now on. You can have the empty room at the top of the house. Now pay attention. We split the takings fifty-fifty between me and the company – for example, if there's six in the cast and three musicians then them plus you means you each get five per cent. Got it? Here's an advance. Can't have you starving. Don't bother to thank me, it's coming out of your share.'

7

Next door to The Moon and the Stars Idris owns a couple of boarding houses, backing on to each other with a courtyard in the middle, in which he houses his company. The buildings were given to him by King Michael along with the theatre. Idris charges a nominal rent – a perk not to be sneezed at, says Bren, when it would cost you an arm and a leg to find lodgings anywhere in the City. Several days after Caro's move up to the attic, Bren climbs the stairs to pay him a visit, trailing a pretty girl behind him. He knocks, twice, but gets no answer, so he opens the door and walks in.

Caro is sitting with his back to them, cross-legged on the end of the bed, staring out of the window.

'What's up?' asks Bren.

Caro stretches out an arm and points, through the sky, to a glimpse of stone skirting-wall hugging the top of the cliff. It is the Palace. The main buildings are set back, out of sight, behind the crest of the hill, and yet the City never doubts that it looks down on them with unsleeping vigilance.

Caro says, 'I'm going to go there one day.'

Bren shrugs. In Michael's day this prediction would certainly have come true, but Brychmachrye's new King shows no sign of reviving his predecessor's patronage of the arts.

Building is Basal Rorhah's passion. Already in Pravarre, in Chatienne, in hot Duccarn and Sogorah of the thousand islands, and even in envious Andariah which long ago lost its best men to the Brychmachrese adventure, people are saying that the white palace King Basal is building on the island of Ksaned Kaled will be an architectural achievement unparalleled in the Seven Kingdoms, far surpassing, in beauty and magnificence, the old Royal Palace of Rouche in Andariah. They are losing out to us in everything now, Basal's subjects crow. Don't they wish they had our King!

In Ksaned Kaled, we hear, the scent of roses and sunshine fills every silken room. You would not believe that it was made for human beings, who eat and shit and bleed and snore, to live in. Oh, we would be drunk and giddy with the sweet cleanliness of it, the fragrance of their baths, the air He breathes. It is the habitation of a God.

The wonders of Ksaned Kaled grow to mythic proportions. In the hearts of the people it has become the seat of enchantment.

All over Brychmachrye men are hard at work on a labour of love, transforming their King's dreams of roads, canals, bridges, docks and drains into reality. The sun has set for good on the parasites – the poets, painters, actors and musicians of the last reign, for truly the Gods never intended those layabouts to take a free ride through life on the backs of honest working folk. Of course the honest working folk still grumble as loudly as ever when the tax collector comes round – only the government has changed, not human nature – but the rancour, and the feeling of being used, has been swept away by a dawning sense of pride in their Kingdom, their King, and in themselves.

Even Bren, one of the few people to have been better off under old King Michael, is not immune to the spell of uncritical adoration being woven around Basal the Great. He had, however, received the strong impression that Caro was determined to stand aloof from the magic encircling Brychmachrye. Caro who is still fighting a war long lost, Caro the self-declared atheist, Caro who practically turns to ice at the thought of being taken for a little Lord – and here he is, mooning through the window like every other young poet Bren has ever known, eating his heart out for the glories of the Court.

Thank you, Gods. Now that You have touched him with the spark of worldly ambition, maybe You can help him see the wisdom in disposing of his more unorthodox poems. Bren is quite sure that Caro has not done this, yet. Still, no point in nagging. Caro and good advice never take kindly to one another. Bren pats the boy's shoulder cheerfully. 'Sure you will. Now turn around and be charming. I've got a lovely girl here to meet you. Roisin, this is Caryllac.'

But Caro sees in her only what he sees in every woman: his own beauty reflected in her widening pupils, his coldness in the warmth of her smile.

'Roisin's just joined us,' says Bren. 'She's going to play Vivienne. She's from Vacled, that's why she's got those beautiful big brown eyes.'

She giggles. 'Is he always like this?' she asks Caro.

'Of course you know,' says Bren, 'that Morwenna got Richenda.'

'Oh!' says Roisin. 'There's your dog. Isn't she sweet. Can I pet her?'

'Fern doesn't bite.'

'Get your shoes on,' says Bren, 'I promised we'd show this lovely girl around the City.'

Walking through the streets of Tsvingtori with Bren is a slow business. Hardly has one of his innumerable acquaintances pumped his hand, vowed to look him up soon for a drink, and slipped into the crowd, before another hails him from a street corner or shop window. As they come up to the terrace of the Clerkden a man calls to him through the open door of a barber's shop. Bren shades his eyes, squints, doffs his hat, and goes over to speak through the doorway in a most respectful manner.

His red face is alight with excitement when he rejoins them. 'That was old Alex Columson, the spice man. Told me his daughter's getting married to Cal Paperman at the end of the month, as if the whole city doesn't know already. Money breeding money,' he tells Roisin, 'Alex the Spice is the richest man in Tsvingtori, and Cal Paperman isn't far behind him. It's going to be the wedding of the year. And it's good news for us. He wanted to tell me he's having trouble finding something suitable for the entertainments. Money no object. I said, look no further, we've got the very thing. He's going to send someone down tomorrow to talk to Idris.' Bren rubs his hands gloatingly. 'This is just what we need for you, Caro. Your play getting its first performance in Alex the Spice's house. You'll be made!'

'He may not want it.'

'What's wrong with you? He'll want it. It's perfect.'

Bren babbles on with his optimistic predictions of fame and fortune, Roisin getting a word in when she can. To Caro, it is as if they are talking about a dead person. He was so in love while he wrote his play that sometimes he would forget to eat, or sleep. Nothing could part him from it. And then he finished it, and he sold it. He has had all the joy he's going to get from it. It belongs to Idris now.

Caro has never felt the sadness of love's aftermath that other poets speak of, but he is sure that this grief, this bereavement he feels after the completion of each of his acts of creation, must be worse. He speeds up, leaving the chatterers behind, and he and Fern come into the Clerkden.

In the far corner, next to the Cripplesteps at the foot of the Temple of Adonac, is something that was not there yesterday: a small brown canvas marquee. A crowd is jostling round it, trying to form a queue. Caro and Fern head over to investigate. Holding tight to her collar, he weasles his way between bodies and under arms until he reaches the front of the queue, and comes slap against the matted chest of a giant guarding the entrance. Caro digs some coins out of his pocket and tries to pass through, but the giant grabs his shoulder. 'The dog, master.'

Caro pays for Fern and they both go in. At first he assumes the tent must belong to some wandering theatre company about to perform, for in the centre is a wooden stage, about twelve feet square and as high as his waist, strewn with sawdust. More people are packing in behind him. A flap of canvas opens behind the stage; daylight and chilly air burst in from a blaze of October sky. A dwarf enters carrying a large brass bell, followed, for ludicrous contrast, by a raw-boned monster of a man whose muscles bulge like a bullock straining at the plough. The dwarf is arrayed in courtly garb, pink and red brocade sprinkled with sequins, gold rings jammed over purple leather gloves. The brute is more or less naked, with a length of blue cloth knotted round his loins. He is pale-skinned, blond, dull of eye. The dwarf struts about on the stage, clanging his brass bell. The crowd ignore him.

Then all conversation fades to a hum of astonishment as a third man climbs on to the stage. He too flexes muscles of ferocious proportions. He too is nearly naked – and he is black, except for his rosy pink palms and the egg-white moons of his eyes. He is black, black, night made flesh.

Exclamations burst from the audience, oo-ing and aw-ing. They push forwards, and those closest to the stage reach

55

up and try to touch his skin, oiled and gleaming as though painted with ink not yet dry. His eyes are unusually bright, full of intelligence. Clearly the antics of the crowd amuse him.

Caro jumps as a hand comes down on his shoulder. 'Here you are,' says Bren, 'I didn't know you liked boxing.'

'I loathe boxing,' says Roisin on Bren's arm.

Caro plucks at Bren's shirt. 'Look, look at him. What happened to him?'

'Who?'

'*Him.* Up there. That man. That black man.'

Bren's roar of amusement brings all heads turning their way. Caro is pink-cheeked with embarrassment. 'Oh Caro, you are priceless. Haven't you ever seen a Southlander before?'

'Is that where he comes from?'

'Sure. They're all like that.'

'Why?'

Bren makes one of his sweeping actor's gestures. 'Why is the sky blue? Why is the sea wet? I guess it pleased the Gods – whatever Gods it is they believe in.'

'Do we have to stay here?' asks Roisin.

Once again the dwarf is prowling the stage, thundering his bell and demanding attention. But the crowd is not ready to settle down. A starry grin lights up the Southlander's face, and he stoops to pluck the little man into the air, dangling him by the armpits with his frogs'-legs kicking madly. The crowd is in raptures.

'Shut up!' screams the dwarf. 'Attend to me, my Lords, Ladies, gentlemen and women, masters, good wives and good little maidens. Today you are about to witness a trial of courage and endurance unprecedented throughout the Seven Kingdoms . . .'

Caro begins to sidle crabwise through the audience, working his way to the centre of the front row. Fern huddles between his legs.

'. . . On my right,' the dwarf flings out an arm, 'Liam Liamson from Rayallah, champion of his Fahl, glorious victor of thirty-six consecutive matches, undefeated, crowned All-Conqueror at this year's Solstice Games . . .'

Bren has caught up with Caro again. 'I know that Southlander,' he whispers. 'I mean, I knew him when he was a boy, about your age. He boxed at Court a couple of times. The

Black Bull of the South, they called him. He's the best. Speaks six languages too. He must have come down in the world a bit if he has to fight for Clerkden crowds.'

Then Bren realises what he has said, and adds, 'As have we all.'

'. . . On my left – or should I say, beneath me – ' the crowd applaud this joke wildly – 'the Black Bull of the South, a name unequalled for courage and honour throughout the Seven Kingdoms. Champion of the world! Unbeaten in all his one hundred and forty-eight matches! Royal favourite of their Graces of Chatienne and Duccarn . . .'

'I took two to one against that Rayallan,' says Bren. 'He must be good for such short odds. Ah – shit, I've seen the Black Bull fight before. He'll knock that runt's block off, you wait.'

A final clang of the bell imposes silence.

Despite their bulk the two boxers move elegantly, fists up and eyes wary. Bare feet swish in the sawdust. There is no other sound but the hushed breathing of the audience.

Caro must have blinked or looked away, for he has missed the split second when the boxers leapt at each other, and now they are fighting at close quarters while the men and women around the stage jump up and down and bay for blood.

They have stopped. Panting for breath, they lie on each other's necks in a lover-like embrace. The dwarf bustles in and separates them.

Many times the rhythm repeats itself: a shuffling, circling dance, the audience on tip-toe wondering who will strike first, and when – then the point and counterpoint of staccato blows that break off as suddenly as they began. Minutes pass. Both boxers have received minor injuries, a split lip, a bruised knuckle.

Slowly comprehension seeps into Caro's bones.

These boxers are fighting not one, but three battles: the two against each other and, more intimately, each man alone against the enemy that is his own flesh. They strive to overcome their fear of pain, the instinct to recoil when a blur of knuckles comes flying at their eyes. They call for greater speed and greater power from excruciatingly slow reactions. The rage set on their faces is anger at the inadequacy of their own nerves, muscles, lungs, hearts, bodies unable to give or take much more. Caro understands. He has stood a thousand times on the edge of this same chasm dividing the limits of one's ability

57

from the goal one yearns to reach. This is their poetry.

And Caro sees that those sensitive souls who call this sport brutal and bloodthirsty are wrong. It is rather the essence of civilisation. These boxers are taking on the animal in themselves, the unreasoning creature that wants to tuck its tail between its legs and run, and are subduing it to their will to win. Every pain they shrug aside and every blow they take as if in passing proves them that much more the masters of themselves. They are alive; they find, in this, the elusive unity of body and mind that Caro has never known. Their flesh and their spirits pull together towards a single end.

The Black Bull staggers and glances round, glassy-eyed, seeing nothing but his enemy. They have punched their way into a world where no sound exists but their laboured breathing and their ringing ears, where there is no object other than the target of vulnerable skin that must continue to be punched as it always has been and will be for ever. In their world, no life is possible outside of the state of conflict. In their world, to surrender is to die, to cease to be a man.

Within about twenty minutes it is clear for all to see that the Black Bull of the South has finally met his match. Bruises puff his face. Blood streams from a deep cut on his cheek, from his nose and broken mouth. One eyelid has swollen, blinding him, and the other eye is bloodshot and glaring. He cannot hope to win. The only question is how long he can stay on his feet. If he admits defeat now, he will save himself from possibly mortal injury, and lose nothing that is not lost already. But he will not accept this.

Blows rain down on him from every side. He crosses his arms over his head, and refuses to let his legs give way.

Don't, Caro prays silently, don't give in, don't let them know, don't let them see how much it hurts. Don't let it hurt. He can't win unless you let him.

Both boxers grit their teeth. The Rayallan's expression seems to say, 'I will beat the admission of my victory from you'. Caro's imagination leaps to join them. He puts words into the Black Bull's mouth:

This is my life. It is everything I live for and the thing I was born to do. I am the best. I have never been beaten. I am the champion of the world. I am the King of Boxers. I am invincible: I am something divine. Once a King, always a King. If you want my crown, you will have to kill me for it.

58

The Southlander will not give in, and Liam the Rayallan will not stop hitting him until he does give in. It looks like murder is about to be committed on this stage, and no one is doing anything to stop it.

'He'll kill him!' cries Caro.

'Why doesn't he admit he's beaten?' demands Bren. 'This is butchery.'

'Do they always kill each other?'

'No, no, they're not supposed to – but sometimes I guess it happens.'

II

The Quarter-Lord's Daughter

8

Alex the Spice did hire The Moon and the Stars to perform at his daughter's wedding, throwing a free meal into the bargain. The happiness of the occasion was slightly marred by the newly-wedded bride herself, when she happened to catch sight of the poet standing alone in a corner of the room, arms folded, his dog at his feet, looking insufferably young and romantic. 'I want *him*,' she wept on her father's chest. 'Is it too late, Daddy?' Her parents managed to pass her behaviour off as the sort of nuptial hysteria only to be expected in a virgin of good family, and as soon as the wedding supper was over the disconcerted groom hurried her away.

As soon as Idris realised no one was going to blame Caro for this incident, he began to think it was all for the best – he had yet to hear of a little sensation harming a play's prospects.

The wedding guests, influential men and women of social standing in the City, praised Caro's play to the skies. The City was on fire to see this new masterpiece. Not since the war had any playhouse enjoyed such popularity, and *The Marvellous Adventures of Vuna's Aphrodisiac Fan* played to full houses until the New Year. Caro's second play, *Good Gossip*, recounting the tribulations of a pair of lovers first separated, then reunited, by a rumour blown out of all proportion, opened in April. It was applauded for its wit and moral by the men with enough education to call themselves critics, and charmed the pit-crowd who asked of a play only that it make them laugh, put a lump in their throats, and leave them with a catchy tune running through their heads. By the end of his first twelve months in the City, Caro's reputation as a playwright was secure.

It was at about this time that he finally gave way to Bren's nagging, and allowed him to pick out several score of poems for submission to the Official Publishers. They were accepted, of course. The only person who had ever doubted it was Caro.

As Bren had long ago warned him, the Official Publishers do not pay their authors. Manual workers, musicians and painters and architects, are venal by the nature of their craft and feel no shame in requesting money, but poetry is a gentleman's art. Nor do the Official Publishers actually publish books in any material sense. Once a manuscript is approved by the board of censors it is contracted out, often by auction, to an individual bookseller who acquires the monopoly on transcribing, illuminating, binding and selling the article. Caro's own booksellers are the minor house of Nolan and Sons, a family concern who were willing to risk a small investment in an unknown poet on the strength of his success as a playwright.

If a book becomes so exceptionally popular that no single bookseller can hope to meet the demand – as with Isumbard Shoemaker's *Homely Rhymes for Growing Minds* or Gertrude Mehah's *Voyages* – the Official Publishers will buy the contract back in and redistribute it between three or four scribe-houses. Caro's work has not been accorded this honour yet.

A great many people – scribes, illustrators, bookbinders, ink blenders, paper and parchment merchants – are trying to earn their daily bread from this system. The poet gets all the glory, and must be content with that.

Having first come to prominence as a playwright, it is inevitable that Caro's work in the less accessible field of poetry should be seen in many quarters (starting with The Moon and the Stars) as of secondary importance. Nevertheless there are literate circles where his poetry is gaining an appreciative audience. The smart set of students at the University consider a copy of Caryllac indispensable: with elegant affectation they starve to buy books. A Pravarrian visitor took Caryllac's second volume home with him, translated it, and published it. Caro is becoming known abroad as a poet to watch. Closer to home there is a group of families in the City, with connections to the pettier nobility, who have tried to take Caro up. So far he has fought shy of this. He can do very well without patronage, he tells Bren. Idris will never make him rich, but they respect one another, and Idris no longer tries to tell him what to write. Caro could never surrender this freedom for the red ribbon of prestige tied around a lapdog's neck.

He has a reputation for bloodymindedness, for speaking and thinking more than he ought. One hears vague rumours about his activities in lower-city pubs, the associates he chooses, crank philosophers, riff-raff, atheists. His company is much sought after by a certain type of student, wranglers and troublemakers, but Caro is difficult to track down, and when they do find him he is always a disappointment. Caro has learned to guard his tongue. From time to time people have been heard to suggest that he holds dangerous, dissident opinions, but on the whole such whispered calumny is set down to an envious desire to blacken his name. Success will always have its detractors.

He has also acquired a reputation as a womaniser and a breaker of hearts, the former somewhat undeservedly, as he doesn't take up the offers of nights of passion from even one-quarter of the women who pursue him so vigorously. Bren is growing rather tired of finding young girls hanging around the boarding-house at all hours of the day and night. He has lost count of the number of times his shoulder has been cried on, often by women he thought of as friends. He could have warned them. They never want to listen. And yet, strangely, none of them try to blame Caro for his heartlessness. Caro, it seems, can get away with anything.

Bren tells Caro, 'You could try to be a bit less . . . brutal, about it.'

'The way you talk anyone would think I enjoy it. I don't encourage them. I tell them not to expect anything and they say it doesn't matter, they don't care – and suddenly next morning it's I love you Caro. What am I supposed to do?'

'You don't have to laugh at them.'

'I don't know who told you that. I never laugh at them. But I'm not going to say I love them when I don't, just to make them feel better. They get what they want.'

'But you're supposed to be a poet. Every poet I've ever known has been madly in love with some woman or other. Why do you have to be different?'

'I'm getting really tired of this, Bren. Every woman I meet thinks she's the one who's going to change me. But I can't *be* changed. Why can't they leave me alone?'

Caro's love poetry is partly to blame, for it is impossible to doubt, so exquisitely lucid, simple and sincere that lovers lost for words copy his out to send to one another, to say, this is how I feel. Nobody would believe that these poems are entirely the product of Caro's imagination. He has no girl in mind. In fact they are the least heartfelt of anything he writes, and he only writes them because, as Bren says, all proper poets do. His collections would look odd without a few love poems. Technically they are perfect. No one has yet noticed that at the centre they ring hollow.

Caro's real love poetry has never been published. It is written in the native, the language of his heart, and even if there were not a ban on works in the native, booksellers would not take these poems because no one would buy them. Most native speakers cannot read: the literate classes want Andarian poetry. Caro only half-minds this. All true lovers are torn between the urge to shout their love from the roof-tops and cherish it in secret. Caro's real love poems do not extol the beauty of golden hair and sparkling eyes, sing his joy when he kisses her lips or bewail his loneliness when they are apart. Caro and his true love will never be parted. She is everywhere around him. In his poems he lies awake beneath her stars, roams through her cornfields blown with poppies, dances in her snow. He celebrates every one of her moods, and never fails to notice what she wears, describing in intimate detail the scents and flowers, clouds and birdsong of each season. She makes him feel at once the thrill of a small boy high in an oak tree, and the sadness of an old man looking into the sunset. Sometimes he, too, is lost for words.

Even if these poems were published, nobody would recognise them for what they are.

Five years have passed. Caro is famous in Tsvingtori. He is hailed and congratulated as often as Bren when he walks up the street. But the prediction he made, gazing across the red roof-tiles at the Palace hidden behind the cliff, his eyes full of some sort of longing, has not come true. So far, the Court has failed to acknowledge his existence.

9

But what's all this? Why this deep prying into the state of Caro's spoilt heart? Bren calls Caro a child of good fortune, a young man with more than his fair share of luck and talent. Caro is the sort of person nothing bad ever happens to. What about the bloody, unbowed Black Bull of the South, ex-champion of the world, still reeling defiantly on the cliffhanger of defeat?

To the relief of some and the disappointment of others, the Black Bull of the South was not killed. A few moments after Caro's outburst, Liam the Rayallan's left jab knocked him mercifully unconscious, and he was carried across the Clerkden to a nearby tavern, where he lay in a stupor for three days. When he awoke, it was to a splitting headache and the belated recognition that there had to be easier ways of making a living.

He has become a professional muscle-man, going around fairs lifting pretty milkmaids on his hands and engaging in trials of strength with oxen. He travels all over the Kingdom, and often goes abroad, for he has itchy feet and an insatiable curiosity. This September afternoon finds him sitting with Bren, Caro and Fern outside the Tar Barrel tavern on the docks, drinking to celebrate Caro's twenty-fourth birthday. Their friendship came about in this manner:

Caro naturally wrote a poem about all that he had seen and thought during the boxing match, and Bren liked it so much he persuaded Caro to rewrite it in court-speech and submit it to the Official Publishers. In time a friend passed a copy on to the Black Bull's extremely literate hands. The Black Bull was amused and doubly flattered: having acquired the literature of six languages, he knew a good poet when he read one. The next time he passed through Tsvingtori he sought the poet out. Their acquaintance did not begin promisingly. Caro was never at his best with strangers, and the sudden appearance of the boxer on his doorstep was like being confronted by one of his poems made flesh: he had forgotten the man was real. The Black Bull was ready to give up the unequal struggle to keep the conversation going, when Bren popped his head round the door, greeted him like a long-lost cousin, and proposed an immediate drink, or two. 'Don't forget to look us up next time you're in town, mate,' said Bren when they parted, and that was that.

Bren turns his face to the sun. 'Lovely day, isn't it?'

The Black Bull nods. 'Nice to have a bit of sunshine after all that rain.'

'Looks like we might have a mild winter after all.'

Their conversation has been ambling on in this inane way for almost half an hour. Caro wishes they would shut up, maybe go away. He likes to be by himself on the waterfront, and often comes down with Fern to sit on a barrel and watch the passers-by, imagining himself into them, giving them characters, families, histories, ambitions. The waterfront breeze is a kingdom of smells: the tingle of salt, the cleanliness of fresh fish, tar hot and cloying, pungent wet hemp, briny timber, the whole spiced with pepper and cinnamon and vanilla tasted in bursts as the wind comes and goes. To his left bales of wool are being loaded on to a merchantman, to his right a Pravarrian ship is disembarking passengers, and on the short docks between them sits a row of fishgutters with their wicker baskets and salt-water tubs. Caro can watch these women for hours. He is in love with all of them, collectively, skinny famine-eyed creatures with long plaits and raw red hands. He is in love with their fishgutterness. He allows to them, as he once allowed to the Black Bull, a poetry of their own in the rhythm of their labour – cut yank slice tug and the fish is disembowelled, beheaded, tossed into the basket, a fresh gleaming mackerel already flapping in their hands. They sing as they work, and their elbows rise and fall in harmony.

> *Oh, all of the fishermen, so I've heard say,*
> *Belong to the Sea and she'll take them one day;*
> *For on the same day that our Jackie was born,*
> *The 'Star of the Evening' was lost in a storm:*
> > *Out on the waves of the west,*
> > *His father and brothers went down with the rest,*
> *And his mother wept under her window,*
> *On the other side of the waves . . .*

Caro hums the tune under his breath. He knows the words of this song by heart: his mother often sang it to him when he was a child, and still he prefers to hear it told by the voices of women. Their hero, Jackie Fisher, grows up to be so brave and handsome you never saw his like, but the girls sigh after him in vain, for he has dedicated his life to the Sea. One day the Quarter-Lord's daughter catches a glimpse of him through her window, and, struck with love, falls on her knees and prays to die if she can't have him:

> *Asdura, Asdura, to you I implore,*
> *Don't let my sweet Jackie go sailing no more.*
> *The waves are so deep and the ocean so wide,*
> *Keep my Jack safe for me here by my side.*
> > *Turn him away from the sea,*
> > *The ship of his heart should be sailing to me.*
> *And her prayers rose up through the window*
> *On the other side of the waves.*

> *Asdura the gentle, Asdura the kind,*
> *To lovers' entreaties is sweetly inclined.*
> *And like the bright lightning that strikes from the skies,*
> *She touched Jackie's heart and she opened his eyes –*

'Caro, Caro, listen to this. Bullocks says it's his real name. Go on, Bullocks, do it for Caro.' The Black Bull complies with an effortless stream of clicks and grunts in the outlandish, Southlandish language. Bren is in transports. 'Good grief! That's never a real language! What d'you think, Caro? He's pulling our legs.'

Caro's opinion of the Black Bull has never recovered from the disillusionment of finding that he chose to give up boxing in order to become something as second-rate as a fairground sideshow. He expresses the required disbelief, and returns his attention to the song. It has just occurred to him that the story might provide some very good material for a play. Jackie has married the Quarter-Lord's daughter, and on their wedding night the Sea storms in a jealous rage up to the gates of the Great God Adonac, Asdura's husband, to demand that the Jackie they stole be returned to her:

> *Jackie was not yours to give,*
> *He'll be a sailor as long as he lives!*
> *And the storm it crashed against his window,*
> *On the other side of the waves.*
>
> *Jack cried in his sleep and he leapt from his bed,*
> *A-tearing his hair and a-clutching his head.*
> *His lady awoke in a terrible fright,*
> *And said, Oh my husband, sleep peaceful tonight.*
> *But he said,*
> *   Oh, can't you hear the Sea?*
> *I've broken my faith and She's calling for me –*

'Bren! Brennain Swithsunson! Hey, Bellthroat!'
Caro groans and looks round. Two men are shouting and waving at them from the corner. One is short and slight, propped on a crutch. The other, taller man wears shapeless clothes and a large pork pie hat, and has a satchel slung over one shoulder.

'I just can't believe my eyes!' Bren shouts back. 'Is it really you?'

'We're coming over!'

Bren is blinking, laughing, shaking his head. 'It can't be true,' he stutters. 'It's an old friend of mine, Paddy Fisher. I haven't seen Paddy for years.'

'Who's the man in the hat?' asks Caro.

Bren is so happy he giggles, girlishly. 'Where are your eyes, mate? That's no bloke. It's Paddy's sister, Annie.'

The friends are reunited in a flurry of handshakes and back-slapping. 'Paddy, you old shit, I can't believe it. Come on, sit down, have a drink –'

'You don't change, do you?' laughs the little man. 'You won't believe this, Bren, but I swear I was saying to Annie as we got off the boat, I said, I bet we see Bren outside the Tar Barrel – didn't I, Annie?'

Annie leans forward to kiss Bren's cheek. He grabs her hand and strokes it, eyes shining. 'Annie Fisher, you lovely girl, you're prettier than ever.'

'You're right,' she tells her brother. 'He doesn't change.'

Drinks are called for and brought, and they all sit down. 'It must be six years at least since I've seen you,' says Bren. 'Where have you been?'

'In Pravarre,' says Paddy.

'You're not joking? Good Gods. What in the King's name possessed you to go to Pravarre for six years?'

Paddy grins. Half his teeth are missing. Those that remain are stained a ferret-fur yellow. His thinning hair, a dusty bronze colour, is combed in limp curls over his ears. He has failed to realise a considerable potential for good looks by being too thin, and too ill, and too nervy, and altogether he gives a strong impression of untrustworthiness.

'It wasn't for the sake of the cooking,' he says, 'I can tell you that for nothing. When did I last see you? Just before you went off on that tour, wasn't it? Well, a few days later I was strolling through the Clerkden, minding my own business for a change, when what should happen but three great officers of the Watch pounce on me and before you could say "I'm innocent", which as it happens I was, there I was back in the Coneywarren. Mystification. So when one of the warders came along I stuck my nose through the bars and said, excuse me, kind sir, but would you be so good as to enlighten me as to the nature of the breach of our blessed and beloved King's law for which I have been incarcerated in this foetid dungheap? So three of them came in and broke my leg again. But in the end – it was a month, wasn't it, Annie? It must have been about a month, because my leg was nicely on the mend. You know one loses all sense of time in that place. Anyway, they had to let me go. They said – and you know how vilely they talk, a pig's grunts would sound more euphonious – they said, you was fucking lucky this time, Fishface, we know you done it but we ain't got no proof. Proof, dear Gods. They don't half long for the good old days when merry King Michael let them string up anyone they could get their hands on –'

At this moment a wind arises from the bay and stirs through Paddy's curls, parting them like a curtain to reveal what Caro has already guessed he will see – no ears, but the scarred stumps of convicted thieves.

'Annie was waiting for me at the gates, weren't you, Annie? I tell you, she is a diamond, this big sister of mine. Waited for me every day from dawn to dusk, didn't you, Annie?'

Bren interposes, 'But none of this explains the six years in Pravarre.'

Paddy continues with his interminable tale of persecution, false accusation, flight. Caro isn't listening. His interest is absorbed elsewhere, by the one who has hardly spoken. Presumably she dresses in men's clothes for safety, but up close she could never pass herself off as anything less than a woman. How she smiles, as if smiling were her most comfortable, most familiar expression. She must have been beautiful once, though Caro supposes she cannot be less than thirty. Strands of dark blonde hair curl at her nape and forehead. Her face is an oval with heavy white eyelids and thick brown lashes. The sunlight reveals fine wrinkles in her upper lip, crows-feet crinkling the corners of her eyes. She looks healthy, happy, rosy-cheeked, calm and sure of herself. Not once has she glanced his way.

Look at me, woman.

'. . . And I found out they'd nobbled the bastard who did it less than a week after we left,' Paddy concludes. 'Picture my chagrin! Six years wasted in loathsome Pravarre. Annie and I were so homesick, we jumped on the next ship back, and here we are, a happy ending. Bugger me, Bren, I never in my wildest dreams thought your ugly mug could look so handsome.'

'You old shit! So, what are you going to do now?'

'I'm going to return to my profession.'

'Which one?' says Annie. Her smile is wearing a little thin.

'Don't nag, dear. I can't help it if I'm torn between vocations. Annie's made me promise to be good, haven't you, Annie? And six years exile is enough to put you off for life. But, since the guild won't let me practise medicine, I'm going to set up as

71

an apothecary. I did a lot of that in Pravarre – Tsvingtori's medical school has a good reputation there, and heaven knows their doctors are even worse bunglers than ours. Annie and I have been saving like mad in hopes of coming home, and I've nearly got enough for a nice little shop in the New City. *And* I've managed to smuggle some herbs in this bag that my old tutors would kill for. So I hope you'll all have the decency to be constantly ill and make our fortune. It's about my turn to put shoulder to the wheel, isn't it, Annie? She refuses to work any more, you see. She's set her heart on us becoming respectable, haven't you, my love?'

Stop smiling and look at me, damn you.

'Good grief!' Bren claps a hand to his head. 'I completely forgot. These are my friends – Annie, Paddy, this is the Black Bull of the South – Bullocks, we call him.'

'I know you,' says Paddy. 'You're a boxer, aren't you?'

'No, I'm retired, like you.'

'Good one,' Paddy salutes with his beer mug.

'And this is Caro – Caryllac – '

Paddy sits forward. 'Caryllac?' he echoes. 'No, wait, don't tell me. Moon and the Stars Caryllac, right? Caryllac the poet?'

Caro looks across at Annie to see if she shares her brother's enthusiastic recognition of his name. Her gaze is wandering mildly through space. Caro says, 'I don't know if there's another one.'

'Ah, what modesty!' Paddy flings his arms wide. 'I embrace you. You're famous, my man. Didn't you know you've been translated into Pravarrian, than which life has no higher accolade to offer – at least, they think so.'

'You've read my books?' Caro asks Annie.

Paddy says, 'I've read everything that came out of Tsvingtori. Annie, Gods bless her, can't read at all, little pearl of laziness that she is. Now tell me, where can I get hold of some copies?'

'I'll give you one,' Caro promises Annie.

Bren, watching and listening, is speechless. What's the boy up to, giving his books away? The bookseller only gives him one free copy, and, ironically, he cannot afford to buy them.

'Caro writes plays too,' says the Black Bull.

'So I've heard. What a man of many parts – tell you what, my Annie, as soon as we're settled in we'll pop along to The Moon and the Stars and take a look at the genius's latest masterpiece.'

Bren is stunned to hear Caro say, 'I can get you in for

free,' which isn't true in the first place, and in the second seems directed exclusively at Annie.

Annie comes down from her cloud, smiles at the company in general, and says, 'What a lovely dog. Is she yours?'

'Yes, she's called Fern.'

'Do you think she'd let me stroke her?'

'Fern doesn't bite. Call her over.'

'Fern,' Annie beckons, 'come here, girl.'

Fern is not best pleased. No one else can smell the faint whiff of heat Caro is giving off, but she can, and she has a pretty fair idea of which human around this table is the cause. Fern shows her teeth and huddles against Caro's leg.

Annie shrugs, 'She doesn't like me.'

'Fern! You bad girl!' Caro slaps Fern on the head, and Fern, to reciprocate, takes Caro's leg between her teeth and bites it, hard enough to hurt. Caro yelps.

Annie's laughter completes his mortification. 'I thought you said she didn't bite.'

'She's just jealous,' he replies without thinking, rubbing his leg and glaring at Fern.

'What's she got to be jealous of?' asks Annie, turning her head to smile at Bren. She doesn't wink, but it's all the same. Not much passes that woman by.

10

Caro doesn't know what she has done to him, but he knows what he would like to do to her.

Awake, asleep, the golden thread of her runs through his thoughts. He dreams of rose petals unfolding to release an overpowering sweetness that makes him want to tear them off, one by one. His hands are on her bare skin. Her breath is musky with the smell of her reluctance, her helplessness, her fear. His fingers dig into her white flesh. He wants to leave red marks all over her. A puff of smoky laughter scatters her substance like feathers; he opens his eyes to find the sun staring at him in surprise through the broken shutters of his attic window.

But it's not love. Caro has read too much, and knows himself too well, to suppose that he has suddenly become like other men. For other men, perhaps, this is how love can begin: the lust to grab and rip apart transforms – once you have her, broken, in your arms – into the tender resolution to keep fast the precious object you have painstakingly mended. Love is the desire to cherish and protect; the longing that scratches inside Caro is the urge to hurt her, bite her, make her cry. She has only herself to blame, with her placid blue eyes and her self-contentment. He's going to wipe the smile off her face. She will be sorry she ever laughed at him.

He shuts Fern into the attic and goes wandering aimlessly, plotting. He knows very well that he has only come out in the hope of running into her. Every time he turns a corner he expects to meet that quiet, knowing smile. He will then express astonishment and say, 'Oh, hullo, fancy meeting you here . . .'

What is he thinking of? This isn't a play. He must act naturally. He must say, 'Oh, hullo – it's Annie, isn't it?' Or maybe he should pretend to forget her name. That might pique her pride. And she will say, 'Oh, hullo, Caro, I'm just –' whatever it was she was off to do. He can engage her in conversation on some innocuous subject for a few minutes, and then suggest, 'If you're not in a hurry, I'll buy you a drink.' He can tell her he's curious to hear about Pravarre. Or if his luck is in and it happens to be around mealtime, he can ask her to share his lunch. In this scenario Annie never replies, 'Sorry, I'm rushed, see you around.' She immediately and eagerly agrees to his proposal, and he takes her to a tavern where nobody knows him. He will talk to her, in a friendly sort of way, show interest in Paddy and their plans to open a shop, and be very careful not to say anything like 'You're beautiful', or 'I can't get you out of my mind'. And after they have chatted for a while, and Annie has had a bit too much to drink, he can remark, as casually as if he has just remembered, 'I promised to give you one of my books, didn't I? Why don't you come round now and I'll let you have it.'

The plot fizzles out here, for everything depends on whether Annie says 'Yes' or 'No'.

As he strolls along, Caro becomes conscious of another new oddity in his behaviour. From time to time he catches a glimpse of a feminine figure in the corner of his eye and doubles back, like a dog on a scent, convinced that it is Annie and that she is searching for him. He pushes against the flow of people, heart thumping, knocking little children over and treading on old women's toes; he has almost caught up with her, when she turns around and is nothing but a stranger, leaving him

74

wondering how he could mistake such an ordinary girl for the most desirable woman in the world.

So he drifts through the early morning, up and down the narrow stepped lanes, light-headed with broken sleep and stupid with desire, led by his nose into the dampest, rankest, oldest quarter of the City, where the decaying houses seem to be held up only by the press of poverty crowded inside them. The sun never penetrates these depths: its decency would be affronted. This is the ocean bed, littered with rubbish and crawling with scavengers. This is where the flotsam sinks and can sink no further. Caro begins to think that he ought to turn back.

About ten yards ahead of him a woman steps out of an alley. She has a scarf tied over her hair, and a reed basket on one arm. Caro shrugs off the irrepressible upsurge of hope – that can't be Annie, not down here – and is about to walk away when she glances over her shoulder. His stomach churns, he can't breathe or move – by the time he has pulled himself together Annie is disappearing up the street. She can't have seen him. He runs – his feet stumble in their haste; there's a string knotted in his belly pulling him after her – until he has narrowed the distance between them to one in which he can conceal himself while keeping Annie in sight.

She hesitates outside a haberdasher's, then goes in. Caro lurks in a doorway. Suddenly, to his horror, he sees a girl he knows only too well heading straight in his direction. He panics and dives for cover into the nearest alley. His breath sounds like thunder in his ears. The girl reappears, standing at the corner of the alley and looking round. A moment later a friend joins her. Caro's relief quickly turns to impatience: those two are gossiping away together as if they have the whole day to waste.

He is sweating. Will they never go? Annie might have come out by now. She might have walked away, vanished. Just as his temper is reaching boiling point, the girls kiss, say, 'See you,' and go their separate ways. Caro dashes into the street, hopping on one foot to shake off a piece of rotten fruit sticking to his shoe. While he is cutting this little caper, Annie emerges. She has taken off her scarf and tied her hair back with a blue ribbon. Caro hasn't seen her hair before. It is thick, straight, and golden-brown: somehow she has contrived to stand in a shaft of sunlight, and his throat constricts on a cry of longing for that illuminated, transfigured goddess. But she still hasn't seen him, and after a moment she starts climbing the street again.

75

For the next twenty minutes Caro trails Annie's footsteps from shop to shop. He has a thousand eyes and ears: half of them are keeping a fix on her, the other half are on guard against attack from the rear by acquaintances or well-wishers. Now and then she stops to finger some goods or to greet an old friend: Caro flattens himself against the nearest wall. In this painful manner, fraught with alarms, they finally reach the sunshine of the market in Sheep Square.

Caro loiters on the porch of the Wool Exchange while Annie considers the fruitmonger's. He hides behind a barrel of apples when Annie moves on to the baker's. At the baker's he buys a roll and gives the wrong coin because his eyes are glued to Annie at the fishmonger's. By the time she has idled her way to the flower-stall, her back to him as she bends to sniff a bunch of purple daisies, Caro has had enough. He's got a plan. As soon as Annie moves on from the flower-stall he'll buy a rose for her, then creep up behind her and brush it against her cheek. That's bound to soften her up.

He is within an arm's-breadth of her when she whirls around, white-faced with panic.

'Oh!' she gasps. Her shoulders slump. 'Oh,' she says again, the colour returning to her cheeks. 'It's only you.'

She smiles, and giggles. Pressing a hand to her heart she says, 'I thought someone was following me. I've been getting goosepimples all the way up the hill.'

Caro's wits are scattered. He blurts out, 'I was following you.'

'No! Really?'

Caro nods. He could kick himself.

'But what on earth for? Haven't you got anything better to do?'

She's laughing at him already. He can tell. This woman doesn't need to open her mouth in order to make fun of him. 'What a boring life you must lead,' she says, shaking her head. Then she notices that he is clutching a rose. The thorns are digging into his palm but he doesn't feel them.

'Is that for me?'

Caro keeps on nodding.

'Really? How sweet. How *poetic*. You're just as sweet as you look, aren't you?'

Annie puts the rose in her basket, and assumes the business-like manner of one who has dawdled longer than she intended. Taking the basket off her arm, she holds it out to him. 'If you're really at a loose end you can pay me back for giving me a fright

76

by carrying my shopping for me.' She slips the basket over his hand and hangs it on his elbow.

'I wish I had the time to go following perfect strangers round the city,' she says briskly. 'Well, let's get on. I've got so much to do. We'd better go back to the fruit-stall first, that rotten brother of mine has been demanding an orange all morning. Six years we were in Pravarre and all he did was complain, and what's the first thing he wants when we get back? An orange. I said, you might as well have stayed there. We'll be lucky if we find any at this time of year. I'm sure they'll be terribly expensive. Oh look, I see some.'

The oranges are uninspiring, shrivelled and yellowish. Annie asks their price, whistles contemptuously, and walks off. Caro digs his hand into his pocket, thrusts all his money at the fruitmonger, grabs the nearest orange and runs after her. 'Here,' he says, 'take it.'

Annie holds the orange to her nose, sniffs it, and hands it back. 'Basket,' she reminds him. 'Listen – ' she pauses, smiles, 'I've forgotten your name, I'm so sorry.'

You will be. 'It's Caro.'

'Oh yes. Well, listen, Caro, are you going to eat that roll?'

'What roll?'

'That roll you're holding.'

He remembers it now, squashed in his fist. 'Oh. No,' he says, about to throw it away. Annie stops him. 'Can I have it? I'm starving.'

'You are? I mean, are you? Wouldn't you rather come and have something to eat?'

'It's too much bother, if you're not hungry. This roll will do me fine.' She plucks it from his fingers and takes a bite. 'Now, let's see. What else is there? We lost everything when we went abroad, so I've got to start from scratch. We'll get some food in first, then the tinker's for plates and pans, and the cutler's, and the potter's for a lamp now it's getting on for winter. And some blankets. Paddy feels the cold terribly. There's no heat in our room, but our landlord's wife lets me use her fire. I should think so too for what they charge. That'll do for the morning. Unless you're bored?'

'No, I – '

'Oh good. It was lucky we ran into each other. I didn't know how I was going to carry everything back.'

The temple bells are celebrating noon-tide as little Caro the

77

donkey, juggling bags and baskets and parcels, follows Annie down the sloping, slippery alley out of which, earlier this morning, she came forth into the day. The sway-backed tenements stand shoulder to shoulder, putting Caro in mind of tired old men propping each other up. Annie stops in front of a three-storied boarding house with green shutters, half-timbered, the plaster flaking off in patches from the mud and straw that sparrows have plundered for their nests. The ground floor is taken up by a ropemaker's workshop: half-mended nets are draped across the windowsills, and from indoors comes the sound of children whining, a woman's thin complaint, and the greasy smell of soup.

'He owns this place,' says Annie, meaning the ropemaker. 'Though why he needs to follow a trade, with his rents . . . And he knows he can get away with it. Is it my imagination, or are there twice as many people in this city as there were six years ago? I feel I hardly have room to breathe. You wouldn't believe the trouble we had finding lodgings. And we had to settle for a room on the second floor, which isn't ideal, with poor Paddy's leg. Still, beggars can't be choosers. And we're lucky in our neighbours. There's a lovely family living in the next room, a young man and his wife who can't be more than sixteen, and their baby! I can't keep away from it. They're country people – from Farzanah, I think, but he's got three older brothers and the farm could hardly feed them as it was. She gets so lonely, poor thing. Of course she hardly knows anybody, and she says she wouldn't have known she was still in Brychmachrye, we speak so differently. And he's away all day. He's found work labouring on one of those building sites in the New City. Can you believe how big it's getting? I can remember when it was open fields, before the war . . .'

While Annie talks she leads Caro up the stairs. 'I hope Paddy's in,' she adds.

I don't, thinks Caro, wishing he had the nerve to say it out loud. How has this woman managed to tie a knot in his tongue? And why is he putting up with it, standing here, listening to her, grinning like an ape when what he really wants to do is run away and hide his head under a stone? Of course Paddy will be in: it seems to Caro that his luck ran out the moment he set eyes on Annie, and the only hope left to him is that in time he will forget this day ever happened.

Annie says, 'He'll be so glad to see you again. He hasn't

stopped talking about you. He's a great admirer of your poetry.'

Caro is so startled he nearly drops all the parcels. This is his cue, the scene he despaired of – he's on, but his timing's flustered and he can't remember the line. 'Annie, I – '

It's too late. The spontaneity is lost. Still he presses on, 'I promised to give you one of my books, didn't I? If you're not doing anything this afternoon, why don't you come round and I'll give it to you.'

Even to his own ears it sounds contrived. On the stage of The Moon and the Stars that split-second dividing sincerity from innuendo would have distinguished the hero from the villain, made the difference between a grateful kiss and a slap across the face.

'How sweet of you to remember.'

'Well, will you come?'

'I don't think I could.'

'Why not?'

He doesn't care any more if he sounds desperate. She's already made a fool of him, parading him around the City like a love-lorn errand boy. But if that's what she wants, fine. Whatever she wants, he'll do. He'll beg if he has to.

'I couldn't take your books, Caro.'

'I'd like you to have one.'

'But they cost the earth. It's too much, really. And it would be wasted on us. I can't read, and Paddy would only sell it. But I mustn't keep you standing here all day with your arms full of shopping. Come in and rest for a bit.'

Their room is tiny, dim, and sparsely furnished. The walls are black with old smoke. Under the window are two straw mattresses less than a foot apart. Paddy is stretched out on one of these, holding up a hand to examine his nails.

'Look who I've brought to see you. Bren's friend.'

'The human hand is a mighty thing,' Paddy tells them. 'A builder of Kingdoms and Palaces, a tiller of fields. Good morning to you, Caryllac.'

There is nothing else in the room aside from a makeshift shelf of a plank on two up-ended bricks, the bags they were carrying when they got off the boat, and Paddy's crutch hanging on a nail. Caro, usually so indifferent to his surroundings, is struck by the incongruity of this setting. Annie doesn't belong here. He has made a great discovery this morning: nothing reveals a woman's character so quickly as a few hours spent shopping

79

with her. Annie has the taste, and moves with the elegance, of one bred for better things.

All at once Caro realises that Paddy is looking at him, reading these thoughts in his face. Paddy grins unapologetically, man to man.

'What's so funny?' asks Annie.

'Some jokes,' says her brother, 'never go stale.'

'What? Oh, never mind. Don't try to get any sense out of him, Caro, he's got none. Caro's been helping me with my shopping – be a love, Caro, and put those things down there – so we're going to return the favour and give him lunch.'

'Haven't we all had a busy morning? Sit down, Caro, take the weight off your feet. I know my Annie, there's nothing she enjoys so much as wearing a man out. I met your friend the boxer in the Clerkden this morning. We admired the new statue of Mathred together. Looks just like Annie, don't you think, Caro?'

Annie tuts, 'Don't be so irreverent.'

'Well, your boxer told me a strange thing. He said the gods of the Southland have animal heads. I'd heard it before, but it's the sort of thing you don't believe until you get it from the horse's mouth. Half of what we hear about the Southland is pure fable. But he assures me it's true, and the curious thing is, although they have animal heads they have human hands. So what I want to know is, which do they worship, their heads or their hands?'

'Here's your orange,' says Annie, tossing it over. 'Caro bought it for you.'

For you, thinks Caro furiously, for *you*, you stupid woman. To make you look at me.

Paddy winks at Caro. 'I shall never eat it. I shall keep it to show my grandchildren for a wonder, and they'll think I'm a doddering old fool when I tell them that this orange was bought for me by the prettiest man in Tsvingtori.'

'Who called me that?'

'My lips are sealed. Try Annie. I'm sure you could make Annie talk, if you put a little effort into it. What do you say, my pearl of wisdom?'

'Are you going to eat it, or shall I put it away for now?'

Paddy throws the orange back to her. Annie puts it on the shelf and, taking one of her new pots, announces that she's going downstairs to get some soup. As the door closes behind her Paddy links his arm through Caro's, leans up against him, and whispers, 'I think this is the moment when I'm supposed to ask you whether your intentions are entirely honourable.'

11

A less honourable state of mind than Caro's would be hard to imagine as the weeks pass. He pursues Annie like one who, bent on revenge, seeks every opportunity to aggravate his grievance. She can't turn around without bumping into him. 'What are you playing at?' she teases. 'What do you want?' Bitch. As if she didn't know. He wanders among his friends with the red eyes of an insomniac. Everybody knows his predicament. Caro – Caro who so rarely wants anything more than to be left alone – wants something he can't have, and it's driving him crazy.

What is he supposed to say? 'Sleep with me'? 'Come to my bed'? 'Make love with me'? How does one phrase such an invitation? The common words are not precise enough. He doesn't want to *sleep* with her. He'd take her in the Clerkden, in broad daylight, if she would let him. He isn't offering love. There remain only the four-letter words which, he has to admit, are pretty resistible. What do men say in situations like this? Caro has never had to ask before.

He fantasises about making love with his hands around her throat; then he comes to with a cold shudder of disgust at his own degradation. He, who abhors violence, can now think of nothing else. She is turning him into a different person, someone vile and brutish and like other men. He is appalled, shamed, enraged by the depths of ugliness his soul contains. He has to put a stop to this. He has to have her.

Bren observes Caro's deterioration with mounting alarm. Usually he'd trust Annie to look after herself, but she doesn't know Caro well enough to treat this problem with the seriousness it deserves. Bren can't remember a single occasion when Caro failed to get something he wanted; and he's never wanted anything as badly as this. So Bren takes Annie aside and tries to warn her, praying that this time his words will be heeded. Annie thanks him for his concern, although it's not necessary – she has no intention of going to bed with a boy half her age, and one twice as pretty as she is to boot.

'Don't worry about it,' she says. 'I don't. From what I've heard, he'll soon lose interest.'

81

For a moment the uncharitable suspicion crosses Bren's mind that Annie enjoys keeping Caro on a string. No, of course not, how could he think that? He knows Annie. Love, and men, have never been a game to her. And she's right: Caro is incapable of sustained pursuit. She's being practical, not cruel. All the same . . . She ought not to see so much of him.

'But I like him, I really do,' Annie laughs. 'He's a sweet boy underneath. He gave me a rose, you know. No one's done that for years. I hope we can still be friends when this blows over.'

Perhaps it is because, by fending off his attentions, Annie has given Caro time to get to know her, that events now take an unexpected turn.

She and Paddy have gone with Caro to The Moon and the Stars, to see his latest play. They take their seats in the gallery, clay pots filled with glowing embers tucked between their feet to keep them warm. Paddy positions himself between his sister and her would-be ravisher, all ears, in a manner of speaking, so that when Caro wants to speak to her he is forced to lean across Paddy, making intimate remarks impossible. Since meeting these two Caro's heart has shown its nastiest side: he had not thought it would be possible to hate anyone as murderously as he hates Annie's unwholesome brother.

After the performance they head down to the Conqueror tavern on Duccarn Street, where the Company will join them later. They find a cosy corner close to the great fireplace; the smoke fills their nostrils, making them slightly sleepy, giving their beer a resinous flavour. While they wait Paddy, for once, lets Annie do the talking, and during the course of this conversation Caro undergoes what can only be described as a change of heart.

They discuss the play, comparing it with others he has written or she has seen, both in the City and in Pravarre. It would be hard to say which astonishes Caro most: the warmth of her praise (he having long lost hope of winning praise from her), or the intelligence of her comments. She doesn't insult him with uncritical approval. She doesn't simper like the women whose flattery is meaningless because they have an end to gain, their slick tongues baying after his flesh . . . Dear God, thinks Caro, suddenly startled by a twinge of sympathy for her, I should understand how she feels. I am the fox turned hound.

This peculiar sensation gives him pause for thought.

Annie is not a piece of meat perversely refusing to lie down on his plate. Listen to her. She thinks, she feels, she has a mind.

She too has ideas and hopes and ambitions. Her judgment is sound; her observations are fair; her respect is worth having. She is his equal, and she knows it.

She deserves much better than to be used and thrown aside. A lifetime's dedication could not begin to equal her merit, or atone for his folly. She possesses every virtue. He sees it now, plain as the daylight she casts all around. She is chaste, truthful, gentle, loyal, patient, perfect. Her kindness never fails, not even towards her brother, scum of the earth; not even towards that proud blind child Caro.

He could bury himself in his own stupidity. How could he have been so arrogant as to presume, for one moment, that she ought to be *grateful* for his interest? Rather he should get down on his knees to her, stay on his knees where her brightness has thrown him.

He alone is at fault. The violence which knotted his muscles, gnawed at his liver, was all his doing, his refusal to admit defeat, his fierce struggle to deny that she had captured not only his imagination, but his soul. Her foot on his breast is as soft as a dove, warm as sunshine. He lived in darkness, chased shadows, until the moment she set eyes on him, and he – stupid, proud, arrogant – vainly tried to cover his eyes and lie to himself. Now he can't stop looking, marvelling, understanding at last what his fellow poets mean when they speak of a surrender more joyful than triumph. He could never hurt her. He'd rather sweat blood than cause her to shed a single tear. The heart he wants to rip out is his own, to lay it at her feet.

Caro lies stretched out on Bren's bed, arms folded, a look of helpless idiocy on his face.

'This is all rather sudden, isn't it?' says Bren.

'I loved her from the moment I saw her.'

'Good grief. It wasn't love you were talking about last week.'

'Yes it was. I didn't know it.'

'Oh sure. She's the first woman who hasn't fallen into your arms, so you love her.'

'It's like a miracle. I never thought this would happen to me. Sometimes I think I'm happy enough just loving her, and it doesn't matter that she's not interested. Bren, you know what it's like when spring comes – there's always a day in the middle of March when you go outside and the wind has changed, and you know the winter is over, and your heart just lifts up? That's how I feel every time I see her.'

'I do know how it feels.'

'I want to give her everything.'

'Like what? Forgive me, Caro, but what have you got to give? You have no money, for a start.'

'I have enough to live on.'

'You don't understand. Listen, Annie – Annie is – well, women like Annie, beautiful women, they know what they're worth. She is older than you, and – well, I guess I'm not giving any secrets away if I say she's been around a bit. At her age her head isn't going to be easily turned by your pretty face. You're not the first man who's been interested in her. What would she want with a boy? A poor boy, like you.'

'I know. I know she's entitled to more than I can give her. I know she'd be a fool to settle for me. I know more about her than you think I do. I can see that she's come down in the world. But that's Paddy's fault, isn't it? And she's so loyal. Six years of exile, for his sake. She takes my breath away. And that's why I love her. It's not just because she's beautiful. I don't even think about that any more. She's perfect in every way. I don't know why the whole world isn't in love with her, she's so kind and intelligent and happy and good. No one could love her more than I do. That must count for something.'

Bren gives up. Caro is in the trance of love which nothing can penetrate: right now he would walk through walls for her. If Annie wants his love put to the test, she can do it herself.

Every night Caro writes another poem, and as the sun rises he sets off through the frosty streets, cracking puddles of ice, to make his way down to the poorest quarter of Old Tsvingtori, rank with the smells of fish-head stew and mouldy cabbage, the underwater kingdom where Annie shines like a lantern that will bring his ship to a peaceful harbour. He passes the fishermen's shacks thrown together from scrap pieces of old boat-wood and discarded canvas, and sometimes, exalted with the prospect of seeing her again, he presses handfuls of coins into the blue fingers of beggars huddled in doorways. He turns into Hemp Alley and knocks on the door of the house with the green shutters. Annie might be in, or she might not. If she isn't, he waits, enduring Paddy's garrulous company and smutty insinuations for her sake.

Other times he may find her cradling the neighbour's baby in her lap, soothing it with old songs and pressing kisses on its fat arms. The child knows her, loves her, and wails whenever she puts it down, a sound very like the one Caro wants to make every time she turns away from him.

'Have you never wanted children, Annie?'

'Yes, very much.'

He can't say the same; but then, Annie is the perfection of all things feminine. He would be willing to share her with a dozen children, he would gladly father a whole tribe on her, if that is what she wants; if that will make her love him.

'But I threw away my chances,' she says, 'and now it's too late. I can't have children.'

'I'm sorry.'

'It's my own fault. It's not so bad, I make do.'

'Why haven't you ever married?'

'Don't be impertinent. Because nobody asked me, if you really want to know.'

This cannot be true. She is covering something up. Is there another man, the ghost of a man whom she loved and still does love, the man she would have chosen as the father of her sons, whom she would have married; whom she lost? Or, knowing she was barren, did he betray her, breaking her heart beyond repair? But that's inconceivable: no man could leave her. Or was it Annie who sent her love away to find a field worth ploughing? It would be like her.

How to make her see that her flaw, in his eyes, is no flaw at all? It means they can be together for ever with no threat of interruption, no unwelcome intruders that he will have to make room for. He says, 'I'm not interested in children.'

'You're still a child yourself.'

'I love you.'

'Don't be absurd.'

She refuses to listen to his poems. If he tries to recite one, she claps her hands over her ears, although she does it with a laugh. She means to laugh him out of his boyish infatuation.

'Go to bed with him, why don't you?' Paddy suggests when they're alone.

'Fat lot of help you are.'

'It's the answer. Once he's cooled his ardour you won't see him for dust.'

'So they tell me.'

85

Why, Annie wonders, is this happening to her? She cannot bear to sit in silence while he bombards her with ignorant praise. Thank goodness she's not vain enough to take him at his word. His poems describe a woman who doesn't exist – who couldn't exist – a woman so much like the Annie she once wanted to be that she could hit him for reminding her.

At some point he always tries to touch her, to hold her hand or steal a kiss when Paddy isn't looking. It is so difficult to ward him off and keep smiling when she's on the brink of screaming at him. It's so unfair. Now that she's old and used-up and not worth it any more, love has come to mock at her in the shape of an honest boy who doesn't know what he's talking about.

At last Caro is forced to take his leave – perhaps he has an appointment with his booksellers, or is needed at The Moon and the Stars, or has been hired to give a reading at some party or dinner in the New City – and when he has gone Paddy tells her, 'You're not being very kind to him, Annie. You shouldn't welcome him with open arms and then kick him in the teeth. Doesn't he tug at your heart-strings just a little bit?' Paddy adopts a moonstruck pose and mimics Caro viciously, 'You're so wonderful, Annie, you're so perfect, you're so pure . . .'

'Leave it alone, Paddy.'

'But you like it really, don't you? You sly little pussy, you,' Paddy nudges her. 'He's a pretty sight, isn't he, Annie? Eh? Prettier even than you ever were, my lovely of lovelies. Come on now, confess – you're sorely tempted, aren't you? What a pity he's so poor.'

'That has nothing to do with it, as you well know. Do me a favour. Take this – this scribble, and put it out of my sight.'

'You mean somewhere where you can't find it? Oh, my Annie. I was convinced that his little verses left you quite unmoved.'

Annie throws a candlestick at him, and is sorry to see it miss.

Caught between them, Bren doesn't know which way to turn or whose side to support, for it is to him that Annie comes with her questions.

'I've told you everything I know,' he says when she persists. 'I don't know what sort of family he comes from, I don't know where he comes from, I don't know what sort of background he has. I don't know where he got his education or who paid for it. I know nothing about his life before he joined us. It's like

86

he fell from the sky. There we were, miles from anywhere, and suddenly this kid appears looking like some heavenly page-boy, his clothes falling off him, hadn't eaten for days, speaking Andarian like a prince.'

'And you fell for him?'

'You know what, Annie? I sometimes think you understand how I felt better than you let on. He needed someone to look after him, and I was curious. No, let's be honest, I was bloody fascinated. I could tell even then that he was someone special. But I kind of thought it was because of what he already was; and then it turned out it was because of what he was going to be. Do you follow me? He's a child of good fortune, our Caro. The thing is, I don't believe, any more, that the reason he's so secretive about his past is because he's hiding something. I don't think Caro would know how to hide anything – look at the way he is with you. He doesn't talk about his past because it isn't important. Not to him. What he is now is all that counts. He's not interested in anything but the here and now, and he doesn't see why other people should be. And if you – if you want to be his friend, you have to respect that.'

'Is it true what they say about him?'

'What?'

'That he's, – well, Paddy would say a free-thinker, but I would say too much like Paddy for comfort, in some ways. You know. That he's an atheist. And other things. I don't like to repeat them. He starts on at me sometimes, but I really don't want to know. I think it's best to treat him like Paddy – I never ask Paddy what he's been up to when he goes out. Ignorance is bliss. But with Caro . . . I can't work out whether he means half the things he says, or if he's just trying to make me worry about him.'

'And do you?'

Annie blushes, but insists, 'If it is true, if he goes around the City slandering the King and dredging up the war, he could be in a lot of trouble.'

Bren chuckles. 'Do you think I haven't told him that? I've warned him and warned him until I realised I was wasting my breath. Caro's not as straightforward as you think. My opinion, for what it's worth, is yes, it is all talk, mostly. It amuses him to unsettle people. He knows he can run rings round most people, intellectually. I can't think why else he does it, because I'm quite sure he doesn't believe it himself any more. As for his religion, your guess is as good as mine. He likes to scoff; but then again, he writes hymns. And he's never fallen foul of the censors, so he's either very devious – '

'Oh no,' Annie interrupts with a smile. 'Not Caro. He couldn't lie to save his life, not about something that mattered to him.'

'There you are, then. So his heart's not really in it. He's a little bundle of contradictions, is our Caro. He likes to keep us on our toes.'

'But Bren, how can you be so sure he doesn't mean it? Even if you're right, it's a terrible risk to take for the sake of a game.'

'Oh, Caro knows what he's about, don't you worry. Listen, Annie, I'll let you into a little secret. I know what Caro's set his heart on.'

'What's that?'

'He wants to be Court Poet.'

'Oh no! Really?'

'It's the only thing about him I'd stake my life on. He's incredibly ambitious. And why shouldn't he be? He knows he's the best.'

Annie starts to laugh. 'What a dark horse! Oh, I'm so glad. How funny he should try to make us all think that's the last thing he wants.'

'He's guarding his rear, isn't he? In case he never makes it. Some disappointments can only be borne if nobody else knows about them. We all do the same; I mean, you're a perfect example.'

'What?'

'Annie, Caro thinks the reason you keep him at arm's length is because you don't love him.'

'I don't love him.'

'Oh, come on, Annie. You don't fool old Bren. I've known you for nearly twenty years and you've always been an honest woman, until now. I know perfectly well what's keeping you away from Caro, and I think you should tell him the truth. Give him the benefit of the doubt.'

'All right, you know him so well, what do you think he'd do if he knew?'

Bren considers this for a bit. 'He might know already. He said he knew more about you than I supposed.'

Annie shakes her head. 'No. He doesn't know. He would

88

show it if he did.' A flat note of bitterness deadens her voice. 'He's a man like all the others.'

12

At the end of November a hard winter descends on Brychmachrye.

In the North a week of blizzards brings drifts of snow deep enough to drown in. News filters south of Ruffash border raids. These barbarians sweep down from their mountain fastnesses on ponies as tough and hairy as themselves, animals reputed to have webbed feet instead of hooves. They swim through snow and feed on human flesh. The Ruffash themselves are said to be cannibals. Their land is not a Kingdom as the rest of the world understands it, because they have no King, and their innumerable tribal chieftains, great and small, are chosen through trial by combat or by the uncivilised method of a show of hands. One would think they had no Gods to guide them.

In Tsvingtori the bay has frozen over. Idris is the only man old enough to remember the last time this happened, way back in the second Henry's reign. The ice-bound docks stand empty. At night ships trapped in their berths are vandalised for firewood. Nothing can come into the City; no one can leave it. Prices double daily. It's all the fault of the rich men, the greedy, the hoarders. Shopkeepers bolt their doors, and the market-stalls have nothing to sell but a few loaves of black bread, wrinkled onions, and pale pork in barrels of brine. Tools drop from frostbitten fingers; the dye-vats have frozen solid; the clacking looms that filled the Weaver's Quarter with chatter have fallen silent, run out of wool. Half the population stands idle, hungry, chilled to the bone.

By day vendors hawk roast chestnuts and rotten potatoes in the squares, unable to beat back the crowd that scrambles for a place close to the brazier. At night the streets are deserted, and the starving wolves with teeth as white and fierce as the winter roam through the City in search of old men, beggars, children, food.

Cats and dogs disappear. Caro keeps Fern on a tight lead whenever he takes her outside, but he may only be risking himself by this: one hears of people murdered for a slab of bread or a hunk of cheese. He goes up to the Official Publishers to beg a loan of the writing materials no longer to be found in the shops, and is told their cupboards too are bare. The paper has been burnt and the parchment boiled down to soup.

The priests, what do they care, snug in their temples? Either they lied or their auguries failed them. No one predicted such a terrible winter. No one prepared for it, except, perhaps, the rich men, who have the priests in their pockets and always keep an eye open for any profit to be made from the misfortunes of others.

One day Bren climbs up to Caro's attic – slowly and painfully, for his feet are an agony of chilblains – to bring him some sad news. Squint Winnie has died. Caro hasn't seen Winnie for years. Soon after they returned to the City she took up with an elderly, respectable tanner, married him, and cut her links with the Company. Bren is in tears. Caro thinks, what's his grief worth if he cries so easily? People are dying all over the City, and Caro has never understood why you should grieve more for your acquaintances than for people you never knew.

Annie has her own griefs. Her neighbour's wife, the mother of her little friend, has died too; she went without food to feed her baby, and now the husband has taken his child and disappeared. Annie doesn't know where they went, or if they are still alive. She keeps herself busy. Annie and Paddy run an open house: they always have something to eat and to share. Annie knows her brother too well to ask how he paid for the food; this winter has repealed all laws except that of survival. The Wardens aren't about to chance their skins for the sake of duty. They shut their eyes and stay put in the Coneywarren, cold and hungry and tired like everyone else.

Annie has to force Caro to eat. He won't do more than match her, mouthful for mouthful, and she has to keep an eye on him, or he'll pour half his bowlful into her own.

The approach of Solstice brings no upsurge of festive spirit: the mood in the City is one of creeping panic. Rumours are going round that the Sun will not return this year. See how weak He is, a feeble glow in leaden skies, hardly rising before He hastens back to His sick-bed. He is dying. This unnaturally savage winter is the beginning of the end of the world.

Food riots break out. Mobs storm the grain warehouses, and, when they find these empty, turn and attack each other. The merchants barricade their houses and the priests closet themselves in their sanctuaries, to pray, presumably. The air is black with the greasy fog of sacrifices. Caro looks at the layer of oily soot topping the snow on his windowsill, and thinks, people could have been fed.

At last the situation becomes so grave that the Court, feeling itself to be in some danger from the rioters, takes action. A few days before Solstice word races round the City that something marvellous, heaven-sent, is about to take place in the Clerkden, and within an hour a great crowd has gathered, stamping their feet in the snow, to hear the address of the Lord Priest of the Palace, Henry filcPeter Farzanah, who has descended to them in the King's name to make the following proclamation:

'If (says his Eminence the Lord Henry) the usual Solstice rituals fail to secure their customary grace, that is, should the Sun not renew His vitality and the days not lengthen their extent in the New Year, then His Divinity the Tsyraec, their dear King Basal, who loves his people with more magnanimity and faithfulness than ever a child was loved by its father, to whom their welfare is more precious than his own blood, has solemnly vowed to offer his own son, the Prince Alexander, as a propitiation for the sins which have displeased the Gods.'

Thus at one gesture of a majestic hand despair is swept away and hope bestowed. Brychmachrye has not been abandoned. The crowd cheer and clap adoringly: the sacrifice of a prince is considered to be infallible magic.

It's enough to make Caro laugh, if he weren't so dispirited by such a display of fatuous ignorance. The custom of human sacrifice died out in Brychmachrye long before the Conquest, and had been banned in Andariah for generations before that. Caro doesn't suppose that Basal Rorhah has any real intention of reviving it now. The King is playing on their ancestral bones, soothing one superstition with another – not unlike, thinks Caro, Bren and his hangover cures. If their Holy Tsyraec really wanted to do something constructive, why didn't he send bread? You can be sure the court isn't starving.

Admirable statecraft, nevertheless: to gain something, that is the pacification of the rioters, for nothing, that is a promise his Grace will never be called upon to keep; and increasing the reverence his people feel for him almost by the way. Even Caro is impressed by the simplicity of it. Oh yes, Basal Rorhah knows his Brychmachrye almost as well as Caro does.

Solstice is celebrated without further incident, and the days grow brighter as Caro sinks further into gloom. The ways of

91

humanity sadden and anger him more in this winter than ever before. He almost wishes the King had been called upon to make good his promise, so that everyone could see how empty it was. He doesn't know which is worse – the sheepish credulity of men and women flocking to the temples and hanging on the priests' every word, or the cold-blooded cynicism of power making capital out of a faith it encourages. These things are two sides of the same bad coin. And he, Caro, he who can see this, he is the one who should be speaking out about it. Sometimes it's difficult to remember why he chose to wait – especially as the Court still shows no sign of taking notice of him.

'You're an intelligent woman,' he says to Annie. 'You don't believe in all this Temple nonsense, surely?'

'You try to be too clever, Caro. Because you can't understand something, you say it can't be true. But there are some things you're not meant to understand with your mind. Yes, I believe. I believe in the Gods, and I believe They shape the world. And our lives. You'd have us believe it all happens by accident. But all you have to do is look at it, and see how everything fits together, to see that it was designed.'

'You can't believe that all Basal Rorhah has to do is crook his little finger and the Sun moves at his command.'

'Don't call him that. You should have more respect.'

'What's he done to deserve my respect?'

'Caro! I don't want to hear any more.'

'He was a man before he became King. And he's still a man, and no better than I.'

'All right, if you know so much, what does bring the Sun back after Solstice? See, you don't know. Wiser men than you weren't too proud to believe in it. You think you know everything, but you don't. You don't know anything and you refuse to believe in anything.'

'I believe we'd all be a lot better off if we stopped crawling around on our knees under these stupid superstitions. If we could throw those off we could stand up and have a good look round, and try to discover what the truth really is. But that's the last thing they want. It's to their advantage to keep us all credulous, can't you see that?'

'I hate it when you talk like this, Caro. You shouldn't say such things, not to me, not to anyone. You don't know who you can trust.'

92

'You know what, Annie? I think you do care about me a bit, despite yourself.'

She can't help smiling at him. Bren was right – Caro's tricks and ploys for catching her out are utterly transparent. Too much affection shines in her eyes, and she compensates with a frosty retort, 'Well, don't get killed just to show me.'

Caro reaches out to touch her. Quickly Annie draws back. His outstretched hand clenches into a fist. He gives her a look of pure hate, pushes back his chair, and stalks to the end of the room.

'What is it?' he cries. 'You let other men touch you. You let Bren hug you and kiss you, but you won't let me near you.'

'I don't want to hurt you.'

'Well you do, all the time. You say you don't want to, but that's all you do. You say one thing and you do another. I don't think you know your own mind.'

'Caro – oh Caro, look. I can't ignore all the things I hear about you. There are enough hearts bleeding over you to float a ship on. I don't want to be another.'

'They were just stupid girls.'

'So am I a stupid girl. Or I would be if I let myself love you.'

'But you could. You're always saying it. Saying you could love me is as good as saying you love me already.'

'I'm ten years older than you. It wouldn't last. And I'm too old to be interested in affairs I know won't last.'

'It will last if we want it to.'

Annie sighs. It's impossible to prevail against his stubbornness, his ignorance of how long life can be, his belief that sheer persistence will turn everything his way in the end. He sounds like a little boy who might say proudly, 'I am five,' as if it were something he'd done all by himself, and not the nature of time which decrees that nothing can last; five will one day become six, and six, in time, old age. Her arms ache to cuddle him. Fortunately he is standing beyond her reach, and after a moment she fights the urge down. Tucking her hands in her armpits she says, 'Every time you open your mouth you prove I'm right. Your life could take you anywhere. Mine's half over. Our affair wouldn't last. Five years from now you won't want to be tied to a forty-year-old woman who isn't even pretty any more.'

'I wish you'd stop trying to talk me out of loving you.'

'But it's all in your head!' she cries. 'There's nothing special

93

about me. I'm no better than any of those other stupid girls, and one day you'll wake up and realise it, and then where will I be?'

'You are better. Why do you always run yourself down? You're different from any other woman I've ever known. I sometimes think you're the only truly good woman in the world, and you don't even realise.'

Tears are pricking behind her eyes. Oh Caro, what's happened to your scepticism? Annie would like nothing better than to laugh and accuse him of not meaning this either; but he means every word of it. Because he doesn't know the first thing about her. He doesn't love her. He loves the idol of his imagination, and when she falls from her pedestal he won't be there to catch her, so don't even consider it, Annie – don't indulge for one moment in the vanity of trust.

She raises her head and says stiffly, 'I haven't spent my life waiting for you to come along. I've had affairs with other men, quite a few in fact.'

The hope, or fear, or whatever it was that prompted Annie to aim this fatal dart, seems suddenly ridiculous, for Caro merely shrugs, either not surprised by this revelation or not interested. 'So what?' He starts to grin. 'I never imagined it was your maidenly modesty giving me the cold shoulder. I'm just as bad. In fact I'm worse. I've been to bed with girls I didn't even want, just because they were there. Sometimes I didn't even know their names. I never loved any of them. I've never loved anyone at all, except you. You mustn't keep telling me that you're not worth it. I know you are. I know how different you are from all the others. That's why I love you. You keep asking me why I love you, and I'm telling you now, it's because you are a fine and honest woman. And that's why I'll never get tired of you. Because that won't ever change.'

He stops there – not because there isn't much more he wants to say, but because his words aren't having the desired effect. Annie looks as if she's about to cry. A visible lump moves in her throat. Her mouth, her hands, are trembling. He's never seen her so unhappy, so upset. Cautiously, he comes closer.

'Don't touch me!' she shouts, swiping at him. Caro traps her flying hand and holds it, astonished by the fever in her skin.

'It's all right,' he says.

She catches her breath and shuts her eyes, an expression of blank surrender on her face like that of an animal which has failed to outrun its predator. He turns her hand over and presses his lips against the palm, expecting Annie to wrench away. She makes no response. He risks flickering his tongue across her skin. Annie gasps.

'Don't,' she says faintly.

He gives her a look from under his brows. Stop it yourself, he dares her, if that's what you really want. His tongue slides over the bump of her wrist and nuzzles up a blue vein to the soft inner crease of her elbow. Annie's arm comes alive like a thing apart from her. Her whole body shakes. Caro fills his hands with her hair and pulls her to him. His breath is hot against her cheek, her lips – his tongue is inside her mouth, licking right down to the tips of her curling toes; and Annie, summoning all her reserves of common sense in the instant before her legs collapse, knees him as hard as she can in the balls.

He crumples to the floor, clutching his groin.

'I know what you can do to me!' she screams. 'Just because you can make me want you doesn't mean you can make me love you – '

She kicks at him, rolling him in a heap through the door and slamming it shut. 'Go away!'

'Oh God,' he moans weakly. 'Let me in, Annie, please.'

'No. I told you not to touch me. It's not the same thing. If you don't know that, you don't know anything.'

'What do you want me to do, stop loving you?'

'I don't care! I don't care! Go away!'

There is a long pause, and then he mutters, 'All right.'

His footsteps fade down the stairs. Annie sits on the floor, and waits, and listens, for a long time, but Caro is not coming back.

Later the same evening Paddy walks through the door and is momentarily suspended in disbelief at the sight of Annie kneeling on the floor beside a little fire in a pot, watching Caro's poems burn.

With an oath he pushes her backwards and thrusts a hand into the flames. The charred parchment disintegrates at his touch. Annie tries to pull him away, and he smacks her face, shouting, 'You cunt, you cunt,' blowing on his scorched fingers between obscenities. The woman has gone mad. She's burning money. Those poems could have been worth something, one day.

95

'He'll have copies,' says Annie calmly, tearing a strip from her petticoat for a bandage. 'Sit down,' she orders. 'Let me see.' The skin of his hand is bubbling with blisters and the fingernails are black. Paddy grimaces, but says, 'It's not as bad as it looks. No, don't bind it, that won't help. Your ignorance astounds me. Go get some hot water.'

Annie soon returns with a steaming pan loaned by the rope-maker's wife. Paddy has had a little time to think things over, and his good humour is partly restored. 'So,' he says, 'you found out where I hid them. Was it by accident, or were you looking?'

'I just wanted to get rid of them. He was here today, and when he left I – I wanted to talk to him, and I couldn't, and I got it into my head that it would help to hold something that was his. Even if I couldn't read them. I only wanted to hold them. I was thinking about him writing them, for me.'

'You have got it bad, haven't you?'

'Shall I wash your hand?'

'Thanks, but I'll do it. Listen, sweetheart, you'd better watch it. You're sailing pretty close to the wind. Caro's taken a lot of shit from you, and I don't think he's going to put up with much more.'

'I tried to tell him today. I really did. But when it came to it, I couldn't. It's so awful the way he looks at me, like I was Asdura or something. If I have to lose him I'd rather he stopped loving me because he got tired of waiting, rather than because he despised me. Oh, Paddy. I told him to go away. And he did. And I don't think he's ever coming back,' she sobs, burying her head in her arms.

Paddy strokes her hair. 'Dear me, big sister, what a pickle. Never you mind. Paddy will think of something.'

13

Mid-February brings warmer weather, and with it fevers, coughs and chills that settle into the bones and lungs of the debilitated population. The hospitals, where in any case only the destitute go, and then only to die, are turning the sick away; and the Cripplesteps, which almost emptied of beggars during the great freeze, are raucous once more with the cries of the blind and the lame, a hazard for any passer-by with a coin in his pocket.

One morning Caro wakes up with a slight cold. He cannot remember ever feeling under the weather before; the passing spots and rashes of infancy left no mark on him. It is hardly an indisposition, merely a bit of sneezing and a thick nose, and he can't think why Bren thought it worth telling Paddy about, nor why Paddy has found it necessary to come right across town to examine him. Especially as Paddy's in no fit state to go anywhere. He drags his bad leg and wheezes at the slightest effort. Paddy, however, takes ill-health in his stride. Worse things than this winter have failed to outsmart him. He is completely the learned man of medicine, taking Caro's pulse, feeling his temperature, tasting his urine, asking him to spit into a piece of cloth, until Caro, despite having no faith whatsoever in Paddy's skills as a doctor, begins to wonder whether there isn't something seriously wrong with him.

'Nothing I can't cure,' says Paddy.

He leaves Caro with the promise that he'll fix something up to put him right. Much later, when the slats of daylight cast through the shutters have crawled up the wall and turned to dusk, Caro hears the street door open. Footsteps come running part-way up the stairs and stop to knock on Bren's door. Bren comes out. He and the visitor talk in murmurs, but Caro recognises Annie's voice, and his heart begins to beat irregularly, as if he really were sickening for something. Annie has never come to his lodgings before.

She says thank you. Now she is climbing the stairs. Now she is standing outside his door. Fern wriggles in Caro's arms and tries to bark. Caro clamps a hand over her muzzle. The door opens. A bright yellow light cuts a swathe through the room, followed by Annie, her face carved into planes and shadows behind the candle.

'Caro?'

He pushes Fern's head under the blankets and sits up, grinning. He doesn't trust himself to speak. Annie holds up the light, peers at him – and bangs the candlestick down crossly on the table.

'I might have known. Well, what *is* wrong with you?'

'I'b gob a code.'

Annie tuts, arms folded, foot tapping, too much the picture of irritation. 'I should have guessed you and Paddy would cook this up between you.'

'What did he tell you?'

'Oh, only that you were dying. Don't you dare laugh. People are. And you never look after yourself.'

He wants to hold her, smooth away the furrows in her brow and kiss the anger from her mouth. 'Come here,' he says, meaning, it's all right, I understand. You don't have to fight any more. I won't make you say it.

'Oh no,' says Annie. She looks around for something to sit on and pulls a stool up to the table, propping chin in hands to take stock of Caro's room. There isn't much to see: four bare walls and draughty gaps between the floorboards, the bed, a brassbound trunk at the foot of it, a plate, cup, knife, inkpot, rolls of parchment and half a dozen books crammed on a high ledge, the table scattered with pens and paper, and the stool she is sitting on.

'So, this is how you live. Can't the wonderful Caryllac afford something better than this? You've got a nerve. I haven't sunk this low yet, I hope.'

Fern breaks free and thrusts her head forth, snarling at the ugly, female voice. Annie pokes her tongue out scornfully. 'Apart from anything else, your dog and I don't like each other.'

'Did you really think I was dying?'

This does not deserve an answer. Annie pinches a drop of hot wax and rolls it slowly, back and forth, between her thumb and forefinger. No, to be honest, she never believed he was dying. Caro's not some insignificant candle to be snuffed out by a random puff of wind. She almost snaps, I knew I wouldn't get rid of you so easily; but they could go on like this for ever, bickering, pleading, circling her cowardice. It was inevitable that she should end up in here, in his room, and she's strongly tempted to simply take what she can get and bury tomorrow. She could climb into his bed right now, without a word. But from where she's sitting, with the candle between them, its brightness blinding her eyes to his expression, it is easier for her to talk.

'Caro, there's something I've been meaning to tell you . . .'

He sits up, abruptly, and she wishes he hadn't, for now she can see his stricken face, immediately fearing the worst. If only it were something as simple as another man, another love, something she could be proud of.

'Caro, you know my people were fishermen, by birth?'

Caro nods. Annie Fisher, Paddy Fisherson – it goes without saying.

'Well, haven't you ever wondered how Paddy, a fisherman's son, managed to get to – pay for – University?'

'I thought you wanted to tell me about yourself.'

'I am. Just listen.'

Her father was a fisherman and her mother was a fishgutter. Caro knows what that means. The lowest of the low. Born to be spat on. They used to live with their cousins in a shack just like the ones Caro passes every day in Hemp Alley. It's funny how you always end up back where you started. But Paddy and Annie had a secret. For as long as she can remember, they had promised each other that they would make a better life for themselves, together. Paddy was a clever child: he was the one who fired her with ambition, but she made the dream her own. Paddy taught himself to read from a book he had stolen. He stole things for Annie too, pretty things, jewellery and trinkets. They were like – what's the word, Caro? – a promise for the future.

Well, when her mother found out that Paddy could read there was nothing for it but school. Charity school, of course. They had no money for anything better. They had no right to aim at anything better. You can imagine how the rest of the fisherfolk made fun of them. Ideas above their station. Her father was dead against it, but Annie was over the moon. All their hopes looked like being fulfilled. An education for Paddy would be their way out. Out, Caro, out for ever from a life of always being cold and tired and never having enough to eat and spending her days gutting fish and waiting to grow old before her time. You know what they called Paddy at that school? Fish-stew. Every child at that school was a charity child, and they all found someone to look down on in Paddy. How can Caro, the child of good fortune, understand what it's like to want things you've been told you can't have – to want *everything*, because you have nothing. All Paddy had was his wits and all Annie had was her beauty, but one day they'd force the whole world to eat their words. She was seventeen, and there were lots of offers, but she didn't want to spend her life standing on the docks night after night, waiting for the boat to come home one man short. Her father beat her for her notions. He said she was no better than she should be.

Charity schools don't keep pupils after the age of fourteen. Paddy needed to get into a Temple school if he was going to go on to the University afterwards, and oh, Annie had set her heart on Paddy becoming a doctor. They would be rich, and wear beautiful clothes, and live in a house with more rooms than people, and be waited on by servants; and people would bow to Paddy and call him Learned. Was that so much to hope for, Caro? Isn't Caro always saying that nothing will change if people are content with their lot? The problem was, Temple schools cost money. Her father said it was worse than if Paddy had got no education at all, he wasn't fit for the life he was born to, he'd end up on the gallows. This looked like turning out to be all too true.

So Annie didn't have to think twice when the rich man saw her in the street and sent his servants down to the fisher shacks to find her. To buy her. And she didn't just do it for Paddy's sake, that's what Caro has to understand. It wasn't a sacrifice. She thought about everything that money could buy her, white bread and gold bracelets and silk dresses and never, never having to clean fish again, and it seemed to her that she had got the best of the bargain.

About a year later her parents died, her father at sea and her mother soon after. Annie put on her best dress and was carried down to the funeral in a litter. Her man didn't want her to go. He didn't want her to associate with that dock-front lot; but he was old, Caro, and she could do anything with him, and all she wanted – all she wanted, Caro, was to see the envy on her cousins' faces when she flashed her jewels. Then the war came along, and her rich man lost all his money, and the University shut down for a while, just as Paddy was about to go up. She and Paddy had to live off her jewellery. He slipped back into pickpocketing as if it were his true vocation – he wasn't joking, Caro. He likes the life.

This lean time soon passed. War makes men rich. There were always rich men willing and able to buy her. So Paddy's University education was paid for, but he never really settled down. He'd got too much into his bad old ways during the war. After he lost his ears the Physicians' Guild wouldn't enroll him, and her dreams of a house in the New City, of respectability and self-respect, were shattered. That was when she started to realise what they really were, she and Paddy: a whore and a thief.

She was a cheat too, Caro. That's what she hates most about herself. She wasn't even an honest whore. She sold herself and then she gave it away on the side to any man she liked the look of, because it made her feel good. It made her feel that her body had not been sold, was still hers to give: can you imagine such perversity? She felt she was getting her own back on the men

100

who'd paid good coin for her. So, anyway, when she told the last of them – her customers – that she was leaving (to go to Pravarre with Paddy, but she didn't tell him that), he gave her a packet of money and asked no questions. Probably he was glad to get shot of her. She'd seen him eyeing up younger, fresher girls. And she had spent her money like water. On top of everything else she was an incompetent housewife. You never think prosperity will end until it all comes crashing round you. Well, that's that, she thought, from now on I'm mouldy second-hand goods, worth less with every year that I grow older.

'So now what do you say to your "good" woman?' she demands. 'I'm not quite what you thought I was, am I? Didn't you know about me? Didn't anyone tell you that Annie can't be bought with love? Why are you so poor? You offer me *this* – this *dump* – when I used to have gold on my arms from my wrists to my elbows. I could eat pearls for breakfast if I felt like it. Well? Well?' She drags her nails down her cheeks and shouts at him, 'Say something!'

'Why have you told me all this?'

'Because I can't stand the way you look at me.'

She is shivering, red-eyed and runny-nosed. Caro leaves his bed and comes to her, taking her cold hands to press a kiss on each in turn, kissing her elbows, the nape of her neck, a salty cheek, any bare skin his lips can find. He winds her hair around his fingers, and asks, 'Did you think I wouldn't love you any more?'

With a cry she throws her arms around him, digging her teeth through his shirt, into his chest. He stumbles on to her lap, and the stool cracks, spilling them across the floor, Caro laughing and Annie crying. He rolls her over and keeps kissing her, holding her face, trying to cram in as many kisses as he can before she stops him. But Annie has abandoned self-restraint. Five months of wanting him and resisting him break loose, and she tears at his trousers with frantic nails.

He catches her wrists. 'Fern,' he says.

Fern is crouched under the bed, hackles raised in disgust. Caro hauls her out by the scruff. 'I'll take her to Bren.'

By the time he returns Annie has undressed and climbed into bed. The candle is snuffed. Caro has nothing to light it with. He is a little hurt to find that she still does not quite trust him. 'You should have waited for me,' he says, although he understands. He too is frightened of what Annie may soon learn about him;

101

of what his love might betray, or hers perceive, of failure. In the dark he removes his clothes and lies down beside her, but she is the one who reaches out first.

And? Did Annie teach him the difference between having sex and making love? Did she bring Caro to the fulfilment of his manhood?

That it was more pleasurable than ever before is undeniable. Caro knew it would be. He enjoyed her enjoyment, found her delight delightful, loved to make her feel loved. In her hands his skilfulness was no longer something demanded of him, but his gift to her, and his body suddenly seems marvellous to him for the power it possesses of making her happy.

She even managed to conquer his grim silence and made him cry out. He supposes she must have interpreted his physical ripple of surprise at his own noisiness as some more normal response – the sort of thing she was used to. She must have thought they were sharing it. But Caro's imagination has its limits. He can guess, almost, what it feels like for her. He can watch and listen. What he cannot do is imagine how the other men felt who once lost their minds and their memories in her arms. Annie cannot change the thing that's wrong in him, and he cannot get that far into other men's skins. He can only read about it, and imitate it as a parrot apes words that have no meaning.

The greatest pleasure is lying with her afterwards in the warm bed, her head tucked into the curve of his shoulder, a smile on her sleeping face. He could stay awake all night, looking at her, and he knows that if he does fall asleep she'll be here to wake him in the morning.

14

They are teased, of course. Half their friends had always known it would happen; the other half could have sworn Annie had more sense. Annie and Caro are so happy they join in the rib-nudging and ribaldry – for lovers, like drunkards, find every-thing amusing. Falling in love is always a comedy. Only the death of love is sad.

The Black Bull asks them, 'Now that spring's here, when are you two going to get married?'

If Caro's friends retained the ability to be surprised by any-thing he said, they would have been surprised now, for he replies, 'As far as I'm concerned, Annie and I *are* married.'

'Oh?' smiles Annie mildly. 'That's news to me.'

She wishes the Black Bull hadn't raised the subject. It annoys her, the way everyone expects them to marry. What business is it of theirs? Can't they see that Caro shouldn't be pushed? He chose her freely. Let him keep that freedom, let him choose her anew every morning; and if – when – one day, she ceases to be his choice, they will at least be able to part cleanly. Caro can't be bound down with chains of law and Temple: that would be the quickest way to lose him. He'd come to hate her. Of course it would be different if children were a possibility.

Sometimes her womb aches with futility, and then she craves, not lovemaking, but to hold Caro in her lap, brush his hair, wash his face, set his collar straight. He nuzzles her flat belly and praises its soft suppleness. He's not aware of hurting her when he rejoices in her barrenness. How can she tell him that she would willingly shave her hair to hang on Asdura's altar, fast, keep vigil, wear her knees out in prayer if she could believe such devotions would give her Caro's child? But two miracles are too much to hope for: to have Caro and his baby would be tempting fate, which never looks kindly on unalloyed happiness. So Annie tells herself she's a silly woman. Why should it upset her, that her lover loves her the better for the very childlessness she grieves over? Crying for the moon only makes you thirsty – that's what her father used to say.

Meanwhile Caro hastens to expound his meaning with the zeal of one bent on universal conversion. 'In the old days, before the Conquest, all a marriage needed to be valid was the mutual consent of the man and the woman. They didn't even have words for "mistress" or "bastard" – Andarian words, you see, for Andarian ideas. They didn't need anyone else's consent and they didn't have legal ceremonies and marriage fees – that's what Andarian marriage is all about, money and property. That's the custom they've imposed on us. But Annie and I are natives, Bryach, and we are married in accordance with our own customs. We choose to live together. It's all in my book.'

The book Caro refers to is the very same one which fell apart in Bren's hands when he was rummaging through Caro's bag of poems. Caro saved the pages and rebound them him-self, unwilling to trust a stranger with the knowledge that he possessed this book. It is entitled *Brishachanah*, which, he tells them, loosely translates as 'The Customs of the Bryach'. Ourselves, he says. He doesn't know whether any other copies survive, and he won't tell them where he found it. The book had been banned almost as soon as it was written, less than ten years after the Conquest, as an act of policy by the men who had come to make Brychmachrye anew in their own image: they disapproved of encouraging the natives to remember their old barbarian ways. Caro enjoys quoting from this book, surprising people with facts their own ancestors had forgotten, such as, did they know that in the old Bryach Principalities the Temple was run entirely by women? Did they realise that their pre-Conquest forefathers and mothers regarded the Great God Adonac as nothing more than a minor war deity? As always when he is speaking of the King, the Andarians, and the Conquest, Caro's anger and indignation swell irrepressibly, and he exclaims, we were once a great nation, and look what they have done to us! They have dishonoured us, humiliated us, raped us; they have even stolen our past from us, and fobbed us off with shepherds'-tales of Prince Foxfoot and Brennain Bryach.

Well, this may be true, thinks Annie, but so are a great many unalterable things. Caro can talk history till he's blue in the face: she knows that she is not married to him. You have to make do with what the Gods send. Her man could be achieving great things, and instead he wastes his talents and energies fretting about events over and done with hundreds of years ago.

He's good at choosing his moments, she'll give him that. He knows when to keep his mouth shut and look obedient. But when he's among his friends or in his favourite 'safe' taverns he throws caution to the winds. He doesn't just toy with treason. He embraces it, passionately. And no one takes him seriously. They don't seem to appreciate that it makes no difference whether Caro means what he says or not. One word at the wrong time, one malicious ear too close for comfort, and the game will be up. Insincerity won't save him. Does he think he's so clever and so talented no one dares touch him?

He brushes her worries aside. Seeing that her fearfulness irritates him, Annie suffers in silence, reflecting that life with Caro is, after all, very much like the one she swore she'd never have. He can't resist the lure of stormy seas; and every time he goes out alone she sits waiting, with despairing certainty, for

104

the knock on the door that will come, one day, to tell her that her man has drowned.

One night in April Annie and Caro are sitting with Paddy and the Black Bull down at the Tar Barrel. Caro and the Black Bull are going at it hammer and tongs, all because Caro accused the boxer of having an unfeeling heart and a dead liver, of being less than a man, because he has no longing for his native land.

'I was a slave,' the Black Bull protests. 'I had to go wherever I was taken. And you know what? In time I came to be glad of it. I'd never have seen the world or had so many adventures if I'd stayed in the Southland. It's a whitened bone of a place. You wouldn't be homesick for it either, Caro – '

'It's not *my* country.'

'I just wish you could see it one day. Then you'd know what you were talking about, for a change. It wasn't meant for men to live in. You'd frizzle up there. Your summers are nothing – Southland winters are hotter. There's no rain sometimes for years on end. And the sand, Gods! It's everywhere, in your food, in your clothes, even in your bed. Sand and thirst and the smell of goats: that's all I remember. Admittedly it makes the oases look a lot more beautiful, but why should I go back there when this whole country of yours is an oasis? There's nothing for me there. In Brychmachrye I can forget what it feels like to be always thirsty. That's a freedom that puts my personal freedom into the shade. Shade, Gods, what a choice word. You Brychmachrese are so spoilt. You sit there on your arse, Caro, preaching to me, and you don't know how lucky you are. You can't love a place just because you're born there, you love it if it's worth loving, and if you don't approve of that sentiment, you go live in the Southland for a while and you'll see that I'm right. I'd rather be a slave again than go back.'

'We have slaves in Brychmachrye too.'

'Galley slaves are different. They're felons. My only crime – will you let me finish? My only crime was my size and a certain native talent for hitting people.'

'I'm not talking about galley slaves,' says Caro. 'Look, I'll tell you what the difference is between Brychmachrye and the rest of the Seven Kingdoms. In the other Kingdoms they have slaves, and citizens, and a King. In Brychmachrye everyone is a slave except the King.'

The Black Bull shakes his head furiously. 'You don't understand. The whole point about being a slave, and I think I can speak with some authority on this, is that you have no protection under the law. You're a piece of property. In Pravarre the murder of a slave is counted as theft, did you know that?'

'What's the punishment in Pravarre for theft?'

'Sometimes a fine,' says Paddy promptly. 'Sometimes hanging.'

'Well, that's what the punishment is for murder here. So when a man kills another man, what difference does it make whether he's hanged for murder or theft?'

All round the tavern heads are turning in the direction of Caro's raised voice. One of a group of students detaches himself from his friends and comes over to stand beside Blue Alanson, a fellow-poet and playwright who has recently enjoyed a minor success at The Mirror of Delights, The Moon and the Stars' great rival; and who is now silent, smiling, concentrating on Caro's line of argument.

'It drives me up the wall when you start shooting your mouth off about things you don't know,' says the Black Bull, nostrils flaring irritably. 'I've been a slave. A slave has no rights. He can't own anything that his master can't take away at a whim. His master can kill him if he wants to.'

'Which leads us to conclude,' says Caro, 'that the King is in the position of our master, and we are in the position of his slaves.'

A sick ache is settling into the pit of Annie's stomach. 'Caro, please – '

'No, Annie,' the Black Bull waves an impatient hand, 'keep out of this. Listen, Caro, obviously it's not the same thing. The other Kingdoms all have more or less the same laws you do, and you all worship the same Gods, but they allow slavery and Brychmachrye doesn't. Why would they need slavery if, as you maintain, it's inherent in your laws and in your religion?'

'How should I know? I don't care what they do in the other Kingdoms. I care about the lies they feed us with here. We're told that we're all free and that makes us better than the rest of the world, when the truth is we're all just as much slaves as you were, because we're not entitled to oppose the will of our masters. Our masters don't need slavery because they found a ready-made bunch of slaves when they came here with *their* laws and *their* Gods. We're not all equal under the law. We're not free. And as long as there's one man who's above the law we never will be.'

106

The student elbows forward, intruding. 'Who are you?' asks the Black Bull.

The student amuses himself by making them a little bow. 'Barney filcBarnard, of the School of Courts. And if I may say so, if you'll forgive the interruption, Master Caryllac is talking nonsense.'

'You tell him,' Blue Alanson cheers.

Barney filcBarnard goes on, 'The King is the King precisely because he *is* above the law. If he wasn't, he couldn't rule. He'd *be* ruled.'

'I don't believe that,' says Caro flatly. 'I don't believe in the Andarian Gods, and I don't believe there's any justification for the sort of absolute power the King has.'

The tavern regulars raise their eyebrows indulgently. Caro has pursued this same topic many times before in the Tar Barrel, but he is a favoured customer and an acquaintance of many, and he is safe from them. For Barney filcBarnard, however, Caryllac is a new experience, and his reputation makes him an exhilarating adversary. The name of filcBarnard will resound through the halls of the Schools if he manages to best this famous poet. So he smiles loftily, secure in his mental training, and asks, 'When you say "absolute power", I want to know what other sort of power you're suggesting there could be. Power can't be effective if it's not absolute, and if it's not effective then it's not power. Now there's a basis on which to justify it: that the alternative would be utter lawlessness.'

'And a good thing too,' quips Paddy. His partners-in-crime among the audience cheer and clap, and Caro waits impatiently for them to calm down before answering, 'That's not what I'm saying at all. I don't mean we don't need laws and all that, obviously we do, and even taxes – ' boos from his listeners – 'but I am saying that I don't think it's right for any man, especially the man who's supposed to be the highest authority and the greatest source of good in the Kingdom – a man we're supposed to believe is divine – to be legally allowed to commit the sort of crimes that would get any one of us in here hanged. That doesn't mean we don't need a King of some description. But once you take away his divine appointment, why does he remain above the law? If the Gods don't put him there, who does? Why is he permitted to rule?'

Barney filcBarnard is floundering in the subtleties of Caro's distinctions. 'What else is a King supposed to do?'

'No, no,' Caro waves his hands, 'that's exactly what he *is* supposed to do. But not because he's the Gods' servant. Because he's *our* servant. Because we need him. Because we permit it.'

Blue Alanson butts in, 'Come on, Caryllac, you're asking us to ignore something that's self-evident.'

'Not everywhere. In some lands the people choose their King.'

'Like where?'

'Ruffashpah.'

Tumultuous roars of derision. 'Call them Kings?' laughs Barney filcBarnard, while Blue Alanson sneers, 'Genius,' and someone at the back cries, 'You want to turn us all into barbarians?'

Caro is not disturbed by their ridicule. He has been working on this novel concept since the middle of winter, during the days of hunger and idleness when all the talk of the Ruffash tribes and their strange customs had started him thinking. His critics cannot be expected to grasp in a moment an idea that has taken him months to conceive. 'We don't have to *be* them,' he explains gently. 'But we don't have to turn our backs on them either. They were our own people once, before the Andarians divided us. We could learn from them. If we chose our King the way they choose their Chiefs, we could have the King *we* wanted, who would have to rule Brychmachrye the way we wanted, and if he didn't suit us we could dismiss him. We'd be in command, instead of always having the strongest forced on us. The King would govern the country for our benefit instead of his own. No, come on, hear me out.'

'All right,' says Blue Alanson, 'amaze us. Who's going to do this "choosing", now that we've forsworn the Gods?'

All around him people spit and touch their lips to avert the catastrophe of blasphemy. Annie's own nerves are on edge. She wants to cry out *he's a child, he doesn't mean it*, to stave off whatever retribution, mortal or divine, Caro so wilfully provokes.

Caro says, 'We can choose. All of us. Every man in Brychmachrye.'

'Why not every woman too?' laughs a heckler. A prostitute thumps him, exclaiming, 'Leave us out of it.'

Blue Alanson sighs, 'Let's not get ridiculous. I want to hear how the genius thinks we should arrange this.'

108

'Very well. I can see you won't be happy unless you have a divine-born as King. But even so that leaves thousands to choose from. Half the Andarians in this country must be descended from Michah the Conqueror. So, we could set up a panel, of noblemen if you like, if you really think you're unfit to exert the power of choice, and then they could sift through the candidates and present us with a shortlist, the way the City Guilds do when the King has to appoint a new Master for one of them. And then we could choose our man from the list.'

'But it wouldn't work,' cries Barney filcBarnard, fighting his way back into the argument.

'It would work. It would work if we wanted it to.'

'It wouldn't work. It doesn't work in Ruffashpah. We'd be mad to try to govern ourselves the way they do. Where's it got them? They have no trade, no towns. They live like animals. They're barbarians. The Gods have given them up as a bad job and left them to their own devices, and that's what their *choice* amounts to. Now what we have been given may not be ideal, but when it fails that's our own fault, because we're human and not divine, sinners and not perfect. But most of the time it does work. Look at the war. I can remember it, just, and I'm not playing down what anybody suffered, but we all know it was necessary. It got rid of Michael Andaranah, which was just about the best thing that's ever happened to this country – '

Close by someone takes exception to this remark and leaps up, ready to give the young whippersnapper a tongue-lashing, but the landlord, who smells serious trouble brewing, is moving between the tables trying to calm people down. 'One argument at a time, please.'

'I suppose you'd rather be a sheep than a barbarian,' says Caro. 'Of course it's all nice and cosy when we're skipping around the hillside without a worry in the world, relying on the shepherd to keep the wolves at bay. But we'd be fools to imagine he does it out of the kindness of his heart. And what defence do we have when he feels hungry for some mutton stew?'

'Metaphors,' says Barney filcBarnard dismissively. 'Just what I'd expect from a poet. I'm talking facts. It's a fact that the Andaranah couldn't have lost the war if they hadn't lost the Gods' favour first. History has proved that again and again. King Basal won the war and he's turned out to be just about the greatest King we've ever had. I don't know how you can fail to see the hand of divinity in that. Why don't you ask the older men here? Ask them how much better off they are now than before the war.'

'That's not the point.'

'Yes it is. The point is, why tamper with a tried and true system? It's simply naïve to think we can usurp the Gods' prerogative and not destroy ourselves in the process.'

'Oh,well, if you're the sort of simpleton who thinks prayer cures boils, you probably see divine intervention every time you crap. Is that what they call learning at your University? Is that what they teach you, to call superstition fact?'

'Caro, please,' Annie begs, 'stop it.'

Barney filcBarnard now recalls something he chose to forget when he broke college curfew to come down here and hang around with the waterfront low life: he remembers that he is a gentleman, and no loud-mouthed jumped-up native has the right to insult him like this. His father would have had the skin flogged off Caro's back for such impudence. Barney's fists clench. The murderous glint in his eyes terrifies Annie. She has seen enough fights to know it is when you have rendered your opponent speechless that you come into physical danger. And Barney filcBarnard is a tall, muscular young man.

Oblivious to menace, Caro is unstoppable. 'The point is that there never should have been a war. We shouldn't have needed one. Maybe Michael was a bad King and maybe he wasn't, but if he was, why did half our fathers have to die in order to get rid of him? There has to be a better way than that. Or do you really believe that because a man can win a war he's fit to rule a Kingdom? Is that how you judge your King? The more men he murders the greater he is?'

The landlord stoops to whisper in Paddy's ear, 'I've had enough. Hanging's one thing, the sort of death you get for not reporting this treason's another.'

'You wouldn't?'

'Not me, but someone might. Nowhere's safe enough for this – '

Hearing the murmurs behind his back, Caro whirls round. 'You,' the landlord jabs a finger at his chest, 'out. And don't come back till you learn to keep your gob shut.'

Caro is already halfway to the door. The speed of his departure takes everyone by surprise, even Fern, who crawls whining from under the table. Then Blue Alanson cracks a timely joke

110

about the kinship of genius and insanity, and those around him chuckle and reach for their mugs.

The tavern yard is full of moonlight. Annie stands outside the door, hugging her arms, looking round – there, in the darkness of the alley that leads to the docks, a glimpse of frosty white breath. Fern trots towards it, tail wagging. Paddy comes out and takes Annie's arm. 'Bullocks wants to stay a while. I've settled up. Your lover owes me, sis. Where's he lurking? Caro! Come on, let's go round the Conqueror and hunt up Bren.'

'Let's go, then,' says Caro from the alley.

As they climb up through the City, Paddy remarks, 'You've made an enemy there, my man.'

'Shut up, Paddy,' says Annie.

Paddy blithely ignores her. 'Typical student. Got a mouth bigger than his brain. That's all they teach you there, you know, to act like you know everything, while they hide it from you that you know nothing. I used to think just like you, Caro. I thought I could change things. Just little things. I never had your big ideas. But do you know, I used to fondly imagine my tutors would like me the better for pointing out the mistakes in their textbooks. Soon learnt the error of my ways, of course. At least I only lost my ears. If they'd had their way they'd have made me blind. Thieving seemed comparatively honest – and anyway I've always liked the life. Gives me a thrill. Rather like the thrill you get from tweaking the noses of people like Barney filcBarnard, I imagine.'

'I'll box your ears in a minute if you don't shut up,' says Annie.

They walk in silence the rest of the way to the Conqueror. Bren is not to be found, and as Annie feels she's had enough for one night she says good-bye to Paddy, takes Caro's arm and steers him homeward. Coming round the corner of The Moon and the Stars, a curious sight meets their eyes. At a little distance from the boarding house a small crowd has gathered to stare, with disconcerting intensity, at the four Palace Guards and the Court Clerk waiting restlessly on the front steps.

Annie drags Caro backwards. 'Don't go there – let's go – '

'I have to see what they want. Don't be frightened. They might not be looking for me. You stay here – '

'No!'

'Yes. Hold Fern. Look after her. I love you, Annie.'

Caro steps into the street and walks forward. Several people in

111

the crowd shout 'There he is!' and 'Master Caryllac!' and others clap and whistle. Their acclaim, like friendly hands of hope and pride, comforts Annie's trembling shoulders. Why, Caro's really popular! Everybody's on his side. Those Palace bullies might find it's not so easy to snatch him away from the hands of his people . . .

Caro bows to the Guards and to the Court Clerk, with whom he converses for less than a minute, the Clerk then taking from his sleeve a large piece of folded parchment that looks, to Annie's eyes, like nothing so much as a warrant. Caro opens and reads it, moving sideways as he does so to give Annie a view of his face. She watches his expression change to – what? Something almost smug, satisfied. He bows again, and the Palace deputation departs, the crowd moving aside to make way for them.

Annie releases Fern's collar and they both run to Caro. He grabs her hand. His is shaking. 'Come on,' he says. Upstairs he tosses the letter on to the bed, throws an arm round Annie's waist and dances her up and down the room, crowing, 'I did it! I did it!'

'What?'

'He wants me!'

'Who?'

'The King! The King! At Court!'

'Oh Caro, no! Really?' She's gasping with relief, delight, a lingering apprehensiveness. 'When?'

'Day after tomorrow. I have to go and give a reading. At his Grace's pleasure. Oh, Annie, Annie, Annie! I knew this would happen! I knew it! It's what I've been waiting for.'

15

The day after tomorrow.

At the lodging house:

Annie sits on the bed and stares at Fern, trying to make the dog react to the power of her dislike. Fern's a sly bitch, making up all friendly whenever Caro's around, then as soon as his back's turned she curls up in a corner and pretends Annie doesn't exist. Caro refuses to believe that the dog hates her. Fern has a pair of supercilious black canine eyebrows, always raised, which seem to boast, I was with him before any of you came along. Annie suspects that even if the beast could talk, she wouldn't part with any of the secrets Annie would so love to know.

This is ridiculous, Annie chides herself. I don't need to be jealous of a dog. She tries to occupy herself with some housework, not that there's much to do in a room so small and empty. Maybe the Court will pay him. Annie tries to steer clear of the subject of money. She doesn't want Caro to get the wrong idea. But he's so undemanding. He should be paid what he is worth. Then they could afford somewhere with a decent-sized bed and a fireplace and enough room so that she didn't have to trip over that dog every time she turned round.

A tune comes into her head. She hums a few bars, and recognizes it as Caro's favourite, *Jackie Fisher*. Annie's dwelt a lot on this song recently: Caro is trying to turn it into a play and keeps asking her to sing it for him. But when she comes to the last verse –

> *His uncles and cousins were putting to sea,*
> *When Jackie came running, 'Don't leave without me!'*
> *He ran up the sail and he pulled from the shore,*
> *And Jackie was seen by his lady no more.*
> *He lies in the arms of the sea,*
> *But the Quarter-Lord's daughter, her arms are empty –*

her voice breaks and she wraps her own empty arms across her breasts.

Caro's where he always wanted to be. There's no doubt that this is one thing he meant when he said it. All his high-flown talk has flown right out the window the moment the King called his name; and Annie should be glad. She is glad. Caro's found a more lucrative game to play, and she tries to be glad for his sake. For her the end will be the same either way.

How can she compete with the elegant young, witty young, beautiful young ladies of the Court? And Caro is so attractive. He's not used to denying himself. He will be unfaithful to her, he's bound to be. She must steel her heart against it.

Annie forgets that a heart steeled too often may turn to stone.

At Court:

Perfume. Roses. The shimmer of beeswax on polished wood, the purple weave of silk carpets. The hush of slippered servants' feet. Exotic fruits and sugar in wine. Above all the whispered laughter, like the smell of cleanliness barely perceptible among those vast spaces of architecture after the hubbub and stink of the City.

The first thing they did when Caro arrived was put him in a bath. When he emerged, pink and tingling, his clothes were gone, and a new suit of soft wool in a shade exactly matching his hair was in their place. Maybe that's all the payment Caro can expect, but he hasn't come here for the money.

The recitation went well, and was much applauded, in their muted, suede-gloved way. Caro has been taken under the wing of a bizarre young gentleman who smells of lavender, wears the latest fashions in magpie satin, has an emerald stud in one ear, and lines his eyes with antimony. The Queen, sitting in a brocaded armchair, indicates that she would like to speak with Caro. She expresses her love of good poetry, her delight in his talents, and her particular fondness for that vivid boxing poem, which her ladies enjoyed so much.

The sibilant music of court-speech hisses all around them, punctuated by giggles or the snap of a fan. The Queen says, 'And the boxer, the Black Bull, did he die?'

Queen Ursula is overweight, red-haired, powdered and placid. Is it true that she slit her youngest brother's throat with her own hands rather than leave him to the mercy of her future husband's soldiers? Caro cannot believe it. This woman doesn't look capable of as much violence as it would take to swat a fly.

'No, Ma'am,' he says. 'He still lives in Brychmachrye, but he's given up boxing.'

'What a pity,' says the Queen.

Someone brushes Caro's sleeve. He looks round. The lady who accidentally bumped into him raises her face to apologise, and then gasps, open-mouthed, her eyes as round as saucers.

'Oh Caro,' she says, 'is it really you?'

The day after the day after tomorrow.

At the lodging-house:

Dawn is breaking when Caro tiptoes into the room. Annie jolts awake, and gazes at him with red-rimmed eyes as though he had risen from the dead. He puts his arms around her. 'You're all right,' she sobs, 'you're all right, you're all right.'

'Of course I'm all right,' Caro comforts her. He tells Annie

114

that everything went well, they loved him, they want him to come again.

'But it's tomorrow already. Why did they keep you so long?'

Caro hesitates. 'I met an old friend.'

'Oh?' says Annie archly. 'You never told me you had friends at the Palace.'

'I didn't know. It was a – a bit of a shock. I'm sorry I'm so late. We had so much to talk about, I never noticed the time.'

'Who was it?'

'Someone from where I used to live when I was a boy.'

Annie caresses his thigh. 'You're very secretive. You'll make me suspicious. What's your friend called?'

'Vivian. Annie, please, I'm exhausted. I can't think straight. I need some sleep.'

Annie lets it go at that. After all, her Caro is clever, and if he wanted to cover up a lie by inventing an old acquaintance, he'd have chosen some more likely name, Henry maybe, or Thomas. Caro crawls into bed. Fern leaps on to his feet and curls up, nose to tail, sighing contentedly. Annie takes this as a good sign. There's no love lost between her and Fern, but they both love Caro, and the dog always knows when she has been betrayed.

16

As the weeks pass Caro increases in favour at Court. For this he has the lady to thank. He has been elevated from the status of servant, which is all his name and birth would have entitled him to, and the King has granted him the privilege of dining with the Court. He is allowed to stand behind the lady's chair and share her plate as though he were a gentleman. She has brought him into her circle of friends, and for many reasons – to gratify her, to amuse themselves, and to annoy outsiders – they treat him as an equal. The Queen has expressed great pleasure in his company; there is some talk of attaching him officially to her Grace's Household. The Palace library has been put at his disposal, and the clerks provide him with parchment, pens and ink upon request. Verses in honour of the Crown Prince's birthday have been commissioned. His enemies grind their teeth with envy – for he has made enemies, of course. Such favour as he enjoys always brings ill-will with it, as if Caro's

115

good looks, his talent, his charm and his luck were not enough to make him either admired or loathed.

The Palace rose-gardens offer as much privacy as one can hope for anywhere at Court, although Caro is always conscious of the eyes watching him, the ears eavesdropping. He walks arm-in-arm with the lady, and asks her, 'Are you happy here?'

She pulls a face. 'It's better than being at home. Arlo's here too – well, not right this moment, he's in the Guards, he's gone to Andariah with Bernard Derondah and my husband – '

'Tell me about him. Why did you marry him?'

'Why – ' she pinches his cheek, 'did you think I was so ugly no one would ever ask for me?'

'I never thought you were ugly,' he protests. The lady laughs, for she knows he's lying. She has always been skinny – bag of bones, Caro used to call her. Her only real claim to prettiness is her exquisitely straight nose. Her brown hair is so thick combs break their teeth on it, but she now wears it in the long plait braided with pearls that custom dictates for ladies-in-waiting, and the style becomes her prominent cheekbones and small chin. She is a lively, cheerful, friendly girl, a breath of fresh air in this Palace of perfumes, and a little of her company soon makes one forget that one had ever thought her plain.

'I hope you didn't take the first one who came along,' says Caro.

'Well, after all that trouble when Grandpapa died, you remember, after you left, I did get sent to the Little Daughters of Vuna for a while and God, Caro! It was gruesome there. I ran away once, nearly – I was going to go to Tsvingtori and find you, I climbed over the wall but I fell and sprained my ankle and I lay there *all night*, I nearly died of pneumonia.'

'Not you, you're far too tough.'

'Charming! Well, after that the Daughters sent me home. Can you imagine the shame? Not even the Daughters of Vuna would keep me. So then Grandmama and Uncle Richard gave me a huge dowry, sort of like a reward for anyone who would take me off their hands. So Arlo was telling Bash – '

'What do you call him?'

'Bash. Everyone calls him that, Caro, I told you. You never remember anything. His real name's Basal Uhlanah, but there's so many Basals here. Anyway, Bash is Arlo's best friend, and I guess he felt sorry for me, and he wanted to do Arlo a favour. I guess he quite liked the idea of marrying into the family too.

And he needed the money. Great jubilation at home, you can imagine. I never even saw him till a week before we were married.'

'What's he like?'

'He's all right. He's about your age, quite good-looking I guess. He has this sort of long face and a big mouth. He's very tall. Actually I don't see all that much of him. He goes abroad a lot. He works for Bernard Derondah.'

'Do you love him?'

'Oh, Caro,' she gives his arm a squeeze. 'That's so like you. Do you know, no one else has ever asked me that. He never asks.'

'Well, do you?'

'Maybe. In a way. I mean I couldn't love him when I married him, I didn't know him. You don't expect to find love in marriage, do you? I was grateful to him for rescuing me, though. Actually, in a way I was kind of in love with him before I met him. I pictured him like my champion coming to carry me away on his white horse. I thought he'd be so beautiful, like Alexander the Fair was supposed to be, you know, when people were struck dumb when they saw him. A bit like you, really. So when I met Bash, I was sort of disappointed, but now that I know him, I do like him. You can't not like him. He's very nice.'

'Do you love him more than me?'

'Caro! You're jealous! Oh how wonderful – and you've no right to be, you never came to save me and I waited and waited.'

'Do you love him more than me?'

'Don't be stupid. I don't love anyone more than you. I loved Daddy as much as I love you but I've loved you longer.'

The lady is a simple soul. Whom she loves, everyone should love, and she regards his honours and privileges as no more than her Caro deserves.

They stroll into the Palace woods, that domesticated pet of a forest where nothing fiercer than a rabbit roams. 'It's all right here,' she tells Caro. 'There's always something going on and at least I'm not bored, much, and now you're here it's almost perfect. But we're so shut in, you don't realise. That's what I hate about it. It's almost as bad as being at home. We're not allowed to go down to the City,' she complains. 'That's why you had to come up. You are so lucky, Caro. I long hopelessly to see the City. I think it's a stupid rule, but this place is full of stupid rules and I have to be good, or I'd be sent home in disgrace. So come on, tell me everything. I want to know all about the City. I want to hear about your friends. Are they nice? Do you tell them about me? Why are you laughing?'

'It's funny,' smiles Caro, 'but down there, in the City, they ask me the same questions about all of you.'

Although the ladies and gentlemen of the Court are not permitted to visit the City, their servants are, and do, bringing with them all the gossip about famous beauties and powerful men. Finally a garbled version of the truth reaches the ears of the one who is always the last to know.

Annie steels herself for a confrontation. But when Caro comes running up the stairs and bursts through the door, shouting, 'I love you, I missed you,' her courage deserts her, and he gives her no chance to regain it. In making love she forgets her wrongs; afterwards, when she remembers what he has done, it seems too late to be angry. Does it matter, in the end, if he has other women, as long as he comes home to her? She might risk what she has if she demands all of him. Better to be happy with as much of Caro as she can call her own, and close her eyes to what he gets up to at Court, which, after all, is another world, and one where she doesn't belong.

She puts her hand in his and they go out for something to eat. At the Tar Barrel they run into Caro's old rival, Blue Alanson, who prostrates himself at Caro's feet in a parody of homage. 'Don't muck about, Blue,' says Caro.

'No sir, yes sir, and may I kiss your arse, sir? If I lick your boots, sir, will you pull some strings for me, sir?'

'Work on it, Blue. That was almost a poem. Your first, would it be?'

'What's going on?' asks Annie. Blue Alanson turns on her. 'Dock-slut,' he spits, 'you've always known which side your bread was buttered on. What's her attraction, Caryllac? Are your women such dead fish you have to take ours? But then you know what they say, don't you? Like father like son. It's funny. I always said you were a bastard – '

'Caro, what's he talking about?'

'He doesn't know what he's talking about,' says Caro through clenched teeth.

'No,' says Blue Alanson, 'you're the one who doesn't know what he's talking about. All that crap you come out with about the purity of being native. You're no more native than Michah the Conqueror was. You're no better than the rest of them, coming in here telling us what we ought to want, and what we ought to think, and what we ought to believe in – what do you know about it, son of a Fahlraec?'

Caro grips Annie's arm hard enough to bruise it. 'Let's go – '

'Go on, get out of here, bastard,' Blue Alanson shouts after them. 'Go back to the Palace, bastard, it's where you belong. Go back to Andariah . . .'

'Don't ask,' Caro tells Annie. 'Don't say anything until we get home.'

Fern takes one look at Caro, tucks her tail between her legs and disappears under the bed. Annie wishes she could do the same. Caro sits her down on the rumpled bed and moves about the room in a fever of activity, gathering together his papers and pens.

'What are you doing, Caro?'

'I have to finish the poem for Prince Hans's birthday.'

'Why don't you talk to me instead? Why don't you tell me what that was all about?'

'It's nothing. A misunderstanding. It's not important.'

Annie takes a deep breath. Say it now, she urges herself. It can't make things any worse than they are already.

'I suppose that girl isn't important either?'

'What girl?'

'That girl you're running around with at Court.'

'I'm not running around with any girl at Court. Where did you get that idea?'

'So what were you doing that first night when you didn't come home till morning?'

'I told you, I met an old friend.'

'Oh yes, Vivian. And I fell for it.'

'Vivvy *is* an old friend of mine.'

'Vivvy, Vivian, Viv, you can call him what you like, it won't make him real, it won't prove you were with him when you were with someone else. You were with that girl. I know you were. So just stop going on about Vivian. I know he doesn't exist.'

Caro stands open-mouthed, exposed, deflated. If Annie loved him less she could have laughed at his absurdity. Her clever little boy, so proud of his quick wits, fondly imagining that gullible Annie would never get to hear the truth. Now he knows he's not as smart as he thinks.

And does that help her? Her pain, his callowness, tear at

119

her heart with equal savagery. The last thing she wanted was to catch him out in a lie. It's humiliating for both of them. Why couldn't he have been clever enough to hide it? If he tells her now that he never meant to hurt her, she would believe him.

'Let me get this straight,' says Caro. 'You think I'm having an affair.'

'Please don't try to pretend it isn't true.'

'With "Vivian"?'

'Don't be disgusting. What do you take me for? Vivian's a man – I mean, you made him up.'

'Did I?'

'Caro, I know! Everybody's told me. They could hardly wait to fill me in on what you were really doing at Court. They say she's besotted with you, poor girl. I could tell her a thing or two. And what about me? I looked like a right fool, saying, but he's with his friend Vivian, he told me. I really believed you, Caro.'

Caro thinks this over, blue eyes visibly weighing up the situation.

'I see,' he says, and sits down.

Why is he suddenly looking so smug? Annie expected contrition, defiance, even denial, anything but the confidence of one about to triumph over his enemies, Annie's tormentors, Annie's own doubts.

'Well,' he says (oh, that irritating smile, the rat who can worm his way out of any tight corner, the magician who always has a spare trick up his sleeve), 'let's make a few things clear. For a start, I did not invent Vivian. You did, if anyone did. And for another thing, it's Vivienne. Vivienne. The Lady Vivienne Floriah, as it happens.'

He's enjoying this, she can tell. He has that look on his face that he gets when he's writing a play and it all comes together, and he can make his characters do anything he wants.

He says, 'She also happens to be my sister.'

Is that it? Is that the best he can come up with? Annie continues to stare at him, unmoved and unpersuaded. This continual lying belittles them both. And such a lie – beyond the bounds of credibility . . .

To her intense annoyance the corners of Caro's mouth begin to twitch. He bites his lips, but the grin is out of control. His whole face is alive with laughter, crinkling his nose, dancing in his eyes – it defeats him, flinging his arms wide, slapping his knees, shaking his sides until it gives him a stitch.

'Oh Annie,' he gasps, clutching his stomach. 'Poor Annie. I'm sorry. I'm not laughing at you. Don't be angry. In fact, I should be angry with you. I don't have another woman. How can you think it? I don't want another woman. Trust me, please. You have to trust me, or you'll make yourself so unhappy. And me. It hurts to be mistrusted when I haven't done anything to deserve it.'

'You're lying.'

'I've never lied to you. I've never had a reason to lie. Well, I told a half-truth when I said Vivvy was an old friend, which she is. But she's also my sister. And she, I suppose, is the one you mean when you say I'm running around with some girl. Fine friends you have, I must say.'

'If she's your sister, why didn't you tell me before, when I asked you who it was you'd stayed with up there all night? I just don't believe you.'

'Ask Blue Alanson.'

'But he said – but you – but it's impossible. She's a Lady, a Floriah, you said, and you're – you can't – you're not really the son of a Fahlraec. Are you?'

'So you're beginning to believe me?'

'Caro, *are you?*'

'No, but you see how everything gets twisted. The Fahlraec was my grandfather, to my shame. And Vivvy's his grand-daughter. She's my half-sister, strictly speaking. Her mother was my father's wife, and my mother was my father's mistress. So there you are. It's not something I'm particularly proud of, and I never wanted it to come out, but I suppose it was bound to once Vivvy opened her mouth. She's – we grew up together, and she's very partial to me. She thinks that the bit of me that's a bit of her is the only part that counts, and she doesn't see why anyone should think I'm not every bit as good as her legitimate brothers. Vivvy's very good at turning a blind eye to anything that – I was going to say inconveniences her, but she's not selfish, she's just careless.'

'But what do you mean, you grew up together? I never heard of that before, a Lord taking his – ' Annie bites her tongue.

Caro supplies the word. 'Bastard. It's all right. You can say it. It won't be the first time I've heard it. And it's not the worst thing I've been called. After all, it's what I am. Let me sit beside you. Listen, Annie, the reason I never told you about this before is because it doesn't matter. No, that's not true, it does matter. It

121

has to make a difference for me because it does for other people. But I wanted to have somewhere where it didn't matter. This is where I belong. I'm a native, a Bryach. You're my people. I mean, look at me. Do I look half-Andarian? I certainly don't feel it. My father's blood seems foreign to me. Here, with you, in the City, I can forget I have it. But up at Court my being a bastard – I mean, the fact that half of me is Andarian, and Fahlraec blood at that, means they think half of me is like them, and it's the only reason why they treat me as someone better than a servant. So now I find I need something I wish I didn't have.

'You know, now that I'm talking about it, I think it's not just Vivvy – all of them up there are past masters at shutting their eyes to unpleasant facts. They talk about us, natives, in front of me as if I'd already thrown my lot in with my father's side. Maybe that's it. Maybe they hate us so much it would be like conquering us all over again if they could get me to disown – despise, my mother's blood. My people. I can't explain.'

'Try,' says Annie gently.

'It's not a very pretty story.'

'Caro, I think it's you who doesn't trust me. I love you, and I want to know. I need to know. You're always asking me to trust you, and I want to – but how can I when I know you're always keeping secrets from me? I didn't keep anything from you, remember? I hated telling you, but it wasn't fair for you not to know. Remember you asked me if I was afraid you wouldn't love me any more?'

'And you were.'

'Is that why you don't want to tell me?'

They sit side by side in silence for a while, until Caro suddenly reaches out to take her hand, and says, 'I do want to tell you.'

III

The Child of Good Fortune

17

Picture a boy, Annie, nearly ten years old, shinnying up an oak tree while a shaggy black-and-white dog named Rose crouched among the roots below. Rose disapproved of tree climbing, an occupation more fit for squirrels than for her boy. Squirrels existed to be barked at and chased and sometimes, to her great surprise, caught. Her boy existed to be worshipped. Whenever she saw him making for this favourite tree she would pursue and snap at his ankles, in order to remind him of his dignity. In return he would pelt her with acorns, just to show her that he wasn't to be bossed about by a grey-muzzled old nanny of a dog.

Rose was the boy's best friend. As puppy and baby they had rolled together in the grass, nipping each other with their milk teeth. Rose was willing to listen to him for hours, her head trapped between his knees while he stroked her ears and told her about school, or village gossip, or his parents, about books and poetry, the things that were wrong with grown-ups, the dreams he would fulfil when he was a man. This boy was set apart from the other village children, always had been, just as the cottage in which he was born stood in isolation on the far side of the oak tree. His mother was like the moon, out of reach and full of secrets. His father was a comet, brilliant, momentous and unreliable. Rose was his peer on earth, his elder sister, his confidante, his comrade and his slave.

Down at the foot of the oak tree Rose scratched the bark and whined. Something strange was going on. Her boy was distracted. He had gone bolting for this tree like a rabbit for its hole, without stopping to tweak her tail or tease her into chasing him. Handfuls of acorns weren't raining down. Rituals were overturned. He was climbing with great haste, and twice he almost missed his footing.

It's a common fallacy, isn't it, Annie, to attribute human thought to dogs. One might almost say Rose was wondering what had got into her boy. True, his mother was absent, but that, though unusual, was not remarkable, and if he and his father chose to come without warning they could not depend on finding her at home. As for his father, the man's abrupt appearances and swift departures were a way of life for all. On that adult Rose had smelt only regret – or maybe it was relief, Annie, an eagerness to get away. Who can guess what a dog's nose knows? On the boy, Rose smelt fear.

If any strangers come, his father had said, go into the cellar.

But this tree was the safest place Caro knew.

His father had ridden away without realising that the strangers were here already. His father had been in a hurry, and hadn't taken time to check the barn. His father hadn't walked in there, as Caro had, to come face to face with two horses he had never seen before, pawing the straw in stalls where they had no right to be. Their glossy hides were covered in scars, their tails viciously cropped to martial stumps. They laid back their ears, rolled their eyes, and gnashed long yellow teeth at Caro: terror took him by the throat and he ran.

Once he was among the branches the panic fell away from him, as it always did. He could rely on this oak tree. Up here, nothing could hurt him. School, parents, village were relegated to earthbound impotence. No one but Caro could climb this tree.

From such a height, danger lost its gravity and became an adventure. He stretched out along the branch and had a think. Fact: there were two strange war-horses in their barn. Strange war-horses meant strange warriors. Since he hadn't seen the warriors, it was reasonable to conclude that they were hiding, and if they were hiding it was because they were up to no good. From this it followed that they must be Rorhah men.

The realisation that evil incarnate was lurking so near at hand gave Caro a wonderful thrill – not the prickling of his spine that he had experienced in the barn, but the heart-stirring glimpse of a chance to do something heroic. Let them try it – whatever wicked plot it was they were hatching. Just let them. They'd soon learn who they were dealing with. He'd show them that his own soldier blood ran true.

Caro locked his heels under the branch and propped chin in hands. From this vantage point it should be easy to spot the villains, creeping around his countryside with nefarious intent. At the same time he could keep an eye on the road from Flormouth, so that when he saw his mother returning he would run to warn her that there were Rorhah men about.

Caro's village stood on the southern slope of a ridge which, just to the west of his house, fell away sharply into a coastal cliff, and to the east rose gently until it became part of the Floriah downs. This ridge formed a minor watershed. Two hours' walk north brought you to the little river Wend, the boundary between the Fahls of Floriah and Mindarah. Caro's village was about equidistant between the two Fahls' capitals: a day's hard riding south-eastwards would take you to Floried, while Mindared, where Caro went to school, was due north. The market town of Flormouth stood at the head of the Flor river estuary, not more than an hour's walk south. Here fishermen from along the coast brought their catch to be salted, barrelled, and shipped inland; here the Quarter's wool was graded and packed before being sent up river to the merchants' agents in Floried.

Caro's mother had grown up in Flormouth. She was a fisherman's daughter, Annie – in a rare moment of confidence, or in an unsolicited attempt to explain why they lived where they did, she had once told her son that she did not like to be beyond the smell of the sea. Most probably, as his father had suggested, she had gone down to the town today, either to visit old friends or to have some corn ground, since the village had no mill of its own. She couldn't be anywhere in the village, or she would have heard their arrival. All the villagers had waved to Caro and his father as they rode through.

And if something had happened to her, something bad – which it hadn't – but if it had, if those strangers had hurt her, or were holding her hostage, Rose would have found a way to tell him.

The road from Flormouth wound over the meadows in a dusty yellow swathe that passed under Caro's oak tree and circled the village green before petering out a few yards from the temple steps. The temple was tall and narrow, with a slate roof. Like Caro's house it was set apart from the rest of the village. For as long as Caro could remember it had been without a resident priest and family, and its upkeep was left to the village women, who regularly dusted the altars and statues, polished the braziers, swept out the dead leaves and renewed the candles. Caro's mother took her turn with the rest – and she was like a Queen in this village, so beautiful and wise. In his daydreams Caro pictured her as Queen Seren, legendary heroine of many a shepherds'-tale, for whose love her husband, Caro's namesake King Caryllac, did marvellous things.

The May sunset was spilling across the sea, and its fiery green light washed up at him from below. With tools slung over their shoulders the village men were tramping in from the fields,

127

and their wives were taking down washing, while billows of mutton-and-cabbage scented smoke puffed from the cottages through holes in the thatched roofs. Speckled ducks nestled on the banks of the pond. In the meadow beyond the cottages cows were ambling in single file along a muddy track, heavy udders swaying, coming home to be milked. Such changes as had taken place since he was last in the village were ones Caro could take in his stride – a door newly painted, a knock-kneed month-old calf, yellow roses in full bloom crawling up the temple walls. His oak tree was rooted in the heart of timelessness, a quiet corner of Brychmachrye undisturbed by war and treason and the crimes of kings.

Nothing ever happened in this village. When Peg-leg Pedrek got drunk and fell down the well, people had talked about it for months. One didn't expect to find adventure and excitement, strange war-horses and maleficent Rorhah men here, in his barn, in this backwater. Their presence was like an arrow shot from beyond the horizon to fall at Caro's feet. He knew that Brychmachrye was at war with herself – his father was fighting in it – but the war was somewhere else. It didn't belong in his village. Having brushed with it this morning, he never dreamt he'd find it waiting for him when he got home.

This morning he had been at school in Mindared, sleeping in the dormitory he shared with twenty other boys. Dimly he had felt a hand nudge him. He opened his eyes and couldn't believe them, for his father was smiling at him – and his father should have been a hundred miles away, winning the war. 'I'm taking you home,' his father whispered. 'Get dressed and come with me.'

When they reached the south gates Caro saw that an army had entered the city during the night. The walls bristled with spears. In the guardhouse his father exchanged a few words with an officer. 'She's safe in the Castle,' he said, 'And the Princes are with her.'

'Your son?' the officer asked. He stroked a hand down Caro's hair. From babyhood Caro had learnt how to tolerate such caresses, for his parents always stood by and watched with a proud smile; they never realised how much he hated being touched by strangers. 'A beautiful boy,' said the officer. He unbolted a small door in the gate to let them out. Caro saw his father's horse, Fearsome, tethered next to a little bay pony. 'It's for you,' said his father. Wide-awake now and game for anything, Caro trotted after his father, criss-crossing the dykes in the marshland south of Mindared. When the sun had soaked up the mist they stopped for breakfast in a roadside tavern. Twelve hours of fast riding followed, until they came to a small town where his father changed horses. 'I have to go back tonight,' he explained, 'Fearsome needs to rest.' Caro swallowed his disappointment and nodded.

By village standards Caro's house was enormous, with three separate rooms and the kitchen. It was the only house between Flormouth and Wendbridge that stood on two floors, and in addition it had a cellar and an attic which was hardly ever used. When he was little Caro had been immensely proud of this house, but since going away to school in Mindared he had realised it was just a cottage. To his father, a man at home in places like Mindared Castle, this little cottage must feel as cramped as a kennel. Less than a minute was all it took for his father's long legs to stride up and down the stairs and right through every room, calling his mother's name. Saddle-sore Caro hobbled after him, and Rose, quivering with joy, brought up the rear.

The house was empty. 'I expect she's gone to Flormouth,' said his father. 'Damn. I can't wait. She doesn't know I've brought you back, Caro, so . . . well, she'll know I was here when she sees you.'

Caro kept his eyes fixed sullenly on his boots, thinking, *Can't you even wait half an hour for her?*

Half of him wanted to plead, 'Stay, please stay,' because he knew that his father was the only one she really wanted to see. And half of him wanted to shout, 'Go on then, go!' so that he could have his mother all to himself. Only it wasn't two different halves of him. His wanting one thing and wanting its opposite was all mixed up together, in the way that he loved them and hated them at the same time. Is it like that for all children, Annie? The feeling of being tugged in a hundred different directions; the feeling that your parents are the only things that stand between you and the world, and that you have to fight both your parents and the world? Everything Caro was proud of he was also supposed to be ashamed of. It was selfish to want things that other people didn't want, or couldn't do, and you don't want to be selfish, do you, Caro? He couldn't say what he did want, because he wanted so many impossible, forbidden, contradictory things. What it came down to, Annie, was that it was the unspoken rule that

129

no one should comment on his father's brief visits and long absences.

Caro had always known that his father was special. The village men doffed their hats and bent their knees whenever they saw him, and they called him Lord. His mother often called him Lord too. Sometimes the villagers called Caro 'Little Lord'. He liked that. When his father wasn't around they let him help with the lambs and scare crows from the cornfield, and the women would pull him on to their laps and feed him dried plums. He liked that even more. There were other things that marked his father out. He could speak court-speech, something no one else in the village could do. He rode a horse. He had a sword, and if Caro was very good he was allowed to touch it. He was always coming and going. The other men in the village never went away, unless it was to Flormouth on market day, and they always came home before nightfall.

Often, on the evenings when his father was at home, Caro would look down from his bedroom window to see perhaps a dozen villagers lined up patiently outside the kitchen door. When his father wasn't at home the villagers always came in through the front door, and nobody bothered about knocking. Caro knew that they were waiting to speak to his father. He knew that his father had power; and it seemed to him that their cottage was a castle.

One day, when Caro was very young, before he had learnt that he wasn't to talk about it, he asked his mother why his father couldn't be with them all the time. Wide-eyed he listened as she explained that his father's greatness was beyond his imagination. His father was a man of influence at Court, a soldier, a Guardsman, and a confidante of the King – which was something, said his mother, to be mighty proud of, and all the more reason not to pester his father or complain when his duties kept him from his family.

Caro was dumbstruck. There was too much pride in his small head: for years it left no room for questions. He gladly accepted his mother's assumption that their loneliness was a small price to pay for his father's magnificence.

On his first day at school the new boys were vying for status by comparing their fathers' occupations. Caro had only a vague idea of what his father did at Court, so he said airily, 'Oh, fighting and things,' and added, 'He's a Prince.'

The other boys, sons of clerks and priests and merchants,

were not prepared to swallow this. 'Go on, pull the other one, big-mouth.'

'He is too. He lives at Court.'

'You're full of shit,' said Brian Brynson the school bully. 'Your father can't be a Prince, squirt, 'cause you'd be related to the King then. You want to tell us you're related to the King?'

A boy with more experience of his fellows might have heeded this warning and backed off. But Caro was not used to animosity, and he wanted to prove his point. If you had to be related to the King to be a Prince, well, 'Then my father's better than a Prince. And he's got a sword. It's this long and it's got pearls in the handle and he put his initials down the blade.'

Awed silence. None of the other boys could claim as much for their fathers. Only noblemen carried swords.

At once the popular opinion of nineteen small schoolboys swayed in Caro's favour, and there, for two terms, it remained. They were as irresistibly eager to be amazed as Caro was to oblige them. At night in the junior dormitory his imagination helped his father to perform heroic deeds of a supernatural improbability rarely equalled in the ancient shepherds'-tales. His father grew taller, stronger, divinely handsome. The King consulted him at every turn. Ambassadors, Councillors and Fahlraecs courted his friendship. He was the stuff of legends, Brennain Bryach and Michah the Conqueror rolled into one.

Caro never thought of these stories as lies. Yes, he made them up, but they could happen. Anything that was possible was as good as true. He couldn't help it if his head was always buzzing with stories. They seemed to fly into his ears out of the air. And his schoolmates were always begging him for a new one. He only wanted to tell them what they wanted to hear.

During the long harvest vacation Brian Brynson went to help his aunt and uncle on their farm near Flormouth, and on the first night of the new term he sneaked into the junior dormitory to announce, with great relish:

'You're a liar, big-mouth. *I* know who your father is. He's Tom Floriah, one of the Fahlraec's sons and not even the oldest – *and* your mother was a fishgutter till your father made her his mistress. My aunt says it's the biggest scandal in Floriah.'

'What's a mistress?' asked one of the smaller boys.

'Like a whore. Caro's mother sleeps with Caro's father and he gives her money. They're not even *married*. Caro's a bastard. Aren't you, shit-face? A lying bastard. My father would take

131

me away from here if he knew this school let in BASTards, BASTard – '

'Why don't Caro's parents get married?' another small boy asked. Brian Brynson turned his venom on this ignoramus. 'Caro's mother's a whore and men don't marry whores, and anyway Caro's father's married to someone else, isn't he, BASTard, BASTard – '

Oh Annie, why did it come as such a shock? Surely even at eight Caro was old enough to know that the daughters of fishermen do not marry men with horses and swords who are confidantes of the King. But he had simply never considered it. They were his parents: they belonged together. Nothing in all his life in the village, among people who loved his mother and revered his father, had prepared him for the moment when a child could sneer, with righteousness, at them.

And that wasn't the worst, Annie. Knowing that their being together was wrong, that they were adulterers and his own existence somehow offensive, that was not the worst, although it took Caro months to understand why it was true. At first, like the other small boys, he didn't appreciate the extent of his parents' wickedness. Brian Brynson took it upon himself to inform Caro's ignorance, pursuing him around the school with whispers of bastard, bastard, lashing off his tongue. And that wasn't the worst either. It's only a name, like potato-head and bug-eyes and smelly. You can grow out of, or grow used to, minding the way names hurt you. When Caro grew older he understood that he wasn't a bastard through any fault of his own. It was his parents' fault – and even that, Annie, even that was easy to forgive compared to the wrong they did him in not telling him. They never prepared him for the moment when he would find out. They abandoned his trust to the mercy of others. And he would never know why. That was the worst of it, the thing that made it more painful the older he became.

You can lie without ever opening your mouth. You can betray someone *by* not opening your mouth. You see, don't you, Annie? Caro couldn't rely on them any more. Perhaps they had thought it best not to tell him, or perhaps they had forgotten, or perhaps they could not be bothered; but if love can be so carelessly betrayed, what reason could his mother have for assuming that his father would not let her down too, one day? They did not come first in Tom Floriah's affections – they came last, and even the little they received from him was practically stolen from those who had a right to it, Tom's King, Tom's wife, Tom's legitimate children. They mustn't pester him for more, in case they drove him away. The goodness of his heart was their only security. They were entitled to nothing. They must thank him for everything. Even his love, like the presents of jewels and toys and books he brought with every visit, was charity.

Up in his oak tree Caro blinked the tears away. If you refuse to let Brian Brynson make you cry when you're eight years old, you certainly don't start blubbering when you're all by yourself and nearly ten. He had more immediate problems to deal with. The horses in the barn were neighing loudly and kicking their stalls. They sounded hungry. Maybe they had been tied up there for days. Maybe his mother had been missing for days. Caro thought, it's not right. If they're not Rorhah men why are they hiding? Why don't they take their horses and go away? People come when they're not wanted. The people I want never come.

Another possibility occurred to him. Suppose the Rorhah men had only left their horses for a little while? Suppose they came back before his mother returned? They'd certainly try to steal his new pony as well, because Rorhah men were thieves, murderers, traitors, everything no decent man could be. Caro devised a plan. If they did come back, he would wait until they were inside the barn, then quickly run over, lock them in, and fetch the men from the village to finish them off. The stealthiness of this plan appealed to him. It was poetic justice. The only good Rorhah was a dead Rorhah.

Far below him Rose uncurled and started to bark. Caro looked down, and saw a cloud of yellow dust moving up the road from Flormouth. His heart bounded, but he held himself back: it might be the Rorhah men. Rose howled rapturously and dashed forward, tail feathering, to greet the dust-cloud now resolving into the shapes of a woman and a donkey. Rose's nose was never mistaken. Immediately forgetting all his schemes for heroism and high drama, Caro scrambled down the tree-trunk, picking up several splinters on the way, and ran to meet his mother.

'Darling,' she laughed, kissing his cheeks, 'what are you doing home from school?'

His head was pressed against her chest. 'Papa brought me,' he said. Under his ear her heart-beat quickened. 'Is he still here?' she asked.

The dust was settling round them. Caro's mother pushed him away and pulled down her hood, shaking the dirt from hair as bright, thick and golden as his own. Every time he came home from school Caro was amazed all over again to see how much more beautiful she was than he remembered. In those first few minutes he always felt that he was looking at her with his father's eyes, and that he loved her not only because she was his mother, but because she was beautiful.

'Never mind,' she said when Caro failed to answer. The flush of pleasure and surprise was fading to two pink spots on her cheeks. 'I know they need him where he is.'

But he could have waited an hour, thought Caro. *I would have.*

'Why did he bring you home, Caro?'

'The Rorhah are going to attack Mindared.'

'Is that what he told you?'

'Didn't need to. It's obvious. The city's full of soldiers, and listen, Mama, the Princess came last night to stay in Mindared Castle, and some of the Princes too. I think Papa brought them.'

She patted his cheek, said, 'I'm glad you're out of it, at least,' and urged the donkey forward. Caro grabbed its halter. 'Don't go up there!' he cried. 'There's Rorhah men around. They put their horses in our barn. Where did you go?'

'Only to Flormouth.' She was laughing at him. 'Don't look so scared, you big silly, they're not Rorhah men. They're friends of your father's who've come to stay with us for a while.'

This sounded highly unlikely to Caro. 'Papa can't know they're here. And I didn't see them.'

'I know. He would have stayed if he'd realised. Oh dear, I wish I hadn't gone out now. They've been hoping to see him. That's why they came here. And for him to come and go without . . . But I suppose it's funny when you think about it, isn't it? Anyway,' she added, 'I'm glad they knew they could come here.'

In the kitchen she laid out three bowls of food. 'There's only two horses,' Caro pointed out, to which she replied, 'Can't one horse carry two men?' slapping his wrist as he tried to filch a chicken wing.

'So where are they?' asked Caro. 'I looked everywhere.'

'Can't have, can you, or you would have found them. They're in the attic.'

'Ugh. What are they doing in the attic?'

134

'Boys who ask too many questions get their noses bitten off. Give me a hand, take this tray.'

'Who'll bite my nose off?'

'Adonac's sparrow.'

'Mama!' Caro scoffed, insulted. 'That's a shepherds'-tale.'

'All right then, smarty, if you know so much you don't need to ask questions. Come on.'

She pulled a ladder from beneath the stairs and raised it up to the attic trap door. Caro asked her, 'How long have they been here?'

'Two days.'

'Why did they come here if Papa doesn't know about it?'

'Try to be a help, not a hindrance,' said his mother mildly. 'I'll go up and you pass the bowls to me.'

She climbed the ladder and rapped on the trap door. Right above Caro's head the ceiling creaked as one of the men in the attic stood up. A hoarse voice demanded, 'Who's there?' in the native Caro spoke with his mother and the villagers.

'It's only me, my Lords,' his mother replied. After a moment the trap door swung back, and the bowls of food were passed up into the darkness. Then his mother clambered into the attic. Caro remained on the landing. He heard the man say, 'Someone was here earlier,' with a pronounced Andarian lisp. 'I think he's gone now. He was calling for you.'

'That was my Lord,' she said.

Caro heard a second man ask, in Andarian, 'What did she say?' The first man translated, and the following exchange became so rapid and acrimonious that Caro could make out no more than a few swear words and the sentences which ended the argument: 'How were we supposed to know? If he talks like a peasant we'd assume it's a peasant.'

The first man asked Caro's mother if her Lord was expected to return. She said she did not think so, 'But his son is here. Come up, Caro, these gentlemen would like to meet you.'

Reluctantly Caro climbed the ladder and hoisted himself through the trap door. He hated the attic. A muddy twilight filtering through the thatch rendered all colours down to shades of grey, and in the corners perpetual night lurked. The air was stale and overheated. His eyes and nostrils itched from the accumulated dust of years, and he could smell something sickening, a sort of sweet ripeness like nothing so much as bad meat. Coughing, he fixed his eyes on a pale splotch hovering in

135

mid-air. After a moment he saw it was a sling. The man wearing
it cleared his throat and said in his accented native, 'So you're
Tom's boy.'

The man's broad, rather flat face was stubbled with beard,
and he had a friendly expression. Caro smiled back. The man
said, 'I understand your father brought you back from Mindared
today?' Caro nodded. 'Do you know why he did that?'

Caro's mother answered for him, telling the man that her Lord
had moved the Andaranah armies into Mindared. Meanwhile
Caro peered around, and spotted the second man squatting on
the floor, the bowl balanced on one knee while he crammed
food into his mouth. Caro said to him, 'Your horses are hungry
too,' but he took no notice.

The first man chuckled. 'I'm afraid Lord Peregrin doesn't
speak the native.'

'Caro knows court-speech,' said his mother, prodding her
son between the shoulder-blades. Obediently Caro performed.
Peregrin, startled at the sound of a strange, childish voice
speaking in his own tongue, looked round wildly, and upset
his bowl.

By now Caro could see quite well. He searched the attic
for some sign of the third man. In the far corner was a straw
pallet with a bundle of blankets on top of it. Their bed, Caro
supposed. Suddenly the bundle stirred; Caro jumped; and the
first man told Caro's mother, 'Lord Kyrah's been feverish all
afternoon.'

'I'll bring his Lordship some water.' Before Caro could stop
her, his mother had disappeared down the ladder, and he was
alone with his father's three friends.

The first man crouched down, grinning. Eyeball to eyeball
with Caro, he said, 'Shall I do the honours, Caryllac filc-
Thomas? My name is Bruno filcAlexander, your greedy friend
is Peregrin Mindarah, and that poor fellow in the corner is
Reyhnard, Lord Kyrah.'

'Is he dead?'

'What did the boy say?' asked Peregrin in court-speech.

'He wanted to know if Kyrah was dead.'

'As near as makes no difference,' said Peregrin.

Caro remembered his manners and spoke in Andarian. 'You
should take him down to one of the bedrooms. He could have
mine.'

'A generous thought,' said Peregrin, looking at Bruno, 'But it

136

wouldn't help. There's no way Kyrah's going to get better. He's stinking the place out as it is.'

'We must wait for what the Gods send,' said Bruno, in the weary tone grown-ups use when a subject begins to bore them.

'You're just too squeamish to put him out of his misery. You've always been a girl when it comes to killing.'

'You mean I don't pretend to enjoy it.'

'He's going to die anyway. Either we can wait for him to rot to death or we can give the Gods a little helping hand and get out of here that much sooner. We shouldn't have come here in the first place. I never liked the idea. I like it even less with Kyrah screaming his head off the way he did last night. We're no safer than rabbits in a trap – we have no swords and there's no way out except down that trap door.'

'You're an ungrateful bastard.'

'I beg to differ. Tom's woman has been kind to us, and our being here puts her and the boy, and the whole village, in danger. Especially if the Rorhah *are* moving on Mindared – and you can bet he won't be far behind Tom. And it's not as if it's their war, these peasants.'

'A just war is everybody's war.'

Peregrin laughs. 'What difference can it make to them who's the King? All they need is some *thing* to worship. Keeps them scared and keeps them quiet. Prop Michael's corpse back on the throne and they'd happily call it a king – '

'I don't find your profanity amusing.'

'They're not fools, you know. They know when they're on to a good thing. You've heard how good the harvest is predicted to be this year, haven't you? Well, it's hardly surprising. The natives know they're working for themselves. No one's got the manpower to collect the rents and enforce the taxes. If this war goes on much longer there won't be much left to win. I'll tell you what, Bruno – what I'd really like to know is, who is going to pay for this when it's all over? Because when we start fighting among ourselves the peasants just go their merry way. They grow fat while we gallop up and down the country whacking each other's heads off. It's so bloody absurd. Thank God it's nearly over.'

'You think so?'

'The woman said it herself. Basal's got us cornered. There's nowhere left to run. So Tom's holed up in Mindared. Much good may it do him.'

'Basal will never get his hands on the Princess in Mindared,' said Bruno. 'Those walls are impregnable.'

Peregrin began to snigger in a way Caro did not like at all, and said, 'That's what Daddy always liked to believe. That's why he never spent any money on repairing them – ' but was interrupted by the sick man at the end of the room who suddenly cried out, 'She'll kill herself before she marries that traitor, traitor, traitor . . .'

'Hullo, Kyrah,' said Peregrin. 'still in the land of the living?'

Caro felt the hot glare of the sick man's eyes boring into him. 'Who's that boy?'

'It's Tom's son,' said Bruno. 'He's called Caryllac.'

'Tom? Is he here?'

'Oh calm down,' said Peregrin. 'He was here, but he's gone back to Mindared. It seems the Rorhah are going to besiege it.'

'Poor Perry,' Kyrah chuckled, 'you won't like that. Isn't it time you went home, Peregrin Mindarah? I'll come with you. We should go, Perry, the Rorhah are going to attack Mindared. I feel awful. Do you think I'm dying? The King's dead. He killed them. He killed all of them. Henry and Asah.'

'No,' said Bruno, 'they're all right. The boy says they're in Mindared, with Ursula.'

'They're only children,' said Kyrah. 'He wouldn't kill them, would he? Not children. So, I hear Tom's gone to Mindared. What a shame. He shames us all. We're holed up here like children, with a child, with a boy. I met your brothers and sisters once, boy. I must say you don't look anything like them. Why aren't you at home, boy?'

'Kyrah, go to sleep.'

'I'm afraid to sleep. If I go to sleep I'll die. My brother wants to kill me. He wants Kyrah. You all want to kill me, I know, I know, I hear you, whispering. You all wish I was dead. Boy!' he shouted, gesturing at Caro. 'Listen. They want to kill me. You won't let them kill me, will you?'

To Caro's relief his mother now reappeared through the trap door. 'I could hear his Lordship in the kitchen,' she said, handing a pitcher of fresh water to Caro. 'What did the woman say?' asked Peregrin. Bruno explained, and Peregrin remarked, 'I should think the whole world can hear him. Might as well send a herald to announce our presence round the Quarter. Save Kyrah the trouble.'

Caro met his mother's steady gaze. 'Go to the kitchen and

put some water on to boil,' she said in the tone which brooked no opposition. 'When you've done that, go down to the stream and pick some comfrey, roots and all, and don't forget to wear the gloves or you'll get stung like last time. If anyone sees you, tell them it's for someone I met in Flormouth and you don't know her name.'

'Mama, no one in the village is a Rorhah man.'

She sighed. 'Just do it, Caro.'

He nodded mutely, only too glad to escape.

Rose was waiting for him in the kitchen. He pulled her whiskers once or twice, and volunteered her to carry the gloves. An evening mist had risen from the sea, soothing Caro's itchy skin and licking away the attic dust. Little clouds nestled sleepily in the hollows of the meadow. His shoes were soon heavy with dew.

Near the stream he found a dead robin. There was no blood on it and its feathers were unruffled: it must have dropped down dead from the sky. Caro hunted around until he found a suitable piece of flat, broad wood, and also, to his delight, a long black-tipped gull's feather which, jammed into a split in the grain, made a perfect sail. Balancing the dead robin carefully on this makeshift boat, Caro cast it off from a rock in the stream and watched it drift and spin through the eddies in the current until it was out of sight. If it didn't sink, it would float to the sea. And then where would it go?

People were saying that King Michael had had no funeral. In the capital, they said, everything was thrown into disorder, and the King's body had been dumped to rot in a temple. The way Peregrin wanted to leave Kyrah. They said that the King's ghost wandered the streets of Tsvingtori at night, looking for souls to eat and crying revenge against his murderer. Caro wasn't sure if he believed in ghosts. They said the King's ghost was all grey and watery – you could put your hand through him if you were brave enough to try – and there was a gory great hole where his heart should be, because the murderer Basal Rorhah had stabbed him to death. And they said that where the King's ghost walked a trail of blood-drops could be seen early in the morning, before they dried up with the dew.

Caro took the gloves from Rose and started pulling up comfrey. If the Rorhah did attack Mindared, as everyone seemed to think they would, then he hoped, with all his heart, that one

139

of them would throw a spear straight through Brian Brynson's guts.

Caro spent most of the next few days up in his oak tree. At ground level the temperature was hot and airless, but a breeze continually stirred among the high branches, and the leaves that shaded him were a dark, glossy green with furry underbellies: their scalloped lobes made Caro think of mouse ears. Sometimes he carried one of his few, precious books up with him, all presents from his father and read many times before; more often he sprawled and dreamed, or watched the countryside.

Plucking an unripe acorn, he peeled the cap off with his fingernails, popped the bitter nut into his mouth, and ruminated. Olwen the goose-girl and Liam the pig-boy had brought their animals to the duck pond, as they did every day at noon, and were sitting side by side to eat their dinner. From the time Caro first learnt to climb trees he had watched these two courting. He could even remember a time when Olwen's hair had been as golden as his mother's. The years had dulled Olwen's brightness and made her stout, and given a stoop to Liam's shoulders, but had brought them no closer to a happy ending. They were the poorest two people in the village. Unable to pay the marriage fee, they could not even afford to build a little cottage in which they could live together, as most of the villagers did. They slept apart, Olwen in a corner of her cousin's house and Liam in the pig sty. The village people said they were bad luck, but Caro thought they were terribly romantic. He was sure that one day Liam would reveal himself as an enchanted hero forced to toil as a pig-boy by some malignant ghost or offended spirit; or else Olwen would turn out to be a Princess disguised as a goose-girl in order to escape her wicked stepmother, and then the whole village would gasp in astonishment and applaud their change of fortune.

Every day, when they had finished their meal, Liam gave Olwen a kiss, and they smiled at each other so shyly you might think all the world was watching, instead of only Caro. Then they went their separate ways, she with her geese to the water-meadow, he with his pigs to the beech wood.

Caro put another acorn in his mouth and turned his thoughts to his latest project. Every man must do his duty, and his, he had decided, was to immortalise the war by writing the

140

greatest epic the world had ever known. Of course it would have to be written in court-speech, the appropriate language for such a noble undertaking. The plot was more or less settled: in the dead of a night bright with the valour of a full moon Lord Bruno sets out, leaving behind the yellow-bellied Peregrin and the mortally-wounded, raving Kyrah ... but maybe the night should be dark and stormy. That would take a lot more bravery. Anyway, Bruno sets out, disregarding the pain of his broken arm because pain has no meaning for him, and gallops across country to relieve the siege of Mindared. In every village he passes through men rise to follow his battle cry – 'A just war is everybody's war!' – and armed only with scythes and staves and great-hearted courage they march on the walls of Mindared, where Caro's father is pacing back and forth, exhorting his troops with dramatic speeches Caro would work out later, and vowing to protect the Princess with his life. 'Lord Bruno will come,' he tells his men. 'You may depend on it.' And then, oh, what celebrations, what vindications of their hopes when dawn breaks to disclose the banners of deliverance mounting the horizon! Caro's father cries, 'Come on, men!' or something like that, and bursts through the gates of Mindared with his soldiers as one behind him. Between them Bruno and Caro's father smash the Rorhah murderer traitors into a bloody pulp; and there is a magnificent parade with trumpets and drums, the heroes borne aloft on thankful citizens' shoulders; and the Princess Ursula, more beautiful than the morning-star, is so grateful she falls in love with Bruno on the spot, and ...

'Are you still in that tree, Squirrel?'

Caro looked down through the branches and saw his mother, much foreshortened, standing hands on hips and frowning at him. 'What are you doing up there all this time?' she yelled.

'Looking for Rorhah men.'

Caro hardly admitted to himself that he was hoping to catch sight of his father, homeward bound.

'Don't be so silly. They won't come anywhere near here. Come down, Caro, I need your help.'

Steam and smoke clouded the kitchen. Caro took his basket of lint outside and sat cross-legged in the grass. Through the open doorway he watched his mother going about her business with her usual calm efficiency. She was cooking a pot of thin soup for Kyrah, baking bread in the oven, boiling stained bandages, and when she had a spare moment she picked up a pair of her son's trousers and put another few stitches through the hole he had torn in the knee. Caro flicked linseeds at Rose, who disdained to respond, and asked his mother, 'How long are they going to stay?'

'Until they're well again.'

'I like Bruno best – don't you think he's the nicest? Mama, do you think Kyrah's going to die?'

'Lord Kyrah to you.'

But Lords dressed in sumptuous finery, velvet, jewels and gold. Lords smelt of scented soap, and spoke like Gods, and walked around with their noses in the air; or more often they rode past, on high-stepping horses, a head and a half above ordinary people. Impossible to believe that those three sick, stinking, quarrelsome men in the attic had once looked as if nothing could harm them.

'Is he really a Lord?' asked Caro doubtfully.

'He's the Fahlraec of Kyrah.'

To have fallen so far was something awesome.

The three men in the attic held a strange attraction for Caro. Every few hours he felt compelled to climb back up there, be with them, study them, and listen to them talk in court-speech. He liked it best when they forgot he was there, for then they spoke of the things they had seen and done with an honesty and wealth of detail that they would never knowingly have used in front of a child. Their conversation was like the chanting of a spell: Caro did not understand half of it, but it had the ring of power. They talked about Tsvingtori, the Palace, Court politics and rivalries dominated by families so great they were known by no other name than that of the provinces they governed. They talked a great deal about the past, their childhoods, and the people they had loved; they talked about the war, the battles they had been in and the ones they had missed, the friends they had made, the friends they had seen die, and the friends who had chosen the other side. They did not talk much about the future. When they did, they sounded as if they did not expect to see it.

Always, when Kyrah awoke, he cried, 'Where is the King?'

Half an hour of this was as much as Caro could bear. The smell, the dustiness, and the monotony of their conversation exhausted him. Panting for breath, he fled from them; he burst into the open air and swarmed up the giddy heights of his oak tree. Perched in the green shade, with the sky wide above

142

him, the sun warm on his knees, the breeze blowing fresh and salty from the ocean, Caro looked down upon the heart of Brychmachrye and saw his home, his village, familiarity and changelessness sealed with a kiss that had become a joke; and it seemed to him that those three men had come from another country altogether.

'Where's the King?'

'Michael's dead, Kyrah.'

'Murdered. Murdered. Perry, how can you kill a God?'

'Go to sleep.'

'There are no Gods,' Kyrah decided.

'Kyrah, the boy is still here.'

'It's a fine time to find out,' said Kyrah, 'when I'm dying.' And he wept.

Caro's mother sat on a bench outside the kitchen door, humming quietly to herself while she knitted. Balls of wool, dyed deep indigo and crimson, were piled in her lap. The evening light was turning dusky. Caro had been reading aloud to her, but the rhythmic click-click of her needles filled him with drowsiness, and he put down his book, stretched out in the grass, and shut his eyes.

'Bed for you, I think,' she laughed.

Caro pretended to be asleep. In a moment she would lay down her knitting, kneel beside him, and stroke his cheek to wake him up. He waited, for a minute or two, until he realised her needles had fallen silent. Something was wrong. He rolled over to look at her. She was sitting stiffly upright, head held at an angle and eyes unfocused as if she could hear something in the distance, or hoped she heard something. Caro held his breath and listened.

Faint at first, but coming closer and growing louder, he heard the sound of hoofbeats moving at a fast gallop up the road from Flormouth.

His mother's face glowed pinkly. Her eyes sparkled and her lips were moving. There was no doubt in her mind. She stood up, smoothing a hand over her hair. Caro tried to say, 'Not from Flormouth, he wouldn't come from Flormouth,' but he didn't think she heard him. Already the hoofbeats had passed their house and were fading northwards, past the temple, into silence.

She looked down and straight through Caro. The needles

slipped from the wool, clattering together on the ground. She threw the wool after them, then covered her face with her apron and ran inside without a word.

Serves her right, thought Caro.

He was too angry at first to be sorry for her. Every day was the same. She put on a smile while she did her chores and tended the men in the attic, she nagged at Caro to help her, and gossiped with him about all the village goings-on that had taken place since he was last at home. Sometimes she said, 'Isn't this nice, Squirrel, just the two of us?' But he saw through her. She lied to him, Annie. Everything she did, every smile, was a sham. She faked being happy when inside, deep down, she was just waiting for his father to come home. Once or twice at night he heard her crying in her bedroom, and talking to herself. He wanted to go to her, to climb in bed with her as she had let him do when he was little; but he knew that her unhappiness was another of the things he wasn't supposed to see, or know, or understand.

He got up to follow her, pausing on the way to rescue the tangle of knitting. She was in the kitchen, kneeling on the floor with her arms around Rose's neck. 'Mama – '

'Leave me alone, Caro.'

He put the knitting on the table and knelt down on the other side of Rose. His mother pressed her face into the dog's fur. The ribbon in her hair had come untied, releasing a stream of gold over her shoulders and down the dog's back. Caro stretched out a hand, but stroked Rose instead.

'Please don't cry,' he said. 'He'll come back. He always does.'

'It's not that.'

Caro said anything that came into his head. 'Mama – Mama – if Papa can't be here the next best place is Mindared, really it is. Those walls are so strong. I've seen them. Nobody can take them. That's why Papa took the Princess there. They're safe. He'll be all right. It's been two years, almost, and Papa's never been hurt, not once – '

'He's a lucky man, your father.'

'I'm here,' said Caro desperately. 'Don't be afraid, please, please don't cry. I can look after you. Papa trusts me, Mama, that's why he brought me home ... ' And, because he had once heard his father say this to her, and hoped it would have the same effect, he added, 'I would die for you.'

His mother giggled. She sat back, wiping the tears from

144

her eyes. Rose licked at her salty cheeks. 'Look at Rose,' she smiled, tapping the dog's muzzle. 'She misses him too, don't you, my girl?'

Rose thumped her tail.

'I miss him too,' said Caro.

'I know you do, darling.'

As she said this she got to her feet, brushed her skirts, fixed her hair-ribbon, and it was as if the last five minutes had never happened. She chucked Caro under the chin and said, 'Aren't we a pair of sillies? We know Papa's needed where he is. We have each other, we mustn't complain. Tell me, Caro, do you know which Princes are at Mindared?'

'I think the two youngest.'

'Henry and Asah? Prince Henry is your age, Squirrel, did you know that? And that poor little Princess is only thirteen. She needs some brave men to look after her right now. And your father is a very brave man. Caro, listen, I want you to remember this. As you go through life you'll find many people who'll try to tell you that telling right from wrong is a difficult business. But that's not true. It's nearly always easy. They use it as an excuse. Do you see what I mean? Because what is difficult is acting on what you know to be right. All his life your father has tried to do this difficult – '

She was interrupted by a scream of pain that, though muffled by two sets of floors, was loud enough to make Caro wince. His mother raised her eyebrows. All she said was, 'That poor man.' She took a jar from the herb shelf and sent Caro to fetch fresh water.

Caro woke up so abruptly he thought he must have been having a nightmare. It felt so real his heart was still pounding. He rubbed his eyes, but the nightmare lingered in orange shadows flickering across the walls. Rose was whining, hackles raised, and scratched at the door. Wolves, thought Caro. Rose always acted like this when wolves came close to the house. He sneezed, coughed, and sneezed again. He could smell smoke. Something was on fire.

The barn, he thought, the horses, my pony! – and ran to the window to see the village on fire. The flames were so strong and bright he could make out the silhouettes of people running about, open-mouthed. The roar of the fire drowned out their screams. Men on horseback were galloping through them,

145

over them, towards his house, and with them came soldiers on foot. The firelight blazed off their armour, but left their helmeted faces in darkness.

Our being here puts them in danger.

His door opened. Rose slipped through and rushed downstairs. His mother came in, fully dressed, holding a candle. 'Put your clothes on,' she said. Caro wanted to run to her and hide inside her arms, but he knew she would only push him away and tell him to do as she said, so he hurriedly pulled on yesterday's trousers and shirt. 'As soon as you're dressed,' she said, 'go down into the cellar – '

Something crashed into the front door and sent the floorboards rocking under their feet.

She changed her mind. 'Caro, get into the chest and stay there. No matter what, Caro, promise me you'll stay there until I come for you.' She went out and shut the door on him. Above his head the trapped rabbits scuttled back and forth. Rose was barking in the kitchen. Once more the floorboards trembled as the front door took another heavy blow, followed by the crack of wood splintering. Their door was being chopped to pieces. He wasn't about to hide in the chest, like a girl, and leave his mother unprotected. How could he ever face his father? Barefoot he ran to the top of the stairs and looked down.

A booted foot kicked away the spars of wood from the doorway and stepped through, and another, and another, until five men had crowded into the little hallway. In the kitchen shutters were being ripped off their hinges, while Rose howled and howled. His mother was standing at the bottom of the stairs. She held the candle in front of her face and stared straight at the soldiers with a deaf-and-dumb tranquillity that, for a moment, held them at bay.

It held Caro back, too. The candlelight filled her eyes and erased her features. She had no expression. She was a blank, dead already – she terrified him.

In the kitchen copper pots rolled clanging across the floor and someone shrieked, 'Get it off me, get it off, mad dog! – ' and all the soldiers were laughing. The men in the hallway stirred forward to take hold of Caro's mother. One ran a hand over her breast, but just then a tall officer stepped out from the kitchen and told them to treat her gently. They released her, and the officer ducked back into the kitchen; as soon as he was gone, one of the soldiers cracked an obscene joke about her in court-speech.

She did not understand Andarian. Her son did, even such crude Andarian as this, and he shook with an anger and shame that went back years. To him these soldiers suddenly looked just like so many Brian Brynsons, and he was so sick of the endless humiliation, infuriated by his inability to retaliate, that he forgot everything except how much he hated them and screamed, 'Shut up, shut up!'

One look from his mother silenced him. Her eyes asked, why didn't you do as you were told? She kept looking at him from behind the candle, as if he had done something so terrible she could never forgive him, and he saw the light snuff out in her eyes just as it had last night, when the horseman she hoped was his father had gone galloping past their house.

Her face drained of blood and her knees buckled. If the soldiers had not moved quickly she would have fallen to the floor.

Two more men in officer's armour now came in, exchanged salutes with the soldiers, went into the front room, looked around, and came out again. The tall officer returned. Everyone stood at attention.

Then a fourth, shorter officer appeared in the doorway. The soldiers pressed back to clear a space for him. Caro watched him walk in, wondering what made this one so special. He stood at his ease in the centre of the hallway and looked around, taking his time, right hand resting lightly on the hilt of his sword.

Someone handed a torch through the doorway. It spat and flared, and in the surge of light Caro saw that this man was hardly a man at all, barely out of his boyhood. None of the other officers were much older. Soon the course of the head boy's slow inspection brought his left profile into Caro's view. A deep brown scar ran down the beardless cheek from a badly broken nose; his left eye drooped, and that whole side of his face was puckered. It was so ugly, and the rest of the face so young, that for a moment Caro felt sorry for him.

Odd, Annie, isn't it, that when they first met Caro's eyes were so full of pity they almost seemed friendly, looking into those green eyes, adder eyes. You know what snakes look like, Annie. They're so evil they're almost innocent. Evil is the only thing they know. They were made that way, like bastards. And he never even blinked. Caro wanted to run, but couldn't move.

147

Isn't it only animals who are supposed to feel that sort of paralysing terror, trapped by the evil eye?

The head boy set Caro free by looking away to ask the tall officer, 'Anything in the kitchen?'

'Only a dog.'

'It bit Lord Olivah, Sir,' said a soldier, 'but we got rid of it.'

The young Commander scratched his chin with his left hand. The two smallest fingers were missing, and there were raw scabs on the stumps. In excellent native he asked Caro's mother, 'Where are they?'

'My Lord is not here.'

He flicked his broken hand in the air. 'Bring that child down.' A soldier ran up the stairs, grabbed Caro round the waist and picked him up. Remembering his mother's dignity as she faced the soldiers, Caro forbore to struggle or protest. He was set on his feet at the side of the young Commander, who now repeated, 'Where are they?'

'I have told you my Lord is not here.'

Two fingers tickled Caro's neck. He shut his eyes and tried not to think about those black crusty scabs touching his skin.

'I could search your house,' said the Commander. 'It wouldn't take long. But why waste my time? This is your son, isn't it?'

Sweat trickled, itching, down Caro's neck.

'I know he's your son. You're Tom Floriah's whore and this is his bastard. Now tell me where they are or I'll kill him.'

A thumb caressed Caro's neck. Caro tried hard not to picture the scabs softening in his sweat, working loose, sticking to his skin. He would throw up if they didn't cut his head off first. He wished he was dead. This was his fault. He should have done as he was told, he should have hidden . . .

The Commander said, with a trace of amusement, 'You don't think I'd do it.'

'Oh, you're a wicked man, you murderer – '

A soldier slapped her in the mouth so hard Caro heard her lip split. 'Don't hurt her!' he screamed, kicking out blindly and bruising someone's knee. Immediately the two fingers let go, but other hands seized his arms and shoulders and hair, and the scabs returned to close around his throat.

'Kill them both,' said a fat officer bleeding from a bitten arm. 'We'll find the others.'

The Commander chuckled. 'I think I'll start with his hand. Hold out his arm, Olivah.'

The fat officer pulled on Caro's wrist so hard his shoulder was almost wrenched from its socket. Caro reeled with pain. He screwed his eyes tightly shut, until his eyebrows were touching his cheeks; he must not look at her, he must not let her see how frightened he was. She must not give in.

He heard the creak of a sword being drawn from its leather scabbard, and sensed, through the fingers that held him by the throat, that all the Commander's muscles were shifting emphasis as he raised his right arm. Caro felt very calm, very ready. If Rose was willing to give her life, could he do less? He would die like the son of a brave man. They would never talk, never.

The cutting edge against his wrist was razor thin, chill, and heavy. It didn't hurt at all. They said it never hurt till later. Maybe his hand was off already and he hadn't felt a thing –

'They're in the attic,' said his mother.

Released, Caro's arm fell numbly to his side.

The Commander asked her, 'Are they armed?' and she shook her head.

Pins and needles shot through Caro's hand. He opened his eyes and flexed his fingers. All there. No blood. Not even a scratch. But with a sword that sharp it should only have taken a second.

Three soldiers moved the ladder into position. The Commander was no longer bothering to hide his amusement, for Bruno and Peregrin were arguing so furiously they could be heard throughout the house.

'It's his fault, screaming his fool bloody head off – '

This panic-stricken voice Caro, to his amazement, recognised as Bruno's.

'We should have killed him ages ago,' said Peregrin.

'Can't you hear them? The bitch gave us away.'

'Well, I think they might have guessed.'

'Kyrah, you bastard, wake up – Gods, I think he's dead – '

'Patience was never his virtue.'

A few seconds later Caro heard the sound of roof-thatch being torn off by bare hands. 'Out here,' Bruno cried, 'We can jump.'

'Don't be so stupid.'

The Commander gave a nod, and one of the soldiers pushed the trap door open with the point of his sword. The Commander called up, 'Lord Kyrah,' receiving in reply Peregrin's disembodied voice, 'He can't hear you.'

Outside Bruno hit the ground with a loud thud and a groan.

'Peregrin Mindarah,' said the Commander.

'I'm here.'

'Come down, then.'

Bruno was being set upon, kicked and punched, though he screamed at them to leave him alone. Peregrin climbed out of the attic and swaggered down the stairs. Caro saw that he was four or five inches taller than the Commander, and of about the same age. He stood with his weight thrown forward on one hip, wearing a casual smile.

If anyone had looked at Caro just then, they would have seen a peculiar sight, for he was blushing, furiously. He had just realised what a fool they had made of him.

Bravery was not required from a bastard. He was in no danger, and never had been. Peregrin, Bruno and Kyrah were the ones the Commander wanted. The Commander had never intended to hurt him. The Commander had known that his mother would give in. He had almost laughed when he said, I'll kill him. He must have known all along where the ones he had come for were hiding. Or, as Peregrin had said, he could easily have guessed.

Caro thought, he did this to me, to my mother, for fun.

It's not as if it's their war. They're only natives, bastards, you're worse than my Dad's dog, Caro, it's a purebred, and you're a bastard. You don't belong here. You don't have a right to anything. You don't belong in your father's war.

'Where's Kyrah?' asked the Commander.

'Up there. But he's dying. If he isn't dead already.'

'You two, bring Lord Kyrah down.'

Kyrah was bundled down the ladder, arms and legs dangling. He looked quite dead and smelt worse than ever. 'Edvard,' said the Commander to the tall officer, 'go outside and see what's happened to Bruno. The rest of you, in here.' He pulled back the curtain to the front room. Caro almost expected him to add, 'And bring us some refreshments, my good woman.' Nothing would have surprised Caro now. They all crowded into the front room. No one was holding Caro. This was the moment when, if he had made a run for it, he might well have got away. But he was too puzzled by their behaviour to do anything other than follow them tamely in.

150

'Put Lord Kyrah down on that table,' said the Commander. This they did; the Commander sheathed his sword, which he had been carrying all this while, and took Lord Kyrah's hand. 'Kyrah,' he said, 'wake up.'

A smile twitched Kyrah's mouth.

'Why don't you leave him alone?' said Peregrin.

The Commander shook Kyrah's hand gently to and fro. 'Reyhnard, look at me.'

Lord Kyrah frowned into the Commander's face. 'Your nose,' he said. 'What's happened to you?'

'Never mind about me.'

'You shouldn't have come here,' Lord Kyrah whispered. 'Perry wants to kill me.'

The Commander glanced at Peregrin, who shrugged.

'Reyhnard, do you recognise me?' Lord Kyrah nodded his chin. 'Will you come with me now?'

'Where?'

'Home.'

A glow of joy suffused the dying man's face. 'Can we see the King?'

'I am the King.'

Lord Kyrah blinked; the happiness ebbed away. 'You're not. I know you're not. I remember. It's not Perry, it's you, you've come to kill me – '

'Oh, don't start him up again,' said Peregrin. 'Leave him alone. You know what he'd say to you if he was in his right mind. It's not fair to take advantage of him when he's dying.'

At that moment all attention was drawn to the doorway, through which the tall officer Edvard led two soldiers carrying a body. Caro wasn't sure whose body it was until he saw the sling, for Bruno's face was smashed beyond recognition. Edvard looked very upset. 'He's dead,' he said unnecessarily. 'Put him over there,' said the Commander. Bruno's corpse was heaped in a corner. Caro's mother stood with her back to the wall, staring into space and biting her cheek.

The Commander turned back to Peregrin. 'I need you,' he said. 'You know Mindared better than any of us. Come with me.'

Peregrin tutted, 'For shame!'

'Don't be such a fool, Perry,' cried Edvard. 'He means it.'

But at twenty-two death is often easier to endure than seeing your equal acclaimed as your superior. The Commander lacked

151

patience for an argument. 'All right,' he said, 'get down.'

'I'm not going to kneel in front of you.'

At a gesture from the Commander two soldiers pinioned Peregrin's arms and dead-legged him until he fell on his knees. The fat officer grabbed Peregrin's hair and stretched his neck out, just as Caro's arm had been stretched. This time, though, they meant business. It took four blows to hack the head from the body. When the two were severed, the soldiers let go of the arms. The torso toppled forward on to its stump, and slid in the gelatinous pool of black blood until it was flat on its belly. Fat Olivah held the head up with a question in his eyes. 'Throw it away,' said the Commander, and it was flung in the corner with Bruno.

Blood had spattered everywhere, lumps and streaks of it over the walls, the ceilings, splashing on Caro's mother, clotting in Caro's hair. The room smelt like a butcher's shop. Caro was retching.

'Edvard, take that boy out, he's going to be sick.'

Edvard took Caro into the kitchen. He cradled the boy with one arm and held the pot with the other while Caro vomited. 'Don't be afraid,' he kept saying, 'his Grace won't hurt you.' Caro felt so dizzy and ill he didn't know where he was. He thought it was his father kneeling beside him, holding him gently and taking care of him. He put his arms around the young man's neck, and fell against his chest.

Over Edvard's shoulder he saw Rose. She lay on the floor, dried blood peaking the fur around her wound. The kitchen was full of soldiers. He felt the sharp studs of Edvard's leather armour digging into him. His gorge rose; he pitched backwards, was caught by Edvard's arm, and vomited until he was throwing up nothing but thin bile.

Edvard picked him up, stepped over the dog's carcase, and returned to the front room. 'What have you done to him?' Caro's mother whispered. 'He's all right,' said Edvard, setting Caro down. Caro swayed, instinctively grabbing at Edvard's arm for support.

In their absence Lord Kyrah had also been beheaded. The Commander wiped his sword on Kyrah's shirt, and sheathed it firmly, as though he intended to let it rest for a while. He smiled at Edvard, and said, 'Outside, everybody.'

A silent dawn was breaking. The flames from the village had died down, and all the birds had fled. Clouds of black smoke smothered the rising sun. The breeze came from the east, carrying fragments of ash, live cinders, and the oily sweetness of burnt flesh. In another hour nothing would be left of the village but smouldering heaps of compost. Caro turned his back on it.

'Throw those torches in the windows,' said the Commander. This was done.

In the minute or so that it took for the fire to catch, Caro was convinced that it wouldn't, that the Gods had worked a miracle and would preserve his home. Soon, though, the whole kitchen was blazing, and moments later gouts of smoke and flame burst from the upper windows. A pot exploded in the kitchen with a great bang, making Caro's heart jump; only now did he remember his toys, his hoard of treasures, owl pellets, sea shells, last year's conkers, his books, the first page of his epic hidden under his mattress, all the presents his father had given him, his clothes – he was wearing nothing but a pair of trousers and a blood-and-puke-stained shirt.

Someone shouted, 'What should we do with the woman and the boy?'

Why don't they go away now? Caro wondered. He had been so sure they would depart as soon as they finished what they came for, leaving him and his mother in peace. He turned around to ask her – but she was gone. He couldn't see her anywhere.

'Why don't we take them to Mindared?' said the fat officer Olivah.

'Where's my mother?'

No one paid any attention to Caro. Olivah continued, 'When Tom sees we've got them – ' but the Commander cut him off with a laugh. 'You don't know your man. Tom would let us chop them into pieces in front of him and never give an inch.'

'He's too stubborn for his own good sometimes,' said Edvard.

They were all so much taller than Caro, talking over his head. 'Wolf cubs grow up, Sir,' said Olivah. 'I think you should kill the bastard, and his dam.'

'When I need your advice, Olivah, I'll ask for it. This boy is guilty of nothing but his parentage, and in any case I don't kill children.'

Sparks caught and blazed on the roof of the barn. The horses were screaming. 'Get those animals out,' shouted the Commander.

'My pony's in there!' cried Caro.

153

The Commander rubbed his chin and looked thoughtfully at Caro. 'Get the boy's pony out,' he ordered. To Edvard he said, 'Bring that child and come with me. You too, Olivah.'

They walked over to the oak tree and stood in conference. The Commander said, 'Olivah, I'm leaving you in charge here. I want them back by the fourth hour and they had better not have any women with them. Also I want you to find the men responsible for Bruno and have them hanged and buried before you leave this place. The men have got to understand that I won't tolerate that sort of behaviour. Edvard, here are the letters for Floriah. You can take this boy with you. After all, Floriah *is* his grandfather.'

'And the woman?' asked Olivah.

'Whatever. Don't bring her back to camp, that's all.'

A soldier approached them and saluted. 'Sir, what'll we do with the horses?'

'Put the pony with Lord Edvard's horse. Bring the other horses to camp – and that donkey.' The Commander raised his voice and announced, 'The horses will go to the first two men over the walls of Mindared.'

The men responded with a rousing cheer.

The Commander turned back to Edvard. 'Get those troops to Mindared within three days. I'm depending on you. And tell Floriah – ' the Commander smiled, and for a moment was no more than a bold boy tweaking the nose of his elders, savouring a joke – 'Tell him to look after the wolf cub. For Tom. Take an escort, four men. You won't need more. Most of this Fahl is pacified now, and I doubt you'll run into any trouble. See you at Mindared.'

The two young men kissed farewell in the Andarian fashion, cheek to cheek with hands clasped, a gesture of friendship and respect. Edvard saluted, about-turned, put a hand under Caro's elbow and marched him away. Caro went quietly until they were out of the Commander's ear-shot. Then he dug in his heels and said, 'You can't take me to Floried.'

Chin up in defiance, he waited for Edvard to cuff him, kick him, yank him onwards. Instead, Edvard bent down and asked, 'Why not?'

Looking back, Annie, this simple little question really was the first basis on which Caro's opinion of Edvard was formed. At the time he thought Edvard must be incredibly stupid. Surely the young man was aware of Caro's status? The words

154

'bastard' and 'whore' had been bandied about freely enough. The general assumption was that Tom Floriah would not dream of sacrificing duty and integrity for the sake of a slut and her half-breed. The Commander's smile had summed it up: *Take him to Lord Floriah*, embarrass and humiliate Floriah. Won't that be funny?

Did Edvard need to have this spelled out? Caro would choke before he'd utter the words. But Edvard was still waiting. He seemed to expect an answer.

At last Caro said, 'I don't go to school there.' He didn't know how else to put it. Clearly it was his father's wish that he should never go anywhere near Floried: that was why he had been sent far away to another part of the country for his schooling. Caro was like a black cloud. Everywhere he went he cast the shadow of shame. His father's real, proper family lived in Floried, and Tom didn't want their happy vistas darkened by the sight of his half-native bastard in the streets of their home. To break this ordinance would be tantamount to co-operating with the enemy. Caro stared hard into Edvard's face and willed him to understand.

Edvard said, 'You're at school in Mindared, aren't you? But you mustn't worry about that. There won't be any schooling in Mindared for quite a while. Floried is the best place for you. Your grandparents will look after you . . .' Half to himself Edvard muttered, 'They really haven't any choice.'

'They don't want me there,' said Caro desperately.

'That is as it may be. They will have to make the best of it. You're under his Grace's protection now, you see.' Edvard squeezed the boy's hand and chivvied him gently, 'Come along.'

Still Caro refused to budge. Sighing, Edvard picked him up and carried him over to the horses. 'I won't go!' Caro protested, while Edvard placed him on the saddle and fitted his feet into the stirrups. 'Please don't make me go, please, please, why are you making me?' Edvard pretended it took all his concentration to string a leading rein between his horse's bridle and the pony's halter. 'I want to stay with my mother,' Caro cried. 'She's got no one to look after her but me, please, please – '

'You know you can't stay here. There's nothing left here.'

'They'll hurt her. Please don't let them hurt her. Can't she come too?'

'You heard what the King said.'

'He said, whatever. He doesn't care. You could bring her if you wanted to, please, you can have my pony if you bring her too, please – '

Edvard opened his mouth, covered it with his hand, took his hand away and was about to speak, when someone shouted, 'Stop her, she's crazy!' and they both looked around to see Caro's mother running towards her burning house. The skirts tangled around her legs, and several times she stumbled, always recovering to keep on running with the same fixity of purpose. Two men started to chase after her, but not as fast as she was running, and the heat soon drove them back. 'Don't look,' said Edvard. He tried to turn Caro's face away. But Caro saw it. He saw sparks fall on her clothes and in her hair. She was covered in flames. She became a small, moving fire running to embrace a greater fire. It ate her up. She melted, and she was gone.

'You're bleeding,' said Edvard. He tore a piece of cloth from his sleeve and dabbed at Caro's bitten lip. Their eyes met. What Caro looked like, who can say? but Edvard had the grace to turn his head, as though acknowledging that any compassion he might offer now would only fester in the wound.

Caro never forgot that. Humility in the face of a child's grief. Not what you would expect to find among the Rorhah men.

Soon the Commander rode away, taking half the soldiers with him. Edvard mounted, called for his escort, and the troop set off. They trotted past the village green, where Olwen knelt under the willows, crooning to a live goose she held clutched against her breast. Above her head Liam's body swung back and forth on a short noose. It had been shot full of arrows.

Seeing them, she stood up. The goose honked and flapped its wings in her face. One of the soldiers sniggered. Her gaze followed them as they circled the green, until Edvard's war-horse pranced forward a step or two, disclosing the small figure of Caro on his pony. Olwen dropped the goose, waved, and sang out:

'Goodbye, Caro, goodbye, Caro, goodbye, Caro . . .'

'I remember now' said Edvard, leaning over, 'your name's Caryllac, isn't it?'

Caro turned his face the other way.

18

So Caro was taken to Floried, and that was how he met his father's family. When they arrived at Floried Castle Caro temporarily lost the use of his legs, and was carried in Edvard's arms through halls and up stairways to the salon where the family was sitting together, drinking tea. Edvard filcLaurentin is his full name, Annie. Of course you recognise it. Yes, he's the Lord Chancellor now, it was the very same man.

You know, at Court they say Lord Edvard and the King are the best of friends, closer than brothers. Nobody understands it. No two men could be less alike. You must have realised by now, Annie, that Edvard was a nice man – a good man. How could such a man have managed to fall among thieves and not see them for what they were? It puzzled Caro too: still does. And another thing. If a good man does an evil thing – does it consciously, for a good man must know when a thing is evil – isn't his guilt that much the greater? Isn't he then worse than the wicked men around him? But Edvard was a weak man too. Only a weak man would have taken the time to humour a small boy's grief.

Try as he might, Caro was never able to hate Edvard. The Floriahs, however, were something else again.

There were so many of them. Cousins and aunts of varying importance were in the room, but no uncles, who were all away at war. Caro's grandfather, the Fahlraec of Floriah, was a rheumaticky old gentleman with permanently wet eyes and an ivory cane. Lady Floriah was a granny straight out of a shepherds'-tale. Her little, wrinkled, powdery, pink-and-white apple of a face was so sweet, Annie, that to look at her you'd never guess she was a vixen of cruelty.

And that thin, rather pretty woman who sat staring straight ahead of her, her features twice as sharp in profile – she was the Lady Isabel, his father's wife. The children clustering around her were proof of the relationship. Her eldest boy, Caro's half-brother Arlo, could with his curly hair and disproportionately long limbs have passed for Tom Floriah when Tom was Caro's age. Arlo imitated his mother in studiously ignoring the young cuckoo Edvard had unceremoniously dumped on their best silk sofa. In the Lady Isabel's lap lay a baby, maybe eighteen months old, bawling for all it was worth, and behind her chair two little girls were hiding. The younger girl was sniffling into her sister's skirt. That elder sister was Vivienne. She was the only one who smiled at Caro, and he wanted to smash her face in.

After they had recovered from the shock of learning Caro's identity, the ladies surrounded Edvard, who was evidently a favourite with them, and clamoured for news of their husbands. Lady Isabel remained in her chair, and said nothing. No one mentioned Tom's name. It was clear the Floriah family was staunchly Rorhah. They were beneath contempt. Caro loathed them. He was filled with a fierce, proud sense of purpose: they could torture him or starve him – and they probably would – but he would never betray his father, never.

When all the news had been exhausted, and the explanations for Caro's presence in their home had been made, Lord Floriah took a deep breath and said, 'But what on earth are we supposed to do with him?'

'Well, he's a bright boy,' said Edvard, 'and well-educated, and Tom – that is, I've been told that he's fond of poetry. He speaks excellent Andarian. Really it's up to you. But his Grace did say that you were to look after the wolf cub. For his father's sake.'

The ensuing silence was finally broken by Vivienne piping up from behind the chair, 'Grandmama, do you have a pain?'

'Hush, Vivvy,' said her mother.

'But Madam, Grandmama looks like she's going to be sick.'

One of the aunts hurriedly offered Edvard a cup of tea. The conversation became general: they discussed the weather, the hunting, the harvest. Caro was so full of hate he felt nauseous and light-headed, drifting in and out of consciousness.

A light hand brushed his shoulder. 'Don't move,' whispered a voice. He opened his eyes and saw Vivienne crouched behind the arm of the sofa. How ugly she was! She had gold studs screwed through the lobes of her pointy ears, and sharp weasel teeth. She was painfully skinny. Her skin was practically yellow. She had no nose to speak of, and her hair was short and thick and woolly like brown lambskin. Caro couldn't bear to look at her. His fist clenched. He was going to lash out at her, drive her away.

'Ssssh,' she said. Taking his fist she prised it open and dribbled a handful of broken biscuit into his palm. 'You must be awfully hungry. Are you really my brother? You're ever so pretty. I wish I looked like you. Everybody says I take after

158

Madam – '

'Grandmama,' cried Arlo loudly, 'Vivvy's talking to *him*.'

'Vivvy! What do you think you're doing? Get away from there at once, you provoking child. Do you hear me? You there,' Lady Floriah pointed at one of the man-servants, 'take that boy away. There's a spare bed in the kitchen, I believe. And give him something to eat.'

The servant took Caro to the kitchen and laid him on a mattress that had been pushed into a corner. A great cooking fire belched heat from the middle of the floor. The kitchen smelt of smoke and roast fat. Everything Caro came into contact with was greasy. He curled into a ball. After a while someone set a plate of meat beside him; later still the untouched food was taken away. Caro pretended to be asleep so that no one would speak to him. He could hear them talking about him. Bastard, they said. Orphan. You can see he's a love-child. If he's anything to go by she must have been as beautiful as they said. Poor little lamb.

Caro made his skin into a wall and sat with his back to it. He shut himself away from the noise and the smell and the people. He was alone in a world that went no further than his skin. He was like the walls of Mindared. Nothing could get in and nothing could get out. He would never break down. He would never let anyone see when they had hurt him. He would never give in and let them make him cry.

Eight weeks were to pass before Caro saw Edvard filcLaurentin again. He spent the first of those eight weeks in the kitchen, being alternately bullied and mothered, eating nothing but bread and tomatoes. The smell of meat made his stomach churn: the taste made him throw up. He never spoke. After a while they stopped trying to coax speech from him. At the end of the week one of the footmen appeared, took Caro by the ear, and hauled him up innumerable flights of stairs until they came to a large, pleasantly airy room high up in the Castle keep. The walls were lined with shelves full of chests, tally-sticks, pots of coloured ink, boxes of candles, scrolls, sealing-wax and ledgers. This, he was told, was the secretary's office, and this gentleman here was Master Gareth, his Lordship's personal secretary. If Caro was a good boy and properly grateful Master Gareth would teach him how to be a clerk, and he could sleep on that camp bed in the corner. But if he was a bad boy, oh my, goodness only knew what Master Gareth might do to him.

Master Gareth persisted for almost a week in attempting to make Caro talk, before giving the job up as impossible. In any case, he told Caro, he could not abide chatty children. Gareth was not a bad master, on the whole, and if he hit Caro more often than the teachers at school had, his beatings were less vigorous, for his arm was out of practice.

Over the next seven weeks Caro ran away twenty-three times. His first escape was the most successful: he slipped through the gates when no one was watching, and had reached the foot of the hill when one of the castle washerwomen, on her way up from the town, caught sight of him, tackled him, and bundled him ignominiously back inside. After this they were wise to him. A sharp-eyed maid at an upstairs window would always spot him slinking through the shadows of the courtyard, and would cry out, 'Gareth's boy's scarpering again!' Whoever was closest would lay hands on him and return him to the office. Master Gareth hit him less enthusiastically each time, and for punishment made him spend hours practising his handwriting in nine styles. Through all this, Caro never said a word.

One afternoon, when Caro had been almost two months at Floried Castle, it happened that Master Gareth was called away on his Lordship's urgent business. 'I may be gone for some time,' he told Caro, neither expecting, nor receiving, a reply. 'I want to find all those pens cut by the time I get back, and if you find yourself idle you can make some new ink and fill those pots.' As always, Master Gareth took the precaution of locking the office door from the outside.

Caro had no intention of obeying the clerk's instructions. At school cutting pens had been viewed as a particularly nasty form of punishment: it was boring, and fiddly, and often painful when slivers of quill worked their way under your fingernails. Caro would rather Master Gareth hit him. Master Gareth was pretty feeble anyway. Caro had more pressing business to attend to. Climbing on to the window-sill, he gazed all around, studying the courtyard, the walls, the guardhouse and the gates in preparation for his twenty-fourth escape. Soon his imagination had liberated itself – in daydreams he was free and running; he was tramping the road to Mindared; he was there, standing beneath the walls no man can conquer, gazing up proudly at the triumphant Andaranah banner of green and silver that fluttered above the severed, broken-nosed head of a man who was still a boy. That head was as lifeless as Peregrin's head, the green venom was dulled in those adder eyes, and Caro's exultant hatred made his heart pound so loudly he didn't hear the key turn in the lock, or the door creak open, and when a girl's voice said:

'Hullo,'

he was so startled he almost fell off the window-sill.

'Remember me?' she grinned. The corners of her eyes turned up, squeezing her lashes together. This, thought Caro, made her look uglier than ever. The only thing that kept him from leaping to attack her was the dog that stood beside her, a shaggy grey hound tall enough to rest its head on her shoulder.

'This is Fletch,' she said, 'he's my dog, my name's Vivienne you know, can I hide in here?'

Caro drew his knees up to his chest, and did not answer.

Apparently silence was as good as an invitation to her. She gangled into the room, twisting a woolly curl around one finger while her eyes roamed over the walls. Her whole air was one of animal furtiveness. In the middle of the floor she stood on one leg, cocked her head sideways, and said, 'Don't you want to know why I'm hiding?'

Of course he did; but he'd bite his tongue out before he asked this girl anything.

'My best friend's coming,' she told him generously. 'Actually she's not really my best friend, that's just what Madam calls her. Her name's Richenda, her father's one of Grandpapa's Quarter-Lords, really I think they want her to suck up to us so that my cousin Richard will marry her one day, but she pretends she comes to see me, when she comes she stays for *weeks* and we have to do embroidery together. Ugh. She's making bedsheets for her wedding chest, honestly, at our age! She's brilliant at embroidery. I'm awful. I thought this would be a good place to hide because I'm not supposed to come here so they won't look. I'll be in trouble later but I don't care. Caryllac – I know why you're trying to run away.

'Stay,' she told the dog. She came over to Caro and put her chin on the sill, her father's brown eyes looking up at him from under her father's brows.

'I wish *you* were my friend,' she said. 'I've been waiting for ages to talk to you. It's really hard to get away, they watch me all the time. Grandmama calls me a delinquent, that's how I knew I'd like you because that's what she calls you too. I tried to run away before, last summer, but I got caught and anyway I didn't really know where Daddy was. They said that if I ever tried it again they'd send me to the Little Daughters of Vuna at Igmolvic and God! it's gruesome there. Richenda's sister got sent and she's an idiot, a real one I mean, she drools and stuff. Anyway I wouldn't be able to keep Fletch if I got sent there so I gave up running away, but we could go. We could go to Mindared together. Fletch can come too, he does anything I say, we'll be really safe with him because he can kill *anything*, but only if I tell him. You don't have to be scared of him.'

'I'm not scared of dogs,' Caro croaked, for his throat was rusty with disuse.

Vivienne whistled. Fletch rose, stretched his long grey hearth-rug of a body, and loped over to the children. 'Up,' she said. The dog stood on his hind legs to put two massive paws, as big as plates, on Caro's knees. Vivienne stroked the dog's head. 'You can pat him too,' she said. 'He won't bite.'

Caro ran a hand down the dog's neck. Fletch lolled his tongue happily and wagged his tail. 'See, he likes you,' said Vivienne. 'D'you have a dog?'

'Not any more.'

'Oh. Oh well, I tell you what. You can share Fletch with me.'

Being the only one facing the doorway, Caro was the first to notice that someone was standing in it. It was the brown-haired boy, the one people could point at and say, that's Tom Floriah's son, no doubt of it. Vivienne realised that something was wrong; she and Fletch turned simultaneously, and her brother sneered at her,

'I knew you'd be here. Everybody's looking for you. You're in big trouble.'

'It's just Arlo,' she told Caro. 'Ignore him.'

'You get away from there, Vivvy,' said Arlo. 'You know what Grandmama said. You've got to come down, Richenda's here.'

'Oh pooh, all they can do is hit me. I don't even feel it any more,' she boasted to Caro. 'I've got a backside like leather.'

'I said get away from him right now.'

'I don't have to do what *you* say.'

'Yes you do.'

'No I don't.'

'Yes you *do*, bastard-lover – '

This was water off a duck's back to Caro. He had a toughened

162

heart and expected no better from any member of the Floriah family. Oh, but Annie, you should have seen Vivvy. That's what hurt him, almost, the way she ran forward all skinny and belligerent, and shouted at the boy Caro still thought of as her real brother, 'Don't you call him that!'

'That's what he is, bastard, bastard – '

'Shut up! You're a horrible sneak! I hate you!'

'Grandmama told us not to come up here, but of course *you* do, you have to make trouble. You think you can get away with anything. Grandmama says Daddy's spoilt you rotten, she says if she'd known what a handful you'd turn out to be she'd have had you drowned at birth, she says that if someone told you to breathe you'd hold your breath till you strangled, she says – '

'Oh fuck off!'

Caro's mouth dropped open. He could hardly believe his ears. These two children of privilege, born in wedlock, nobly-bred, were brawling like a couple of street-brats. He would never have used such foul language, not in a million years. He would have gone supperless to bed for a week.

Arlo swung his fist back and smacked Vivienne across the face. Surely this couldn't be happening. Gentlemen did not strike ladies. She shrieked and hit back, while Fletch, forbidden to lay a claw on Arlo, whimpered and buried his nose in his paws. Caro had no such inhibitions. He jumped from the window and charged.

'Don't!' Vivienne screamed. She caught his wrist and the momentum pulled them both off balance, tumbling in a heap of arms and legs to the floor. Arlo doubled up with laughter.

Red-faced, Caro tried to struggle free of her. He'd been made a fool of again. Arlo was her brother – of course she wouldn't want some bastard to hit him. Then she tugged Caro's hair and made him look at her. The red weal stood out on her cheek. She was looking at him in exactly the way his father used to when he had done something reckless and stupid. And Caro thought, *I am her brother too.*

Annie, remember last winter, when it was so cold your blood froze in your veins and your hands and feet went numb? You went inside and sat by the fire, and your toes started coming back to life, and it hurt, Gods, it hurt, but you knew it had to hurt if you weren't to lose the use of your limbs. That was how

163

Caro felt. It hurt, as if Vivienne had thrust her hot hand in and taken hold of his frozen heart.

'I'll kill him,' said Caro.

'No,' she said with the breathlessness of one who has just averted disaster, 'you mustn't. If you hit him he'll tell Grand-mama, and she'll have you whipped.'

Of course, thought Caro, how stupid of me. Of course he and Arlo could not have a fair fight. Arlo had the right to hit Caro whenever he pleased. Caro had no right to strike back. It doesn't matter, Caro told himself, it doesn't matter, it doesn't matter. There has to be another way.

Seeing that his legitimacy had won by default, Arlo yanked his sister to her feet and led her from the room. Fletch followed, tail between legs. Only when they were in the corridor did Caro hear Vivienne protest, 'You'd better watch out when Daddy comes home . . .'

19

Edvard filcLaurentin arrived early in the next week. He was leading the vanguard of the King's retinue on its triumphal progress to Tsvingtori, and he came with some of the more important officials to spend the night in Floried Castle. News of the victory had preceded him by several days. The new King had done the impossible. For him the walls of Mindared had fallen at last – although from the inside, torn down brick by brick. A legend could have no firmer foundation than Mindared's humbled stones.

Nevertheless Edvard's visit was eagerly welcomed, both for his own sake and for the information, good and bad, that he brought concerning the fates of those individuals with whom the Castle was most concerned. He in his turn was, it seemed, quite bizarrely concerned with one particular small individual now residing high up in the Castle keep; less than an hour after he had ridden through the gates he was standing in the doorway of the office, unannounced, and he said to Master Gareth, 'Leave us.'

Master Gareth gathered up his working papers and bowed and scraped backwards through the door. Caro remained sitting.

'What are you doing here?' he asked.

164

'I want to have a talk with you, Caryllac filcThomas. Lord Floriah tells me you've been trying to run away.'

Caro shrugged.

'Where is it you want to go?'

A place that had lost all meaning. A majestic emblem of resistance, brought low. 'Nowhere,' said Caro. 'Anywhere. I don't care. Away from here.'

'Well, I want to tell you something. It's no good just running *away* from somewhere. You have to have somewhere you want to run *to*. If you have no destination in mind, every other place will be the same as the one you left.'

'Nowhere can be worse than here.'

'Are they cruel to you?'

Caro couldn't answer. Two months ago he would have said yes, but his gauge of cruelty had been shot to pieces, and he had no idea what the rest of the world might think unacceptably cruel. They hadn't kicked him to death or sawn his head off, or strung him up in a tree to use for target practice. Being grateful to them for this was another matter.

Edvard said, 'I know it's hard for you – '

'You don't know anything.'

'Caro, listen to me. Even if you do hate it here, life is full of things we hate and don't want to do. We can't keep running away from them. We have to face them. If you learn to face things here, to endure them, it will make you tougher. And that's no bad thing. You are an intelligent boy. I think you understand your situation. I know it's through no fault of your own that you've been brought to this, and I know it's not fair that you have to live in accordance with circumstances, but that is the way of the world. Your life isn't going to be easy, not here, not anywhere. No one's is, come to that. I've also done things, and seen things, that I would like to run away from, but part of being a man is learning to accept one's responsibility for circumstances, and – '

'You're full of shit,' said Caro.

Edvard sighed and looked depressed. Then he forced himself to perk up, put on a fake smile, and said brightly, 'Come over here. I have a present for you.'

'I don't want anything from you.'

'It's not from me.'

'I don't care who it's from,' Caro cried as Edvard drew his sword, 'I don't want it.'

165

Edvard knelt down beside him, and carefully laid the sword across Caro's knees. 'Look,' he said.

Caro looked. A sword this long, with pearls in the handle. He shut his eyes. Blindly his fingers traced the initials etched in the clean steel.

He said, 'He's dead.'

'Yes, he is.'

But Caro had always known that one day his father would not come back.

Edvard said, 'Your father never ran away. He stood his ground to the end and he died with more courage than I can ever hope to have. He was truly a noble man. He was good, and brave, and you can be proud of him. You should try to make him proud of you.'

How? thought Caro. He's dead.

The weight of the sword made his legs ache. He thought, this sword didn't do my father much good, did it? Or my mother. Or me.

'I don't want it.'

'But it was your father's. You must want it.'

'I don't want to kill people.'

'Just because you have it doesn't mean you have to use it.'

'Doesn't it?'

'Now you listen to me, Caryllac filcThomas – '

'Don't call me that. I'm not an Andarian. Take it away, please. Take it away and leave me alone.'

A weak man, Annie. He should have clouted Caro round the ear, reminded him who he was and whom he was speaking to. But Edvard took the sword and put it back in his scabbard. He said, 'Nothing can make up for it. I know that. I only want to help you. If it ever gets unbearable here – if they're cruel to you, or turn you out – if that happens, I want you to get in touch with me, at Court. It's not as difficult as you might think. If you ever need me, I promise you I'll help you all I can.'

He was turning to go, when a girl's screams echoed off the Castle walls from the other side of the courtyard. Someone had broken the news to Vivienne.

20

'I stayed there for almost nine years,' Caro tells Annie.

'Did they throw you out?'

'They probably would have, but I left first. I always meant to leave, but it would have meant leaving Vivvy. I couldn't leave her there by herself. We didn't have anybody but each other. Well, there was Lord Floriah. He doted on her. She wormed permission out of him for me to use the Castle library. That's where my book comes from. She asked him if I could have it and he said I could take what I liked, since no one else was interested. She could wind that old man round her little finger. She's such a funny girl – you know she's still not at all pretty, but she's a real little fascinator. I was her slave. That dog, Fletch, and I, we followed her around everywhere. We did everything together.'

'And now?'

'I don't know. For years, you know, I couldn't imagine life without Vivvy. And then after I left I never expected to see her again. I still haven't quite grown used to her being a grown-up married woman. She's much happier at Court than she ever was at home, though, so that's one good thing. She seems to have calmed down a bit.'

'So what happened, to make you leave?'

'That was because of Vivvy too. Remember those treason trials they had about six years back, just before you went to Pravarre? One of Lord Floriah's bosom buddies from his youth got caught up in it somehow. I know because I opened the letters my Uncle Richard sent from Court. The news practically killed him – Lord Floriah, I mean. Of course he was a sick old man to start with. Everyone knew it was only a matter of days before he died. And Vivvy – she went wild, wilder than ever. She always was uncontrollable, and she got worse and worse as she got older. Naturally I was blamed for it. The evil influence of my bad blood. But Lord Floriah always indulged her, and I think it was because of her that he became quite fond of me. He wouldn't let anyone try to split us up – and her grandmother knew some pretty subtle ways for breaking children's spirits, I can tell you. I probably would have broken, without Vivvy. To her it was like a goad to a mad bull. Forbidding her to do something was a guarantee that she'd do it or die trying. Well, what happened was that, a few days after Lord Floriah fell ill, she went missing, and they didn't find her till past midnight. She was fooling around in the hayloft with one of the grooms, dead drunk. Even faithful Caro was pretty shocked. And some fool – probably that wretched Arlo – went and told her grandfather, and that finished him off. He was dead the next morning. Then Gareth told me that the family was planning to pack Vivvy off to that place she always went in holy terror of, some cave full of mad spinsters and half-wits – '

'The Little Daughters of Vuna at Igmolvic.'

'That's it. That's where the Andarians dispose of their un-marriageable daughters. Of course her mother and grandmother had been dying to get her off their hands for ages, and with Lord Floriah gone there was no one to stop them. No one to protect me, either, for that matter. So I packed up my poems and left.'

'The famous bag,' Annie smiles.

'Yes, well, I didn't know I'd written so many. I hid it from everyone, there, that I wrote things. Except Vivvy. There was nowhere in the office where I could keep them without Gareth or someone finding them, so she hid them for me, in her room. She wheedled Lord Floriah into giving her a chest with a lock on it. He never even asked why she wanted it. Oh, and Fern, she gave me Fern for my eighteenth birthday. I think Fern is Fletch's half-sister. So after nine years that was all I had to take, Fern and a bag full of poems. That night I walked out – it's funny, all my elaborate plans for running away and in the end it couldn't have been easier. Everything was in confusion and the guards left one of the gates open. And a week later I met Bren, and the rest you know.'

'Caro – ' Annie fingers her dress anxiously, 'that man – the one you called the Commander – he was – he's the King, isn't he?'

'Didn't I make that obvious? Taking some time off from the war to have a bit of fun with a bunch of peasants.'

'Don't talk like that. It frightens me. I suppose he can't know who you are, I mean, whose son you are. Can he? Or he wouldn't allow you at Court.'

'I don't know whether he recognised me straight away, but he knows who I am now. Vivvy blurted it all round the Court the moment she saw me. Typical Vivvy, completely open, no pretence, unable to see why everyone shouldn't be as glad as she is that her long-lost bastard brother has suddenly turned up in the last place you'd expect to find him. You'd like her, Annie. And she's very popular, which has helped me a great deal. I hardly ever see the King, not to talk to. He doesn't seem to be very interested in poetry. I have more to do with the Queen. And Lord Edvard. He hasn't changed a bit. Still trying to be my friend. He couldn't be prouder of me if he were my own father. He's very fond of Vivvy, too. In fact I think he's a little in love with her, but then half the Court is. And of course with her being married, and him being Edvard, there's nothing doing.'

'Caro – '

'Yes?'

'I see now why you hate the King.'

'But I don't, that's just it. I don't hate *him*. It's not personal. When I was younger I did hate him for what he did to my family, but I know now that I'm not the only one. Terrible things happened to thousands of people. That was the war's fault, not Basal Rorhah's fault. He knew no better. I'm sure my father did pretty much the same things when he had to. He was an Andarian. And I'm not. I'm not. And even the war probably wasn't Basal Rorhah's fault. If Michael was as bad as they say then something had to be done about him. And what they did was fight a war. And that's what I hate. I hate the fact that all that bloodshed and suffering changed nothing – one day there'll be another war when one of Basal Rorhah's descendants doesn't come up to scratch, and then another war, and another, because it's self-perpetuating. I hate the King, not the man who is the King. I hate the religion that tells us it's our duty to be happy with the world as it is, and then murders us if we're not. I hate everything that the King and the Court and the Temple stand for. I hate him because he's Andarian. Well, you see, there's lots of things I hate about this world, but I don't hate him, he's just a man. I can't make him any different from the way he is. Like I said, he's just a snake. In a different sort of world he might have been a different sort of man, and to that extent he's a victim too, a slave of circumstances. Listen, is that Bren calling us? What time is it?'

Caro goes to the window and opens the shutters. Bright sunshine lights up the room. 'Dawn was hours ago,' he says. 'Are you sleepy?' Annie shakes her head. 'Then let's go get something to eat. I'm ravenous, and not, for a change, for you. Come on, Fern.'

IV

The Willows of Babylon

21

Edvard filcLaurentin has reached the age of thirty-seven and has no wife, though not for want of women willing to have him or families who would have welcomed the connection. When young he was handsome and agreeable, and while he had no property of his own, his intimacy with Basal Rorhah held out prospects for limitless advancement. Even now there can be no better catch than a bachelor Lord Chancellor, given that the Princes are barely out of their cradles. They're little terrors, those two boys, teasing the Court girls and pulling their hair; and when the girls run sobbing to their mothers those ladies smack them, and tell them how lucky they are, for those boys promise to take after their father, and you never know, daughter, you never know.

Edvard can see no good reason to get himself married, aside from love, and that's one trap he's thankful never to have fallen into. As the younger son of a minor family, he has no patrimony to bequeath. His only income is his Court salary, which he feels he fairly earns, and he will not take favours from the King. He would hate anyone to accuse him of trying to profit from a friendship worth treasuring for its own sake. He keeps his integrity intact and knows he is respected for it. Heirs and their provision would be a burden to him – a family would make too many demands on his time and energy. He is celibate out of financial necessity, on principle, and by inclination.

He works hard, and has aged badly, unlike his friend the King, who retains all the enthusiasms of youth. Even when they were young men in the Guards, when Edvard was by far the better-looking, Basal was the one the girls preferred. Edvard has never envied him for this: he has known Basal too long and loves him too well. Basal has always been someone out of the ordinary, someone marked out by the Gods. Edvard has no false ideas about himself. He will never be loved as Basal is loved. He wasn't made to be an object of veneration, desire, and fear. If a woman loved him for himself, well, that might be a temptation, but in his position, how could he ever be sure? In any case, passion embarrasses him. He does not know how to express it.

His lesser friendships have not withstood the tests of time and change. Against the better judgment of the entire Council, and against his own inclinations, Gilles Mehah was appointed Treasurer; it was only because they did not think Basal could be mistaken that they did not press harder for an alternative choice. And of course Basal was not mistaken. Gilles soon displayed the same genius for finance that he had shown, in the war, for the logistics of supplies, and he's now become as obsessed with money, the breeding of money, as Bernard Derondah always was with rank. And Edvard has never been fond of Fredric Olivah, that fat bore.

Over the last few years Edvard has been taking an interest in the careers of the fatherless Floriah children. Someone needed to accept the responsibility for them: their mother and grandmother had allowed them to grow up without discipline or education. Edvard used his influence to obtain a post for Arlo in the Guards, and he arranged Vivienne's appointment as a lady-in-waiting. When he heard that she was married he did wonder, very briefly, why he had not thought of her for himself, before realising that it would have been an exceedingly foolish thing to do. No two people could be more likely to make each other miserable than a pensive middle-aged bachelor and a heedless adolescent girl. If he'd really been serious about taking charge of Vivienne he should have married Tom Floriah's widow, and given himself some legal rights over all Tom's offspring. As it is, Edvard knows how it feels to be disappointed in children. Arlo will not be cured of his bullying tendencies, and no amount of gentle reprimanding can force the slightest notion of propriety into Vivienne's head. As for Caro, Edvard never forgot him, but through the years his work kept him so busy that he could do no more than spare the boy a thought from time to time, and wonder how he was getting on. Arlo refused to talk about Caro – refused to admit that Caro was alive – and all Vivienne ever said on the subject was, 'He was my best friend. He ran away.'

No one whose life has been closely bound up in that of Basal Rorhah's can fail to believe in the force of destiny, and so, when Caro appeared at Court as none other than the famous poet of whom they had all heard so much, Edvard was less surprised than one might think. Clearly there is nothing his influence can do for Caro that Caro has not already achieved by himself. Yes, Edvard is proud of him, doubly proud that he has managed to overcome the stigma of his birth and all his other misfortunes to prove that his blood, however wrongly acquired, does run true.

He has invited Caro to lunch with him. He often does this,

for the pleasure of Caro's company, the intelligence of his conversation, and the comfort of feeling that a real friendship is growing between them. Today, however, he has a matter of some urgency to discuss with Caro, all the more urgent due to its having languished in Chancery for the past three months, handed up from clerk to clerk until it finally reached him. No one wanted to take the responsibility for acting on it: they know what favour Caro stands in.

The meal has been carefully catered to Caro's idiosyncracies: bread of a whiteness never seen in the City, fresh butter, black-eyed beans stewed in wine, five types of cheese, fruit and nuts. Edvard dismisses his servants and takes a roll of parchment from his drawer. Handing it to Caro he says, 'I wonder if you can shed any light on this.'

'What is it, Eminence?'

'Someone has made out a deposition against you. It came in last April, but these things always take an interminable time. It's only just come to my attention. Read it, you'll see what you're accused of.'

Caro reads it with no change of expression, except, once or twice, to chuckle. When he has finished it, he asks, 'Am I allowed to know the name of my accuser?'

'Strictly, no.'

'Let me guess, then. It's probably one of two people. But Blue wouldn't risk it – he wouldn't like anyone to think he had done it out of jealousy. So let's see. My accuser is a gentleman, by birth at any rate. A student of the School of Courts. Am I warm, Eminence? If I suggested that his name is something like Barney filcBarney, would your Eminence tell me I'm right?'

'You know him?'

'Hardly. I met him once. I got the better of him in an argument and this is his revenge.'

'These are serious accusations, Caro. Denying the Gods, slandering his Grace, advocating violence and fomenting popular unrest. Men have lost their lives on the mere suspicion of such crimes. It seems rather an extreme method for obtaining revenge.'

'Your Eminence knows me. I have my pride. After all, orphan bastards don't have much else that they can call their own. Does your Eminence believe that I could take his Grace's money, serve in his Court, and accept the honour of his favour if I really held these opinions?'

175

'Then you're saying these charges are entirely unfounded?'

'Eminence, may I ask you a question?'

Another man, one with a more robust conscience, would have said, no, you may not: you are on trial here, not me. Caro did not use the words 'orphan bastard' carelessly. Edvard's eagerness in cultivating their friendship, his present concern to find an acceptable explanation, and his willingness to believe in Caro give his weaknesses away. Caro has been studying Edvard, exploring his possibilities, for months, and he is fairly confident in identifying Edvard's character as one eaten up with loneliness and oppressed by unacknowledged regrets. Why this should be so, Caro can't say, and he really doesn't care. It simply is so, and he can use it.

'Of course you may,' says Edvard.

'Do you believe in the Gods?'

'Undoubtedly.'

'Your Eminence believes that they have corporeal existence, with faces and bodies just like ours, and that their features look just like they're portrayed on the temple statues; that they have lusts and jealousies and bicker and squabble? Your Eminence believes that Vishnac has a running feud with Isen Mathred because she plucked his eyes out to get back at him for looking at her in the nude, and that she made the Sun and Moon from them just as a sort of by-the-way? Your Eminence believes that one divinity could rebel against the rest and take those omniscient deities by *surprise*? And that an immortal like Adonac could actually die? And then be resurrected for no better reason than that Asdura cried for him? That the Gods are, basically, glorified human beings, and the worst sort of human being at that? Because I can't believe in it.'

Edvard is laughing. 'No, no one expects you to. You're an educated young man. If the gods really were so full of contradictions the world would be completely disordered. The common mind needs something it can grasp, something not too far removed from itself. That's why those legends spring up, and there's not much point in trying to eradicate them because the majority of people will never have the level of education necessary for a more sophisticated understanding. Of course one can never really understand the Gods, and I don't presume that my views are any truer a representation of what they really are, but I personally tend to think of them as pure intelligences, masculine and feminine, light and dark, fruitful

176

and sterile, hot and cold and so on, balancing the world. How can I put it? Personifications of qualities – and of virtues. And everything on earth which possesses those qualities and virtues, is really a reflection of the Gods.'

'Well, that's how I understand it,' says Caro. 'But either I didn't put it half so well as you, or this student Barney has a very unsophisticated mind, because he obviously missed my meaning. I never said that I didn't believe in the Gods. I said that I didn't understand them. In the native the two words are very similar, and we were talking in the native, so maybe that's how he got confused. In fact what I really said was that it was difficult to understand why, if they love us, they allow us to fight wars. I didn't mean that that proved they didn't exist. I wouldn't be so presumptuous. I know when things need to be taken on faith. And I did say that maybe there was a better way, but what I meant was that if we couldn't find it, it was due to our own shortcomings, our lack of divinity. And I still do believe that there must be a better way to sort out our affairs than by war and violence, a way that would be constructive and not destructive. Is that a crime, Eminence?'

'I don't know, Caro.'

Caro is wise enough not to press his point. The combination of sincerity, flattery and perplexity turning round in Edvard's mind should do the work for him.

Edvard's philosophy of life is a patchwork cobbled together from circumstances, each one dealt with as it came along. He is forever rearranging it, discarding pieces that no longer fit and putting the rest into new relationships with one another. The only consistent thread is that of a lifelong devotion to one man, which holds the patchwork together and alone makes sense of it. If this thread should come unravelled, Edvard's life would fall apart. Instinct tells him this: it's not something he wants to pick at too closely.

There is, however, another thread, one that Edvard and Caro are unaware of sharing, though it lies at the root of Edvard's sympathy for Caro, and is the reason why, despite everything, Caro feels a certain respect for Edvard. It is their profound belief in the perfectibility of human society. Edvard's view is that no single man's labour is equal to this task. It inches forward slowly, generation by generation. Talking with Caro makes him realise that these ideals are never lost for good – they reappear in fresher hands and stouter hearts, borne aloft

177

triumphantly as though they were a new discovery.

'If it is a crime,' says Edvard slowly, 'it's one I've been guilty of all my life. I never wanted a war. None of us did. But there didn't seem to be any other solution.'

'Eminence, does his Grace know that these accusations have been made against me?'

'There isn't enough time in the day for all the work his Grace has to do. He can't be expected to deal with everything. That's why he has a Council, and that's why we're empowered to make the decisions he would make for himself.'

Having said this, Edvard takes the charge sheet from Caro and puts it in the fire.

'Thank you,' says Caro. 'Eminence, if you'll forgive my curiosity, can I ask – '

'Yes, what, Caro?'

'Does his Grace subscribe to your understanding of the nature of the Gods?'

'His Grace believes what it is right for him to believe,' says Edvard, a little sharply. What this really means is that he doesn't want to admit that he has no idea of Basal Rorhah's opinion on the subject.

22

Caro tells no one about this little incident. He doesn't expect any of his friends to see it in quite the same promising light that he does; and he wants, above everything, to keep Annie from worrying about him.

In her extreme old age, when she will have outlived Basal's son and Basal's grandson and all her friends and relations, when the bad is blurred with the good in her memory, and remembered with equal fondness, Annie will look back on these times as the happiest she ever knew. Her Caro has finally settled down. He is honoured every bit as much as he deserves. He is busy, successful, admired, and prosperous. They have enough to live comfortably, although he won't hear of moving out of their tiny attic. He treats her to pretty dresses, and sparkling baubles for her ears and throat. Of course the gems and frocks don't really matter, but all the same they are an added sweetness, like the spice of Court gossip, the romance of great names, which he brings down to her in unsatisfactory dribbles. So like a man – he says he can't see what's so fascinating about who's sleeping with whom, who's feuding with whom, which beauty the King took to his bed last night and whose noses are out of joint. But Annie has people relying on her for their information about what goes on Up There. She can't help luxuriating, just a little, in the envy of her friends. They warned her not to fall for Caro, and now she's showing them just how wrong they were. She was ready to give up everything for Caro – and instead she has Caro *and* everything she ever wanted. Her man has so much luck it brushes off on all around him. In fact, the only blot on Annie's utter contentment is the torture of being forced to learn to read.

'Now come on, Annie. You're not stupid, you're just not trying. You should know your letters by now. It's not difficult.'

'But what's the point? Even if I did learn to read I can't speak Andarian, so what's there for me to read? And don't say you'll teach me Andarian, or I'll throw this slate at you.'

Caro, as always, has an answer. He writes little poems for her and leaves them lying about the room. If Annie wants to know what they say, she has to struggle through them by herself. Her heart persists when her brain wants to give up. Each poem is like a kiss. They are something to hold on to, to be read again and again, painfully, lovingly, whenever he leaves her to go up to Court.

She knows it's wicked to be jealous of his sister. Really she ought to be thanking the Gods he hasn't fallen into the clutches of some more dangerous woman. She tries not to look for faults in Vivienne, although honestly, from what Caro says, his sister does sound like a thoughtless, selfish, spoilt young lady. Of course Caro can't see that. To him Vivienne is perfect. He fantasises about how much Annie and Vivienne would like each other, and Annie plays along, secure in the knowledge that it's a harmless, impossible dream. She never thought the day would come when she'd be glad to be a fisherman's daughter, but that's what she is, and Vivienne is a Lady, and they can never meet.

Meanwhile, up at Court, Vivienne is importuning Caro, 'Teach me the native.'

'No thank you. What for? You can hardly read and write your own language properly.'

'Don't be mean. I just think it would be interesting, that's all.'

'I know what it is. You hear your maids gossiping behind

your back and you want to know if they're talking about you.'

'Of course they are. I'm so interesting. No, actually, Caro – I want to hear what they're saying about *you*. They're all madly in love with you, you know, but you're so good you couldn't be gooder.'

'I am married, Vivvy.'

'I wish I could meet your Annie. But even if I could I wouldn't be able to talk to her about you, because you're such a pig you won't teach me native. Does she tell you you're a pig? I bet she does. I bet she knows how to keep you in line. Oh, life's so unfair,' Vivienne sighs. She has not lost the habit of fidgeting incessantly while she talks, waving a hand, hopping from foot to foot, twisting a curl around a finger that now and again flies to scratch at her nose. 'Anyway,' she goes on, 'people here don't think that's any reason. They all think you're frightfully straight-laced. They don't care about being married or not married.'

'So I've noticed.'

'My friend Maude positively dies for you, it's sickening.'

'Which one is she?'

'Oh Caro, don't pretend.'

'But all the women here seem the same to me.'

'You liar, you know her. She's the one you said made you feel like she wanted to eat you. Maude Vacled, the one with the big bosoms. See, you *have* noticed her. Don't you think she's pretty? She's Elinor Vacled's sister. And don't tell me you don't know who she is.'

'How could I fail to recognise such an elevated person as his Grace's mistress? I kiss the ground the patronising bitch walks on.'

'Oh Caro,' Vivienne giggles. 'She is, though. Don't let her hear you said that, she'll go running straight to his Grace. Except I think he'd rather get rid of her than let you go. I mean there's lots of Elinor Vacleds dying to take her place, but there isn't another you. His Grace thinks a lot of you, her Grace told me. He said you were an ornament of the Court. Oh Caro, this is something you don't know. The King of Andariah, King Henry, he wrote asking his Grace if he would, well, kind of lend you to his Court for a while. Your poetry's really popular in Andariah, her Grace told me so.'

'And what did his Grace reply?'

'Her Grace said he said you were a poet and not a painting,

180

and you had a mind of your own and it was up to you, and besides, since you're more or less a member of her Grace's Household she could decide whether to ask you or not. But she said she wasn't going to because she didn't want to lose you, you're the brightest star in her Court.'

'In that case, should you be telling me?'

'I thought you'd be pleased. You don't want to go, do you?'

'As it happens, I don't, but even if I did I couldn't do much about it, could I?'

'Well I don't care, I don't want you to go. Arlo and Bash are going to be back next month, I need you here.'

'He's your husband, Vivvy. You shouldn't dread seeing him.'

'Oh, I don't mind Bash, he lets me do what I like. It's Arlo. You know how he was always such a pig, well now he's ten times worse. I want you to be here so he can see how famous you are and how wonderful their Graces think you are. He's going to be *green*,' she exults, savouring the prospect.

They are interrupted by a footman, who has come in search of Vivienne to tell her she is needed by the Queen. Vivienne kisses Caro and runs off, hair unkempt, heels flying. Caro walks on in solitude, puzzling over the things Vivienne told him.

He has no desire to take up the King of Andariah's offer – to go and serve in a foreign land would be almost like a self-inflicted punishment for having too much fame and talent – and yet, he can't decide whether the behaviour of the principals involved is out of character, or not. The Queen is so inert she would always prefer inaction to action, not asking to asking him. But Basal Rorhah must have had a preference: the prestige gained by sending his sought-after poet abroad in the manner of a literary ambassador, set against the prestige to be gained by keeping for himself a treasure that other Kings desire. It makes Caro wonder whether he really might be worth something to the King – and if so, how much? Not him personally, not Caro the orphan, Tom Floriah's bastard, but Caryllac the famous poet, Caryllac in fact just like a painting, or like the victory at Mindared and the Palace of Ksaned Kaled. A piece of somebody else's legend. A decoration for his Grace's Court. Basal Rorhah left the decision to his wife, knowing that she would do nothing. Was it so that history would say, he was the great architect of Ksaned Kaled, he was the great and sole patron of Caryllac?

Engrossed in these speculations, Caro strolls aimlessly along a gravel path, until the sound of a pebble plonking into water

181

recalls him to the present. He has wandered into a part of the Palace grounds unfamiliar to him. A glossy box hedge separates the path from a herd of red and white cows grazing in the sunny meadow, and on the other side of the path a stream rushes gurgling over smooth brown rocks. Willows trail their branches in the water, dappling and rippling it with sparkling light and shade. Edvard filcLaurentin is sitting on a marble bench under one of the willows, throwing stones into the stream. Caro makes to retreat, but Edvard has seen him and calls him over.

'I'm sorry, Eminence, I didn't mean to intrude.'

'You're not intruding. In fact I'm glad you've come. Did you want to speak to me?'

'No, Eminence, I was just walking. I'm surprised to find your Eminence alone.'

'I'm not, really. My Guards are about somewhere.' Glancing up the path, Caro sees a glitter of metal through the willow branches and hears the low murmur of voices. 'Come and sit down with me,' says Edvard. 'I always enjoy talking to you. I'm afraid I've been indulging in a little homesickness. It's this place. It reminds me a little of my home. You know, I haven't been home since – well, since just after the war ended.'

'Your Eminence has more pressing calls on his time.'

'Unfortunately that's true. One hasn't much time to think of oneself, or to do the things one would like to do. I'd like to go home, for a while, but I don't suppose I ever will. This really is a beautiful spot, isn't it? I've heard people say that heaven must be like Ksaned Kaled, but I don't know. Ksaned Kaled is very beautiful, but it's all by human design. All those coloured fields of flowers laid out in squares. There's something too regimented about it. I think the human spirit would revolt if it had nothing but an endless Ksaned Kaled to look at. This here, though, is Brychmachrye as the Gods made her. I can't imagine anywhere more beautiful.'

'I know what you mean, Eminence.'

'Yes, I think you do. And you express it so beautifully too. I believe those are my favourites of all your poems, Caro – your landscape poems. There's so much more than description in them. There's real feeling.'

'The ones you've read are nothing, Eminence. I have some others, written in the native, much better, I think.'

'You write in the native?'

'If I can speak a language I have to write in it. The thing

is, every language is best suited to a particular sort of poetry. Court-speech has more logic, more flexibility, more nuances – more precision. But the native has more passion and warmth. You speak the native, don't you, Eminence? I could show them to you, if you like.'

'I'd like that very much. But it's just occurred to me that I'd like to ask you a different favour. With all the building projects going on there's no telling which part of the grounds are going to be touched next, and I know his Grace has been thinking about constructing an artificial lake, somewhere around here. If that happens, this place will probably go, and I'd like it if you could put it down in words for me, capture it so to speak, before it is destroyed. I did think of having a painting made, but that would only be a view from one angle. You could put all the angles in.'

'Your Eminence has only to command.'

'I know that. I prefer to ask. I would pay you for your trouble, of course.'

It's on the tip of Caro's tongue to retort, I don't want your blood money.

Edvard spent the whole of the war fighting at Basal Rorhah's side. The war lasted for two years, and in that time Edvard's assistance in the destruction of Caro's home, the murder of three unarmed men, the abandonment of a woman to death by rape or fire, and the abduction of an orphan cannot possibly have been the only reprehensible thing or even the worst thing he found himself compelled to do. Years ago he confessed to Caro that he had done things he wished he could run away from. Who knows how many faces he sees when he looks at Caro? Faces of the men, and women, and children who did not succeed in salvaging themselves from the ruin the war made of their lives.

That Edvard believes himself to be exceptionally fond of the young poet is, in Caro's opinion, neither here nor there. He suspects another motive behind Edvard's friendship. Caro, the sole survivor, rising from the ashes of war to attain prosperity and fame, is in Edvard's eyes a sort of living proof that no permanent damage was done. Edvard's avuncular generosity is nothing more than guilt. And why should he feel guilty unless he knows, even if he won't admit it, that the things he did were wrong?

'What do you think?' asks Edvard.

Caro replies, 'Now that I've seen this place, I couldn't but write about it. And I'd be honoured if your Eminence would accept the dedication. Please don't talk about money. Your Eminence has already given me more kindness than I can ever repay.'

23

There's something about Annie. She has changed in some way. Caro cannot help noticing it. It's not just the way she looks, though she has become even more beautiful. Her smile is deeper, her eyes are brighter, she has put on a bit of weight, her skin is softer and clearer. She is, in short, blooming, and that makes Caro anxious, because he's sure he isn't the one who brought this about.

She has withdrawn from him. She's not listening to him; her thoughts are far away. He can no longer arouse her desire merely by touching her hand. She has shut him out, and there is nothing Caro hates so much as the feeling of being shut out, excluded, not needed. Is it something he has done? Doesn't she love him any more? Has she found another man to fill the lonely hours when he is away at Court?

Paddy knows what's up, but he's not telling. All he will say is that Annie has been a very stupid girl. Don't be too hard on her, Caro, he advises, she's made things hard enough for herself.

Caro confronts her and demands an explanation. The truth is worse than he could have imagined. Annie is going to have a baby, and what's more, she has known she was pregnant for three or four months, and never breathed a word. She was afraid to talk about it, in case she lost it. She makes a stab at apologising, saying it wasn't a lie when she told him she couldn't have children, she really did think it was impossible. It was an accident, and she's sorry – but she isn't sorry. She's over the moon. A baby, Caro, a baby! She's always wanted a baby. She's so happy. Isn't it wonderful?

No, it is not. How could she do this to him? How could she be so selfish? She knows his feelings. He doesn't want a baby. He can't bear the thought of it. She'll have to get rid of it, please, Annie, please.

Just listen to her! She springs to its defence. The baby is all she cares about now. He should have known something

184

had gone wrong the moment she started shutting him out. He should have realised a usurper had come to push him aside. Annie has already made her choice. If she has to give up one of them, it won't be the baby. She loves it. She loves it more than she loves him. Oh, he knew this would happen.

She'll fight tooth and nail for this baby. It's more than she ever dared to hope for, because she's had three abortions already and –

'You what?' says Caro.

'Three. Three abortions. And another one I lost before I had time to get rid of it. After what they did to my insides I never thought I could conceive another child.'

'You whore.'

'That's right, throw it back in my face. It was so wrong that now you want me to do it again. You're no better than the rest of them. You loved me until you got what you wanted, and if I want something else that's just too bad. Well, I am a whore and I don't care, I'm your whore, you've kept me a whore – '

'Oh, I see. That's what all this is in aid of. You think I'm going to marry you.'

'I thought we were married already? Or was that just more of your talk?'

'You know what I mean. You've never trusted me, and now you think you can trap me into doing what you want.'

'What *I* want? What *I* want? When have we ever done what *I* want? You're the one who always gets what he wants. You've had it so easy all your life. I guess that's why you wanted me – I was the first woman who ever said no to you, and your pride couldn't stand it. Well I'm still saying no. No no no. I'm going to have this baby and if it's got to be a bastard that's fine with me. I wouldn't marry you anyway, even if you went down on your knees. Being a kept woman suits me just fine. It's what I do best. And if being a whore was good enough for your mother it's certainly good enough for the mother of a bastard's bastard – '

'Don't you dare bring my mother into this.'

'Oh God, the sacred parents of the wonderful Caryllac, too holy to talk about . . .'

The look on his face makes her realise, but too late, that what she has said can never be forgiven.

They stare furiously at each other for a minute; then Caro turns on his heel and walks from the room.

Annie's eyeballs are burning. She lies down on the bed, exhausted and numb. Caro has been gone for hours. Perhaps he isn't going to come back.

She would have done anything for him, but this. Why, of all the sacrifices she would gladly make for him does he have to pick on the one thing she cannot do? She would rather die herself. This is probably the last baby she can have. Why is he trying to make her choose? Can't he see that she wants this baby because it's his? There is no choice. The baby can't live without her. Caro can, oh, so easily. He may have already decided to leave her.

They were so happy. Everything was going so well. This can't be the end of it. Oh dear Gods, she would give anything to take back the terrible things she said. He can't just walk away from her, he can't. She loves him so much. That sort of love must have the power to draw him back.

And it does.

He is standing in the doorway, twisting his hat in his hands. Fern leans against his knee. He looks oddly unsure of himself, as if he might after all turn and go away again. His face is filthy. He is covered with tar and dirt, his hair stands up in spikes, his clothes are torn, his lip is bleeding, and there's a bruise darkening on his right cheek.

'Oh Caro, what have you done to yourself?'

'Went down to the waterfront and got mugged.'

'Are you all right?'

'It was some of your brother's friends. They recognised me and let me go. Gave me my money back too. Must be my lucky day.'

Not knowing how else to respond, Annie smiles, tentatively. Caro smiles back. She holds out her arms. He takes a step through the door – then he leaps across the room and buries his face in her lap.

'I'm sorry, Annie.'

'I'm sorry too.'

'No, no, don't be. You were right. I was wrong. I just needed some time to think it through. If you want this baby you must have him. I only want you to stay with me. I love you, Annie. Don't ever leave me, please. Promise.'

'I promise.'

'I couldn't bear it.'

'You won't have to. I'll never leave you. I love you. That's

186

why I want the baby. He'll be your baby too, and I'll love him twice as much because of that.' Annie starts to laugh, happy and relieved. With Caro it's always either tears or laughter, mountain peaks of joy or deep oceans of despair. But who wants a quiet life when they can have Caro? 'Anyway,' says Annie, being practical, 'we shouldn't start thinking of the baby as he. It might be a girl. I think I'd like a daughter.'

She hugs Caro, pressing his face into her dress. It's in there, on the other side of her skin, mocking him. It has won. Nothing can dislodge it from its throne beneath her heart. Annie will go away if he doesn't pretend to welcome it. I hate you, he tells it. You thief. You usurper. The gentle motion of her firm, round belly against his cheeks and mouth makes him want to vomit.

As soon as he hears the good news Bren rushes off to buy a little wooden rattle and a pottery lamb on wheels pulled along by a leather strap. 'It's crazy,' he tells Annie, finding her alone, 'but I almost feel like the granddad. Please can I be sponsor?'

'You know we can't enrol this baby in the Temple. We're not married, whatever Caro says.'

'But surely now – '

'No. We don't talk about it. Don't mention it to him, please.'

'No fear of that. I hardly ever see him these days.'

Paddy, alone among their friends, is less than delighted. He tells Caro that Annie knew perfectly well she ought not to get pregnant again. Those butchers – Paddy spits – tore her around something awful. She almost died of the last one. This baby could kill her if she carries it full term, or it could as easily miscarry – but trying to get rid of it would kill her more certainly than anything.

'You're not happy about it, are you, Caro?'

'You expect me not to care that she's probably going to die? If she hadn't told me she couldn't get pregnant I'd have made sure this never happened. I never wanted a baby. I want her. I want her to live.'

'Don't get in a stew. There's always a risk, but ten to one she'll be fine. She's a tough old bird. Don't blame yourself. It's what she wants. She wanted the other babies, you know. It was the fathers made her get rid of them. Said they'd get rid of her if she didn't.'

Which is the last thing *you'd* have wanted, thinks Caro. And

187

Annie, how could she? Money makes all the difference. It paid her to get rid of those other babies. But with Caro it's different. Caro made the mistake of loving her. Caro can't put his foot down because this time she'd choose the baby. So what does that make her love worth? Whatever the price of a baby's life is, Caro doesn't have it.

Paddy disgusts him. They all disgust him. He avoids Bren. The thought of his beaming red face and burbles of joy is more than Caro can bear.

He flees from their congratulations, but it even pursues him to the Palace. Vivienne hugs and kisses him, dancing with glee at her prospective aunt-hood. How on earth did she find out?

'My maid told me, she got it from Elinor Vacled's groom who heard it from one of the leatherers in Duccarn Street. It is true, isn't it? You must be so happy! Annie must be so pleased, is she pleased? Tell her I think about her. Tell her I would come but I'm not allowed, but I know what I'll do, I'll send my maid. I want to give her a present. I'd make something for her, only you know how rotten I am at embroidery and things. I know, how about a dress, a lying-in dress? Oh, I hope it's a girl, you can name her after me. Your daughter is bound to be absolutely gorgeous.'

'It's a boy,' says Caro.

'Is it really, are you sure? Have you had the auguries taken already?'

'No, I just know.'

Soon he finds himself summoned to speak with the Queen, who is happy to tell him that it has finally been decided to make his position in her Household official. With it come a handsome salary and the award of sleeping-quarters at Court for his personal use. No explanation is given for this sudden decision. The Queen gives him a motherly smile, without referring to or even hinting at Annie and the forthcoming baby. She must be aware of their existence – if Vivienne knows something, the whole Court knows – but the Court clerks have access to the Temple records of births and deaths and marriages, and while no one is going to bother arguing that scatterbrained Vivienne out of the notion that Caro is truly married, the rest of the Court consider Caro's woman to be no more than what Annie described herself as being: a poet's eccentricity, his quaint little love affair with some native piece from Tsvingtori docks, his whore.

Caro returns to the City in a bad mood, not much improved when Annie says that Idris wants him to call in at the theatre.

Idris gets straight to the point. 'When are you moving out?'

'I wasn't thinking of it.'

'Weren't you? Well now, Caryllac, I put up with the dog, and I put up with the woman, but I'll be buried if I'll put up with a baby in my lodging-house. I turn the girls out if they get pregnant. I don't see why you should be any different. You're paying rent for one person, not four. And it's hardly as if you're working for me any more.'

'I'm working on something for you now.'

'What, that *Jackie Fisher*? Give over. I haven't seen anything from you in six months. Blue Alanson could have knocked it up in half the time, while you've been too busy knocking other things up.'

'I don't need this – '

'I need *plays*, Caro. You work for the Court now, and that's all right and proper and as it should be, I'm not saying it isn't, but I need my rooms to house my Company. And it's not as if you can't afford a place of your own, now that you've got your Court appointment.'

'My God, is nothing secret?'

'You know how the good news gets around. Now listen, Caro, I want you and your dog and your bit in pig out by the end of the week, and that's all there is to it. If you should ever happen to finish another play, you know who to bring it to; but let's be honest, your heart was never really in the theatre. We've done some good business together over the years, let's not spoil it by losing our tempers now. Just to show you there's no hard feelings, I could put you in the way of a nice set of rooms in Chicken Street, if you're interested.'

'Don't tell me. You own them.'

'Do you mind? As it happens they belong to my sister's grandson. He's got his poulterer's shop on the ground floor. You'd get a nice bit of fowl there cheap, and the rent's reasonable too, for the area. I've been telling him to hold it for you, just in case.'

Knowing he'd be lucky to find anywhere suitable by the end of the week, Caro finally agrees to go and look at the place. The lodgings on offer take up the whole of the first floor above the poultry shop, and consist of three rooms, cheaply but adequately furnished, looking on to the noisy street. The rooms are connected by a corridor, running the width of the house, its unshuttered windows commanding a view of the courtyard, which contains a well, a small flock of ducks dabbling in a yellow puddle, a large bloodstained wooden block, and a bucket half-filled with chicken heads and giblets. The entire house smells faintly of rotten eggs. The landlord bows and says it would be an honour to welcome a tenant as illustrious as Master Caryllac, before quoting an outrageous rent. Caro bargains him down, and they shake on it.

'You've got your way,' he tells Annie when he returns to the attic. 'We have to move. Happy now?'

'That's right, blame me. It's not my fault. This room was never big enough for us.'

'I didn't want to move. I like it here . . .'

For half an hour they squabble and shout and accuse each other of selfishness. At last Caro exclaims, 'Do you know what we sound like?'

'What?'

'Vuna and Vishnac, having a row. So who I am to talk? I'm sorry, Annie, I'm being absurd.' He sits beside her, resting his head on her shoulder. Annie weaves her fingers through his. 'It doesn't really matter,' he says. 'It's only a room. If you'd like, we can go and look at the new place now.'

'Oh yes, let's.'

Annie is eager to please and be pleased, to mend the rift. Hasn't her clever Caro done well? The lodgings are everything she could wish for. There's so much space, and it's closer to the market, and she won't have so many stairs to climb. Three rooms, Caro, what will we do with them all? A room for them to sleep in – they can put the baby's cradle in there, when he comes – and a room for cooking and eating and talking to friends, which still leaves one room where Caro can work in peace. It's better, Caro, isn't it? We'll be happy here. She hugs him and he kisses her. Everything is perfect.

24

The day set for Caro and Annie to move into their new lodgings coincides with the return of Bernard Derondah's embassy from Andariah. Vivienne has been pestering Caro to make sure he's at Court for the welcoming ceremony – she wants to show Caro off, she can't wait to see Arlo's face – but Caro is glad of an excuse to stay away. He doesn't want to be blamed for any trouble which might arise between him and his half-brother. At

190

best Arlo is an irrelevance, at worst an unnecessary complication, and Caro will be happy to keep out of his way if Arlo will keep out of Caro's.

The move is quickly completed, as their possessions are so few, and he and Annie are discussing the possible purchase of a rug for the bedroom when someone comes rapping frantically on the front door. Annie goes to open it. He hears a woman ask breathlessly, 'Does Master Caryllac Thomasson live here?'

He goes into the corridor to see Vivienne's maid standing in the doorway, flushed and tearful. 'Do you know this woman?' asks Annie.

The maid tries to push past her. 'Oh Master Caryllac, please come,' she beseeches, 'it's my Lady – '

'What's happened?'

'I don't rightly know – some trouble with my Lord and my Lady's brother, they haven't come home with the embassy. It's something awful, everything's turned upside down, and my Lady won't let me see her – I didn't know what else to do, so I came for you. She'll see you, Master, please come – '

'All right, I'm coming. Let's go.'

'Caro! – '

'I have to go, Annie – '

They hurry through the streets of the City and head up the cliff. The maid is so distraught Caro can wring no sense from her, and he races ahead. At the Palace a group of Vivienne's friends and their servants are gathered outside her closed door, biting their nails and looking useless. Maude Vacled runs to greet him. 'Thank God you've come,' she says, taking his arm.

'What's happened?'

'No one's sure exactly, but Arlo is dead. Bash killed him, in Andariah. Some sort of fight over a woman, can you believe it? Bash hasn't come home either. You'd better go in and see her. I don't know what she might have done to herself. She's in a terrible state.'

Caro slips through the door, shutting it behind him.

Vivienne is spread-eagled on the floor, so completely motionless that for one dreadful moment Caro fears she must be dead. Then he sees that she is breathing, in sharp, shallow gasps. He sits down beside her, touches her shoulder. 'Vivvy – '

'Do you know what he *did*?' she screams.

'It doesn't matter. I'm here now, Vivvy, it's all right. Now try to sit up, calm yourself. You'll make yourself ill.'

191

'I wish I was dead!'

'No you don't. Just think how unhappy that would make me.'

'You don't care about me. No one does. I'm horrible and ugly.'

'Oh Vivvy, you're not – '

'He didn't have to marry me. He didn't have to if he didn't want to. He was Arlo's friend.' She begins to thrash about, crying, 'I can't believe he's dead. It's a lie. He'll come back like you did, he's not dead. Everybody's lying to me. I hate them, I hate them . . .'

Caro hauls her up from the floor and wrestles her, kicking and shrieking, to the bed. Her nose is bleeding. He yells for someone to fetch a doctor. Vivienne claws at his arms, screaming that she wants to jump through the window, she wants to die, Arlo's dead, Daddy's dead, Caro's gone away . . .

Her maid arrives with the Queen's physician, who succeeds in forcing a dose of poppy syrup between Vivienne's clenched teeth. 'She'll sleep now,' he tells Caro. 'Rest is the best cure for cases of hysteria.'

'Do you think we could be left alone, please?'

Before he goes, the physician puts the bottle of syrup in Caro's hands, advising him to give the patient another dose if she should wake. From time to time servants sent to inquire after her knock on the door; at one point the King's own valet appears. Vivienne's maid brings a meal for Caro, and he nibbles at it, hardly noticing what he eats. Just after midnight, Vivienne stirs.

'Daddy?'

'No, it's me, Caro. Here, drink this. It will help you sleep.'

'I don't want it. I want Daddy.'

'All right, just drink this first. Come on, drink it, please, or – or Daddy will be angry with you.'

'Daddy's never angry with me.'

'Then drink it for me, please.'

At last she falls asleep again. By now Caro is so exhausted he can hardly keep his eyes open. He leans his head against the bedpost, and is just drifting off, when Edvard filcLaurentin comes quietly through the door. Not perhaps the very last person Caro expected to see, but one of them, and he cannot conceal his surprise. Why didn't his Eminence send his servants, like everybody else?

Edvard picks up a chair and sits beside Caro. 'How is she?'

'She wants her Daddy.'

Caro didn't mean to say that – it seized the chance and sprang from his tongue, no more than the truth and yet sounding like an accusation. Edvard looks at him, rather sadly, then rests his elbow on the chair-arm and puts his face in his hand, like a man too tired to think. For a while neither of them says anything; until Caro, thinking that conversation will be easier to endure than this pregnant silence, remarks, 'You didn't need to come, Eminence.'

'I couldn't sleep. I thought I would probably find you here, and I wanted to see how this little one was taking it. It's good she's sleeping. I've only just come from the Council. We've been up half the night, discussing it. You realise it's a bad blow for all of us, to be publicly humiliated on another Kingdom's soil.'

'What did happen?'

'A sordid business. Vivienne's husband, Basal Uhlanah – '

'Bash,' Caro interrupts. 'Vivvy always calls him Bash.'

'Does she? I wouldn't know. I wasn't very well acquainted with him, as he was very rarely here. Presumably you know he was in Lord Bernard Derondah's employ? He was a very gifted young man, a linguist, very quiet and capable, not at all the sort of boy you'd expect to find in the middle of a mess like this.'

'You talk as if he's dead too.'

'He might as well be. Duelling is a capital offence, and he was, if anything, more at fault than Arlo. He became romantically involved with one of the ladies at the Court in Rouche. I suppose the only people who know all the facts of the case are the two young men involved, and of course that hothead Arlo is dead now, but from what Lord Bernard tells us, it seems that when the time came for them to set off home, Vivienne's husband announced that he intended to bring the young lady with him, and was going to divorce Vivienne and marry her. A lady of very good family as well, I believe, some kin to King Henry. Which doesn't help things at all. As far as I know he had no grounds on which he could have divorced this little one – whether she'd have wanted to divorce him is not for me to say, although I never did think he was the right husband for her. However, that was in her family's hands. So, it transpires that Arlo felt called upon to defend his sister's honour, and challenged young – what did you call him? – Bash. And was

193

killed in the duel. We don't know where Vivienne's husband is now. Apparently he has run off into the east of Andariah with his young lady. We're going to press King Henry to make some attempt to find him and send him home to stand his trial, but I shouldn't imagine he'll let himself be caught very easily. And so far Henry hasn't shown much willingness to co-operate. A huge joke, it seems, and of course the lady's connections incline him towards mercy. It's an embarrassment for us – and as for this poor little one, I don't know how she will bear it, losing both of them at once. Well, I suppose time will have to take its course to put this right. I only wish there was more I could do.'

'You're very good to us, Eminence. We've had nothing but kindness from you.'

'It's good of you to say so,' says Edvard. 'I only wish you really meant it.'

Now it is Caro's turn to look away, his glib tongue temporarily robbed of speech. He would never have expected such directness from Edvard; and Edvard seems to have surprised himself, for he too can find nothing further to say.

Another uneasy silence follows. It is the middle of the night – the candle has burned down to its stub and gone out. No one remembered to shut Vivienne's windows, and the full moon glazes the walls with an honest light, daytime shades of colour simplified to black and white. The Palace is slumbering. Caro and Edvard sit side by side, enfolded in an isolating peacefulness that makes them feel they are the only two people awake in the whole wide world.

Edvard asks Caro, 'Have you ever forgiven me?'

'For what, Eminence?'

'Oh Caro, come now. Even though you've managed to put it behind you, it's not something any human being could ever forget – and I hope you don't think so little of me you imagine I could forget it either.'

Caro takes a deep breath. If Edvard wants to talk about it, there seems no reason not to oblige him. So Caro tells him the truth. 'I never blamed you, Eminence. I wanted to, I tried to. I wanted to hate you. But I couldn't. My father was a soldier, remember? And soldiers have to follow their orders.'

'Yes – well – that is as it happens. Caro, there's something I've been meaning to tell you for quite some time – right from the very beginning of our acquaintance, if I may call it that.

194

I happen to admire you. I think that in many ways you're a remarkable young man, not least in the way you have managed to overcome adversity and achieve as much as you have. Perhaps nothing could have held you back. I value your good opinion, and because of that I'm anxious, perhaps selfishly so, that you shouldn't think worse of me than I deserve. Caro, you remember that night – of course you remember, I'm putting this badly – when we were about to leave for Floried, and you said – you asked me to bring your mother too? I want to tell you that I would have. I meant to do it. I wouldn't have needed his Grace's permission, and in any case I'm sure he wouldn't have objected. But I was never given the chance.'

'Is that supposed to make a difference?'

'Caro, you really ought not to speak to me like that.'

'You invite it, Eminence.'

Edvard reflects on this. Then he says, 'Perhaps I've been taking too much comfort from my good intentions. As you say, it's the outcome, not the intentions, that counts.'

'I said I never blamed you. If you blame yourself, I'm sorry, but there's nothing I can do about it. My mother knew what she was doing. She was an intelligent woman and she never did things on the spur of the moment. It was all thought out. She knew that my father was in Mindared, and she knew you were going to attack it and that sooner or later you'd succeed. And knowing my father as well as she did, she knew he would rather die than surrender. And she didn't want to live without him. That's all there is to it. She loved him, so she died. Simple, really.'

'Well, your father was a very easy man to love. I think you take after him in many ways. Everyone who knew Tom thought very highly of him. I respected him immensely. I was his friend, you know.'

'And Bruno's friend, and Perry's, and Kyrah's.'

'Yes, they were my friends. Surely you don't imagine the war was easy, or, Gods help us, fun for any of us? We didn't enter into it lightly. In fact – well, this is probably something you don't know. When it first became obvious to us that Michael would have to be removed, we approached your father – he was our Captain, in the Guards, and we all looked up to him, even his Grace. He was like an elder brother to us. Well, at first your father was very much in favour of the idea. We might not have gone ahead at all if we hadn't believed we had his support. But

195

then he began to think it would be possible to force an abdication. Of course it was completely unworkable – we can't have a new King as long as the old one is still alive, and two Kings would have been twice the disaster of one Michael. Then your father wanted to put one of the Princes in Michael's place. But that would have opened the door to perpetual warfare. There'd have been no peace until one of the Princes managed to kill all the rest. We believed we needed a clean break, and that was when your father broke with us. Michael was actually killed on the very same day, not more than a half an hour after we had finally concluded that we shared no common ground with Tom. We couldn't afford to give him time to act against us.'

'I see. Well, my father did always have more honour than sense. It's true. He loved his duty and his honour and his damned sword more than he loved my mother and me. Why should he have given his life for a King who was already dead? And my mother loved him more than she loved me. Vivvy's really the only one that I have left.'

'Surely that can't be true. I don't want you to think that I've been prying into your private life, but it's common knowledge that congratulations are in order.'

'Oh yes, there's a little Caro on the way.'

'You seem convinced it will be a boy.'

'Sons for the mother, daughters for the father. It's bound to be a boy. My life goes round in circles. Have you ever been in love, Eminence?'

'A few infatuations when I was a boy. They never came to anything. But they were pretty painful while they lasted.'

'Cured you for life, did they, Eminence?'

Edvard checks his laughter so as not to wake the patient. 'They must have done, and I can't say I'm sorry. Friendship's a much better way to go about bestowing one's affections. There's less pain and a great deal more pleasure. Friends are what makes life worth living – at least I've always found it to be so. Friendship is reliable, while love – you're always afraid of losing it, aren't you? Perhaps love is something so precious it's almost not worth the anxiety of having it. I don't discount the possibility of one day being struck by the thunderbolt, but at my time of life it seems unlikely.'

A notion suddenly comes to Caro, right out of the blue. He can't think why it's occurred to him, unless because it's so improbable that a man like Edvard should go through life without loving anyone. Caro hesitates, fearing he may be about to blunder into an area where Edvard permits no intrusion. Still, it's worth exploring, if he can find a way around Edvard's guard. Cautiously he suggests, 'Of course, your Eminence has the honour of his Grace's friendship.'

'Yes,' Edvard smiles, a little shyly. 'That's one of my great blessings. Naturally, in our present positions and with our responsibilities, the nature of our friendship has altered considerably from what it was when we were children. But I like to think that he still needs me – not only as a Councillor, you know, but as a friend.'

'If you'll excuse my curiosity, Eminence, I'd love to hear the story of how you and his Grace became friends.'

Edvard was only waiting for the invitation. He is more than willing to tell Caro all about it, perhaps because no one else has ever asked, or found the state of Edvard's heart quite as fascinating as Caro does. Edvard says that when he was a child he lived on his father's estates in Rayallah – Rorhah as it was called then – and was taken first to play, later to share tutors, and above all to form useful connections with the Fahlraec's son. How amusing to remember that at first he and Basal were sworn enemies, because Edvard, as the elder, felt he should be the one to dictate their games and amusements. But Edvard wasn't born to be a leader. There was always something irresistible about Basal. It wasn't arrogance, more a confidence that he would get his own way, and that everyone else would prefer his schemes once they understood them. Oh, Basal knew how to make things happen. You could never guess what he might dream up next. He swept Edvard along with his energy; Edvard was the voice of prudence, always afraid that Basal's ideas were too dangerous or too forbidden to put into practice. The boy Basal had a fearlessness bordering on the foolhardy; and he sometimes displayed a streak of violence, or passion, that you might mistake for cruelty. But Basal was never cruel. He simply simmered with impatience at the slowness and dullness of others. Edvard, by comparison, was a very ordinary, unimaginative child, and at times it still seems incredible to him that someone like Basal should have sought for, and treasured, his friendship.

Edvard talks until dawn, laughing, remembering, lingering over parent-defying adventures and scandalous practical jokes, all of Basal's invention. Caro listens, and one might accurately say that the dawn is as much in his comprehension as in the sky. He feels that he has never really understood Edvard filcLaurentin, or Basal Rorhah, until now.

25

'You don't see what I mean,' Vivienne tells Caro. 'I never loved Arlo like I love you. I had to love Arlo because he was my brother, like I have to love Madam because she's my mother, even though I sort of hate her too. I guess in a way he was good for me, he pushed me around and told me what to do and what I shouldn't do. I never know for myself. Oh Fern,' she giggles weakly, 'don't lick my face, you'll give me spots.'

In hopes of cheering Vivienne up a little, Caro has brought Fern to visit her. The giggle is a good sign: Vivienne hasn't laughed, or smiled, for weeks. She ruffles her nose through the dog's fur and sighs, 'Mmm, Fletch-smell. I still miss him awfully. I wish I could have another dog.'

'A great big ferocious dog for a ferocious little girl.'

'You should boss me around more, Caro. I'd appreciate it.'

'You know you've always had me in the palm of your hand.'

Vivienne bites her lip. All Fern's good work is undone; Vivienne's face crumples and she bursts into tears. 'Oh Caro, you're so nice to me and I'm so horrible.'

'You must stop thinking like that.'

'But it's true, you don't know. You don't know what awful things I used to think.'

'It doesn't matter now.'

'Yes it does. It matters for ever. Caro, when I was really little I used – I used to hate you. I'm so sorry. I used – ' she hiccups – 'I used to wish you were *dead*, I did, because then Daddy would be home with us all the time. I thought you took him away from me. I didn't understand. And then when you came to live with us, and I saw you, I don't know, I just couldn't hate you any more. I felt sorry for you but I liked you too, I couldn't help liking you, you just looked so nice and I knew we were going to be friends. I wish I'd never wished that, I hate remembering it. I'd hate it if you were dead. I expect you despise me now.'

'Of course I don't.'

'I had to tell you. It's been preying on my mind ever since I heard about Arlo. I mean, if I died tomorrow, or something, I'd want to have told you, so that you could forgive me.'

'There's nothing to forgive.'

'Caro, you know when Daddy died, I felt like it was my fault, I was being punished for being so wicked. And anyway, I know now that you don't stop loving people just because they're dead.'

Caro tries his best to jolly her out of such morbid thoughts, but Vivienne will not be comforted. Weeks have passed with scarcely any improvement in her condition. She lies in bed, staring at the ceiling, dozing fitfully at odd hours of the day and night, her sleep broken by nightmares. She keeps lapsing back into a fever, and picks listlessly at her food. The physician says it is only the shock of sudden grief on over-excitable female nerves. Time and rest will mend her. Caro wishes she would try to exert herself a little more, but he hasn't the heart to push her.

Vivienne's affliction and the circumstances surrounding it are a source of great interest to the entire Court. She has many well-wishers who bring flowers, presents, and Court gossip. The Queen often comes to sit with her, patting her hand and advising her to resign herself to the will of the Gods. Edvard filcLaurentin is also a frequent visitor, though he finds little to say to her.

'He makes me nervous,' Vivienne complains to Caro.

'He's concerned about you.'

'He is not. I know what he wants. He's always been leering after me. It gives me the creeps, because he's not – you know – he's not like a proper man.'

'What do you mean?'

'Well, listen. When he and his Grace were younger they – ugh, I don't know how to say it – they were like, you know, like Lord Edvard was his Grace's woman.'

'How do you know that?'

'Everybody says it. It must be true. I mean, most boys go through that, don't they, before they're married? That's why Grandmama never wanted Arlo to come to Court. But most boys grow out of it. They get married. But Lord Edvard's never got married, and that's why, so you see it must be true. You should be careful with him, Caro. You're just the sort of boy horrible old men like him go after.'

Caro smiles, 'I think I'm safe enough.'

'Well, I wish he'd leave me alone. I wish they all would.'

Determined to be on hand whenever Vivienne should need him, Caro is spending most of his time at Court. His lodgings – he tries and fails to think of them as home – don't offer much of a welcome when he goes there. Annie's fat stomach proceeds her as she follows him from room to room, wearing him down with her complaints. That third one is always present, a creature curled inside her, biding its time, sniggering at each harsh word and angry insult that drives them further apart.

Annie makes sour remarks about living with a stranger, and hints, without coming right out and saying it, that Vivienne is revelling in being the centre of attention. Annie is spoiling for a fight, and Caro can't face that, so he goes down to the Conqueror for a quiet drink and the chance of some civilised conversation with literary-minded friends in which the words Court, Vivienne, Annie and baby are never mentioned. The person he does run into, however, is Bren, who is sitting in the corner with a few members of the Company. Caro tries to avoid being spotted, but is caught in the act. Bren bears down on him. Caro dredges up what he hopes will be a neutral subject, and asks, 'Seen much of the Black Bull lately?'

'Bullocks went off to the wine fairs in Duccarn three months ago. Of course you wouldn't know that. I can't remember the last time we saw your face down here. You know, Caro, when you were first called up to Court nobody could have been more happy for you than I was. I never dreamt that once you got what you wanted you'd turn your back on all of us. We miss you, you know, even if you don't miss us.'

'That's not true. It's not my choice to spend so much time at Court. I have obligations.'

'And what about Annie, eh? Don't you have any obligations to her? I hate to see her moping around in those big empty rooms while you're having fun at Court.'

'I am not having fun.'

'If you ask me, it's about time you married that poor girl, that's what it is.'

'I'm not asking you,' says Caro, losing control of his temper, 'so shut up.'

'Oh, excuse me, Lord Caro. Sorry I spoke. Of course you're far too good for us now. You use people and then you drop them, that's what you do. I hope you're proud of yourself. You'd just better watch out. It won't last. I've been through it myself, and when it's your turn to get dropped by the Court and you come back down here you may well find all your friends have forgotten you.'

Caro gets up and goes home, ready now for the fight he walked out on. Annie is in the bedroom, hemming baby blankets. 'I've fallen out with Bren,' he tells her, 'thanks to you.'

'What have I done now?'

'What did you have to go on at him about us getting married for?'

'I didn't. Quite frankly, Caro, I really don't care any more. If it's going to go on like this I'd be better off by myself.'

'Do you mean that?'

'Oh, I don't know. I don't know. I keep promising myself I won't nag at you. I don't know why I do it. It's just so miserable being here by myself all the time.'

'I love you, Annie.'

'I love you too, but what's the point if you're never here?'

'It won't last for much longer, I promise. But right now Vivvy needs me. I can't desert her – and I don't think you'd really want me to. Surely you couldn't trust a man whose own sister couldn't rely on him?'

'You always know how to twist things round so you come out in the right.'

'I will be here more, I'll try. I have no time to myself either. I've hardly written anything for weeks.'

'I see. You want to come home to write.'

Caro sits beside her. 'Don't put words in my mouth that aren't in my heart,' he says, taking her hand. Annie trembles, too proud or ashamed to ask. He knows he ought to make more of an effort. Annie wants him to kiss her, embrace and desire her. He wishes he could. But that bump in her belly comes between them. He can't bring himself to touch it.

Annie kisses him on the cheek, an affectionate peck. He doesn't respond. They haven't made love for weeks, and Annie aches for it. 'I need you too,' she whispers, running a hand up the inside of his leg. Annie is well-trained in all the tricks for arousing a man's desire, though she never thought she'd stoop to using them on Caro. She kisses his neck, then his ear, then his mouth. She will be a whore for the sake of a fuck. She can't stop herself; and she hates Caro for bringing her so low.

Not wanting to offend her, Caro gives in. He makes love carefully, avoiding her stomach as best he can, and her swollen blue-veined breasts with their darkened nipples. Annie wraps her legs around him. It takes all his self-control not to pull away.

'Got a bad taste in your mouth?' asks Annie afterwards.

'It can't be good for the baby.'

'That's your excuse, is it? Don't talk to me. I don't want to listen. Go away and do your writing. It's what you came home for.'

Another time Caro comes home to find Paddy installed beside the blazing fireplace with his feet up on the table, reading one of Caro's books and looking very much at his ease. 'Hullo, my man,' he greets Caro cheerfully. 'Haven't seen much of you lately. The Tar Barrel's pretty lifeless these days without your little lectures to get them going. Or would you rather I didn't remind you? Every man must serve his master, and he who pays the piper calls the tune, isn't that so, Caryllac?'

Caro tracks Annie to the bedroom and demands, 'Is he living here?'

'Just for a while. He had no where else to go after the ropemaker's burnt down – '

'The house with the green shutters? It burnt down?'

'The day before yesterday. Didn't you hear about it? Aren't your great Lords and Ladies aware of anything that goes on down here, while they're up in the clouds? The whole of Hemp Alley was gutted. Half a dozen people were burnt alive. Paddy was lucky to escape. He's got another place lined up to go to in a couple of weeks, but in the meantime I said he could stay here. I didn't think you'd mind. You're never here anyway.'

'I don't want that parasite living in my house.'

'What else could I do? Leave him in the gutter? When it comes to your sister, who isn't even your proper sister, nothing is too much trouble, but when it comes to my brother you want to shut the door in his face. Well, I'm not having it. I want him here. It makes a change to have some company.'

'You only know one way to live, don't you? I thought we were different. I thought you came to live with me because you loved me. But all you and Paddy know how to do is spunge off men. You're out for what you can get.'

'I get precious little from you, that's for sure!'

'You've had everything from me. I've given you everything you wanted. You wanted these lodgings. And now I can't even call my home my own.'

'Well then it's lucky you've got somewhere else to go, isn't it?'

And so they go on quarrelling, relentlessly, for hours and days. They now seem to crave fights as once, not so long ago, they craved each other's bodies. He comes home to quarrel. She looks forward to his return, so that they can pick up the argument where they left off. Eating, sleeping, working, and rational conversation merely fill in the time between bouts. Any niggling sin of omission or commission is a sufficient excuse to start turning the well-worn grindstone of accusations and resentment. Only exhaustion can enforce a temporary truce.

During these lulls one of them will always say, 'I don't want to fight with you,' and the other will laugh, 'Neither do I, it's ridiculous.' They embrace, apologise, and promise that things will be different from now on; as if they didn't know that the argument will erupt again as soon as it has regained its strength.

'I love you, Caro.'

'I love you too, Annie.'

But neither Caro nor Annie is sure that they mean this, any more.

26

November brings the last trading-ships of the season into Tsvingtori harbour, but still no word on the whereabouts of the missing Lord Bash Uhlanah and his adulterous lady-love. Nothing can now be expected from Andariah until the spring, if then. His Grace King Basal is reluctant to leave the matter unresolved, and Bash is therefore tried in his absence, found guilty of murder, duelling, shameful misconduct and treason, and sentenced to death. All his property is sequestered. Arlo is also tried posthumously on all the same charges but that of murder, and also found guilty; his goods and chattels are made over to his family. Vivienne is declared a widow, and her dowry, a very handsome sum, is returned to her. His Grace kindly takes it upon himself to visit Vivienne and explain the situation, pointing out that she will have control of her dowry, and that she is free to marry again, should she wish to do so. The choice will be entirely her own. Vivienne is overwhelmed by this display of royal benevolence – that *he* should come, in person, and go to so much trouble just for her!

'Oh Caro, you can't imagine how I felt. I thought I would

die when he came in. I tried to get out of bed to prostrate myself, but he stopped me. I didn't know where to look. And I was such a mess, I wanted to hide. He was so nice I can't tell you. I never thought he was like that at all. You know what he called me? He called me kitten. No one's called me that since Daddy. I think he's the nicest man in the world, after you. He said I should eat more and fatten up and get pretty again. He said I was pretty, Caro! I mean, I know he was just saying it to make me feel better, but if his Grace wants me to try and get better I really *have* to try, don't I?'

A few days later Caro is surprised, and delighted, to find his sister up and about in a flurry of activity. It soon transpires that he has the King to thank for re-animating Vivienne's spirits, for his Grace has just paid another visit and scolded her, in the most gentlemanly way possible, for over-indulging her grief. Vivienne recounts every word the King uttered. He said that he stood in the place of a father to her. The Queen needs her, he said. He said she used to be like a little ray of sunshine. He said everybody misses her happy laugh and pretty face about the Court.

Vivienne's maid is unrolling a bolt of black mourning silk across the carpet. It's a present from the Queen, and look, Caro, Maude has given Vivienne this beautiful pair of black doe-skin gloves. And see this, Caro, this dark purple Farzanah lace? It's really rare. His Grace gave it to her. Oh, and Lord Edvard has given her a little embossed book of devotions, how dull.

'His Grace said Arlo wouldn't have wanted me to lie in bed and pine away. He said I have to try and enjoy life twice as much now, for Arlo. That's true, really, isn't it, Caro?'

Ingenuous Vivienne, trusting in the simple sincerity of kindness. Caro is less inclined to take Basal Rorhah's amiability at face value. He would like to know the real reason behind this sudden upsurge of interest in Vivienne.

Is it to gratify his wife? Vivienne has always been a prime favourite with the Queen, and Caro can see for himself that Vivienne's absence has deprived the Queen's Household of much of its animation, and nearly all its good humour. Maude Vacled has complained that the King doesn't spend half as much time in the Queen's apartments as he did when Vivienne was around to liven things up. So, is Basal Rorhah considering his own domestic comfort when he tries to hurry Vivienne back to her duties?

Or – much more likely – is it for Edvard's sake? Caro is beginning to think that there is something in what Vivienne said – or at least, that she was right to assume that disinterested kindness was not the only motive behind Edvard's frequent visits to her sickbed. The other things she whispered about Edvard Caro dismisses as the unimaginative gossip of banal minds. Edvard likes women, all right. He definitely likes Vivienne. During the course of one of their conversations, soon after the onset of Vivienne's illness, Edvard confided to Caro that he had indeed once wondered, briefly, in a speculative way, whether he might not have offered for her if Bash had not got there first; but, Edvard laughingly added, this was only after she was safely married to another man, and so there was no danger of speculation becoming intention.

In any case, said Edvard, he would probably not make any better a husband for Vivienne than Bash had. The last thing she needs to do is rush straight from one mismatch into another. They would never suit. They are too far apart in age; they have not a single interest in common. Edvard has repeated these arguments so often, it can only be because he is trying to talk himself out of the notion that he ought to wed Vivienne.

Caro doesn't for one moment suppose that Edvard really loves his sister, but he can see that Vivienne is exactly the sort of girl to appeal to a rather lonely, aging bachelor. Until her illness damped her down she was vivacious, chatty and carefree, and she would exert all the charm of an opposite on Edvard's staid conscientiousness. She is also quite evidently in need of some man of good sense to look after her, and that, for Edvard, is a more attractive sensation than passion.

Caro's unvoiced opinion is that, since the choice of her next husband has been left up to Vivienne, it's probably just as well if Edvard refrains from setting his heart on her. However, it's quite possible that for reasons of his own the King would like to see his Chancellor married. And if Edvard wants Vivienne, it can't cost the King much in time or effort to win the girl's trust and push her in the direction of his friend. Basal Rorhah is renowned for his love of practical jokes, and, apart from anything else, it would be great fun to watch Edvard being led a merry dance by a scatter-brained girl almost half his age.

The days leading up to the Winter Solstice bring a new scandal, casting Vivienne's stale griefs into the shade. Proud Elinor, the Lily of Vacled, has been sent away from Court in

205

disgrace. She fell foul of the law of nature and got herself with child, and then aggravated her guilt by concealing the pregnancy from his Grace until it was too late to do anything about it. She will have to give birth to it now, but the child, a half-royal bastard with too much noble blood in its veins, will not be allowed to live to be a danger to the Princes, and Elinor's beautiful face will never be seen at Court again.

Vivienne astonishes Caro by sobbing her heart out over this drama. 'But you never even liked her,' he protests.

'I know, but it's so sad. Elinor must want her baby, she could easily have got rid of it if she didn't and nobody would have been any the wiser, and then none of this would have happened to her. Her Grace says, when we talk about it – not about Elinor, she never mentions Elinor or anything like that – but when we talk about babies and things, her Grace says it's natural to want babies with the man you love. You must know. Annie's having your baby, because she loves you. It's so awful for Elinor never to be able to see his Grace again. I'd die if it was me. It's awful for his Grace, too. He's a good father, he really is, he's always nice to me and you know how he loves little Prince Hans. It must have been a terrible decision for him to make. I don't know how Elinor could have done it to him, except if she didn't really love him, but if she didn't, you know, nothing makes sense. Everything's so unfair. It seems so unfair on the poor little baby, to be born just to die. I do understand, I know why it has to be like that, I know it's right really but it just seems wrong.'

What can Caro say? He has walked this same knife-edge, and it is no credit to him that he did not get his way. He of course can only bully and sulk: the King gives an order and it is done. But is cruelty any less cruel because it is done for reasons of the heart instead of reasons of state? He, Caro, he who of all people should know the difference between right and wrong, has behaved no better than the King, and the realisation sickens him. Annie is risking her life – Annie might die for the sake of the thing she wants. Caro should be able to understand that. He was so proud of his courage and vision and single-mindedness – and when it came to the point he didn't respect those qualities in the one he loves best. Here's Annie acting as he ought to act, when he's been acting like a King. He has done nothing but blame her. They might have so little time left together. He has wasted too much of it already.

Chastened and contrite, Caro goes home resolved to mend his ways, to spend more time with Annie, to show her more tenderness, and to summon up some spirit of welcome for the son who is now an active, kicking presence inside her.

Caro and Annie talk far into the night, patching up their differences. Annie goes off to bed feeling happier than she has for months. Caro cannot sleep. His head is buzzing and he has work to do.

He spreads his materials across the table, intending to get on with the collection of hymns he is preparing for the Queen. She has commissioned a set of twelve, one for each month, each dedicated to the guardian deity of that month: blind Vishnac for dark January, strength slumbering; Urac for March, when soldiers polish their swords and oil their armour, anticipating the summer of warfare ahead; Asdura for the sweetness and promise of April; the Sun in the splendour of June, Vuna in the passion of August, Isen Mathred in the abundance of September; Great Adonac for the fires of December, the pinching frost and the remembrance of mortality. These hymns are not for public consumption. One copy only is to be made, and her Grace is bringing a famous illuminator, said to have the finest hand in the Kingdom, from Mehed to inscribe Caro's words on sheets of vellum edged with gold, already on order from the most illustrious parchment-merchant in the City.

Queen Ursula abounds in a simple and fervent faith. She is, after all, married to a God. Even if this article of faith were not the linchpin holding the Kingdom of Brychmachrye together, Basal Rorhah's career and the force of his personality would have helped inspire the legend that he is more than human. Which is all to the good, as far as Caro's concerned. The incompetence of a Michael Andaranah would only have confused the issue. Caro sees no harm in encouraging the Queen's conviction that her dear Caryllac, such a decent young man, shares her faith. Why bother to disillusion her? Why distress an already weak intellect? Her influence goes no further than her apartments, and she is of no importance save as the official source of Caro's income. There is nothing to be gained by overturning her misconceptions: she is not of Edvard filcLaurentin's calibre. She will be sorry to lose Caro, of course, but she will never understand why it had to happen.

Something is going to happen. Caro can feel it, in his water as Bren would say. Probably it will take the shape of an external event. A fresh wave of treason trials, perhaps, the last mopping up of civil war leftovers. Such a possibility has been rumoured. Or it may be a popular uprising, or an eclipse. Caro will know when it happens. He is ready, his ground is prepared, he lives in daily expectation of a signal to proceed. The suspense is disrupting his poetry. He has difficulty abstracting the Gods. They keep turning into portraits of people he knows – a crapulous Adonac with Bren's beefy face, propping up the gates of heaven and bellowing a tavern welcome; ridiculous caricatures. Vishnac as Edvard, devoted and blind. Elinor Vacled a sluttish Asdura, her heart swollen with ambition and pride, who aspired to divinity, and was destroyed.

He cannot concentrate on the Queen's poems. Edvard says the gods are images of perfection; how can Caro waste his time trying to describe a perfect circle when all around him the tattered, untidy lives of men are crying out to be heard? When Brychmachrye herself suffers daily abuse in silence? It is as if everything he has ever seen, or heard, or thought is coming to the boil at once inside Caro's skull, bubbling with a single, comprehensive significance that reveals its own form, its own poem, and bursts forth faster than Caro can write it down.

In part it is Elinor's story, and Annie's story, and all the sad little stories he has heard of maids from the Palace violated by men they had no power to resist, men who used them for half an hour's amusement and then, when complications resulted, cast them out to fend for themselves in the streets of a City that can always make room for bastards, for it is the head and heart of a bastard nation. It is Caro's story, and Brychmachrye's story; it is the story of spoilt promise and wasted chances.

His poetry stutters and fumbles over the need for absolute clarity. He begins it in native, starts over again in Andarian, goes back to the native version, and before he knows how it could have happened he has lost any sense of a distinction between the two, choosing here a word from his mother's tongue and there a word from his father's as each offers the greater precision of meaning. This poem cannot afford to respect the struggles Caro has always made to keep the two languages separate in his mind. It draws on every part of him, overriding his resistance. It forces those parts to co-operate, subdues their mutual antagonism, until Caro, absorbed in the effort to prove equal to the demands of this poem, forgets that he believed a bastard must always be at war with himself, denying his Andarian half, hating the impurity that will not permit him to be wholly native. While he writes his heart is at one with the blood that makes it beat. He is both his father and his mother, he is Annie and Vivienne, Bren and Edvard, he is the whole of Brychmachrye in one flesh. He is the son of a fishgutter and the grandson of a Fahlraec, and he must rejoice in it, for at last he understands – or his poetry understands – that his bastardy is the essence of his genius, integral to his fate: who else but a bastard could put words in the mouth of Brychmachrye? This poem ought to sound piecemeal, wrong, incomprehensible as the yappings of mongrels; and yet to Caro's ears it is a seamless unity. He has never expressed himself so clearly.

Later he will have to pick this poem apart and re-write it, twice, filling up the gaps that the loss of the foreign words will leave in each language. It will be interesting to see how the two versions differ once they are separated. That's when the real work will begin, all hard slog and no inspiration. Caro has the feeling that this is how it is always going to be, from now on. His poetry has found its voice. It will resist any attempt to return to the old division between pure court-speech and pure native. Caro will have to be both its scribe and its translator. But he must try. This poem will be of no use to anyone, unless everyone can understand it.

27

One evening at the beginning of February Caro returns from Court to a house overrun with women – Annie's friends, the poulterer's wife and elder daughters, several neighbours from up the street, and the midwife, a friend of Paddy's but highly recommended, who bars Caro's entrance and tells him she doesn't need any men under her feet, she's had more than enough experience in helping women and babies through difficult births, thank you . . . Fortunately Paddy has been hanging around waiting for Caro, and takes him away to the Conqueror, where Bren has lined up a row of beers in expectation of their arrival. Former hard feelings are brushed aside. The important thing is to keep Caro's mind off Annie. Paddy tells dirty stories, and Bren fills Caro in on all the Company news – they've found a new playwright, a refugee from one of the provincial travelling companies who decided to chuck in the roaming life, turn his hand to the pen, and seek his fortune in Tsvingtori. A nice enough bloke and an old stager; knows his craft like the back of his hand; but he hasn't got Caro's touch. There's no poetry in him, just solid workmanship, and he knows it himself, more's to his credit. He'd like to meet Caro, if Caro will condescend. Don't put it like that, Caro slurs, of course I will. Midnight passes and the tavern gradually empties. Mind if I shut up? asks the landlord, eyeing the last three customers slumped over their mugs. They can put their heads down on the table, if they like. He can see they're too drunk to go anywhere.

Early next morning the landlord's wife is sweeping up to a background chorus of snores, when one of Annie's friends comes in, asks for Caro, sees him, and shakes him gently awake. Bleary-eyed, Caro raises his head and wonders what's going on; then he wakes up sharply and remembers. Is Annie all right? The friend smiles, yes, it wasn't easy, at one point they even thought they might lose her, but she's fine now, she's pulled through just fine.

Something is wrong, though. Caro can see it in her face. She doesn't want to tell him. It's the baby, isn't it? Well, she says, Annie's afraid you'll be disappointed. She said you wanted a boy –

'It's a girl?' says Caro incredulously.

He rushes home. The women are celebrating together in the living room, drinking wine from a keg brought up by the poulterer's wife and gabbling nineteen to the dozen. Caro goes into the bedroom. Annie is sleeping, her hair matted in rats'-tails, dark rings around her eyes. Caro bends over the cradle. Here she is, the cause of all this alarm, two filmy blue eyes staring straight through him and on top of her head a full complement of tight, woolly brown curls. She takes one look at her father, fills her lungs, and bawls for all she's worth.

'Oh Caro,' says Annie sleepily.

'She's crying.'

'Pick her up, then.'

Caro fumbles around, terrified that one touch of his hand might crack the eggshell fragility of his daughter's awkward skull. At last he manages to scoop her up, an untidy tangle of blankets and swaddling clothes. She blows a bubble of spit at him.

'What do you think of her?' asks Annie.

'She looks like a frog.'

'Takes after you, I guess. Whose hair is that?'

'My father's.'

He perches gingerly on the edge of the bed, wishing Annie would take the burden from his arms. 'She's still crying.'

'Put your finger in her mouth.'

Caro offers his little finger. His daughter sucks it, greedily, eyes shut, the expression of blissful contentment on her face matched by the dawning stupefaction on Caro's.

Annie watches them for a while, then says, 'She must be hungry. Give her to me.'

'In a minute.'

'It's all right, isn't it, Caro? I mean, you were so sure it was going to be a boy.'

'No,' says Caro, 'she's perfect. She's the one I wanted.'

Isn't fate full of strange twists? Caro feared he would lose Annie to their son, and instead, Annie has lost Caro to their daughter.

'Look, Annie, look, she smiled at me.'

'It's just wind.'

'She knows who her father is, don't you, my sweetheart.'

Well, Annie wanted him home from Court, so really she ought to be pleased. Official summons are the only things that can drag him away from his daughter's side. Annie loves her daughter none the less for having taken over Caro's heart. On the contrary, she's amused: watching him play with the baby fills her with the same tender indulgence she once lavished on other people's children. Sometimes her heart still leaps and warms towards him. If only it could last. They might have a chance to be happy together, treating each other kindly for the sake of the child in whom they both have a stake, whom they both love. But Annie doesn't have much faith left in the staying power of Caro's affections. Just wait till the baby learns to walk and talk, to have her own opinions, to demand something of him! No, Caro's infatuation won't last. He's too much in love with himself.

Once Annie would have died for him; now she would kill to protect her child, and that's the difference. Her daughter is a part of herself, and Annie loves her as she does her own eyes, her nerves, her soul. When her daughter cries Annie feels the pain, in her womb, in her breasts. Caro merely panics. He rushes to her cradle at the first hint of a whimper, but Annie is the one who can soothe her with a little gentle rocking, calming two beating hearts. To Caro, every cough is an occasion for terror, certain symptom of a fatal illness; every coo and gurgle is an attempt to talk, further proof of his daughter's prodigious intelligence. He parades her among his friends, never doubting that their compliments are completely sincere. Privately Annie thinks the child is rather ugly, and doesn't take after Caro in the least. But that's irrelevant. Plain or pretty, clever or stupid, she will be her daughter's mother and raise her, watch over her, feel proud of her, until the day she dies. Of no other love in her life has Annie been able to say this much: that it will not come to an end.

Fern's jealousy knows no bounds, but she too has been supplanted – one snarl, one hungry look, and Caro packed her off to stay with Bren until she learns to know her place.

The baby's cradle looks like one of the Clerkden notice-boards. Caro has pinned little love-poems all over it. Annie reads them, and is troubled with foreboding, though whether for herself or her daughter she can't say, because they are one flesh. Oh daughter, she thinks, he loved me too, once. Daughters can't choose their fathers. Women choose their lovers. In the end we have to protect ourselves.

28

Absorbed as he is in his daughter, Caro cannot drum up much interest for the wax and wane of Court affairs. Nothing new ever happens at Court. It's the same old round of petty rivalries and meaningless feuds and shipwrecked friendships and endless backbiting that has always gone on and always will. These things go in one ear and out the other: Caro's head, spinning with the joys of fatherhood, cannot accommodate them.

Nevertheless he has noticed, because he is in the habit of noticing things, that Vivienne seems much more like her old self these days. She's somewhat quieter than she used to be, and has acquired a little polish, or maturity. And she's taken up with some new friends, older, more sophisticated women. And Edvard seems more preoccupied than ever. But none of this has really registered in Caro's thoughts. He is happy for Vivienne, and relieved that she is no longer making heavy demands on time he would rather spend elsewhere. He obeys when he is sent for, fulfils his duties, and takes his leave as soon as he decently can. The Queen's poems have been completed: that's another nuisance out of the way.

Between the birth of his daughter and the beginning of April the sum of time Caro spends at Court amounts to less than a week, all told. In the second week of April the Lady Maude Vacled invites him, in his anomalous role as part-guest, part-entertainment, to a lunch she is giving to celebrate her birthday. They are dining out in the Palace grounds, under the fragrance of the blossoming May trees, enjoying the warm spell of spring weather. Musicians from the Queen's Household stroll up and down, diverting their senses with elegant airs. The Queen of course has been invited, and of course has declined. She rarely leaves her apartments. Caro comes armed with poems, including a short, flattering, rhyming bit of nonsense written in the Lady Maude's honour. He arrives late, apologising and looking around for Vivienne. Strange – she is nowhere to be seen. Yet parties are meat and drink to her, and the Lady Maude is her most particular friend. Is she ill? A relapse? Maude laughs at the question, says no, looks arch, and asks him to amuse them. He obliges. Later, when they are lounging on rugs spread over the grass, drinking wine, Maude takes a seat beside him, leans forward, and begins to speak in a confidential tone:

'I would have invited Vivvy, but you know how it is. I don't bear her any ill-will, actually I'm pleased for her, but in my position one can't be too careful. Especially after the trouble with Nell. After all, I'm still a lady-in-waiting, and much as I adore Vivvy, my first duty is to her Grace.'

Maude seems to expect him to understand what she's talking about. Not wanting to look ignorant, Caro racks his brains. Vivienne has got herself into a scrape again, that must be it, and she hasn't dared to tell him. This hint about ladies-in-waiting, that must be a clue. Now that he comes to think about it, on the few occasions over the last two months when he has been in the Queen's apartments, Vivienne has been conspicuous by her absence. He asks Maude, 'Has Vivvy lost her place, Lady?'

Maude laughs hugely. 'Oh no. Her Grace would never do that. She prefers to pretend not to know.'

Caro looks blank. Maude flutters her fan coyly, then snaps it shut and taps his knee. 'Now now, there's no need for all this native prudishness. You don't have to pretend with me. I owe my place at Court to Nell. You must be pleased, surely. I know we were when it happened to our family. It is an honour, and your favour's safe.'

The face of the young man opposite her is a study in bewilderment, which, after a moment, Maude begins to share. She isn't usually slow on the uptake, but this seems incredible. 'You really don't know?' she asks.

Think, Caro. Fit together all the little details vaguely noticed, never dwelt on, and soon dismissed. Vivienne in a bloom of happiness; Vivienne taking uncharacteristically great pains with her appearance; Vivienne walking as if on clouds. Vivienne – why didn't he see it before? – in love. But not with Edvard, a man practised in resigning himself to disappointment. Edvard more morose than ever, new lines of bitterness carving his mouth. Vivienne unwelcome in the Queen's apartments, when she was always so popular in that quarter. The slight, almost involuntary cooling of the Queen's attitude towards himself, and the visible pains she takes to overcome it, as if to say, it is not your fault.

Love, regrets and jealousy swirling in the rose-water of the Court. Caro could have smelt it if he'd stopped to think. Especially after the trouble with Elinor. He hasn't had much time for Vivienne these last weeks, but when they have been together, her conversation has lingered, lovingly, on the splendour, the perfections, the all-encompassing wonderfulness of the King.

'Not Vivvy,' says Caro.

Too late to deny it. He knows it is true. It all makes a horrible sort of sense. It happened right under his nose and he didn't see it, he didn't stop it, and now it feels like someone cut him or he cut himself and has only just realised, seeing the blood.

Maude is laughing again. 'Isn't that just like a brother. Always underrating their own sisters. Vivvy's quite as attractive in her way as you are, and just as popular with the opposite sex. Though I say it of my own sister, Nell was rather raw meat. Vivvy has a piquancy, and you know what they say, a change is as good as a rest. None of us – Caro, Caro, where are you going? Caro, come back here . . .'

He runs off, not caring in which direction as long as he gets away from their music and their laughter. Once, in a corner of the gardens, he stops to throw up, then walks on at random, heart pounding against his empty stomach. Not Vivvy. How could she? How could she let that man touch her? That filth, that murderer, that employer of Caro's. He's so ugly. And why would he want her? His Court is full of willing women who are also beautiful. It's an honour. Why settle his fancy on a sallow, noisy bag of bones?

Caro needs to sit down. He needs to think. Think, something he's done far too little of lately.

As if he could have stopped it. Are your intentions honourable, Sir? My attentions are always an honour, bastard.

Nothing happens by accident. The King's whims, the King's pleasures are his fate. That is true in principle – religiously true, one might say, of every subject in Brychmachrye; and it is particularly true, historically true, of Caro.

If he gave way to his first instinct and stormed up to her rooms, hit her, shouted at her, and dragged her away from this place, he would still change nothing. Fate, though often incomprehensible, is unescapable. The King isn't sleeping with Vivienne for the conscious purpose of injuring Caro. He is doing it because he has to. Fate is the weaver controlling the loom, and where Caro differs from most people is in understanding the pattern being woven for him out of other people's lives. The King had to make Vivienne his mistress, just as Elinor Vacled had to become pregnant with a royal bastard she would not be allowed to keep, and Caro had to become so famous that the King would seek to number him among the treasures of his Court; just as Bren's wagons were the ones which had to pick Caro up, and the three men in his mother's attic had to be betrayed to the young Commander, and Edvard had to be the one who took him to Floried and to no other place, and he, Caro, had to have a native mother and an Andarian father. These circumstances are the planets in his constellation. Vivienne is his falling star, his earthquake, his eclipse, the sign he was waiting for. In taking her, Basal Rorhah has at last taken everything from Caro. This is what was bound to happen. It has the structure of a poem. Each line follows on from the one before and leads on to the next. It can be construed in one way only, and no other. Vivienne's loss of virtue is a simple metaphor, designed to be understood by a poet who is himself a metaphor, a bastard, half-native and half-Andarian like his country.

He goes into the Palace and walks along the mostly deserted corridors, passing a few servants, nodding to a few clerks, until he comes to two Guards standing outside a closed door. In this part of the Palace there are few sounds but the eternal scratch of pens pushing, the drudgery of government. Caro rarely has a reason to come here, and the Guards look surprised to see him. He says, 'I'd like to speak to his Eminence, please, if he is free.'

The Guards do not demur. They know their Lord Chancellor is always happy to spare a few minutes for her Grace's Poet. One goes in to announce him. Edvard looks up from scrolls of parchment and smiles, 'I didn't expect to see you today.'

'Can we talk privately, Eminence?'

Edvard dismisses his clerks and Guards, who shut the door behind them. 'Is there something on your mind, Caro?'

'I've come to tell you I'm leaving.'

Perhaps Edvard chooses to misunderstand. He says, 'Have you come from the lady Maude's party? You've had a lovely day for it. I'm glad you came to see me before you go, it's time I took a little break. Would you like some tea? I don't drink wine when I'm working.'

'Leaving,' says Caro. 'Leaving for good. Leaving Court and never coming back.'

Edvard takes a closer look at him, observes the whiteness around Caro's mouth, the over-bright eyes, and smells the faint sourness of vomit on his breath. 'Are you ill?' he asks. 'Please, sit down. Something has upset you. Tell me what it is. You know I'll do what I can for you.'

'You can't do anything. You can't even help yourself. Why did you let him do it? Everyone says you're the only man at Court who can talk him out of doing something. Didn't you succeed in making him listen? Or didn't you try? I'd have preferred you. At least you would have taken her honourably, and not made a whore out of her.'

'Are you referring to the lady Vivienne and his Grace – '

'Of course I mean that filth. It's even rubbed off on me. I've colluded. Being his servant. Writing his poems. Being another one of the little prizes he waves under the noses of the other Kingdoms. Anyone who has anything to do with him gets dragged into the dirt too. This is a corrupting place.'

'Remember what you're saying. I know it must have come as a shock – '

'No, it didn't. That's just it. I'm not surprised. It's part of the pattern. I love something so he has to take it. All he has to do is see something good or sweet or pure and he has to ruin it, he has to make it his and smear it all over with his filth.'

Edvard stands up, 'My Guards are outside this door,' he

warns Caro. 'If you cannot control yourself this instant I will be forced to call them in.'

'Do it, then.'

There follows a minute, feeling like an hour, when Edvard might or might not call his Guards. Caro cannot be sure. He doesn't much care either way. Edvard proposed this test: let him decide what constitutes passing it.

Edvard does not call his Guards.

He sits down again, and makes a business of rolling up his parchments, putting them to one side, arranging all his pens and other clutter neatly. When there is nothing left to occupy his hands, he rubs them across his face and then folds them on the table. His jaw is set, his expression both stern and sympathetic. 'Is it because of the lady Vivienne?' he asks, 'or have you always hated his Grace?'

'I don't hate him. He can't help being an evil man.'

'Come now, Caro, you are talking like a child. You've disappointed me. I expected better of your intelligence than to find you are still nursing grudges for something which you know was at worst an accident, and at best unavoidable. Or if nothing else, I would have hoped you had more honour than to eat the bread of a man you consider to be your enemy. His Grace, your enemy. What an absurdity! You seem to think the war was fought for the express purpose of injuring yourself.'

'Why bring the war into this?'

'Because that's at the root of this, isn't it? You've never forgiven us – you've never understood. You still have the understanding of a boy. You've hated me all this time, haven't you? When I was doing you the credit of believing you had grown up sufficiently to be capable of friendship.'

'I've said I never blamed you. The war has nothing to do with this, well, except circumstantially. I know why it had to happen. I know why you fought the war – '

Caro pauses. He is being led into a line of argument he did not mean to pursue –he didn't come here to discuss the state of Edvard's soul. Edvard is the one who seems unable to deal with any subject except as it relates to himself; and now that he has raised it, why not put him straight once and for all? So Caro repeats, 'I know why *you* fought the war. I've lost count of the number of times you've told me about it, trying to persuade me that it was right, you had to do it, you had no choice – I mean, who are you trying to convince? Yourself? I'm not the one who keeps talking about the war. You are. You're the one who thinks I have some good reason to hate you. You're so convinced that I ought to hate you that you won't believe me when I say I don't. But I don't hate you. I understand you, which is better. You never fought the war because you believed it was right. It might have been or it might not, but the reason *you* fought in it is because you love Basal Rorhah. And that's why you're eaten up with doubt about it, and that's why you keep asking me if I forgive you. You doubt the purity of your own motives. Don't you?'

Attacked by surprise from behind, the walls of his secret penetrated, Edvard's defences are in disarray. He cannot deny it, and there is no time to waste wondering how Caro could have guessed. He will have to feint and parry. 'No, Caro, you have it backwards. You're right, of course, I did – I do love him, but I didn't fight to make him King because I loved him. It was the right thing to do. I loved him first because of – because he was – because of everything about him that made him the man he was. Is. Because he was meant to be King. I didn't do it because I hoped I would gain something from being his friend. I don't think love is worth much if it's given only to get.'

'You've certainly proved that, at least. Well, you have a neat way of rationalising it. You're good at that, aren't you? I suppose you've learnt to be, or I don't know how you could have lived with yourself this long. But what I've never been able to understand is why you're ashamed of it. It's no crime to love someone, even if they're not worth it. I even think it's better to love another man than to love nobody at all. Maybe love is a better reason, I mean, maybe it is more excusable to fight a war out of love than because you believe it is the right thing to do. Maybe it's more human to be guided by your heart instead of your head. You know what people say about you, don't you? The reason why you never got married? Because you used to be his lover when you were young.'

Edvard pales, and says angrily, 'I don't know where you heard that ridiculous old lie, but I will not even give it the honour of a denial.'

'Don't bother. I don't believe it, and even if it were true it's not important. I think that your feelings for him are a great deal more complicated than that, so complicated that you can twist around in them and pretend they're not what they are. You like to think your actions are weighed up on the basis of

218

your principles and your beliefs – you pride yourself on your virtues, your tolerance and your open-mindedness and your dedication, and your kindness to bastards and orphans. But really you only have one guiding principle. Him. The bits of you that make up their own mind are the bits of you that he doesn't need. Of course you would say that obedience is your duty, but there's a difference between a man's obedience and a dog's obedience. Dogs obey out of love. You're not his friend. You're his dog. You love him so much you let him trample all over your integrity and then you have to ask a bastard to forgive you. It's better to be dead than be a shell like you. You've given him your whole life. You've wasted it. He doesn't care about you. If he did, he could never have done what he's done with Vivvy. And you shut your eyes and tell yourself you don't mind, anything he wants is fine with you. You don't know how to want anything any more. You're not even a person.'

Caro runs out of breath and sits down, rather suddenly. Edvard's shoulders are hunched around his ears as though he wishes he could fold himself out of existence. His fingers are an agonised tangle of knots. Caro wonders whether any of the things he has said have taken Edvard by surprise.

'I'm sorry,' Caro apologises, 'I didn't mean to make this personal.'

'So this is why you came to Court. You hate me this much.'

'How many times do I have to tell you? I don't hate you. I don't know that I could say I like you, exactly. That doesn't come into it. But I respect what you could have been. Perhaps I am your friend, if that's possible. Has anyone else tried to get to know you as well as I have? Has anyone else ever bothered to talk to you about it?'

'To further your own purpose.'

'I only think you should be honest with yourself.'

'What do you want from me, Caro?'

'I want you to understand why I'm leaving. I need somebody here to understand, and you're the only person at this Court who's worth anything. I feel angry for you, even if you don't know how to be. I'm angry at the way you've been used, and wasted. You're a sort of metaphor too, I mean, an example. You are what happens to people in this world, the world we have made that chews people up and empties them. You go wrong because everything has gone wrong. I can see why so many people want to be King, and why they fight to achieve it. In this world, everyone who is not a King ends up having their soul snuffed out because they're treated as less than human. But wars, Kings, you know, none of it has to happen. I used to think that it all went wrong with the Conquest, because that was wrong. Which it was. It was something you had no right to do, depriving us of our freedom and destroying our integrity as a nation. But then again that is the tendency of our world, the system we've devised for governing ourselves. It has to get rid of freedoms, and integrity, and the opportunity for choice, in order to maintain its own stability. What if we chose not to live this way? But we daren't, because the Gods will be angry, and if that doesn't deter us the King will soon shut us up. I don't know whether there's anywhere in the world where things are different, but I know that it's possible. Anything we can imagine is possible if we have the courage to try for it. We've boxed ourselves in with our Gods and our Kingdoms and our laws and our conviction that everything is static, that this is how it's always been and consequently can't be changed and can't be made better. People believe that, you know. They don't even bother to think about it. They don't know how to think. Right from birth they're taught to substitute superstition and blind faith for thought. It's like a great wall they can't get over. They can't think, so they kill instead. If you don't like your King, kill him, have a war, and since you can't think of anything better put another King in his place. Why doesn't anything ever *improve*? Why can't we learn? Edvard, didn't you ever wonder why, if the Gods really intended Basal Rorhah to be King, they didn't simply make him Michael's eldest son and thus save us all a lot of bloodshed? You see? Unless the Gods actually enjoy seeing us kill each other, in which case they're not the Gods you thought they were. We can't go on being slaves to Gods who don't exist. There has to be a better way. We have to find it. We have to be free to use our intellects, instead of having them blunted at birth. We have to have the freedom to change things, or we might as well not be alive. We might as well be animals. Now I could stay at Court for the rest of my life and become rich and even more famous and the Grand Old Man of Letters, but I'm not going to lend it my support any more. I'm not going to pretend I agree with it when I can see that there must be a better way. That's why, don't you see, that's why I have this gift, of words, not for myself, but for the whole of Brychmachrye. Do you understand?'

Edvard says, 'That deposition.'

'Yes?'

'Everything in it was true?'

'Yes.'

'You are throwing away your career. If you persist in this, you will die. You realise that, don't you?'

'Yes.'

'I can't protect you.'

'I don't want your protection. I only want you to understand.'

'Oh Caro. God help me. Get out of here, please, quickly, before I do what I should have done half an hour ago and call my Guards.'

29

Because Caro has long ceased to confide in her, more than a week passes before Annie comprehends what he has done.

He's been acting strangely all week. He seems to have embarked on a binge of frantic activity, working all day and far into the night. Annie wonders if he takes time off to sleep. He hasn't come to bed with her for days. On two occasions royal messengers have arrived with official summons from the Court, and Annie has passed these on to Caro, receiving for her pains a grunt of acknowledgment from the fair head bent over a table piled high with books and papers. She assumed he would be going up to Court the next morning, or the day after, as these summons usually request his almost immediate attendance on the Queen. But Caro has not stirred from his room. Annie lies awake at night, alone, puzzled, and increasingly alarmed. Has Caro fallen out with the Court? If he has, it can't be the Court's doing: they are still sending for him. And Caro ignores them.

Something must have happened the day he went up to give a reading at that lady's birthday party. Annie is sure of it. He arrived home unexpectedly early the same afternoon, and she could tell there was something different about him the moment he walked through the door. She could see it in the way he moved. When he crossed the floor she could have sworn his feet barely touched it, as though his body had no weight to bring it down to earth.

While she busied herself preparing dinner her eyes kept straying back to where he sat, wrapped in thought, close to the fire. Maybe it was only the way the light flickered across his face, but he suddenly looked so much younger than she was used to, so clear-skinned and beautiful, that her heart leapt into her throat. It's easy, when you live with someone day in, day out, to gradually stop noticing what they look like. The sight of Caro lit up among the shadows reminded Annie forcefully of the day they first met, and her own startled, irritable response to his attraction. She had thought then, this one's too damn sure of himself.

She recalls, too, Bren's story of how they found Caro under an elm tree in the middle of nowhere, a boy dressed in rags, hungry and evidently lost, who nevertheless seemed sure of where he was going. I'd never seen anyone so beautiful, Bren told her, and I couldn't keep my eyes off him. Skin deep, Annie had remarked sourly, for this was at the time when Caro's courtship was wearing her down, and she wanted to think badly of him. Bren had shaken his head and stated, no, I knew right away that he was someone extraordinary.

Bren's conviction that Caro's outer loveliness denotes an inner lovableness has, like Annie's, been rattled considerably since then.

Caro takes a rare break from his work and wanders into the living room. His fingers are cramped from writing. He crouches by the hearth and stretches his hands out to the warmth. Annie sits across from him, nursing the baby. He has hardly spoken a word to her for days. The flames' reflections dance in his eyes and make them glitter, fanatically. Less than a year ago he used to look at Annie like that. Now he seems unconscious of her presence. There's a look on his face that she recognises. Men have smiled in her arms, just like that, after making love. And she suddenly realises that the reason Caro looks so different is that she has never seen him smile like this, this dreamy daze of exhaustion and contentment, before. Not in all the time he loved her.

'Caro?'

'Mmm?'

'Just out of curiosity. Have you ever been unfaithful to me?'

'No.'

She believes him. How can you be unfaithful when you don't feel? Caro never gets carried away in the heat of the moment. She says, 'It meant nothing to you, did it?'

She speaks to him and he doesn't hear, doesn't answer.

222

Ask him no questions, thinks Annie, and he'll tell me no lies.

She dares not leave the child alone with him. In his state of uncommunicative elation he cannot be relied on to hear her cry. On market day Annie goes downstairs to ask the poulterer's wife if she will mind the baby. My pleasure, says that good woman. She loves babies, and, as she tells the neighbour who pops in soon after for a chat, she feels sorry for that poor Annie. Of course the woman was a fool to get mixed up with poets and that lot, they're all touched in the head. He won't make an honest woman of her, you know, not even now this little duck's come along. And he dotes on his child. But he's got ambitions, oh yes. We reckon he's angling for a lady, and with his looks, dear Gods, he'll be unlucky not to catch one. I keep an eye on my daughters, I can tell you. That boy is trouble. And when he's home, my dear, you should hear them argue! Though it's all been a bit quiet of late. A bit too quiet, you mark my words.

It is early in the morning, a late touch of frost lingering in the air and crisping the vegetables on the market-stalls. Annie's route takes her through the Clerkden. A crowd of housewives and other early risers is buzzing excitedly around the temple notice-board. Annie sees a couple of friends, and waves to them. They exchange glances. Others turn to look at her. Her two friends pick up their skirts and come running over, followed by half a dozen women Annie doesn't know so well, acquaintances and friends of friends. They press in on her, all talking at once of their sympathy, their outrage, their disbelief, their pity. One offers a bed in her house to Annie. You know what it is, says another, it's mixing with his betters, them great ones, has addled his brain. And her poor daughter, with a madman for a father. Hands on her arms and shoulders push Annie towards the notice-board. Even those people who don't know her to talk to are aware of whose woman she is, and they clear a space for her. You know how to read now, Annie. Read it.

There is a signature at the bottom, but Annie has already recognised the neat, clerkish script. The same handwriting taught her to read, and wrote for her poems in the same clear, simple native as this. Pinned to the temple's own notice-board, Caro's beautifully-worded invitation to tear the temple down.

Her eyes aren't focusing properly. In any case she doesn't need to read beyond the first verse. She knows how it will go on. She has heard him hold forth on the subject countless times in the Conqueror and the Tar Barrel. But he'd thought better of it – oh, she trusted him, she believed he had thought better of it once he came into favour at Court. She believed it was a game. Like Bren, she believed he didn't really mean it. But he did. All the time. And now he's done it.

Annie thinks she will faint, when someone cries, 'The Watch!' and everybody scatters. Annie is swept along in the rush, dropping her basket and losing a clog. Separated from her friends in the panic, she runs blindly, home to Caro.

Downstairs the poulterer's wife lifts triumphant eyebrows at the sound of raised voices overhead, and asks her neighbour, 'What did I tell you?'

Annie is crying in the bedroom. She won't come out. Caro has given up trying to explain to her. She doesn't want to understand.

Bren can't understand either. He has brought Fern back, saying that he won't risk keeping her, not now. He doesn't want to be accused of helping Caro in any way. Idris has already made a bonfire of every copy of Caro's plays he could lay his hands on. For half an hour Bren has stayed to berate Caro on his total lack of responsibility, his sheer foolhardiness, his utter failure to consider the welfare of Annie and the child, not to mention his own safety. Which leads Bren on to the topic of ships, escape, flight abroad, the absolute necessity of speed.

Patiently Caro points out to Bren that the Coneywarren will not send the Watch for him today, nor possibly for quite some time. He is still officially a member of the Queen's Household, and consequently under the protection of the Court. No action can be taken against him without written authorisation from the Palace. This it will take them at least a week to get: Lord Edvard filcLaurentin has often complained that the ratchets of bureaucracy turn painfully slow.

How dare Bren suggest that Caro has not considered his daughter? Caro loves that child so much he sometimes wishes she had never been born. How can one justify bringing children into a world like this? Bren will remember that Caro was not the one who wanted children. He knew it would complicate matters.

Annie and the baby will not be harmed. How can Caro be so sure? Because their great King doesn't kill children. He said as much in Caro's hearing. He punishes criminals, not their innocent families. So, Caro admits he's a criminal? Legally, yes, of course. This is a world in which speaking the truth is an offence. Morally, no. That's all very grand and splendid, Caro, but who's going to look after the girls, who's going to feed them, who's going to put a roof over their heads when he's gone?

They will manage. Caro is going to leave his daughter something better than a material inheritance. She will be proud of him. She will understand. She will know that he did this for her. To Caro she is all future generations. They will remember that he had the courage to speak. To keep silent is to acquiesce. To know the truth and refuse to speak it is to accept that men are incapable of understanding and striving for it. And if he accepts that, he is no longer Caro. In silence he would, truly, throw his life away.

'There's no talking to you,' says Bren. 'You've finally lost your mind.'

But there are a few people in the City who do not agree with Bren. When night falls they come to tell Caro so. Everybody knows where Caryllac the Poet lives. They have passed his lodgings many times, pointing it out to curious visitors. Tonight they walk through the shadows and scratch quietly on his door, expecting, perhaps, that he has already been taken from them, or if not, that he will not welcome the intrusion of ordinary men. He is Brychmachrye's Court Poet, whom they have often seen in the street, from afar, envying and admiring him, wishing they had the nerve to make his acquaintance, although he is said to be ambitious and proud, the grandson of a Fahlraec – what then can equal their surprise, to find themselves sitting in Caryllac's home, speaking to him of thoughts each had believed he was alone in thinking? Individually they arrive, five men unknown to one another before tonight. Five free intellects trawled from a City of twenty thousand.

Unaccustomed to the liberty of free speech, they are bursting to tell their stories. Two are students, brought together by the intuition that they thought alike, and hoping to find in Caro answers to the questions they do not dare ask their tutors. One is a doctor, who thought he would go mad attempting to reconcile the evidence of his eyes with the received truths prescribed in the textbooks. Another is a middle-aged teacher from one of the Guild-schools, a mathematician and an amateur astronomer, who trusts they will not think he is deranged, but it's his observation that the earth moves round the Sun. The last is a young Priest of Asdura, nudged into a Temple career by a devout mother, who awoke one morning to the realisation that he had no faith, and from that day to this has been unable to make sense of his life.

'I'm not going to tell you what to do,' says Caro. 'You're free men. You can make your own decisions. But I could do with some help, if you want to help me.'

Over the past week Caro has produced a number of little parables in ballad form, simply-worded in Tsvingtori street-native. For an example, he reads one out:

Once upon a time there was a peaceful greenwood inhabited by deer. Then the greenwood was invaded by wolves, who, being stronger and more cunning than the deer, subjected them to their rule. You are happier like this, the wolves assured the deer, because we protect you from conquest by some less considerate predator: surely the fact that we are obliged to eat one or two of you from time to time, in order to keep our strength up, is but scant reward for our kindness and hard work. After all, we are a higher class of creature, for we are civilised carnivores while you are backward grass-eaters. Any deer who protested against this line of argument was promptly eaten, and soon the deer forgot how to protest. Then it came to pass that the wolves grew dissatisfied with their King, who always claimed the choicest joints of meat for his own jaws; and they tore him to pieces. But the wolves could not agree on who was to take his place, for each wolf considered himself the one best fit to be King, the strongest and most cunning, and so their war continued until they had all perished. Was that power and wisdom, or greed and folly? The deer observed how their oppressors had destroyed themselves, and, being once more in possession of the greenwood, they assembled and debated, and chose from out of their number a modest young stag who promised to wear the crown only for as long as they should be satisfied with his rule. And the greenwood was prosperous and peaceful once more.

In the middle of this recitation the door opens, and Caro glances up, hoping to see Annie. Instead he meets Paddy's ferret-grin. Paddy limps into the room and stations himself against the back wall. Caro frowns, and carries on reading. When he comes to the end of the poem Paddy breaks into loud applause, clapping and exclaiming, 'Brilliant!'

226

Caro ignores him. 'Is it all clear?' he asks the others. He has been careful not to indulge himself in elaborate invention or complicated simile, anxious to put his message across as straightforwardly as possible. They nod, and praise the poem, assuring him that he has not failed.

'And it's so clever,' adds Paddy. 'You could pass it off as a shepherd's-tale and no one could hold you responsible for what evil minds might read into it. One can see why you're the Queen's Poet.'

'Excuse me,' says Caro.

He takes Paddy's elbow and leads him into the corridor. 'What are you doing here?'

'You know me, bored and born to hang. I didn't want to miss out on the fun. I say, I recognise that medical fellow you've got in there. His name's Arnauld Caryllacson. We were at the college together. I guess it took him a lot longer than me to get disillusioned.'

'Annie's in the bedroom if you want to see her,' says Caro. 'She won't talk to me.'

'Can't say I blame her, poor bitch. She's never understood you. Hang on a minute, Caro. I came round here because Bren asked me to. He's in a state about Annie – and about you, but he despairs of you. I'm supposed to try to talk some sense into you.'

'You're wasting your breath.'

'And don't I know it. When you set your little heart on something nothing can turn it aside. Annie should know that by now. Look, Caro, I know you and me have never exactly seen eye to eye, and I know you don't like me – and to be honest I've always thought you were nothing more than a pretty face. All that farting around licking arse at Court, I thought that's what you really wanted. I never thought you'd have the guts to do what you did today.'

'Don't tell me. You want to lend me your support.'

'You seem to be doing all right on that score without me. So if it's all the same to you, I'd rather be hanged than buried. I don't think you're wrong, mind you, I just think it's not worth it. Now I think I'll go comfort my big sister.'

'Paddy – ' Caro lays a hand on his arm. 'Talk to her for me. Tell her I never meant – tell her I'm sorry this had to happen to her.'

Back in the room he hands the poems out among his new apostles. He gives them each a roll of parchment, and asks them

227

to copy the poems out and distribute them secretly around the City. They must take care not to compromise their personal safety. For this reason, it's better if they are not seen with him or near his lodgings again. He doesn't want sacrifices. He wants witnesses.

'You're sorry?' says Annie. 'You never meant? What balls. You planned this. From the start.'

'Not this precisely. I knew it would come to something like this in the end.'

'So tell me, where do I fit in? How was I necessary to your great plan?'

'I never meant to love you. I just saw you and it happened. It was an accident. A happy accident, for me. I never thought I'd be able to love anyone.'

'You were right there.'

'That's not true, Annie. I have loved you. If I ever did you any wrong it was in trying to make you love me back. You knew I would hurt you and you were right. Loving you is the only selfish thing I've ever done in my whole life. It's the only thing in my life that wasn't part of a plan. I loved you for yourself.'

'Oh, Caro. You never loved me. You don't know how to love. You think all it takes is to be good in bed. And you don't even enjoy that, do you? You're a fraud. You have no heart. You're the coldest person I've ever met. You're obsessed, that's what it is. Obsessed. You've punched yourself in the head so many times you can't think straight. All you ever think about is what happened to you – you're wrapped up in this feud you've dreamt up. Avenge your mother, avenge your father – it comes first and last with you. Let me tell you something. When you first told me about what happened to you in the war, about how your mother died and how they took you to your father's people, I thought it was so tragic I practically fell in love with you all over again. I was so afraid for you. I guess I was always afraid that something like this would happen. You don't know what that's like, to be always afraid for someone. The more I loved you the more frightened I was for you, until I tried not to love you so much because it was so unbearable to be so frightened all the time. But you never thought about my feelings. I just had to put up with it. And now you're doing the same thing to our daughter. She's going to have to make

228

do with being an orphan. Just like you had to. Is that what you want for her?'

'She will understand.'

'Will she? Who'll explain it to her? How can I make her understand when I don't understand myself why you're doing this? The King doesn't care what you say, the Court doesn't care, nobody cares, nobody thinks anything about your stupid ideas except that you've gone completely mad ... And trying to make me believe you don't hate the King. You do hate him. You hate him so much you might as well love him. He's the one you're doing all this for. You're like Fern, biting the hand that feeds you. Nobody's impressed. You're going to be killed, Caro, killed, and this fool Annie just sits here like a clod waiting for it to happen.'

'Looking forward to it.'

'Oh, you think I'm enjoying this? You think it's fun to think that every footstep I hear coming down the street is coming to take the father of my child away? The baby's frightened too. She knows that something's wrong. She won't eat and she cries all night, not that you'd notice. I have to think of her, Caro. What am I going to tell her? That her father didn't love her, that he chose to abandon her?'

'Stop it, Annie. You know that's not true.'

'I'm going to have to tell her that her father was a traitor.'

'I am not a traitor.'

'You are. In every way. You've betrayed me, and our child, and your friends, everyone who's ever wanted the best for you, you've pulled the wool over everybody's eyes. And I'll have to tell her that her father was a selfish bastard.'

'I won't let you keep her.'

'Oh, what will you do, have her buried with you? That's real fatherly love, I must say.'

'My sister will take her.'

'The pure and noble Lady Vivienne. Not so pure now, is she? The whole City knows whose bed she's warming. But I guess it doesn't matter to you which whore brings our child up. You're surrounded by sluts, aren't you, Caro? It must be your pretty face. I wish to God I'd never set eyes on it.'

'Why don't you leave, then?'

'I'd have left yesterday if I had anywhere to go.'

'Then stay here. The rent's paid for the next quarter, so that's a weight off your mind, I'm sure. All you've ever thought about is money.'

'Look!' Annie laughs, flinging her arms wide. 'Look! You can't hurt me any more.'

Her voice breaks, and she runs from the room in tears. Caro does not go after her. He knows she is only crying for herself. He dips his pen, and continues to write from the point where she interrupted him.

It wouldn't be true to say that Caro's single-handed mutiny has thrown the City into turmoil. Everyone, right down to the fishgutters on the docks, has heard the news that he's turned traitor, and everyone is mildly, pleasantly scandalised. But the disestablishmentarian content of his poems has made little impact on the illiterate, uneducated majority of the population.

Even if they could read, they would not see what relevance his poems held for their lives. They do not live in the rarefied air of the cliff-top. Unlike Caro, they have no sense of their place in the march of history. Today is what concerns them: today's petty irritations, a shoe that needs mending, an aching tooth, a mistake in their work that must be laboriously corrected; today's humiliations and griefs, the debts that cannot be paid, the master who must be placated, the death of a loved child; today's pleasures, large and small, the favourite meal eaten with relish, the shoe well-mended, the job well-done, the friend they are reunited with, the woman they make love to. Kings come and go: daily life never changes. These are the real human sufferings that no government can free them from, the real human joys that no government can provide. Government, like hunger, poverty, hard work and death, is a constant of their existence, the will of the Gods, to be endured when it bears down on them and otherwise thought of as little as possible. Governments are well able to increase the sum of human misery, but rarely, if ever, has a man thanked his government for contributing to his happiness.

Where Caro's poems have succeeded in making people sit up and take notice is among the class he had least interest in reaching: those with education and money and vested interests. They bought his books. They patronised his plays. They feel he owes his place at Court to their original support. They made him. They were proud to count him as a member of their City. And now the ungrateful bastard has turned on them.

The most prominent citizens go in a body to the Coneywarren and demand that the Wardens take action. What do you expect us to do? those harassed officials reply. We can't arrest the Queen's Poet for writing poetry. His house is being watched. That's all we can do for the moment. The Palace has been informed. We await our instructions.

30

I have to speke to you. My room. Fifteen minits.

Much more than a quarter of an hour has passed since this crumpled note was pressed into Edvard's hand as he came out of lunch. He was in two minds whether to respond to it or not. The business with Elinor Vacled had been very unpleasant, and he is reluctant to get involved in a similar crisis. In the end, however, he concluded the appeal must be desperate: he would not have been called upon had there been anyone else who could help. And so here he is, drawn by dead affection and charitable principles, folding the scrap of paper up and putting it back in his pocket before knocking on the door. Immediately he hears the muffled bang of a trunk-lid slamming down, and a moment later the door inches open. Vivienne looks up at him. Her little face is pinched and white.

'Oh, it's you,' she says. 'I didn't think you were coming.'

'What is it, Lady?'

'You'd better come in.' She stands aside to let him pass, and closes the door. Edvard realises that, aside from her latest gift from the King, a lapdog ball of white fur and wet black nose called Fluff, he and Vivienne are alone in her room. He sits down, suggesting, 'Shouldn't you call your maid?' not that the lady has much reputation left to protect.

'No,' she insists, 'I have to speak to you alone.'

Vivienne looks quite frantic. Elinor looked just the same when she came begging him to intercede with the King on her behalf. His refusal evoked such a stream of tears and filthy slander that at last he was forced to have Elinor removed from his rooms. Elinor was arrogant and boastful; he had never seen her charms; yet even so it was a struggle for him to turn his back on her distress. His past fondness for Vivienne may make her case harder to deal with.

Fluff leaps on to his lap, demanding caresses. The warmth

231

of the dog under his hand softens Edvard's stern intentions, and he asks her gently, 'Are you in trouble, Lady?'

She sees what he means and starts laughing at him, a high-pitched humourless giggle. Edvard hopes he isn't about to have a hysterical girl on his hands. 'It's not me,' she says, 'it's not me in trouble this time. It's Caro. Look, come here – ' she pushes the dog to the floor, grabs Edvard's hands and pulls him over to the trunk, throwing it open. 'Look,' she cries, 'look, look.'

The open trunk emits a strong, feminine aroma of cloves and dried rose-petals. It is full of dresses, stockings, smocks and petticoats, and on top of her clothes lies a thick bundle of handwritten sheets of parchment. She picks these up and holds them out to Edvard. 'Read them. Just read them. Just read them.'

'Pull yourself together,' says Edvard harshly. 'I know what they are.'

'You've seen them too?'

He heard about them first. The Coneywarren Wardens were obliged to refer the matter through Chancery. And only yesterday more concrete evidence was put into his hands. He takes Vivienne's bundle and flicks through it. As he suspected, it contains several copies of the poem he was shown, although hers are written in the native, and his was in court-speech. The gist of the story is the same: a native country girl, blue-eyed, golden-haired, apple-cheeked sweet innocence, comes to work as a maid at the Palace. She is hoping to catch a handsome groom or gardener for her husband; but instead, she catches the green adder eye, the rapine unfingered claw, of a great Lord. Like a God he is accustomed to taking what he wants and never hearing the word no. No is a word she is not free to utter. Conquered, ravished, pregnant, she loses her job and ends up keeping what is left of her body and soul together by working as a prostitute on Tsvingtori docks. But surely, thought Edvard when he first read this story, they cannot all go the same way, or . . . Or what? Or the City would have more whores than customers. He has never really wondered before what happened to these girls. He always assumed they went back to their people.

The heroine of this ugly and all-too-true history dies, inevitably, in giving birth to a bastard boy who, although blue-eyed and golden-haired, can never be a true Brychmachrese. He has been cheated of his patrimony. He will grow up with a mongrel language that is neither one thing nor the other, a fitting tongue for the voice of a raped nation. Edvard can trace the outline of Elinor Vacled's story in this poem; he can even appreciate the imaginative skill that has succeeded in extracting a fable of universal application from the misfortunes of a few score girls. He remembers that Caro is fond of speaking, and thinking, in metaphors.

He asks Vivienne, 'How did you get these?'

'My maid brought me the first one. Someone gave it to her in the market. I couldn't read it – you see they're all in the native, and Caro wouldn't ever teach me. But she translated it for me. I nearly died. Even I can see what they're really supposed to mean. He used to talk like this a lot, when we were younger, but I never really listened to him then. Anyway I thought he didn't think like that any more. I thought he was happy here. So anyway, I told my maid to bring me all the ones she could find. I thought there'd only be a few, I mean, how many can one person write? But there's hundreds of them, thousands, maybe. My maid says they're all over the City. Look – that's not his handwriting. My maid says there's other people helping him, no one knows who. She says he even goes into the Clerkden and down around the shipyards, and places, and reads them out, and people come and listen.'

'Yes,' says Edvard, 'I heard about that.'

'I don't know what's happened to him!' Vivienne cries. 'He's not a wicked person. I mean, look at that one, that one about the maid – you can tell who that Lord is really supposed to be, but his Grace isn't like that and Caro knows he's not. He's always liked Caro. Do you think his Grace knows, I mean about these?'

'You should be able to tell me that.'

It was a cheap, snide dig, and Edvard immediately regrets it. Vivienne colours up and defends herself, in disjointed exclamations, 'I know you think I'm a terrible person – but I wouldn't tell on Caro, not even to his Grace – I know you hate me too now, everybody hates me, but it's not my fault. You should understand how I feel – I love his Grace, I can't help it. No one else has ever been so good to me – I don't see why I should get blamed – It's me, you know, this is all because of me, Caro hates me too now, that's why he's doing this.'

'No it's not,' says Edvard.

For almost three weeks Edvard has been sitting on the information lodged against Caro in Chancery, making excuses to the Wardens through his clerks. Inaction seemed the best course,

233

as it did not require him to make a decision. It now occurs to him that Caro must have relied on this, trusting to his judgment of Edvard's character; and Edvard begins to feel that he has acted, or rather not acted, out of sentiment. He could never have kept it secret for long. The Temple is involved – the Lord Priest Henry filcThomas is losing patience with Edvard's inertia – and if Vivienne is aware of what Caro is doing, others at Court must also know. How then can the King not know? But if he knows, why is he allowing the charade to continue? The trench Caro is digging for himself is already deep enough to bury him twice over.

'We have to stop him,' says Vivienne. 'You were always his friend, Eminence. Can't you do something?'

'I didn't want to betray him,' says Edvard vaguely, leaving, in his own mind if not in Vivienne's, some doubt as to which 'him' is meant.

'Please,' Vivienne begs, 'I don't know what else to do.'

'Let me think. You understand that his Grace will have to be told? It should come from one of us. All right. I'll do it. I think that's best. It's my responsibility. I'll tell him tonight, after the Council meeting. It will take a few hours to draw up the warrant. I can stall, but not for long. Until morning at the latest. What you must do is go down to the city and warn Caro. That will give him this afternoon and tonight to get away. Can you do that, Vivvy?'

'I'm not allowed to leave the Palace.'

'I've thought of that. I'll write out a permit for you. That will get you past the gates. Take your maid, she knows where Caro lives. Don't be afraid. If anyone finds out, I'll take it on myself. You can say that I ordered you to go. After all, Caro is your brother. You'll be forgiven, don't worry. You want to help him, don't you, Vivvy?'

She nods, mutely.

'All right, then. You wait here. I'll send one of my clerks with the permit in about half an hour. Don't lose heart, dear. We'll save Caro's life in spite of himself.'

And Edvard goes off to set these plans in motion, congratulating himself on having found such a satisfactory solution to his moral dilemma.

Caro returns home from giving a public reading on the docks with rotten egg splodged all over the front of his shirt. He has a cut above his eye where a stone hit him, but it doesn't matter. The slops poured on to his head from upper windows; the children who run up and slap him and then scamper away, screaming, as though he were a ghost; the abuse and foul names hurled at him; the acquaintances who turn hurriedly in the opposite direction when they see him coming; none of it matters if he succeeds in making just one man or woman in the crowd hear his words through the whistling and jeering of the hecklers. That one person, that one receptive soul, is worth enduring all for.

Caro rubs a hand across his hair. It's stiff, and sticky. He picks out a tomato seed with his fingernail, and begins to smile. They're throwing metaphors at him now.

He goes straight to his room, sits down, and writes. Some hours later, as dusk is drawing in, he gets up to light a candle, and realises that the house seems unusually quiet. Now that he comes to think about it, he hasn't heard the baby cry. He feels hungry. Annie is no longer speaking to him, but she still feeds him, and he opens the door to see if she has put a tray of food down. The corridor is empty. Every room is empty, with the silence of abandonment.

'If there is no other business,' says the King, 'I would like to draw the Council's attention to the matter of Caryllac Thomasson, poet of her Grace's Household.'

Edvard looks up to find them all staring at him – Bernard Derondah, Henry filcThomas, Gilles Mehah, every member of the Council aside from the King himself, who is examining the sheet of paper in front of him. Edvard's start of surprise tells them all they need to know. They look away.

'I believe you are all familiar with the young man in question,' says the King. 'And I am surprised that not one of you gentlemen, my Councillors, saw fit to mention his treasonable activities to me.'

Once again all heads swivel in Edvard's direction. Edvard stifles a sudden urge to laugh. They might as well point fingers. *There's the culprit, Sir, it was his job to tell you.*

'Have you failed to appreciate the serious nature of Caryllac Thomasson's offences?' asks the King. 'Both verbally and in writing he is attempting by subtle means to undermine every foundation-stone of this government, although so far, I trust, with little success. He has abused the hospitality of our Court

235

and belied the favour with which we honoured him; he has done his best to foment unrest not only outside these walls, but within them, and if you, my Lord Chancellor, thought this matter so trifling it did not merit my attention, I would have hoped that you, my Lord Priest, would have wished to express the Temple's concern. At best I can credit you with the charitable, if misguided, desire to shield me from the distressing realisation that we have nurtured a traitor in our bosom. At worst I am forced to conclude that you were all in ignorance of Caryllac Thomasson's seditious activities, which he has been perpetrating, unchecked, for at least three weeks. I do not want to be told that you did not know. It is your duty to keep yourselves informed. Or what use are you to me?'

The other Councillors hang their heads and look small, though Edvard knows they are all silently blaming him for the dereliction of duty which has brought this undifferentiated wrath down on their fifteen heads. Edvard is struck with the impulse to leap up defiantly and shout something dramatic, but as no words come to him he remains in his seat, as sheep-like as the others.

'Edvard – ' says the King.

'Yes, Sir?'

'As you are my Chancellor I would take it as a kindness if you could arrange for a warrant to be drawn up for Caryllac Thomasson's arrest. And please try to ensure that the operation takes rather less than three weeks. Here is the charge sheet.' The King hands the paper to a clerk, who takes it around the table to Edvard. The King continues, 'Bearing in mind that Caryllac Thomasson remains a member of my wife's Household, it would be inappropriate to involve the Coneywarren in this case. Please see to it that his arrest is carried out by Guards of my Household, by tomorrow morning at the latest, and that he is brought to the Palace to be kept in custody until his sentence is determined. If there is nothing else you wish to discuss, gentlemen, you are dismissed. Good evening.'

The Council rises. One of the footmen at the back of the chamber pulls aside a tapestry that conceals a small door. The King goes through this, into his private offices. Edvard half-expected to be asked to accompany him. The other Councillors leave one by one. Gilles Mehah nudges Edvard in passing, and says, 'I wouldn't like to be in your shoes, Ned. He's livid.'

Edvard brushes Gilles' hand away, and sits down again in

the solitude of the empty Council chamber. He feels sick. He can hardly believe what he saw tonight. He feels that he has not looked properly at his fellow Councillors, his old comrades-in-arms, for years. Gilles – what has happened to Gilles? In his time he was one of the bravest men Edvard knew, always to be found in the front line of battle singing at the top of his lungs. Henry filcThomas faced a starving Clerkden mob and never turned a hair. Bernard Derondah was an intrepid sailor in his youth – once during the war, when they were moving troops along the coast from Mehed to Gurnah, a storm came up, and Edvard will never forget how Bernard paced the deck shouting, keep those sails up! We can beat this bitch! while the rest of them were puking over the rails.

So it has happened, as Edvard feared it would, and so gradually that there was never a point where they could see what was being done to them, and resist. Perhaps they did it to themselves. As Caro said, they colluded. They all tremble when Basal raises his voice and wish they could fall flat on their faces. Would age have diminished us in any case, Edvard wonders, or have we been deliberately reduced in stature? Every man who is not a King will have his soul destroyed and become less than human. Caro said that too. Caro says and sees too much, and Edvard can no longer shut his eyes to it.

What use are they? No use at all, thinks Edvard. We're fifteen old war-horses who've been gently led out to pasture. A clerk could do what I do. I chivvy my staff and sign papers. I would have followed him to the ends of the earth. I would have died for him. I would willingly have grown old in his service. I only asked, in return, to be valued. Dear Gods, please let it not be bitterness making me feel like this. Bitterness is a victim's emotion. But surely I have earned the right to something more.

Down in the City, outside the Tar Barrel, Caro has run Paddy down to earth. The landlord refused to let Caro cross his threshold, but Paddy has agreed to come out and speak to him, on the understanding that they hold their conversation down at the end of the street.

'You still with us?' Paddy quips. 'Somebody up there must love you.'

'Where's Annie?'

'It's funny you should ask me that. She came round to my room about five hours ago, with my niece. She asked

237

me for some money and I gave her what I could spare. Look, keep your dog back. I'm telling you what I know. She said the money was for the fare to cross the bay to Harbourferryport. She might have been lying – you know she doesn't trust me to keep a secret. She wouldn't tell me anything else, I swear. Go ask Bren, he might know.'

Edvard returns to his apartments to find Vivienne waiting for him. She jumps up eagerly when he enters and asks, 'Well?'

He has to pour himself a drink and gulp it down before he feels able to control his anger. What does she imagine, this betrayer of her own blood? That the King waved a hand and forgave Caro's crimes? Is that what she hoped to achieve with her wiles?

'We had an agreement, Lady,' he says icily. 'I trusted you. Why did you break it?'

'What do you mean? Haven't you told him?'

'There wasn't much need.'

Vivienne's forehead wrinkles. 'You mean he already knew?'

'You're a pretty little dissembler, but it won't wash with me. I know you told him.'

'But I didn't.'

'You didn't?'

'Oh Edvard!' Vivienne stamps her foot. 'You stupid old man. We never needed to tell him. He knew already. He's known for ever. He just wanted it to come from us, he gave us a chance, he gave us three weeks. And we didn't. Oh God, he'll never forgive me. You didn't tell him that I knew, did you? Please say you didn't – '

Edvard grabs her shoulders and shakes her, hard. 'You *have* been down to the City?'

'No – '

'You haven't warned Caro?'

'No, no, no!'

'You promised you would do it.'

'I know, but I was so scared. This is the most awful thing that's ever happened to me. It's horrible for me, you can't imagine. Caro's gone and he's never going to forgive me for – for you know – for loving – and if I went to him and his Grace found out he'd be so angry he'd never forgive me either. I don't want to make him hate me too. And anyway I've thought about it and it's Caro who's in the wrong, he shouldn't be saying such things, it's wrong and it's mean, and it's not fair to make me pay for it, it's not . . .'

Her nose is running. Can this snivelling, shameless, self-centred chit be Tom Floriah's daughter? Caro is the only one of Tom's children worthy of the name. Disgusted, Edvard lets go of her, and she backs against the wall, wiping her face with her sleeve. She's spineless, thinks Edvard. And I have been no better. For years and years.

Tonight he has been confronted with himself twice over; first, the erosion of his self-respect in the Council's trembling uselessness; and now, the cowardice of his heart in this pathetic girl's helpless love for a man already tiring of the amusement he found in her. Vivienne's feeble excuses echo his lifetime of rationalisations. He had always admired Vivienne for being lively, frank and opinionated – and now she, like him, has been pithed, de-boned, by the acquiescence of adoration. And it seems to Edvard that such a love, stifling protests, swallowing demands, is no virtue. It demeans the lover, and makes a monster of the beloved.

He should never have asked her to go to the City. She's not equal to it. Edvard is suddenly ashamed of himself for having tried to use her. Torn two ways, between two courses of action, he appropriated Vivienne; faced with a choice, he avoided it by asking her to do what he would not do himself. She should have been the one to tell Basal. Even if he knew already. She should have earned that little bit of gratitude, imaginary as it might be. Edvard ought to be able to do without gratitude by now. He asked her to betray her duty, while he fulfilled his. But on the other hand, he only suggested it because Caro is her brother. He thought she would want to be the one to help him. While he, Edvard, betrayed him.

Still Edvard can see there is no simple decision to be made. It is not absolute righteousness ranged against absolute wrong. His sense of practicality tells him that much of what Caro says is stupid, misguided, and unrealistic; his self-perception, heightened in the mirror of the evening's events, tells him that much of what Caro says is true. Caro is a traitor; Edvard's duty is to the King he made and serves; and if, despite all this, it remains his instinct to save Caro, why doesn't he do it himself? Why doesn't he undo the character-building self-denial of the last twenty years and give way, at last, to an impulse?

He fumbles in his pocket and pulls out a silk handkerchief.

239

'Here,' he says, 'blow your nose. Better? Now listen to me, Vivvy. I've just asked my staff to draw up a warrant for Caro's arrest.'

Vivienne tries not to scream, stuffing her fingers between her teeth. She looks at Edvard desperately. He says, 'Do you want to go down and warn him now? There is still time.'

'I can't.'

'All right. Just go back to your room, and don't worry.'

'I can't. I really can't. His Grace is expecting me. If I went to see Caro he'd wonder where I am. God, look at me, I'm a mess. I can't go to him like this. He'll know I know.'

'Don't fret. All the Councillors know, and he'll assume someone told you. I think he'd be more surprised if you weren't crying. Go on, run along and see him now. Maybe your tears will do Caro some good.'

'What are you going to do, Eminence?'

'Better you don't know. In case he asks.'

Bren tries to shut the door in Caro's face. Caro wedges a foot in and shouts, 'Tell me where she's gone. I know you know.'

'She asked me not to tell you. If you have anything to say to her I can pass it on.'

'She's taken my daughter.'

'Her daughter. *Her* daughter. Annie isn't your wife. You've got no claims on them. Now get your foot out of my door or I'll break it.'

'I'm not leaving until you tell me where they are.'

'They're somewhere where they'll be safe. Safe from you.'

'Where?'

'I'm not going to tell you. Listen, Caro, leave it alone. I can't help you any more. You're beyond help. But I can help them. Leave Annie be. Soon it won't matter anyway – ' Bren breaks off to clear his throat, and says hoarsely, 'Go away, Caro. I don't want to see you. I try not to think about it. To my mind you've been dead for years.'

Fern is bored, whining and tugging on her leash. Caro takes his foot from the door and walks away, but halfway down the stairs he hears the door creak open, and turns around to see Bren looking down at him from the landing. Fat tears of grief are dripping from the tip of Bren's bloated nose. They embarrass Caro. He would feel foolish, apologising or saying goodbye, and so he turns around again and walks home, conscious of the two

240

Coneywarren Guards close behind him who have dogged his footsteps back and forth across the City.

He walks past The Moon and Stars. New doors, painted a glossy red, have been fitted on shiny brass hinges; the plaster stars have been replaced and the moon freshly gilded, and colourful posters are plastered where the cracked slates once hung. The playhouse has been restored to its former glory, a far cry from the shabby ruin that seven years ago welcomed Caro, the single-handed saviour of its fortunes, with open arms. And now Idris has burnt his plays. He walks past the Conqueror, whose landlord used to be glad to take Caro's money and let him talk all he wanted. Having Caryllac as a regular was good for business. He walks through the Skirtchasers Alley, where the whores once tucked flowers in his collar, and up the Street of the Booksellers, past the fine new wooden house of Nolan and Sons, purchased with their profits from an unknown poet. He walks through the deserted Clerkden, past the marbled temples and Guildhalls glistening in the moonlight, past the beggars curled up together, snoring, on the Cripplesteps. From this height he can see the bay, rippling dark blue and silver like the shot-silk hangings in the Palace salons, sequinned with the reflections of stars. He can hear the faint musical chimes of ships' bells from the merchantmen rocking at anchor.

A great City: a wonder of the world. Caro wouldn't have believed, when he first came here, that he would grow to love it. He hasn't served it so badly. For a while he was Tsvingtori's favourite son, the dream of every starry-eyed provincial. He was the young lad from the country who found the streets of the City were paved with gold. He went to Court, and saw the Queen. The child of good fortune. What was it the Company used to call him? Our lucky charm. A hidden treasure. An ornament of the Court. So let them bury their treasure under the earth of Brychmachrye, for they are too dazzled by the legal tender of their fool's gold to know the worth of what they could be.

He climbs the stairs to his lodgings and goes into his writing room, sits down, sharpens his pen, and begins to write. Fern stretches across his feet, tail thumping contentedly. This is how it began, she alone with Caro, Caro alone with his poetry. This is how Edvard finds them when he arrives, just after midnight.

241

31

'If I were going to run away I'd have done it three weeks ago,' Caro tells Edvard. 'I suppose I have you to thank for delaying the inevitable?'

'I can't gain you any more time. My clerks are drawing up a warrant for your arrest and Basal wants to send his own Guards for you. They'll be here in a couple of hours. There's an Andarian ship at anchor in the bay, taking the ambassador's daughter home for her marriage. They're waiting for the tide to turn before they set sail, which should be just before dawn, I think. I see that your house is being watched, and presumably they'll follow us down to the docks, but they can't prevent me from taking you on board, and once you're on board you're on Andarian territory and no one can touch you. The ambassador's wife is a friend of mine. They'll take you. You'll be safe in Andariah, and they'll be glad to give you refuge.'

'So I've heard,' says Caro. 'Anything to spite Brychmachrye.'

'The Kingdom will survive without you.'

'I'm not leaving. This is my country. I've done nothing wrong. Why should I punish myself?'

'Caro, I am trying to save your life.'

'Why?'

Edvard sweeps the question aside. 'This isn't a game. If you don't leave tonight you'll be taken back to the Palace and in less than a week you'll be executed.'

'That seems a fairly good reason why *I* should want to scarper. But I asked you why *you* are trying to save my life.'

Edvard opens his mouth, but it's full of platitudes not worth uttering: every life is precious, while there's life there's hope, don't throw your young life away . . .

This tidy, sparsely-furnished room, smelling of ink and badly-cured parchment, its collection of books and papers arranged with clerkish precision, reminds Edvard of another room in which he once talked to Caro, high up in Floried Castle's keep. In fact they seem to have had this conversation before: it's your father's sword, Caro, you must want it.

'Caro, remember you said to me, years ago, in Floried, that you didn't want Tom's sword because you didn't want to kill people?'

'So why am I trying to kill myself?' Caro smiles. 'Actually, there's something I always wondered about that. Why did you bring that sword to me? By rights it belonged to Arlo.'

'I know that. He did get it in the end – I gave it to Lord Floriah and he gave it to young Arlo. But you seemed to me the more proper person to have it. You're the most like your father of any of Tom's children. I thought so then, and you're more like him now than you ever were.'

'Stubborn, you mean. Well, there you are, one can't fight one's own blood. You look done in, Eminence. Why don't you sit down? Have my chair. I've been sitting most of the day anyway. It's all right, Fern, he's a friend. This is my dog, Fern. You may have seen her once or twice in Vivvy's room. I've been wondering what to do with her. I thought I had a friend who would look after her, but he's disowned me. Maybe you could take her with you when you go. She doesn't bite – well, hardly ever. I think Vivvy would like to have her. Fern was a present from Vivvy originally, for my eighteenth birthday.'

'Forgive me, but the fate of your dog is not my primary concern. I came here hoping I could make you listen to me.'

'I'm listening. You just won't make me change my mind.'

Edvard does look tired, grey around the mouth. His eyes are stinging with exhaustion. He rubs his long hands across his face, and coughs. 'Would you like something to drink, Eminence? Some water?'

'Why did you come to Court in the first place?'

'To torment you,' Caro grins.

'This isn't funny.'

'I'm sorry. I came because I was sent for. You know that.'

'You needn't have obeyed. You could have left the country then – or, if this is what you were really after, you could have refused to obey and insulted the Court by doing what you're doing now.'

'I had to come. I'd always hoped the Court would send for me. I needed that distinction. Who'd be listening to me now if I wasn't the Queen's Poet? If I'd written these things when I was only Caryllac of The Moon and the Stars, everyone would have accused me of envy, or thwarted ambition. I had to make them see that I mean what I say. I had to have every honour it was possible for me to have, so that everyone could see what I stood to lose. And I have to show them I'm willing to die for it. To go abroad now would be like saying I only mean it up to a point. Anyway, everybody has to die sometime. You have to think of death as something you can use, like talents and

243

opportunities, and turn it to advantage instead of wasting it. I'm not going to flee into the arms of some foreign King who'll manipulate me like a thorn in Basal Rorhah's side. That's what you're suggesting, isn't it? But if I did that I would feel like a traitor. And I will not serve Kings any longer.'

'You don't know what you're saying. You can't imagine what it's like to die the way you will.'

'There are worse ways to go. Look at you. Buried under your wasted life. You couldn't see the truth when it stared you in the face. I was only ten years old and I could see that if you have to kill people in order to put things right, then it can't be right. You could have seen it if you hadn't pawned your integrity for romance. You should have realised the war was a mistake, Basal Rorhah was a mistake, the whole thing was one big mistake and we have to tear it down and start from scratch. That's the great adventure worth dying for.

'You and I, Eminence, we're two of a kind. You're not like most of the others at Court. They're only concerned with promoting their own self-interest. You wanted something more. You wanted to be something better. You love this country as much as I do. You wanted to improve things, but you've never really known how. I suppose you thought Basal Rorhah could do it for the both of you. And now you realise you've just compounded the error. It's not so easy for you, I can see that. You've lived in the heart of the stinking corpse all your life. You can't even smell it any more. I know you do what you can to mitigate it, but don't you see, that doesn't help put things right. If you try to lighten the pain a little you only lessen the incentive to seek a real cure.'

'Sometimes,' says Edvard slowly, 'I wish I'd died in the war.'

'With all your ideals intact, I know. I was right about you, wasn't I?'

'I expect if you weren't I shouldn't be here.'

'So what is it, don't you love him any more?'

Edvard has to think about this. The impulse to come here was obeyed on the spur of the moment, a sort of reaction against the cumulative submissiveness of everyone around him. He hasn't examined his motives clearly; and Caro is now forcing him to do so.

He says, as one who has only just realised it himself, 'I will always love him. One can't slough off a lifetime of devotion as if it had never been. He has become what he is because

244

we allowed it to happen. But I'm not going to be his dog, as you put it. I saw myself today, you know, in the Council. Basal was furious because none of us had told him about you, and we all cowered. Fifteen pathetic jellies who used to be his equals. I can't remember the last time he took any advice from me. He doesn't need it. He's a monster of competence. He's taken everything we had to offer and now he doesn't need us any more. And none of us has the guts to stand up to him. We used to, but he – well, maybe it's not him, but time and circumstances have made us small. You know I slaved to put this Kingdom back to rights after the mess Michael made of it. And today I realised I'm surplus to requirements. I'm a glorified clerk.'

'And you think you were made for something better? You're trying to bundle me abroad out of wounded vanity?'

'What more do you want from me?' Edvard exclaims. 'I have broken the law and betrayed my King in coming here to try to save you, I've destroyed my career and will almost certainly be banished from Court, if not worse, and I have broken the friendship that was the most important thing in the world to me. Can I ruin myself any more thoroughly to your satisfaction?'

'My heart bleeds for you.'

'Oh, bury yourself, Caro. I don't know why I bothered. I came here because I don't want to see you die. And yes, I came here to salvage what's left of my self-respect. I can't stand by and do nothing. You haven't done anything that deserves death.'

'Well then, what matters is that you came. That you tried. Not that I live.'

'If you die it will all have been for nothing. And speaking as my King's Councillor, I must add that I think it would be a mistake to kill you. It would only lend you credence.'

'Well, that's it, isn't it? If the foundations of your government weren't so shoddy I wouldn't have to die. They could tolerate dissent. The fact that I have to be silenced proves how precarious they are. I've dared to express my lack of faith in the Temple, and the King, and the way you run things, so you have to dig a little hole for me and put me out of sight. I've forced your hand. In killing me you prove my point. And what disturbs you most is that I'm not afraid. Fear is the tool by which you govern, and if it loses its effectiveness you have nothing with which to hold us down. Death is nothing. You don't get rid of me that easily. People will remember me. A few people will. They'll remember that I chose to die for this, that I was silenced because you could not afford to let me speak, and that alone will make them think there is something in what I say. And there will be others after me. They'll hear about me and they'll have the courage to follow my example. You won't be able to kill them all. A Brychmachrye worth loving can't be built on the bones of her bravest men.

'I know what sort of death I'm facing. I'm not walking into this blindly. Years ago, when I was travelling with the theatre company, we were in Farzaned when a man was executed for treason. You might remember – he tried to assassinate that fat Fahlraec of Olivah at his nephew's wedding.'

'Yes, I do remember.'

'That was when I first started to think about it. I've always known I was fated for the same sort of end. You might almost say I've looked forward to it. If I had the choice, I would rather be buried. You know I'm not a believer. There's no heaven, and you certainly can't sail to it. I've never set foot off these shores and I have no intention of leaving them when I'm dead. I love this country. Leaving it, dead or alive, is the worst thing that could happen to me. I'd rather die than go abroad. I believe I would die if I went abroad. I'd be an uprooted tree. This is where I belong. I was born here, I breathe this air, I speak our languages. Brychmachrye is my life. You know that. I let you read my poems. Worst things I've ever done.'

'I thought they were beautiful.'

'Not as beautiful. Not half as beautiful. There's no words for what I feel. I feel that when I write about our country I detract from her. I steal a bit of her beauty and spoil it by trying to copy it. So, when you bury me I'll be giving something back. I'll be a little bit of Brychmachrye. For always. Since I have to die it's comforting to know that, even dead, I'll be of some use to this country. The worms will eat me, and my bones will crumble into earth and feed the grass. I like to think that I will make this land a little greener. I like knowing that I will always be here. When you and Basal Rorhah and Lord Olivah and all the others are ash in the winds of history, I will still be here. I'll be something solid. I'll be the ground under my daughter's feet. So I'm happy. I win. Would you mind going now, Eminence? And please, take Fern, give her to Vivvy. I don't have much time and there's some writing I want to do.'

246

32

Nothing is said to Edvard when he returns to Court, although he does not doubt that Basal knows where he went. In his absence his rooms have been discreetly searched, and a quantity of documents, including some private copies he has made of Caro's Brychmachrye poems, have been removed. Hourly he expects to be summoned into Basal's presence and stripped of his posts and honours, but no one comes for him, and later the same morning his clerks inform him that Caro is now in custody in the Palace cells. That afternoon a distraught Vivienne comes, with Fern and Fluff romping close behind, to weep on Edvard's shoulder because Caro refused to see her. Edvard says that Caro knows best. He had been wondering whether to visit Caro himself, but now he understands that Caro has nothing left to say.

Several days pass, and it seems that Edvard is to be forgiven for his impulsive gesture, for he is invited to an audience alone with the King. Basal offers him a glass of wine and tells him, 'That was a very unwise thing you did.'

'Sometimes one acts on one's instincts.'

'It would appear I judged him more accurately than you did. He wouldn't run, would he?'

Edvard does not reply. He has just noticed a pile of the poems which were taken from his room, stacked neatly on the table next to the beaker of wine. Basal observes him, and says, 'They were very instructive. You can keep them, if you like. It would be a shame to destroy everything he's written, and there's nothing objectionable in those. I know you're fond of the boy, Ned. There's a great deal of his father in him, isn't there?'

'He doesn't like to think so, but I agree with you.'

'A brave boy, but wrongheaded. Tom all over again, I would say. And one doesn't like to make the same mistakes twice. That's why I wanted to speak to you first. I thought you'd like to know what's been decided.'

'I assumed he would be executed.'

'No, I don't think that would help anybody. I'm sending him abroad, to the Southland.'

'Exile?'

'The Southland is a country for hotheads, if you'll forgive the pun. After all, Caro's crime is an intellectual one. A physical punishment would be inappropriate.'

'But Basal, you can't do that!'

'Is that your opinion as my Chancellor?'

'Yes – no – ' says Edvard in some confusion. 'I don't know – I thought – Caro thinks he's going to die. He wants to die – that is, he said – he told me he would rather die than go into exile. That's why he didn't run.'

'Am I now to gratify the wishes of traitors? That foolish young man is little more than a boy, and I have no desire to deprive him of his future because of what amounts to an admittedly serious, but childish prank. Youthful exuberance commits follies that time teaches one to regret. His exile will last only for as long as he chooses it to. When he is prepared to admit his error, he can come home.'

'It would be kinder to kill him quickly than to break his heart.'

'Please don't be sentimental, Ned. I don't wish to be seen as the villain of this rather silly little poem. Nor do I wish to be remembered as the murderer of one of this Kingdom's greatest poets. I think it's better for all concerned if he goes off and cools his heels in the Southland for a while. In time he'll come to appreciate the advantages of a way of life which he now professes to despise. He can even take his dog, if the Lady Vivienne can bear to part with it. I really think I'm being more than fair.'

'As it pleases your Grace,' says Edvard. 'But I'd like to be the one to tell him. Do I have your leave?'

'If you think that's best.' Basal gives his crooked smile. 'I trust your instincts. So far, they seem to have coincided with my intentions.'

Edvard tells Caro, he wants to break you, and all Caro says is, I see.

When Edvard has gone he pulls a stool up to the window. Standing on tip-toe he is able to look through the bars of his cell. It's like Floried Castle, he told Edvard. I've come round in a circle. Vivvy can keep Fern. I don't think the Southland would agree with her. She has too much fur for a hot climate.

The evening sunlight slanting through the window warms Caro's face and neck. He can just catch a glimpse of a corner of the gardens, the dewy whites and velvet reds of the roses, and beyond the gardens the newly leafed woods where a thrush is singing in the willows, and a cold stream sparkles over mossy brown rocks. Beyond the woods, cows graze at pasture; beyond the Palace walls, fields of ripening spring corn and meadows

248

awash with daisies and dandelions, thatched villages, muddy duck ponds, bramble hedgerows and scarlet berries, damp shadowy forests mulched with last autumn's fallen leaves, the delicate unfurling of young bracken, the sheep drifting across the downs of Floriah, the blossoming apple trees of Uhlanah, the rocky wilderness of Kyrah, the purple heather of the northern moors, the great central mountains thrusting their naked spine out of the earth, capped with snow that melts to rush in torrents to the Wastryl, over cataracts, to the sea. Clouds are rising from the west, shimmering grey and pink – like a fresh trout's belly – with the promise of rain. Caro can smell it, an acrid dustiness in the air.

At Floried Castle he had made his skin into a wall and sat with his back to it. Be like the walls of Mindared. Never break down. Don't give in, don't let them know, don't let them see how much it hurts. He can't win unless you let him.

At Floried he had refused to speak. In the South it will make no difference. They do not know his language. He can speak, or not: no one will understand him.

The walls of Mindared have fallen, undermined by a man who knows the price of all things. The value of treachery, the expendability of friendship, the cost of exile.

Caro never considered this possibility: that the thread of his fate would run out, but leave him alive. Empty years stretch before him, an existence with no purpose but the determination not to give in. He drinks in the view of green fields, wet flowers, cloudy skies, and assures himself, over and over, I will remember this: it is printed in my heart and I will take it with me, and I will never surrender.

But when Basal Rorhah had threatened to kill her son, Caro's mother broke. Every man will break if you find his weakness. Caro knows this, in his water. The hot sun of exile evaporates defiance. In the South he will forget the smell of rain and the sound of his own voice. His tongue will cleave to the roof of his mouth. His poetry will shrivel. His throat will run dry. The thirst for home will bring him to his knees, in time. He also will be broken, first in his spirit, and then in his pride.

Bren's liver packed in during the winter following Caro's exile, and he bled to death from his mouth. Next summer the Black Bull returned to Brychmachrye with a bride he had met treading grapes at the wine festivals in Duccarn, and he settled down in Tsvingtori to work as a translator for the Official Publishers. Annie's disappearance relieved Paddy of the obligation to pretend that he was still serious about becoming an apothecary, and three years later he was hanged for picking pockets in the Clerkden. Idris Owenson lived to be a hundred and four and died in his sleep.

Vivienne's lap-dog fathered a litter of peculiarly-shaped puppies on Fern; these little mongrels became all the rage at Court. The King arranged a marriage for Vivienne with a nobleman of rank, and she went to live on her husband's estates in the foothills of Buranah. Her place as lady-in-waiting was taken by a Lady Heloise, who came from a minor family in Laurinyah and had a hunched back. She bore her disfigurement with fortitude, was well-read and mild-mannered, and in time Edvard married her. He recognised her affectionate heart, and she seemed to need protection.

Annie Fisher lived to be almost as old as Idris. She married an uncle of the friend with whom she went to stay, a widowed farmer with three half-grown children who brought her daughter up as his own. When the girl was a grown woman and herself a wife and mother, Annie did tell her the truth about her father, but Caro was dead by then, like Basal Rorhah and Edvard filcLaurentin, ashes on the sea, and Annie hardly remembered what he looked like. She could only say that he had been a handsome man.

Hundreds of years later, when transportation was so advanced one could cross Brychmachrye in less than twenty-four hours; when medicine and welfare had made such strides that few could remember how the Cripplesteps had got its name; when Tom Floriah's sword was a museum piece, laughably feeble compared to contemporary weaponry; when people said, look how far we have progressed, hunger and poverty and illiteracy are things of the past; when history was no longer an epiç poem and had become a science; when happiness was measured by the barometric fluctuations of the economy – Caro was exhumed, and research students were allowed to spend three years at the taxpayers' expense analysing, explaining, and paraphrasing his poetry. Fragments of his plays fetched high prices at auctions, and were tenderly restored by scholars who believed they knew what he meant to say, until his plays resembled the eroded marble pillars of national monuments held together with cement. He was remembered and studied, not for

250

his courage, which they thought naïvety, and not for his ideas, which seemed to them quaint, but for the most accidental of his achievements, the forging of a bastard language out of the union of old native and old Andarian. These languages died: his survived and supplanted them.

Tsvingtori City Council hired a team of archaeologists to identify the place where The Moon and the Stars theatre had stood. The archaeologists succeeded in pinpointing it in a part of the City knocked down by a bombing raid during the last war: a housing estate had recently been erected on the site. An important ceremony was then held, and a large brass plaque with the legend THE FATHER OF LITERATURE, CARYLLAC THOMASSON, POET AND PLAYWRIGHT, LIVED HERE was riveted on to one of the brick walls.